Vale

Rebecca Farnworth has work   ebrity ghostwriter.
She lives in Brighton with her husband and three children.
This is her first novel.

Valentine
Rebecca Farnworth

arrow books

Published in the United Kingdom by Arrow Books in 2009

1 3 5 7 9 10 8 6 4 2

Copyright © Rebecca Farnworth, 2009

Rebecca Farnworth has asserted her right under the Copyright, Designs and Patents Act, 1988
to be identified as the author of this work.

This novel is a work of fiction. Names and characters are the product of the
author's imagination and any resemblance to actual persons, living or dead, is
entirely coincidental

This book is sold subject to the condition that it shall not, by way of trade or
otherwise, be lent, resold, hired out, or otherwise circulated without the publisher's
prior consent in any form of binding or cover other than that in which it is
published and without a similar condition, including this condition, being imposed
on the subsequent purchaser

First published in Great Britain in 2009 by
Arrow Books

Arrow Books
Random House, 20 Vauxhall Bridge Road,
London SW1V 2SA

www.rbooks.co.uk

Addresses for companies within The Random House Group Limited can be found at:
www.randomhouse.co.uk/offices.htm

The Random House Group Limited Reg. No. 954009

A CIP catalogue record for this book
is available from the British Library

ISBN 9780099527190

The Random House Group Limited supports The Forest Stewardship
Council (FSC), the leading international forest certification organisation. All our
titles that are printed on Greenpeace approved FSC certified paper carry the FSC logo.
Our paper procurement policy can be found at www.rbooks.co.uk/environment

Typeset by Palimpsest Book Production Ltd,
Grangemouth, Stirlingshire
Printed and bound in Great Britain by
CPI Cox & Wyman, Reading, RG1 8EX

To my fantastic four:
Julian, Joe Amelie and Lola

Acknowledgements

Thank you Maggie Hanbury, my fantastically wise agent, I really appreciate everything you do for me.

Thank you to everyone at Random House especially Mark Booth and Charlotte Haycock.

Thank you Anna for your insights into the acting world. *Dahling* you were marvellous!

Thank you Alison for being the voice of reason and calm in a sea of wittering.

Thank you Claire Jones for always believing I could do it. You are a star shining brightly in the darkness of self doubt!

Thank you Ali for all those emails to cheer me through when it was most needed.

And thank you Isobel Williams who got me going on the right track in the first place.

1

Valentine's Day Mascara

Valentine Fleming took a long hard look at herself and despaired. *Mirror, mirror on the wall, who has the fattest bum of all? Is it me in these trousers? Should I even be wearing trousers to the audition? Jesus Christ my arse looks VAST! What was I thinking of, wearing black Capri pants with my backside? I should be in a reality freak show for people with massive arses; they could call it Arse Swap.*

She was just hours away from auditioning for the part of Titania, the fairy queen, in *A Midsummer Night's Dream*, but instead of channelling her character's magical and powerful qualities she was gripped with self-doubt and blind panic. To make matters worse the audition was on her least favourite day of the year – Valentine's Day – which also happened to be her birthday. Up until a year ago Valentine had loved having a birthday on the fourteenth of February. How she used to enjoy strolling down the road, flipping through her impressively large bundle of mail, noting the looks of envy coming at her from the women she passed, who weren't to know that they were seeing birthday cards. And yes, it was shallow, but did that make her a bad person? Did that mean that she had deserved what had happened on this day a year ago?

It was imperative not to think about that now. She had to focus on the audition. But it was no good. Suddenly, as if she'd been wearing Dorothy's ruby slippers, she was transported back to the scene in Café Pasta, Covent Garden. She was sitting opposite Finn Steele, the love, she was sure, of her life. She was blissfully happy and felt ever so slightly smug that she had a date on this night of all nights. She neglected to reflect that Finn wasn't in fact her boyfriend; he was someone else's. After six months of their affair Finn had just revealed that he was finally going to leave Eva, his girlfriend – something he'd been promising to do from the moment he and Valentine got together. It was a perfect moment. Too perfect to be true, apparently, as into the lovers' idyll stormed an angry-looking blonde who would have been pretty were her face not puce with rage. The girlfriend. For a second Valentine remembered thinking it was remarkable that her face was very nearly the same colour as the deep red roses she was carrying, and wasn't that taking accessorising a little far? Then the red-faced blonde violently hurled the bouquet at Finn, causing his carbonara sauce to splatter into his eyes. While he shouted that she had blinded him, she screeched that he was a two-timing bastard. Then she left and Finn ran after her, begging her to forgive him, declaring that he loved her and only her. In the aftermath of their affair ending so publicly and so painfully Valentine had developed an almost pathological hatred of red roses and Italian food, which was a shame as she'd always loved Penne alla Vongole.

She should have hated Finn after that. God knew she had cause. Instead she still loved him, still hoped that one day they could get back together. Now she picked up her phone, hoping he'd texted (the fifth time she'd checked in an hour) and even as she did it she despised herself for being such a cliché. What becomes of the broken hearted? They compulsively check their phones and stalk their exes on Facebook. Technology had a lot to answer for. There was no text and she was torturing herself by even looking, but she just couldn't help it. Finn was the itch under her skin, always there. It hadn't helped that they'd met up since the break-up – always on his terms, always for sex. Ten times to be precise. Valentine remembered every single detail of every single encounter. Every time had been intoxicating, intense but ultimately disastrous for an addict like Valentine. It had stopped her moving on and getting over him, left her in a permanent limbo.

Oh God, thinking about him now was not going to help. Would he be thinking about her? Fat chance. He was most likely bringing his girlfriend champagne and flowers in bed, pulling out a single red rose from the exquisite bouquet and lightly caressing her body with the petals, switching between the flower and his hands and tongue, turning her on and STOP! She put up a mental roadblock sign in her mind. If she carried on like this she would be guaranteed to balls up the audition. She turned her thoughts from Finn to another ruthless scrutiny of her arse – really, Trinny and Susanna had nothing on her. There was no getting away from it: the trousers were a disaster. She looked more Beth Ditto (no offence Beth, lovely girl and all that) than Audrey Hepburn in them. She frantically flicked through the clothes in her wardrobe, growing ever more desperate. When she couldn't find anything she ended up pulling everything out and dumping it on the floor in frustration, creating a hideous jumble of garments and giving her even less chance of finding something suitable.

'You're going to be late if you don't step on it, V,' her flatmate Lauren advised, standing at her bedroom door, smoking. She'd just got out of bed but still looked stunning in a turquoise silk kimono. She resembled the Hollywood actress Diane Kruger with her sculpted cheekbones, slanting blue eyes, full lips, perfect skin and long, naturally blonde hair. When Valentine had first met her at drama school seven years ago, she had never imagined that they could be friends. Lauren seemed completely out of her league and frankly what kind of masochist wants to be friends with someone who would always outshine them? But they had bonded as witches in a student production of Macbeth, discovering they shared the same wicked sense of humour. In Lauren she found a best friend who kept her going, even through the darkest times. Sometimes she didn't even notice her beauty.

'Don't smoke near me!' Valentine wailed. 'You know I've given up and this is my weakest hour!'

Lauren narrowed her eyes. 'I hope you haven't been obsessing about *him* again. I know what today means to you, but you've got to get a grip.' Lauren loathed Finn so much for his treatment of Valentine that she couldn't even bring herself to say his name. While Valentine told her friend most things, she hadn't let on about the secret meetings. She felt too ashamed and too conflicted to confide. Lauren's best qualities, her unflinching honesty and her straight talking, could also be her worst. 'He's a gutless bastard who nearly destroyed you, remember?' This was the mantra Lauren had tried to drum into her, with limited success it had to be said – hence the ten shags. 'You've got to focus on the audition. You must have a core of steel.' The latter comment being her other mantra.

'I am! I do!' protested Valentine, whose core felt more like jelly. She avoided looking at Lauren, who could always tell when she was lying.

'Well, I'll leave you to it then.' Lauren blew a smoke ring at her.

'No!' Valentine begged. 'This is a 911 situation!' Both she and Lauren were convinced that 911 sounded more twenty-first century than 999, which always strangely reminded them of Michael Buerk and his TV programme with its dramatic reconstructions of people rescued from potholes. 'You've got to help me!' This was the torturous ritual Valentine went through with every single audition. The mad, headless-chicken panicking that she had nothing to wear, the worrying that she wasn't pretty enough / thin enough / blonde enough / straight-haired enough / tall enough / small enough to get the part. Casually Lauren walked towards the heap of clothes, picked out a black wrap dress, a pair of black leggings and black pumps and handed them to Valentine. 'Try these,' she said calmly.

Quickly Valentine slipped off the rejected outfit and put on Lauren's choice, triggering another frantic self-appraisal in the mirror.

'You don't think the dress makes me look too—'

She couldn't get the words out before Lauren cut in, 'No, you look great.'

'Are you sure I don't look a bit—' Valentine persisted, but Lauren had stuck her fingers in her ears and was singing 'la la la' at the top of her voice. It was fair enough, Valentine reasoned; Lauren had endured this routine many, many, many times.

'What about the make-up?' Valentine asked. The trick about audition make-up was that you were supposed to look as if you weren't wearing any. God knew the natural look was fiendishly hard to perfect.

'Maybe a tiny bit more blusher,' Lauren advised, advancing towards her with a brush and adding the merest hint to Valentine's cheeks.

'Not too much!' Valentine protested. 'You know I always go red under pressure.' She took one last look in the mirror. Would she do? She'd tried to emphasise her large green eyes – her best feature, she always thought – by curling her lashes and with subtle eye make-up. She'd spent ages blending in her foundation, covering up the few freckles on her nose in case the director didn't like them, and she was wearing the most natural-coloured lipstick she had. Even though she was hyper self-critical she knew she wasn't bad looking, could admit on her good days to being pretty. However she also knew that she didn't fall into the beautiful category so effortlessly occupied by Lauren. But then Valentine always underestimated her looks, probably because she'd had so many rejections at auditions and because she lived with Lauren. She didn't realise how attractive and sexy she was, with her sensuous lips and beautiful eyes. And she was constantly obsessing over her weight; being a natural size twelve was no fun when you were always up against size-eight and size-six skinnies. She sighed as she tried to tuck one of her curls back into place and cursed her mother yet again, from whom she had inherited her wild chestnut hair. Why hadn't she been born in an era that appreciated curls? Say the eighteenth century? Then again, there would have been no Pringles, no teeth-whitening toothpaste, in fact no toothpaste and no George Clooney.

'Knock em' dead kid and we'll have a birthday drink when you get back, plus I'll give you your present,' Lauren said as Valentine headed out of their top-floor flat. Downstairs in the hallway the post had arrived. Let there be a card from Finn, Valentine prayed as she feverishly went through it. But there were just cards from her mum and brother, and several of her friends, along with three Valentine cards for Lauren. If she hadn't been her best friend Valentine would have had every reason to hate her.

She walked rather despondently to the bus stop, then tried to pull herself together. She really needed this part. She hadn't had an audition for five long months, which felt like for ever. She often thought that being a struggling actress was like enduring a series of humiliations and living on perpetual tenterhooks. There was the endless waiting for auditions, chipping away at her self-esteem, not helped by other people forever asking her what she was in at the moment, reminding her that she wasn't in *anything.* When she replied she was between jobs they'd exclaim cheerily, 'So you're resting. All right for some!' Valentine would smile politely and resist the impulse to tell them to fuck off. Then there would be the moment of hope when she actually got an audition, but it was hope mixed in with a large measure of insidious doubt that she wasn't pretty enough / thin enough, etc. etc. to get it. There was the audition itself where nine times out of ten she was treated like total shit by the director and didn't get the part anyway. Then there were those all-too-brief times when she got a part and even if it was tiny and the pay was rubbish (as it invariably was) it somehow made up for everything else and kept her going.

And when she wasn't acting there were the humiliating jobs she had to do just to survive. Her 'theatre in education' work, for example, which sounded worthwhile but always seemed to involve trying to get testosterone-charged Lynx-wearing teenage boys interested in *Macbeth* while ignoring their sexually suggestive comments. There was her temping work, which she loathed. To make it more interesting she used to practise her acting skills and go into jobs as different characters, but she'd had to abandon this when she had pretended to be from Bulgaria and her boss had been Bulgarian. What were the chances of that? Having to fess up had been deeply embarrassing.

And there was her work as a children's party entertainer.

She winced in recollection of the most recent booking, for which she had dressed as the sugar plum fairy to entertain twenty precocious six-year-old girls. It had gone wrong even before she arrived at the party, as she'd had to borrow Lauren's pink leotard, two sizes too small. Consequently she'd ended up showing far more cleavage than was probably acceptable for a children's birthday party and the thong had nearly caused her a serious gynaecological injury. Lauren had taken one look at her and burst out laughing, calling her 'Porno Fairy'. And she'd been right – Valentine had been whistled at all the way to the party by white van drivers who'd called out lewd comments about where they'd like to stick their wands. Valentine had retaliated by giving them the finger and shouting that she knew where she'd like to stick hers, and been witnessed by several mothers with small children – they wouldn't be booking her for a party any time soon. And things had only got worse. At the party the children, who were all spoilt, rich darlings, were already on a wild sugar rush, and had turned their noses up at every single game Valentine had suggested and kept doing *whatever minger* hand signals at her. Meanwhile the father of the über-obnoxious birthday girl, Harrison Foster-Twat Arse or something (a city banker type in chinos, a garment for which Valentine had an irrational hatred) spent the entire time leering at her cleavage or trying to grope her. She winced at the memory. *Please let me get this part, God.* She didn't believe in God, but maybe if she succeeded in acting she would undergo a rapid conversion.

She anxiously looked at her watch. Where the hell was

9

the bus? A woman passed by clutching an unfeasibly large bouquet of red roses, a smug I-am-not-a-sad-singleton expression across her face. Valentine felt the familiar wave of nausea at the sight of the red roses and looked the other way. It really was time to stop channelling Marnie from that Hitchcock film. Just at that moment a double-decker bus sailed past her with one of the actresses from her old drama school plastered across it, advertising her latest film, and almost blinding the unsuspecting public with her incredibly white, perfect teeth. It was Tamara Moore or NTM (No Talent Moore) as Valentine and Lauren called her. Valentine liked to think that she would not have begrudged her fellow actor her success if she had been supremely talented, but Tamara had all the acting range of an eleven-year-old girl and that was probably being disrespectful to the eleven-year-old. Her trajectory to almost instant fame was due entirely to who she was, or rather who her parents were. She was the daughter of an extremely successful actress and a rock-star dad. Nepotism was alive and kicking in the acting world. In fact, all the people from Valentine's year who had gone on to do well were the sons or daughters of established actors. While some had talent and deserved it; others like Tamara did not. Valentine's mum was a midwife and her dad, who had died three years ago, had been a psychiatric nurse, both extremely worthwhile professionals, and Valentine was proud of them. However, sometimes, when there had been no auditions for a while Valentine did have the odd dark moment when she thought she might have made it by now had she been better-connected. She had talent – she had won the prestigious Olivier award in her final year – but that apparently wasn't enough. But she didn't just dislike Tamara because of her talent bypass; Tamara had made it her mission to undermine Valentine at all times and had also flirted outrageously with Finn. Valentine had often wondered if there'd been something going on between them.

She took a deep breath, trying to centre herself and instantly regretted it as she inhaled what seemed like the entire vehicle emissions of Westbourne Park Road. She spent the next five minutes coughing and thinking she was going to die of lung cancer on the spot. And what would her epitaph be? Here lies Valentine Fleming, failed actress, single, leaving behind no children. Her funeral would just be attended by her mum, brother, aunt, and friends. There would be no one giving speeches about how they remembered her Lady Macbeth and how her Rosalind had defined a generation. There would be no one eulogising about how unfair it was that she had never got the Oscar for Best Actress. No large plasma screen showing her finest moments in stylish black and white, while 'What a Wonderful World' played and there wasn't a dry eye in the church. There would be no white coffin (did that say tacky or timeless chic? She couldn't decide) in front of the altar decorated with lilies and white roses, only a cardboard one because her mother was very eco-aware and would have insisted on sustainable materials. She probably wouldn't allow any flowers at all unless they were grown in this country, because of their carbon footprint. Valentine would end up with a wreath of nettles and hogweed. In fact her mum probably wouldn't let her have a church funeral at all, but would bury Valentine in the back garden, next to the two deceased cats and five hamsters, in some kind of humanist ceremony. She cheered herself up by reminding herself that she'd be dead and wouldn't know anyway.

Twenty minutes later, when her bus still hadn't turned up, panic had well and truly set in. She rifled through her purse, which only contained a solitary fiver, not enough to get her to The Circle Arts Centre, the theatre on Baker Street. She'd have to get a taxi some of the way and then leg it. There then ensued a further five frustrating minutes when every single available taxi ignored her outstretched arm as if she'd suddenly become invisible. In the end she had to practically stand in the middle of the road, risking death to flag one down. The cardboard coffin, hogweeds and burial next to the hamsters might be coming sooner than she realised. Finally one stopped. She got in and quickly explained her cash crisis to the taxi driver. 'We could go via a cash point,' he replied.

'No, there isn't time; I've got to get to an audition. I'll run some of the way,' Valentine said, willing him to put his foot down.

'Oh you're an actress are you? Would I have seen you in anything?' the cabbie asked, pulling away maddeningly slowly, as if he had only just learned to drive.

Fuck, why had she mentioned the audition? She hated telling strangers about her profession; they always asked that question.

'Probably not,' she replied, trying to keep the edge

from her voice. She was buggered if she was going to give him a run-down of her CV. She didn't ask him how long he'd been driving a cab or when he'd passed the Knowledge. But that was the thing about revealing that you were an actress; it gave other people carte blanche to ask personal questions.

'Perhaps your big break's round the corner,' the cabbie persisted. 'What's your name and then if you make it I can say that I've had you in the back of my cab. Driven you, I mean!' The cabbie gave a raucous, dirty laugh at his own joke, worthy of Sid James in his *Carry on* roles, while Valentine rolled her eyes and squirted a shot of Bach Rescue Remedy into her mouth to stop herself telling him to piss off.

'Candy Beaver,' she lied, instantly regretting giving herself a porn-star name, and quickly got her copy of *A Midsummer Night's Dream* out of her bag as a barrier to further conversation. She liked to get to auditions in plenty of time, but at this rate she would have just seconds to spare. She chewed her nails (a disgusting habit she knew and promised herself that if she got the part today she'd stop doing it) and squirted more Rescue Remedy into her mouth. You couldn't OD on it could you? After what seemed like two minutes the meter hit five pounds.

'That's your lot,' the cabbie said cheerfully, pulling over. 'Good luck in the audition Candy,' he called after her as she thrust the fiver at him and opened the door. Then she started running, thinking bitterly that if she had been No Talent Moore the driver would have taken her all the way. Then again if she was NTM she wouldn't be going

13

to an audition for an off-West End play in the first place. Almost instantly her hair, which she had so carefully arranged into an elegant bun, started breaking free and cascading down her shoulders, leaving behind a trail of pins. A bad omen. Curly hair was like marmite and aroused strong feelings in people, which was why she preferred to keep it tied back at auditions.

Fifteen minutes later, dishevelled-haired, red-faced (the extra blusher had definitely been a mistake) and out of breath, she burst into the theatre building. She was nearly ten minutes late – a complete audition no-no – and saying the bus hadn't come would sound pathetically lame. She'd blown it. There was no one in the foyer and guessing that they were all in the theatre she tentatively knocked at the large green door in front of her. There was no reply. Bollocks, what should she do? Stay out here? Or go in? But say they were in the middle of a scene? She pressed her ear against the door straining to hear anything. Nothing. She knelt down and tried to look through the keyhole but something seemed to be blocking her view.

She was just about to get up when the door opened and she found herself staring straight into a denim crotch. A very nice one, she had to admit – just the right proportions – but oh God never mind that now! She just hoped it wasn't the director, or maybe it would be good if it was. She had never gone the casting-couch route before but frankly right now she was willing to try almost anything to get a part. Hastily she averted her gaze upwards into an amused pair of dark-brown eyes, owned by a very handsome man. Surely too striking to be a director?

He had leading man stamped all over his gorgeous face and his broad-shouldered, sexy, lean-limbed body, all six foot two of it by her reckoning, though it was hard to be sure from the position she was in.

'I don't usually have this effect on women on first meeting – I'd say usually halfway through the second date,' he said smiling, his brown eyes with a very naughty glint in them. Was he flirting with her?

Valentine felt at a horrible disadvantage. She hastily scrambled to her feet and stuck out her hand. 'Valentine Fleming. I'm so sorry I'm late.'

'Really? A Valentine on Valentine's Day? But isn't it a boy's name?' he asked as he shook her hand. His hand felt cool and firm. Valentine prayed that hers didn't feel sweaty. She did so hate a moist palm herself.

'Yes, it's a boy's name,' Valentine replied, trying not to go into surly teenager mode – people were always telling her this. 'I was born on Valentine's Day and so that's why my mum chose it.'

'Happy birthday then,' the good-looking man said. 'We've got a bit of a theme here as I'm Jack Hart. Harts and Valentines, we go together.' All right he was good looking, but he also seemed a bit of a wanker.

'So you're not the director, are you?' Valentine asked, surreptitiously trying to smooth down her wild hair as she followed him into the theatre. She paused for a moment, trying to orientate herself in the space – there was a stage in the middle of the room, and tiered seats on three sides, which could probably seat two hundred. She liked the feel of it.

'Nope, another actor like you. The director's just nipped out for a fag, said he'd be back in a minute.' His dark-brown eyes moved over her appraisingly. 'You might want to do up your dress before he gets back, unless it's deliberate, in which case, very nice.'

Valentine looked down. The wrap dress had unwrapped. Her come-to-bed black lace bra was on full display. Usually it was strictly reserved for the bedroom, as it was ferociously scratchy and totally revealing but she'd had to wear it as she'd run out of clean lingerie.

'Don't worry, it could have been worse. I once did a whole audition with my flies undone,' Jack continued.

'Did you get the part or just show yours?' Valentine muttered sarcastically, feeing that Jack Hart, although undeniably attractive, was way too cocky. She would have bet money on him having gone to public school and then to Oxford. He had that kind of easy confidence that only came with money and privilege and always getting what you wanted. She was self-aware enough to admit to having a slight chip on her shoulder, having gone to a rubbish comprehensive, and coming from a very non-theatre family, where the only books in the house were John Grishams and Dan the *Da Vinci Code* Brown's, and the only family trips to the theatre had been to pantomimes.

'Both, actually.'

Jammy bastard. She turned away and pulled her copy of *A Midsummer Night's Dream* from her bag, wanting to compose herself for the audition.

'Love the hair by the way, very pre-Raphaelite.'

Damn, it must be looking wild.

16

'And I wouldn't bother reading that,' Jack said, seeing her book. 'I had a quick chat with Vince, the director, and he wants us to improvise.'

The horror, the horror, the horror! Valentine had one of those heart-of-darkness, staring-into-the-abyss moments. She *hated* improvising at auditions. You never knew quite what you were supposed to be doing and as you didn't know the other actors there was none of the feeling of trust, which was what improvisation was supposed to be based on.

'So what part are you up for?' Valentine asked, her heart sinking – all those hours she'd wasted getting into the role of Titania.

'Bottom,' Jack replied, grinning wickedly. 'So you're in love with me.'

'Yeah, only because I've been drugged!' Valentine shot back.

At that moment Vince, the director, walked into the hall. He was a small, intense-looking man in his mid-twenties, dressed in a long black military-style coat several sizes too big for him and scruffy Converse trainers. Valentine immediately switched into charm mode and introduced herself, shrugging off her irritation with the arrogant Jack. Vince, who she noted had a moist and limp handshake, then launched into a long and frankly tedious explanation of how he saw the play, during which Valentine could feel her eyes glazing over. Sylvia, her agent, had raved about him, saying that he was an up-and-coming director; he'd been to Oxford and was well-connected and bound to be destined for great things. 'Get in with him now, darling, is my advice. And you never know who'll come and see the show – it could be your big break.' When Valentine had first signed up with Sylvia she had hung on her every word, convinced that success was only just round the corner. Now she was wise to Sylvia's tendency to exaggerate.

Jack caught her eye at one point and she saw his lips twitching.

Bugger off, she felt like saying. *I need this part!*

Vince's vision included having the forest scenes set in a giant club with Titania as a hip DJ, who along with her husband Oberon had a sideline in selling hallucinogenic drugs. 'So right now I want you and Jack to improvise a scene in a club. I'll say no more than that, but Valentine, I want you to make the first move. I'll put some music on to give you some ambience.' He walked over to a portable CD player and pressed *play*. Dance music pulsed through the theatre, while dread filled Valentine's soul. Then he sat down cross-legged on one of the front-row chairs and leaned forward, looking like an expectant gnome. It was at moments like this that Valentine wondered what had ever possessed her to want to act. Perhaps she should have gone into nursing like her mum. Admittedly there was her phobia of hospitals to overcome, but maybe she could have had aversion therapy or watched back-to-back episodes of ER to get over it. And that way she'd have a steady job where people respected her and did not expect her to humiliate herself on a regular basis. Then she tried to clear her mind of everything. She'd bloody well improvise her arse off . . .

2

Thong and Dance

'How did it go?' Lauren called out from the kitchen, where she was sitting at the table flicking through a magazine and cracking open pistachio nuts, when Valentine let herself into the flat later that night. Valentine slumped down at the worn oak table. The kitchen was an eccentric mix of fifties-style cabinets, a dresser full of mismatched but pretty crockery sourced from charity shops, an old-fashioned butler sink with a leaky tap, and bright egg-yolk-yellow floorboards and walls because Lauren said yellow was good for lifting the spirits. Right now the yellow was doing fuck-all for Valentine's spirits; she put her head in her hands.

'That bad?' Lauren asked sympathetically.

'It was impro,' Valentine muttered darkly.

Lauren took a sharp intake of breath. 'Mother*fucker*!' She'd recently become addicted to *The Wire* – the gritty police HBO drama series set in Baltimore, which had caused her swearing to go up a gear – even though Valentine had told her time and time again that only Americans could get away with saying 'motherfucker' and then only drug dealers, cops, rap artists or Samantha in *Sex and the City*. However Valentine was prepared to let this one go; the impro had, after all, been a motherfucker kind of moment. With some effort she raised her head. 'I had to improvise a scene where I was a sexually predatory older woman, trying to seduce a much younger man. I had to dance suggestively and then kiss, or rather snog this other actor. I felt like I was doing some kind of floor show for the pervy director. In fact it will probably be best if I don't get the part, as fuck knows what he intends the play to be like!' She clasped her hands together in anguish. 'God, why does this happen to me? Why can't I get an audition for the RSC!'

'Wine?'

'I'm sick of my life! It's not fair. I can't go on!' Valentine hammed it up, deliberately mistaking Lauren's meaning.

'Ha fucking ha. Come on, let's have a drink. It's your birthday!'

'Happy birthday to me,' Valentine said miserably.

'Oh cheer up, Lily and Frank are coming up in a minute and if you're depressed Lily will give one of her pep talks and I won't be able to stand that.'

Lily and Frank rented the first- and ground-floor flats respectively of the three-storey Georgian house Lauren had inherited from her uncle in Westbourne Park, just five minutes away from the Portabello Road. On paper that made Lauren sound like a spoilt trustafarian. In reality the house was falling to pieces with damp, a roof that needed redoing, erratic plumbing, no central heating and Lauren had no money to do it up. Nor could Lauren sell the house, as Lily and Frank were sitting tenants. Valentine often felt as she looked out the window from their shabby, bohemian living room on to the beautifully restored pastel-coloured multi-million-pound Georgian houses opposite, that their ramshackle home was like an ancient boat moored in a sea of wealth. Any minute now they'd spring a leak, the water would come pouring in and they'd be lost, but in the meantime they had to keep going, papering over the cracks, painting the flat in the brightest colours. It was like a metaphor for her life.

Lily was an actress in her early seventies who still got occasional parts in BBC radio dramas and Frank was a retired sax player in his late sixties. He suffered from arthritis in his hands, or he would still have played. Instead he spent his time selling antique jewellery on the Portabello Road market and cultivating vegetables and marijuana in the greenhouse in the shared garden, smoking to alleviate the pain – the marijuana that was, not the vegetables. Lily and Frank were a couple but refused to move in with each other, claiming that they liked having their own space too much. They had met in their twenties when both of them were married to other people and despite falling in love, they had stayed married to their partners and only met up again ten years ago when Frank's wife had died and Lily had divorced her husband. Depending on her mood, Valentine either thought it was wildly romantic that they were together now or tragic that they had wasted all those years.

As if on cue Lily knocked at the door and called out, 'It's only us; just wanted to see how the birthday girl got on!'

Valentine rolled her eyes and muttered, 'You'd have thought Lily of all people would know that I don't want a bloody post-mortem!' She adored Lily, who had an absolute heart of gold, but her habit of always asking the girls about whether they had an audition or, when they had them, how they did, drove Valentine to distraction.

Lauren shrugged. 'She means well.' And she called out, 'Come in.'

Lily and Frank walked into the kitchen, both of them wheezing away in harmony. 'So darling, how did it go?' Lily asked, as soon as she had got her breath back. 'You didn't let me wish you good luck. I had checked your horoscope this morning and everything was looking in fantastic alignment.'

'It was OK,' Valentine lied, wanting to avoid the analysis.

'Anyway, happy birthday! This is from both of us.' Lily handed over a small, expertly wrapped parcel, which Valentine unwrapped to discover a sweet, diamante bracelet – Lily had an eye for an accessory. As usual she looked stylish in a black forties-style jacket nipped in at the waist and a black and white checked pencil skirt, red suede ankle boots, her silver-white hair cut in a sharp bob, her face carefully made up. Lily had not let herself go. Not for her the sexless old-lady uniform of nylon trousers with elasticated waistbands, fleeces with paw prints and flat Cornish pastie-style shoes. Lily still put in the effort and Valentine admired her style.

'And here's mine to you.' Lauren handed over a present, and Valentine ripped open the paper to reveal a gorgeous red silk tea dress that she'd coveted for ages from one of the Vintage clothes shops on Portabello Road.

Frank held up a sleek silver cocktail shaker and a bottle of vodka. 'Birthday Martinis all round?'

'Thanks all of you,' Valentine said, standing up and hugging her friends in turn. She was touched by the gifts and Frank's offer of cocktails, especially since he was a reformed alcoholic in AA. 'Even though I wonder what I've got to celebrate.'

Lauren rolled her eyes. 'Lucky for you it's your birthday or I'd tell you to stop being so sappy.'

Valentine ignored her and continued in a mock-dramatic voice, 'The audition was just another humiliating incident in my life as a failed actress. The only thing I want right now is oblivion.' She had a sudden flashback to the moment she'd kissed Jack. He had been an amazingly good kisser. Valentine always set great store on how men kissed. It was a failsafe equation: good kisser equalled good in bed. Bad kisser equalled invariably the opposite. If he didn't know what to do with his lips and tongue you could forget about the other bits.

'You got to snog a fit lad though, didn't you?' Lauren put in, as if reading her mind. 'And let's face it, it's been a while since you've seen any action.'

'That's right,' Lily piped up, 'it's been six months since your last romance.' And four long weeks since she'd last seen Finn, not that Lily knew that.

'He wasn't good enough for you,' Frank declared,

23

vigorously shaking the silver cocktail shaker like a pro.
The 'he' in question was Samuel – a lawyer Valentine
had gone out with for two months in an attempt to snap
herself out of her fixation with Finn. It was doomed from
the start. He didn't get acting and she didn't get the law.
Whenever Valentine socialised with Samuel and his friends
she felt like a performing monkey, expected to entertain
them with her 'hilarious' anecdotes about the theatre
world. Valentine surveyed her friends' faces and said
sarcastically, 'Thank you so much for reminding me on
my birthday that not only am I a failed actress, but also
that I'm single as well.'

'Sam wasn't so bad. He looked lovely in a suit. And
he had that gorgeous leather briefcase – calfskin wasn't
it? Quality product.' Lily and her accessories.

Frank poured out the cocktails and passed them round,
commenting, 'Still, that Sam was much nicer than the
one before – what was his name? Finn or something. He
was a right bastard, excuse my language. No hang on,
what was it? A gutless bastard who nearly destroyed you.'
Bugger Lauren and her mantra. Valentine flinched at the
mention of her Finn's name. Maybe one day she'd be
able to hear it without feeling as if someone had punched
her, but she wasn't there yet, not by a long way.

Lauren came to her rescue and said quietly, 'We don't
talk about him, Frank.'

Valentine took a large slug of the Martini and nearly
choked, it was so strong. Her mobile rang. It was bound
to be her mother wishing her happy birthday and
bombarding her with questions about the audition.

Wearily she picked up her phone, steeling herself for another *How did it go, darling?* conversation and walked into the hall. But suddenly things looked up, because it was Sylvia telling her that she'd got the part. A surge of happiness washed over her. Hurrah! She would be working again! She was not the sad reject actress no one wanted! She was just single! She glanced back into the kitchen where everyone was looking expectantly at her and did the thumbs-up. They beamed back at her in response.

'You start rehearsing next Monday,' Sylvia told her. 'By the way,' she continued in what Valentine knew was her agent-pacifying-client voice. She suddenly felt wary, suspecting something was coming up that she wouldn't like.

'I did mention the nudity to you, didn't I?'

Valentine crashed. This was too cruel. 'Whose?' she demanded.

'Well, it's not full-frontal, but you and the other fairies will be wearing nipple tassels and thongs.' Not words that Kiera bloody Knightly had ever had to hear, Valentine thought bitterly. And before Valentine could reply that no it bloody well wasn't all right, Sylvia pressed on, 'Think of it as a burlesque performance. It's so *now*. And Valentine, it has been five months since you were last on stage. You need to be seen.'

Not all of me! Valentine wanted to say. But she knew Sylvia had a point. She really needed this part. 'Thank you, Sylvia, you're right. I accept the role,' she replied, in her actress-making-the-best-of-things voice.

In the kitchen Frank was high-fiving Lily and Lauren. 'Hey, why that face?' Lauren asked as Valentine walked back into the kitchen and once more slumped down at the table. Slumping was all she seemed to do these days.

'I might have to do it practically nude,' Valentine muttered, picking up and draining her seriously strong Martini.

'Is that all?' Lauren scoffed. 'Stop making such a thong and dance about it! She paused to look at Frank, checking he'd got the pun. He winked and Lauren carried on, 'What's the big deal? Remember all those men who have stripped off, like Daniel Radcliffe in *Equus*? It's much worse for men to do naked than women. Just think how they get judged on the size of their dicks.'

'Two words – shrivelled members,' Frank said wisely. 'You know how cold theatres can be sometimes and how bright and unforgiving the lights – a lady's always going to look better in the buff.'

'I'll be a laughing stock,' Valentine persisted, 'and I might have to wear . . . she hesitated, the full horror only just beginning to sink in – 'nipple tassels! I may as well go the whole hog and sign up to be a lap dancer at Top Totty.' Top Totty was a lap dancing club round the corner and when times had been particularly hard both she and Lauren had considered signing up – well only after they'd both drunk too much wine. They'd always changed their minds by the morning.

'Don't be silly,' Lily put her oar in now, 'you are going to be performing Shakespeare; you will be naked for art! I've done it! I bared all as Cleopatra!'

Valentine and Lauren exchanged eye-rolls, knowing that this was a signal for Lily to take a long and meandering walk down memory lane, or rather mammary lane. Ten minutes later as tumbleweed was blowing through the flat and Lily was finally coming to the end of her story, Valentine's phone beeped with a text message. 'It's probably Vince telling me I have to have group sex on stage with the fairies and Bottom,' she said darkly, opening the message, 'and I expect you'll all tell me that's no big deal so long as there's no actual penetration involved.'

But it was from Jack – sexy, arrogant, too-gorgeous-for-his-own-good Jack. She read the message out loud to her friends. '*Happy Birthday Valentine, so glad you got the part, looking forward to working with you, Jack x.*'

'Oh, how smooth can you get?' Valentine scoffed, secretly disappointed that it wasn't from Finn.

'He sounds lovely!' Lily exclaimed. She was like a bloodhound in trying to sniff out a potential love interest. 'A new play and maybe a new man. I imagine your eyes will lock when you see each other across the rehearsal studio and that will be the start of a great love!' She really was incorrigible.

'I know where his eyes will be locking; I bet he can't wait to see you in your nipple tassels!' Lauren teased. 'I've got some Agent Provocateur ones in my bedroom if you want to practise.' That wasn't all knowing Lauren, who had a comprehensive selection of sex toys in her bedside cabinet. Valentine gave her the finger.

Lily piped up again, 'If you're worried about the lack of costume you really must take up pilates, so good for

27

your core muscles and your pelvic floor. And if you look after the pelvic floor . . .' she paused, searching for the word.

'What? I'll be able to shoot ping pong balls from my vagina? I don't think Vince has thought about that yet, but give him time,' Valentine retorted, adding, 'Sorry Frank.'

'No offence. Saw a great show like that in Bangkok when I was on tour with the boys. Never forgotten it. Never to this day.' Frank became unusually animated. 'She shot the balls right across the room, with such velocity, nearly took my eye out with one. And that would have taken some explaining to the missus, God rest her soul, wouldn't it? Sorry love, some bird blinded me in one eye with a ball she fired straight out of her—'

'Right, I think I get the picture,' Valentine intervened.

'I wish I had!' Frank replied. 'But my flash didn't work.'

Cue much giggling. Valentine picked up the now-empty cocktail shaker. 'I need more alcohol to numb my senses. Any requests? I'm going over the road.'

Fortunately (or unfortunately for their livers) the off-licence was opposite their house. It stood defiant, painted a poisonous shade of green in the middle of a row of designer shops. On the right was a chi-chi shop selling unnecessary accessories to pampered pooches, and on the left a horrifyingly expensive clothes shop which was so extortionate it only ever had one garment displayed in the window, but you never knew how much it cost because it carried no price tag. The off-licence owner had been the victim of several armed robberies and had recently turned his shop into a fortress where the wine and the staff were behind bulletproof glass and you had to point out what you wanted. Every time Valentine walked in she felt like some kind of addict getting her fix. Still, it was cheap, and the two students who worked there in the evenings were such sweethearts. They were behind the glass now, listening to XFM – Robbie, a tall, blonde surfer type who was studying philosophy and Tom, a dark-haired, chocolate-eyed Johnny Depp lookalike, who was studying English.

As soon as they realised it was Valentine the two boys went into one of their favourite routines of pretending to be in a Texan jail on death row with Valentine as their firm but fair female governor. They had a number of scenarios they liked enacting with Valentine, mainly inspired by films set in prisons – it really was very boring working in the store. They'd spent the previous week working on their homage to *Silence of the Lambs*, with the boys playing Hannibal to Valentine's Agent Starling, holding up bottles of Chianti and exclaiming how well it had washed down the brains they'd just eaten. Valentine really wasn't in the mood right now, but felt she couldn't really stop them. They put their hands up in supplication against the glass and assumed hangdog expressions. 'We've been real good, ma'am. Promise you'll put in a good word for us at the parole board,' Tom said.

'And ma'am,' Robbie added, 'may I say how awful pretty you look today.'

'You may not,' Valentine replied, doing her best Susan

Sarandon accent. 'You should only be looking at the Bible.'

'But ma'am,' Robbie put in, 'respectfully we haven't seen a female body in a real long time. Couldn't we just look at you a while longer in case our appeal is rejected and we get sent to the chair?' Robbie managed to put a quiver in his voice and Valentine made a big deal of putting her hand to her head, to show that she wasn't unsympathetic, but she was also firm, so she said, 'Just tell me if you still have the three for two offer on?'

'Oh yes ma'am, for you ma'am, definitely.'

'Very well then – I'll have a bottle of Pinot Grigio and two bottles of Cabernet Sauvignon and step on it. I have to go to church with my husband for evensong.'

'Yes ma'am!' the boys exclaimed in unison, then raced round the shop collecting the bottles. As she paid they all dropped out of character as Tom asked hopefully, 'How's Lauren?'

'Do yourself a favour and forget about her,' Valentine replied.

'I can't,' Tom said with feeling. Valentine smiled ruefully. Lauren had a rule that she never went out with younger men or arts students, so Tom failed on both counts. He had even promised to switch from English and go to medical school, a sacrifice indeed as apparently he couldn't stand the sight of blood. But there wasn't much he could do about his age. It was a case of complete unrequited love.

'And Valentine?' Robbie called out, just as she was leaving the shop, 'You really do look pretty tonight.' In turn Robbie carried a bit of a torch for Valentine.

'Thanks Robbie,' Valentine replied as neutrally as possible – she liked him, but not in that way, and she couldn't afford to upset him because of where he worked. God forbid she might have to walk further to get her liquor.

Upstairs Lauren had dealt out the cards ready for a game of Hearts. The four of them regularly played and were fiercely competitive. Lauren and Valentine had first got into cards when they'd toured round Holland with a student production of *A Winter's Tale*, staying in a number of different Center Parcs. Even now, five years on, the adverts for the British Center Parcs still had the power to give both the girls nightmares. It was off season and they were practically the only guests staying at the camps. It felt a little bit like being on the set of *The Shining* – well, there was no snow, no Jack Nicholson, no child saying 'redrum' every five minutes – but apart from that it was exactly the same with the ominous feeling that they were the only people for miles around and that any moment one of their number might go stir crazy and get a bit wayward with a bread knife . . . Cards was just about the only thing that kept them sane as they had no money – that and learning to drink very, very cheap wine. It had been a joy to discover that Lily and Frank shared their passion for cards.

They played a couple of rounds, Frank for once losing.

'You might have lost at Hearts,' Valentine told him, 'but at least you'll never have to wear nipple tassels!'

'Who says I don't, young lady?' Frank teased her.

Lily rolled her eyes. 'Honestly Frank, you'll give her nightmares.'

'I'll let you know in the morning; I'm going to bed now,' Valentine announced.

'To sleep, perchance to dream of sexy Jack,' Lauren said wickedly, adding, 'The tassels are in the top drawer. I've probably got some ping pong balls as well.'

'Pervert,' Valentine answered back, but waved sweetly to Lily and Frank.

It was only when she was in bed at midnight that she finally got the text she'd longed for. *Happy Birthday V. Can you come over? x.* She didn't hesitate for a second.

3

Can't Get You Out of My Head

'I was beginning to think you weren't going to turn up.'

It was after one, Finn was leaning against the door-frame of his Richmond flat looking sexily dishevelled, his white shirt unbuttoned showing his toned, tanned chest. Valentine's heart flipped over in love and other relevant parts tingled with lust. The rational Valentine thought that not turning up was much more Finn's style. But then Valentine the addict lightly kissed Finn on the lips and murmured, 'I'm here now.'

'God, I want you,' he said, pulling her to him and kissing her. A hard, passionate, hungry kiss. Clearly talking wasn't on Finn's agenda. Valentine never knew how to play these clandestine meetings. Sometimes (say four out of ten) Finn wanted to drink wine, talk and then get down to it; the other times it had been straight down to it. Now he was undoing the buttons on her dress, the one Lauren had just given her for her birthday, and when he got frustrated he ripped them open, causing several to fly off and the delicate silk fabric to tear.

'You've got such fantastic big tits V,' he said throatily. This was possibly the only time Valentine liked hearing big linked with her name. She didn't think her tits were that big – a thirty-two D to be precise – but Finn's girlfriend was waif-thin and flat as a pancake in that department. Finn caressed her fantastic big tits, then ducked down and sucked her nipples, igniting a white-hot fire in her Agent Provocateur silk briefs. For a few minutes she enjoyed the feeling of being so turned on, but she knew Finn too well. She knew what was expected.

She slid down to her knees and, unbuttoning his fly, released his stiff cock, or his 'fantastic big cock' as she told him. A good average, in reality. Though saying that would not go down well – definitely not as well as her. If she was really honest she thought blow jobs were over-rated, but try telling a man that. She supposed it was a turn-on feeling so powerful, knowing how much the recipient was being aroused. But on the other hand there was always so much to think about – watching the teeth, making sure you didn't gag if they became too enthusiastic, trying to avoid lockjaw if it was going on too long, then the whole to swallow or not to swallow . . . She liked it best if it was quick. But right now she wanted to make love, wanted to feel the connection with Finn, wanted him inside her. Sneaking out of the flat so Lauren didn't know what she was up to, crossing London, giving him a blowie and then going on her way (which had happened twice out of the ten times) did not make her feel sexy and empowered, but slightly sordid, as if Finn had dialled for a delivery BJ in much the same way as a pizza.

He was enjoying this one a little too much. If she wasn't careful it would go all the way. But suddenly he put his hand on her shoulder and said, 'Come into the bedroom. I've got something for you.'

He had spread red rose petals all over the bed, and there was a bottle of champagne on the bedside cabinet. 'Happy Birthday V,' he said, leading her on to the bed. Valentine winced at the sight of the red petals. The rational Valentine wondered if he had remembered it was also the anniversary of their break-up. But the addict Valentine took over again, helping Finn pull off her dress and stripping off his clothes. She lay wantonly back on the bed, drank champagne with him, then writhed with pleasure as he trickled it over her body and kissed and licked it off, and by the time he reached her Agent Provocateurs she really didn't care. And then he was inside her and they were fucking. Everything else melted away as waves of pleasure rippled through her and the thought went through her mind that for now at least he belonged to her. And oh, this was going to be so good, this was so good, she was nearly there and it was going to be so good coming together. But, hang on! *That was quicker than usual*, she thought as Finn groaned and oh babied and oh Goded to his climax. Maybe he had something else in mind for her? But after the briefest of kisses he disengaged and flopped down on the bed next to her.

'That was fucking amazing, V,' he murmured, peeling off the condom and throwing it on the floor. Then to Valentine's deep disappointment and frustration he fell asleep. It had been four weeks; she had expected more.

She lay next to him for a while, enjoying the feeling of his body next to hers. He was so gorgeous, his skin golden-brown all over and without a blemish; his face was so handsome, resembling Jude Law in *The Talented Mr Ripley*. Some people, Lauren for instance, thought his looks were too pretty-boy, but Valentine thought he was just perfect. She couldn't resist him. Knew she should, but couldn't.

When they'd broken up she managed six weeks without speaking to him, resisting all his texts, calls and emails. She had been trying to build up the core of steel as directed by Lauren, but maybe not hard enough, because one night when he'd called begging her to see him and she was missing him particularly badly she'd given in. And after that time it became even harder to resist him. And so began the exquisite torture of being the other woman again, seeing him once or twice a month and always on his terms. Finn kept promising that he would leave Eva when the time was right, but the time never was. He couldn't leave her while she was in such and such a play as she'd be devastated; her dad was ill or some-thing else. Thinking about it did not make Valentine feel good about herself and she knew if one of her girlfriends was behaving in such a way she would really think that they had lost the plot. The trouble was she loved Finn like she had never loved another man. Their affair had been so intense and passionate. She sighed. Thinking of the past always made her feel blue. She wished Finn would wake up, hold her, tell her that he loved her, but he was out for the count. She traced a finger along his shoulder hoping he would wake up, but he batted her hand away in his sleep and turned over. She, on the other hand, wasn't at all sleepy; she felt totally wired.

She sat up in bed, looking round the room for evidence of his life with Eva. Finn was always claiming things were rocky between them and that Eva had moved out, but she was never sure how much to believe. On her last trip to the flat Valentine had discovered a set of her exquisite black lace La Perla lingerie. The size six on the label was like a slap in the face. She was double the size of the woman! The subsequent downward spiral had been particularly bad. Now she crept off the bed. Ugh! She stifled a 'fuck' as her foot squelched on the condom. She threw it in the bin and headed for the chest of drawers where she could see Finn's phone beckoning her over. She just had to see if there were any new pictures of Eva or the SGF [skinny girlfriend] as she thought of her. She knew she shouldn't – it was borderline stalkerish behaviour and plain wrong, but she couldn't stop herself. She gave a quick backward glance at Finn to check he was still asleep and picked up the phone.

A whole new set of pictures of Eva greeted her. She resembled a twenty-something Elle Macpherson, with her long limbs, waist-length honey-blonde hair, cheekbones and pouty sexy mouth as she reclined on the bed, giving Finn a come-hither look wearing the aforementioned skimpy underwear. Valentine was only slightly comforted by the next photo where the SGF was topless. Flat as a pancake. But Valentine's feeling of superiority lasted less than a few seconds as she reflected that these pictures did not show a couple on the brink of a break-up. Jealousy coursed through her and without thinking clearly she deleted the photographs. Regret swiftly followed. She was an idiot. If only she'd left them then every time Finn looked at the pictures he would be reminded of what the SGF hadn't got and remember Valentine's 'fantastic big tits'. It just showed that stalking did not pay.

Suddenly her own phone beeped. She quickly put Finn's phone down, looking behind her guiltily to make sure he hadn't woken up, but he was snoring quietly now. She rifled in her bag for her mobile, praying the text wasn't from Lauren asking her where the hell she was. To her surprise the message was from Jack: *Would it be wrong of me to tell you that I keep thinking of that kiss? Look forward to seeing you at rehearsal J x*. That was unexpected. She was flattered that Jack had texted her again. He was very attractive and it was unusual in her experience for a man to be so open about his feelings. And he had been a good kisser. A very good kisser. But he was not for her. Valentine got back into bed next to Finn and curled her body round his. He hated being touched when he was asleep and always protested that he got too hot. Sure enough Finn immediately moved to the opposite side of the bed, eluding her even in sleep. Valentine tried not to mind too much. She was here, lying next to him on her birthday; that was all that mattered.

She was woken the following morning by Finn sliding his hand over her breast and his insistent early-morning erection pressing into her back, 'I must clean my teeth!' she exclaimed, making a dash to the bathroom. 'Don't be long!' Finn ordered, pulling off the duvet to show off the good average standing to attention. Valentine hastily washed her face and cleaned her teeth. This time Finn was a more considerate lover, and took his time pleasing Valentine. And then he'd rounded off his performance by telling her he loved her. And that was exactly why, she reflected on the Tube journey home, her body still throbbing from their antics, she couldn't get him out of her head.

But by the time she got home, the ecstasy had been replaced by the agony. She crept into her bedroom without waking Lauren, swapped her dress for her PJs, then headed for the kitchen and reached for the peanut butter. She was never going to be a size six, so what was the point of even trying?

Lauren caught her as she shovelled toast into her mouth. 'I'd go easy on that if I were you, V, given the nipple-tassel situation,' she teased. Lauren never ate breakfast, only drank black coffee and smoked a cigarette. Who did she think she was, a bloody French existentialist?

Valentine shrugged; she was well on her way to the familiar pit of misery that followed a meeting with Finn and nothing could stop her now. 'Where are you off to anyway?' she asked through a mouthful of toast, seeing that Lauren had her coat on.

'I've got some modelling job; it's bound to be shit,' Lauren replied bitterly. She loathed modelling but it was good money and given her stunning looks she found it fairly easy to get work when she wasn't acting. She generally took her revenge by seducing the best-looking male model on the set. Lauren had the most amazing sexual confidence. She really did believe she could have any man she wanted, and her beauty helped her have her way. She was also a serial seducer, who couldn't see the point of relationships and turned her nose up whenever Valentine, a hopeless romantic, told her that she simply hadn't met the right man yet.

'Stop porking out!' Lauren ordered, walking out of the kitchen.

'Don't shag anyone I wouldn't,' Valentine called after her, trying to cheer herself up. So long as Lauren didn't bring back another model like her recent Russian conquest, whom both girls had called Dostoevsky behind his back. Trust Lauren to have the latest must-have lover. Dostoevsky was gorgeous, all high cheekbones, brooding dark eyes, raven-black hair, sculpted abs, and couldn't speak a word of English. That, of course, had been exactly how Lauren liked it. But Valentine had not enjoyed his presence in their flat one little bit. As he was Russian he was used to the biting cold and favoured wandering around stark naked, save for a large Cossack hat. She wouldn't have minded if he'd possessed anything to be proud of but the Russian had more of a party sausage than a saveloy.

Valentine took another savage bite of toast. At least she hadn't fried it Elvis Presley-style with banana and white bread. Then again, maybe she should. What difference would it really make to her career if she got fat? The phone hadn't exactly been ringing off the hook with auditions now she was slim and she couldn't see her part in the Shakespeare leading to greater things, whatever

spin Sylvia put on it. That was the thing about seeing
Finn; it always made her doubt every area of her life,
made her feel such a failure. But maybe if she porked up
she might actually get some work. She'd have to get *really*
fat, possibly morbidly obese, then she could corner the
market in fat women roles – though she was struggling
right now to actually think of any. There was the mother
in the Johnny Depp film *What's Eating Gilbert Grape* who
tragically dies. There was poor Shelley Winters in *The
Poseidon Adventure*, who wasn't even that fat and what was
her fate? She saved one of the other passengers, only to
die of a heart attack. The message in the movies rang
out loud and clear: fat people copped it.

And what about Finn? He was hardly going to want
her in that state, even if her fantastic big tits would probably get even bigger. OK, this would have to be the deal:
after she became a wildly successful super-sized star she
would slim down dramatically and then have surgery to
get rid of all the flabby skin – maybe even become a size
six – and Finn would realise that he couldn't live without
her; he'd leave Eva and they'd all live happily ever after . . .
What complete bollocks!

She threw her toast into the bin and crawled back into
bed, alternately daydreaming that she and Finn were
together and then tormenting herself with imagining what
he was up to with the SGF. Late afternoon she finally
emerged and reached for her laptop. No post-Finn misery
fest was complete without stalking him on Facebook. He was
too lazy to up load pictures on his site, except for his
official Stage photograph in black and white, but the SGF

wasn't. Eva just loved to show off her fabulous life and had made her profile accessible to everyone, so when Valentine logged on to her site there was all she needed to know for extra torture ammunition. Finn on a mini-break with the SGF in Florence, looking loved up; Finn on a stag weekend in Prague with his mates looking the worse for wear but still gorgeous; Finn staying with friends in the country.

If she hadn't been so in love with him Valentine might have seen that actually Finn was selfish, narcissistic and always sought out people who would give him an easy life, even if he didn't especially like them. He had chosen many of his friends purely on the basis that they were wealthy and had second homes in the country or in Italy or wherever. Deep down Valentine knew that one of the reasons Finn couldn't bring himself to leave Eva was because she came from a wealthy family. Finally, with her head swimming with images of Finn's lovely life without her, she texted him. She always made herself wait as long as she could, a tactic which she hoped said *My life is so full, I've hardly given you a moment's thought.* And her message would be casual, cool and sexy. This time she went for: *That was delicious; I can't wait to taste you again . . . Vx* But sending the text brought no relief because now followed the agony of waiting for a reply, which sometimes came and sometimes didn't. Often Valentine wondered whether it would be better not to send the message in the first place, but she always did. She was truly Pavlov's dog.

* * *

She was still in her PJs an hour later, hunched over the screen, when Lauren stormed back from her modelling job, bitching about the photographer who had made her pose endlessly.

'And why aren't you dressed?' Lauren exclaimed. 'You got the part, so what's the problem?'

'I know, I know,' Valentine replied guiltily, switching off the laptop. There was no way she wanted Lauren to know about Finn. Usually she explained these blue periods as anxieties about work, but this time she had work. She'd have to lie, something she hated doing to Lauren of all people. 'It's just that I'll do the play and nothing will come of it.'

'You don't know that. It might lead to something else, but it won't lead to anything if you carry on lying in bed and filling your face with peanut butter.' Lauren, although not unsympathetic, believed in tough love and pulling yourself together. Her dad had run off with her mum's best friend when Lauren was seven, hence her core-of-steel mantra. 'Anyway, aren't we supposed to be meeting your mum and Lottie for cocktails?'

'Yes,' Valentine muttered.

'Well hurry up and get dressed; I'm desperate for a drink.'

Lottie, Valentine's bohemian and eccentric aunt, was easy to spot in the bar, as in the sea of little black dresses and suits she was wearing a bright-green velvet dress, purple suede boots, and her hair was a vibrant red, matching her red lips. As soon as she saw them she waved frantically, causing her many gold bangles to jingle loudly on her arm. Valentine's mum Sarah was already at the table, chalk to Lottie's cheese in a navy wrap dress, her curly chestnut hair uncoloured, subtle make-up on. Lottie, a former actress, was flamboyant in both the clothes she wore and in her personality. Sarah was calm and laid back. After the happy birthdays and exchange of gifts (Lottie had bought her a set of gold jangly bracelets like her own that Valentine was unlikely ever to wear and her mum had played it safe with Valentine's favourite perfume, Coco Mademoiselle) Lottie proceeded to bombard her with questions about her new role. Lottie had been the one who had encouraged her to go to drama school in the first place. She'd acted until ten years ago, when she'd finally abandoned her dream and had become a drama teacher at a sixth-form college in Barnet.

'I should warn you that I might have to wear nipple tassels,' Valentine said grimly, the comment mainly directed at her mum.

Lottie laughed uproariously. 'She's hardly going to be bothered by that, is she darling! She probably had her hand up someone's vaginal passage most of the morning!'

Valentine rolled her eyes and said in a loud voice in case anyone had overheard, 'She's a midwife! Honestly, Lottie!'

'So do you think anything will come of the play?' her mum asked when she could finally get a word in. There it was: the reality check, the icy bucket of water on her dreams. Much as she loved her mum, it was a real bone of contention between them that Sarah had never seemed .

to take Valentine's acting career seriously. Valentine couldn't help thinking that her mum would have been so much happier if she had followed her into nursing. She'd lost count of the times she'd tried to explain that an acting career was not like nursing – it did not follow a single trajectory upwards. It was up and down – mostly down in her experience to date – erratic and uncertain. She shrugged. 'I don't know.'

Sarah sighed. 'I see all these actresses on the TV and I think, why isn't it you? You're just as talented. More so, I think. You as well, Lauren.'

'You just have to accept it,' Lauren replied, used to Sarah's comments.

Valentine hated having this conversation with her mum; they'd had variations on it for the last twelve years. From the moment Valentine had decided, aged fifteen, that she wanted to be an actress it had been like hitting a wall of resistance from her parents. They just didn't get it; in their world you got a job, followed a steady career path and ended up with a pension. The arts were for other people, not them. Thank God for Lottie, who had always been her champion and encouraged her in her dream.

Valentine rolled her eyes, while her mum continued on the topic most likely to wind everyone up.

'And why hasn't your agent lined you up with anything else, V?' She hesitated. 'You've had her for nearly five years, haven't you?'

Valentine knew that her mum was only saying these things because she cared and because she worried about her not having a proper job and not having any money or security, but right now she wanted her to button it.

'And offers of work haven't exactly been flooding in,' Valentine said bitterly, finishing the sentence for her. 'Isn't that what you were going to say?'

'Not exactly,' her mum tried to pacify her. Valentine took a very large sip of her cocktail.

'Now, this is not a helpful conversation, is it?' Lottie put in, 'Sarah, I have tried to explain to you about how the acting world works. You simply can't apply the same principles to it as you can to nursing!' Lottie was getting quite heated now. She hated it when Sarah appeared to have a go at Valentine and she always came to Valentine's defence, as if re-enacting scenes from her own life. She had also been hitting the cocktails, judging by the blast of pure alcohol she emitted every time she opened her mouth.

'Well, at least with nursing you get a regular salary,' Sarah replied, also getting defensive now Lottie was involved.

'Money isn't everything,' Lottie shot back.

'You know how hard the acting world is, don't you! I just don't want Valentine to end up bitter and frustrated—'

'Like me, you mean!' Lottie cut across her.

Oh Jesus, not the full sister-on-sister row! Valentine looked around the bar and saw that they were attracting the attention of the other drinkers.

'No, of course I didn't mean that! But can you seriously say that if you had your time again you would go into acting? You were so bright, Lottie, you could have done anything.'

Lottie seemed to be turning pale with anger; her nostrils

flared, she shook back her long red hair and slammed her fist on the table, causing her many gold bracelets to jangle furiously. 'Acting is what I was meant to do! I have no regrets about following that star, even if I didn't get to appear in *Holby* Fucking *City* or *Pride* and Bollocking *Prejudice* on the BBC, which seems to be your only measure of success. I loved it! And I was good at it. And yes, I wish I'd had the career of Kristen Scott Thomas, but I didn't! And now I teach and I probably do have a bit of an alcohol dependency problem, but I am not bitter and frustrated. *Je ne regret rien!*' Another slam of her fist on the table and a frenetic jingle of bracelets. She was formidable in anger, and Valentine suddenly remembered seeing her play Martha in *Who's Afraid of Virginia Woolf?* She really had been mesmerising.

'And I would take this from anyone but you! You who have it in your power to set your daughter on the path to success.'

Valentine stared at her aunt, wondering what on earth she was talking about. While her mum had never been exactly enthusiastic about her acting she had never stood in her way.

'Don't you even go there!' Sarah hissed at Lottie, her eyes blazing, her normally calm – I'm a midwife you can trust me, and this won't hurt that much – expression replaced by one of pure rage. 'We're supposed to be celebrating V's birthday; this is not the time.'

'Shall I get some more drinks in?' Valentine attempted to cut across the two women, but nothing was going to stop them now.

'It's about time she knew the truth! It could make all the difference to her, and you know it!'

'I said don't go there!' Sarah repeated. Valentine had never seen her mum look so impassioned.

'Oh don't worry, I won't tell her now, but if you don't tell her soon, I will, because Valentine has a right to know.' Lottie took a deep breath as if trying to calm herself. 'V, I'm really sorry. We shouldn't have behaved like this; it was your night. I'm going now, but I'll see you soon,' and before Valentine could say anything else her aunt blew her and Lauren a kiss and swept out of the bar without a backward glance, her green velvet dress billowing out behind her.

'What the hell was that all about?' Valentine turned to ask her mum, but Sarah was putting on her jacket and doing up her buttons with trembling fingers. 'I've got to go too,' she said, opening her purse and counting out the money for the drinks. 'This should cover the bill.'

'*Mum!* Tell me.'

'I'm sorry love, I've got to go. I'll call you tomorrow, sorry.' And with that Sarah got up and practically ran out of the bar.

'Am I in a Mike Leigh film?' Valentine asked Lauren. 'Do you have any idea what the hell they were on about? Do you think Lottie has early onset dementia from all the drinking?'

Lauren considered. 'Maybe you're fantastically rich and your mum has been keeping it from you all this time so you don't turn into Paris Hilton.' They drank another round of cocktails, continuing to speculate wildly.

The events of the evening had one good effect though, as Valentine realised when she got home: she'd barely given a thought to Finn and she hadn't even checked to see if he had texted. It was a good feeling. Though inevitably it didn't last and like an addict craving her fix she logged on to Facebook. The SGF had uploaded more pictures, nauseatingly entitled *The Day After Valentine's Day with my love*, of the two of them on Hampstead Health – looking spectacularly loved up and photogenic and, Valentine was glad to see, cold. But wouldn't you like to know what he was up to the night before? Valentine thought. For a fleeting second she thought of emailing her, but no, that really wasn't Valentine's style. She couldn't blame the SGF. She was just in love with Finn as Valentine was. And Valentine was the other woman. She was in the wrong.

She woke up suddenly the following morning to the sound of Lauren knocking on her door and informing her that her mum was there. She got up and found Lauren making a cafetiere of coffee in the kitchen while Sarah sat at the table, looking uncharacteristically tense. Valentine gave her a quick kiss on the cheek and sat down. Her mum looked terrible, as if she hadn't slept at all; there were dark shadows under her eyes and she didn't appear to have brushed her hair before coming out. It was most unlike her.

'So is this about what Lottie said last night?' Valentine asked.

'Lauren, could you spare a cigarette?' Sarah asked, stunning both Lauren and Valentine.

'*Mum!* You don't bloody smoke!' Valentine exclaimed in outrage. She couldn't have been more surprised if her mum had demanded a line of coke, she was so fervently anti-smoking. It had been the only bone of contention between her mum and Chris, who couldn't do without his roll-ups.

'I need something and it's too early to have a drink.'

Lauren expertly made a roll-up for Sarah and lit the cigarette for her, while Valentine looked on, thinking that she was having some kind of hallucination. Sarah inhaled and spent the next few minutes choking.

'See, it's not big or clever, is it?' Valentine said sarcastically, while Sarah shot her a filthy look and carried on trying to inhale.

'I could quite enjoy this,' Sarah spluttered.

'Well you're not going to get the chance; this is your first and last cigarette, young lady!' Valentine declared, mimicking her mum's exact words when she had caught her having a fag while leaning precariously out of her bedroom window, aged fourteen.

Sarah made a few more attempts to smoke, then reluctantly handed the cigarette back to Lauren, who tactfully said, 'Right, I'll leave you guys to it. I've got a casting.'

Suddenly Valentine felt apprehensive, she clasped her cup of coffee for comfort. What if it was something really awful, like her mum had cancer? She could even feel her eyes filling with tears at the prospect. 'So what's this big thing you have to tell me, Mum?' she asked tentatively. 'You're not ill, are you?'

Sarah shook her head, 'No, no! It's nothing like that.

I'm sorry, Valentine, maybe Lottie is right and I should have told you before. I honestly thought I was doing this for the best.'

'Mum, please just tell me!'

Sarah took a deep breath and said quickly, 'OK then, there is no easy way of breaking this to you. This is going to be a real shock.'

She hesitated.

'*Mum!*'

'Chris wasn't your father.'

'What?' Valentine exclaimed, her mind scrambling to make sense. 'I don't understand.' She suddenly longed for a cigarette herself. She really was in a Mike Leigh film. Either that or *Mamma Mia*. But her mum didn't look as if she was about to burst into an Abba song – she definitely had more of an anxious Brenda Blethyn expression than a I'm-still-hot-and-I'm-nearly-sixty Meryl Streep look.

'Your father was someone I met before Chris. We had a fling and I fell pregnant with you.'

Valentine was about to say something sarcastic about contraceptives, remembering only too well her mum's lectures on the subject when she was a teenager, but Sarah's serious expression stopped her. 'I was only nineteen but I knew I wanted to keep you. He – your father – moved away before I could tell him. When you were a year and a half I met Chris, fell in love with him and the rest you know.'

Did she? Valentine was reeling from the secret her mum had kept from her for all these years.

'So who's my father then?' Valentine asked. She suddenly felt very wobbly. She thought she knew everything about her background and now it appeared she didn't. Her mum clasped her hands together as if she was praying before she replied. 'He's Piers Hunter, the film director.'

Valentine let out a hysterical laugh; the news just seemed too incredible. Piers Hunter was one of Hollywood's most successful film directors. He'd made a string of blockbusters which had grossed hundreds of millions at the box office. 'Mum! That is just insane! Are you feeling OK?' Oh God, perhaps her mum was going mad – the stress of coping with Chris's death and Valentine's brother Matt's recent drug conviction.

'I met him through Lottie, when he was directing a play she was in. It was purely a physical attraction, to be honest. I knew there wasn't going to be any future in it, but he was very good looking and charming. Our fling or whatever only lasted a couple of weeks.'

'I just don't understand why you didn't tell me before,' Valentine said. It seemed very out of character for her mum not to be completely honest.

Sarah fiddled with the sleeve of her jumper, clearly not finding this conversation at all easy. 'You were just a baby when I married Chris; he was to all intents and purposes your dad. He was the one who brought you up, who loved you like his own.'

'So he – Piers – knows about me then?' Valentine asked slowly, trying to piece together the jigsaw of her life, which suddenly felt wildly mixed up.

'I don't know. Chris thought that we should tell him about you so when you were five, I wrote him a letter, but heard nothing, but I wrote again when you were ten, then fifteen, and finally when you were eighteen, but there was no reply. I suppose I took his silence as his answer; that actually he didn't want to know you. Don't be too angry with me, V.'

'I'm not angry, Mum,' Valentine said, getting up and hunting down Lauren's Rizlas and tobacco and quickly rolling herself a cigarette. This definitely counted as an emergency. 'Just completely and utterly shell-shocked.' She lit the cigarette and inhaled deeply. 'Does Matt know?'

Sarah shook her head, 'Of course not!'

'So now I've got a father I never knew and my brother is my half-brother and the man I thought was my dad wasn't.' She felt on the verge of hysteria, but then looked at her watch and sighed. She desperately needed time to take in the news and work out her feelings, but in half an hour her first rehearsal started; she couldn't be late.

She felt in a daze all the way to the theatre. She had never even suspected that Chris might not be her real dad. It was like being told that after all the world was square. True, she and Chris had absolutely nothing in common. He had never understood her driving ambition to be an actress and at times that had been difficult, but that wasn't such an unusual scenario between father and daughter. And in all other respects he'd been a great dad, easy going and warm. Valentine had been devastated when he had died three years ago from a heart attack. And now she had a famous dad. A famous dad who apparently didn't want to know. Suddenly she understood exactly why her mum hadn't wanted to tell her, as an insidious feeling of rejection washed over her. She tried to summon Lauren's core of steel, but found herself silently crying. First Finn had rejected her and then she'd found out that her real dad didn't want her either. She was so lost in her thoughts that she completely missed her stop. She ended up having to run to the theatre, late again.

4

Fairy Queen

She walked into the theatre to discover the actors sitting in a circle on the floor with Vince standing up in the middle as if to emphasise his superior status. Shit! She was hardly going to be able to creep in unobserved. She hesitated at the doorway. Vince was in full flow. Suddenly he noticed her. 'Ah, Titania! We were wondering what had happened to you.'

'I was drugged by a fairy and then fell in love with a donkey; you know, the usual scenario,' Valentine said, walking towards the circle, aware of twenty pairs of eyes on her and feeling like a naughty schoolgirl being ticked off. Vince didn't crack his face.

'Sorry, the bus was late,' she mumbled, sitting down next to an actress called Kitty, whom she'd worked with before. She could hardly give the real reason: sorry, I've just found out that my real dad is an internationally famous film director. Emotionally I'm a bit shaken up right now.

'Well, if you could try to be on time, Valentine,' Vince

said a little tersely. 'The rehearsal period is tight, with just four weeks.' It was only to be expected. It was very rare for companies to have a longer rehearsal period, especially in off-West End productions where the actors were getting paid a pittance.

'Sorry,' Valentine repeated, and looking up saw Jack sitting opposite her, his long legs stretched out in front of him. He grinned broadly when he caught her eye. Suddenly she remembered the text he'd sent and the kiss that had led to the text. She was surprised how disconcerted she felt. Get a grip, woman! It was just a kiss in an improvisation!

'Anyway, now we finally have our Titania we can do the introductions,' Vince continued. 'You all know of course that I'm Vince Powell-Lancaster.' Or VPL, Valentine thought and fought the urge to giggle. 'So now over to you. It's crucial that we bond quickly as a company given that the play is going to be pushing the boundaries and contain scenes of nudity.' Valentine noted that none of the cast looked thrilled by that last comment; she obviously wasn't alone in dreading it. 'So can we go round the circle, tell us your role and three significant things about yourself.'

'Cringe alert,' Kitty muttered.

'So who wants to start?' Vince demanded. There was a pause, during which Valentine lowered her eyes and made a thorough investigation of her shoe; please don't let it be her! She hated doing this kind of thing.

'OK, I'll go first.' It was Jack. Valentine looked up. 'I'm Jack Hart,' he said confidently. 'I'm playing Bottom.

I'm Gemini. I hate bullies and my favourite film is *The English Patient*.'

Valentine almost did a double take; that was *her* all-time favourite film. She had been bitterly disappointed when Finn had told her it was one of the most boring films he had ever seen. She looked at Jack with a new feeling of respect and again he caught her eye and smiled. He really was very good-looking. Though possibly he was too testosterone-charged for Valentine, who liked pretty boys, and a little too hairy judging from the chest hair visible from the v of his black shirt. She had one of those repulsion/attraction moments as she tried to imagine the extent of the body hair. Would he, horror of horrors, have a hairy back? Like a beast? Like a sexy beast, it had to be admitted. Finn had hardly any hair on his chest. In fact Valentine sometimes worried that she was hairier than he was and a phone call from him inviting her over would always trigger a frantic deforestation of body hair by razor, which was frankly annoying as she preferred to wax.

Sexy, hairy Jack had broken the ice for everyone and they all followed suit, giving their star sign, a pet hate and their favourite film. Vince, or VPL as he would for ever now be known to Valentine, probably wanted them to say far more meaningful things – like when I read Chekhov my life changed and the Stanislavsky acting method is the only one to follow blah blah blah, but he couldn't expect to get trust right away. Valentine tried to work out what the actors were going to be like from their comments – Toby, in his mid-thirties, was playing Theseus the duke and

Oberon, and sounded a sweetie. He disliked liquorice and his favourite film was *Some Like It Hot;* Alexander, (or Xander as he wanted to be called) the actor playing Demetrius, one of the young lovers, sounded a bit of a tosser. He hated the congestion charge and his favourite film was *Top Gun*. Would he turn out to be the wanker in the cast? Every company had one; it was practically the law and was usually someone with a super-sized ego who thought they were a much better actor than they really were. *Xander,* Valentine thought, *it could be you . . .* Or then again it could be Emily, the ravishingly pretty girl sitting next to Jack. She was playing Helena, one of the leads, and was straight out of Oxford; she hadn't bothered with drama school. Valentine suddenly realised why she looked familiar; she was the daughter of Tilly Wilson, a very successful actress who was in practically every single costume drama on the BBC. Doubtless Emily would not be doing off-West End for long with those connections. On top of that she sounded way too pretentious: her favourite film was Ingmar Bergman's *The Seventh Seal* (not exactly a barrel of laughs); Kitty, who was playing Hermia, hated Starbucks and her favourite film was *Pulp Fiction* – she even had the same stylish black bob as Uma Thurman's character, but hopefully not the same heroin addiction; Rufus, a boyishly good looking black actor whom Valentine had met at a very unfortunate casting for a music video, which gave both of them carpet burns – enough said – hated four-by-fours and his favourite film was *Reservoir Dogs*. He and Kitty were bound to get along.

And that left Valentine. 'I'm Valentine, I'm Aquarius,' she hesitated, trying to think what to say next. She could hardly say that she hated red roses and Italian food – she would sound like a total mentalist. 'I hate paying bills and my favourite film . . .' – another hesitation, 'I'm really not copying you Jack, but it would have to be *The English Patient.*'

'It really is,' Kitty put in. 'She's watched it over twenty times, haven't you?'

Now she really did sound like a mentalist. She caught Jack's eye and he smiled at her again. Cue another attraction/repulsion moment.

More input from Vince followed, inviting contributions from the actors, but only every now and then. Vince liked the sound of his own voice. A lot. Valentine still wasn't wild about Vince's vision of the wood as a giant nightclub and the fairies, herself included, as decadent, pleasure-seeking nymphos. But Shakespeare was such a genius that even if directors like Vince did go off on one, the language and drama always shone through. Well, that was the thought she would hang on to, she told herself. And every now and then when Valentine found herself looking in Jack's direction, he would grin conspiratorially or roll his eyes if Vince was sounding particularly wanky – which was quite frequently. Valentine arched her eyebrow back in return, a gesture she was very proud of having perfected. She decided that she knew exactly the kind of man Jack was. There was always an actor like him in a company as well as 'the wanker' – a charming good-looker whom everyone lusted after. Well, good luck to him and to the other women in the cast — especially Emily, who could barely drag her eyes away from him, and indeed to the men — Toby seemed pretty smitten also. Jack was not Valentine's type and that was that. She was here to work and she needed the part to go well. She was not going to be distracted by a man, however gorgeous, even if he did love her all-time favourite film and had liked the way she kissed.

At one they broke for lunch, to Valentine's relief, as she was freezing and had a numb bum from sitting on the floor. Everyone headed off to the nearest pub, of the traditional seen-better-days variety. Valentine found herself next to Jack. He clearly did not believe in small talk. 'So did your boyfriend take you out on a romantic Valentine/birthday dinner?' A question guaranteed to warm Valentine's heart — not.

'No,' she mumbled, 'I haven't got a boyfriend.' *Just an ex who calls me for sex, whom I can't stop loving.*

'What about your girlfriend?' she asked, wanting to deflect his attention. 'Nope,' he shook his head emphatically. 'Don't have one. So did you get my text?' He looked at her, his deep brown eyes serious, searching and very lovely she had to admit. 'I meant what I said.'

'Meant what?' Valentine asked, deciding for once in her life to play it cool. 'Oh, the kiss! I'd completely forgotten to be honest.'

A sceptical look from Jack, 'Well I'm glad you got the part, even if you seem to have selective amnesia. I just hope you're OK at learning your lines.'

'Ha fucking ha,' Valentine shot back. 'And I'm looking forward to seeing you in a donkey mask. And by the look of the hairs on your chest . . .' she reached out and peaked inside Jack's shirt, which was very forward but she couldn't resist being cheeky, 'they could always be used to make the donkey fur, given that the costume budget is bound to be tiny.'

'What's the matter with you, Valentine? Never seen a real man before?' Jack asked, doing up one of the buttons on his shirt and laughing at her. 'I didn't have you down as batting for the other side.'

Valentine curled her lip at the expression. 'Oh please, what public school did you go to?'

Jack shook his head. 'Didn't. And anyway you should be gentle with me, sweet Titania; this is only my second role out of drama school. I may have seemed all cocky last week but actually I was shitting it.'

'I'd never have known,' she replied slightly grudgingly, remembering how he had oozed, yes bloody *oozed* confidence and remembering her own dishevelled entrance. 'So how come you're only just out of drama school, given that you're no spring chicken?' She was aware that she was doing that thing of being rude to someone when actually you quite like them, but was enjoying herself too much to stop.

'I'm thirty, cheeky pants.' He gave her a considering look and Valentine cared enough about his opinion to flick back her hair, put her shoulders back and stick her chest out. 'I'm guessing two or three years older than you.'

'Three,' Valentine admitted, slightly peeved that he didn't think she was younger.

Jack continued, 'I was training to be a barrister but I hated it. Well, I liked the court bit. It was all that slaving over the cases every night that got me, so I jacked it in. I'd always wanted to act, anyway. So how about you?'

'Well, it's hardly been a glittering career since leaving drama school,' Valentine said dryly. 'I mean, I didn't expect overnight success, but Jesus, it's tough.'

'So what have you done?' Jack continued. She could tell that he was fresh out of drama school – all these questions. She felt like saying *Look I'm twenty-seven and I'm in a frigging off-West end play, go figure!* Instead she replied airily, 'Theatre mainly,' praying he wouldn't press her further as she'd only been in small productions, with the exception of a short run in the West End in *Jane Eyre*. And I've done some TV and a film.' Another prayer that he didn't press her as that included a non-speaking part in an advert for low-fat oven chips (oh the glamour, but at least it hadn't been for feminine hygiene products like one of her friends), a part in *The Bill* as a heroin addict and shoplifter – but as everyone gets a part in *The Bill* that didn't really count. Plus she had been a murder victim in *Waking the Dead*. She was in two scenes: one where she had to scream, just before she was strangled (giving her quite a terrifying double chin worthy of Jabba the Hut, she thought when she saw the episode) and the other when she was lying on the slab, looking blue – definitely not a good colour for her. And there'd been her film role, where she played the wife of a brutal drug dealer who was about to turn him over to the police. It had been a fantastically gritty and demanding part which Valentine had thought was easily her best work, and so had her agent, but unfortunately the film didn't get a distributor and so was only seen at film festivals. She sighed and took a sip of her mineral water. Just talking about her flatlining acting career depressed the hell out of her.

'Well, I'm sure it's just a matter of time with your talent and good looks,' Jack answered.

Valentine frowned at him, unable to work out if he was being genuine or taking the piss, so she sarcastically replied, 'Yeah right – in the meantime Keira bloody Knightly has my career.'

'Um, she's very beautiful, but—' Jack gave her one of his appraising looks again. 'You're much sexier and you've got breasts. So you win.'

Valentine pulled a face of mock-indignation and put on her best Southern Belle outraged accent. 'Why, Mr Hart, you've only just met me and you mention my breasts!'

Jack shrugged, 'We're halfway there as I saw your bra at the audition and you've looked inside my shirt. I've got to prepare myself for what will be the awesome wearing of the nipple tassels. Far better if I get your breasts off my chest, so to speak. In fact I think it would be a good idea if you showed me them now and then I can stop fantasising about them,' Jack carried on, his eyes with a mischievous, naughtiest-boy-in-the-school sparkle in them.

Valentine folded her arms protectively across her chest and said, 'The tassels are still up for discussion.'

Jack shook his head. 'Oh there will be no discussion; you'd better start practising. I could coach you.'

'It's not funny, Jack. VPL has booked Twirlies to be the fairies – they're arriving next week.'

'What are Twirlies?'

'Professional dancers. I am going to look like a sumo wrestler compared to them.'

At this Toby, who was sitting next to Jack, gave Valentine a sympathetic look and said, 'Don't worry, Valentine. Jack's making too much of the whole nudity thing because he's new to the business. Do you wear contact lenses?'

Valentine shook her head, wondering why he'd asked.

'Oh, it's just that if you did I was going to suggest you didn't wear them on stage. If you can't see anyone else clearly, you imagine that they can't see you either!'

Valentine smiled, appreciating Toby's effort. 'That would be good, but I've got perfect eyesight and this seems like the one time that will be a disadvantage.'

'I've got twenty-twenty vision too,' Jack put in. 'And I don't see any problem with that at all.' He winked at Valentine.

Toby said, 'I don't know why Jack is sounding so pleased with himself. Last I heard Vince had his heart set on having Bottom naked when he was transformed into the donkey.'

Jack shook his head disbelievingly. 'No way!' But Valentine was secretly pleased to see he looked ever so slightly anxious.

'I can see why Vince wants that,' she put in, sounding earnest. 'It makes that whole scene between Bottom and Titania more sexually charged and dynamic. You know Vince wants to push the boundaries with the play and get himself a name and what better way than with a bit of male nudity? It always gets the critics very overexcited.'

Jack's confident persona was crumbling before Valentine's eyes, especially when Toby put in, 'Bloody freezing in that theatre though, isn't it? I can't say that I'd like to get my kit off in those conditions. The cold can do terrible things to a man's . . .' he paused, 'Well there's no way to put it delicately really, is there . . .? To his todger.' At that he slapped Jack heartily on the back and said, 'Cheer up! We could always get in a fluffer before you go on stage; you know, to inject a bit of life in the old boy.' Toby was so clearly taking the piss and Valentine was struggling not to laugh. But Jack was well and truly taken in now.

'What do you mean, a fluffer? I thought they were only used on porn films.'

'Oh no! It's an ancient theatre tradition whenever male nudity is involved. Of course the fluffer has to be careful not to overstimulate the member, just do enough to make it look presentable,' Toby deadpanned. 'It's a real art – only an expert can achieve that slight tumescence but not a fully fledged erection, which obviously causes problems.'

'How come I never heard about this at drama school?' Jack demanded, a picture of outrage.

'It's just one of those things that they like you to find out for yourself,' Toby said evenly.

'Well, I'm not going to do it – not the nudity or the fluffer bit. I didn't sign up for this when I accepted the part. I'm going to phone my agent.' And with that he got up and practically ran out of the pub, scrabbling in his pocket for his mobile.

Toby and Valentine both gave in to the laughter. 'Toby, that was genius!' she spluttered.

'Not bad was it? I just didn't want you to feel uncomfortable about what you have to do.'

'You're a real sweetheart,' she said and leant over and gave him a quick kiss on the cheek and then laughed again, thinking of the shocked expression on Jack's face.

After lunch VPL once more corralled the actors into a circle while he stood in the middle. 'OK, listen up everybody. Before we talk about the text anymore,' – *translation*, thought Valentine, *before I talk about the text anymore* – 'I thought we'd spend some time doing some trust exercises. Because the play is going to contain some nudity we need to really come together and bond as a company.' VPL looked even more intense than usual and Valentine sneaked a glance at Jack, pointed at him and mouthed, 'You naked.' Jack frowned; he obviously hadn't discovered Toby's joke yet. But then he mouthed back, 'You nipple tassels.' Valentine stuck her tongue out.

Unfortunately this was the moment VPL chose to look at her. 'Anything you want to share, Valentine?' he asked sarcastically, 'because sharing and trust is going to be very important for all of us.'

Valentine shook her head, having a feeling that she'd

be for it now. 'OK, you can be the first to experience the trust that we're going to have. I want you to stand in the middle of the circle.'

Shit! Valentine hated trust games. HATED them! Extremely reluctantly she got up and walked into the middle of the circle. She felt horribly exposed. 'Now everyone come closer and form a tighter circle round Valentine,' VPL continued. 'Valentine, I want you to close your eyes and fall forward. The others will catch you and then push you back so you are moved round the circle.' The rest of the company had now regrouped themselves around her. 'OK, we're ready for you,' VPL spoke. 'Just close your eyes and fall backwards.'

Very reluctantly Valentine did as she was told. There was that sickening moment of falling through the air when it felt like no one was going to catch her and then someone did and gently pushed her backwards. She tried to relax, but it was not a pleasant sensation as she was passed round the circle, not knowing who was touching her. Suddenly she was pushed forward and caught under the arms by someone who staggered under the weight. 'Christ! I think I've put my back out!' It was Xander. She opened her eyes. Great, now she felt like a complete porker. So much for building trust.

'What? Over a little slip of a thing like Valentine?' Jack moved in front of Valentine and to her surprise picked her up and swung her round in his arms as if she weighed very little. When in fact at last weigh-in it was nine and a half stone. It was such a delightful sensation and so sweet of Jack, Valentine couldn't help laughing.

'You can put me down now,' she said after he'd swung her round a couple of times, 'and thank you.'

After he'd put her down he bowed and kissed her hand. 'Any time.'

Valentine felt swept off her feet in more ways than one.

5

Much Ado About Something

Valentine had always thought that Lauren was completely unshockable, but as she told her the news about her father later that night her friend was left speechless. Not even a *motherfucker* escaped her as she sat there open-mouthed. Finally she pulled herself together enough to ask, 'So how do you feel, V?'

Valentine sighed. 'All over the place. Part of me wishes that mum and Chris had told me the truth, but then again I understand why they didn't. I don't know if I could have handled knowing that my real dad didn't want anything to do with me.'

'You'd have ended up like me after my dad walked out – hard-hearted and unable to commit, but with a core of steel,' Lauren only half-joked. Then she shook her head, reassessing. 'No, you would have tortured yourself and it would have shredded your self-esteem. I can see exactly why your mum didn't want to tell you. But now you know, what are you going to do?'

Valentine shrugged. 'I just don't know. I mean Chris,

to all intents and purposes, was my dad. Maybe I should forget about Piers. I've lived twenty-seven years without him and it's been fine, but then I think maybe I should contact him and try and get to know him. I feel that if I don't I might not ever really know myself. But then again I don't know if I can bear it if he rejects me.' She paused to bite her thumbnail. 'Oh God, does that sound like a trailer for *Oprah*?'

'So long as you don't bounce on the sofa and whoop when Piers and you get invited on to talk about your relationship,' was Lauren's reply. 'I'd have to disown you for being a total tit.'

They spent the rest of the night Googling Piers. He had made over fifteen films but never won an Oscar; he had homes in LA and London and had been married to Olivia, a famous American actress, for over twenty years, which surely had to be something of a record for Hollywood. He had no other children. The pictures on the web showed a distinguished-looking man with blonde hair and chiselled features who was still handsome in his fifties. Valentine found herself staring at his photograph and wondering what kind of man he was, wondering if she had inherited her green eyes from him.

Later, when she was in bed, she called Finn, wanting to confide in him. But she only got his voicemail. Eva was probably back from filming. From now on she'd have to wait for Finn to call her. She felt lonely and hated being the other woman. Just as she was drifting off to sleep her phone beeped with a text. It wasn't from Finn as she had hoped, but Jack; a flirty, teasing, *Fleming, I'll get you back for the fluffer lie x.* She was about to send back a cheeky reply, then she thought, *what the hell,* and phoned him.

'Going to spin me another story, Fleming?' Jack said sleepily. Valentine had a not unpleasant image of him lying in bed.

'I was actually phoning to say sorry. No hard feelings?'

'There would be nothing hard if I had to go on stage naked, believe me. Anyway, it's me who should apologise. I realise it was out of order teasing you about your costume. I didn't mean to make you feel self-conscious.' Jack went up again in her estimation. 'I may have a hairy chest but I am evolved.'

Valentine had a sudden urge to ask if he had a hairy back. She felt she could deal with a hairy chest, but she wasn't at all sure about a hairy back. Maybe he could get it waxed.

They stayed talking on the phone for the next half-hour – swapping gossip about what they thought of the rest of the cast, and verdicts on plays and films they'd seen recently. All innocent subjects but there was a definite undercurrent of attraction in their banter. Jack was so easy to talk to – funny, charming, self-deprecating and very flirtatious. Flirtatious was good; it seemed ages since she'd flirted with anyone. The conversation was also a welcome reprieve from having to think about her big news. In fact she would probably have stayed talking to him for longer, but at midnight his doorbell went.

'Shit,' he said with feeling, 'I'd better get this. See you tomorrow, Valentine.' A beat. 'Nice talking to you. Did you know what a sexy voice you have?'

For the first time in a very long time, she didn't think about Finn as she fell asleep.

She woke early the next morning and forced herself to go for a run. Usually she loathed running, but the spectre of the nipple tassels and the Twirlies was very motivational. The exercise helped clear her head, and by the time she got home she had made a decision: she was going to contact Piers. It wasn't easy composing the letter.

> *Dear Piers, I hope this doesn't come as too much of a surprise but I am your daughter Valentine. Twenty-eight years ago you may remember you had a brief relationship with Sarah Fleming; well I am the consequence!*

The exclamation mark was a mistake; it made her sound like a crazy person. She scrunched up the paper and threw it in the bin. Her second, third and fourth attempts weren't much better. Valentine gave a sigh of exasperation. Every version she came up with really did sound like a trailer for Oprah: *This week multi-award-winning, successful film director Piers Hunter discovers he has a long lost daughter! Here they are on the sofa with me!* In the end she kept the letter brief and to the point.

> *Dear Piers, my name is Valentine Fleming. I know this is probably going to sound like a bolt from the blue but I believe that I am your daughter. Twenty-eight years ago you had a brief affair with my mother Sarah Fleming. It was while you were directing* The Importance of Being Ernest *in Oxford.*

I am an actress, living in London. I am not looking for anything other than the chance to meet you.

She finished by giving all her contact details and enclosing one of her black and white publicity shots. She also mentioned the play she was in. She hesitated at the post box. Could she really deal with the feeling of rejection if he didn't reply? She posted the letter. Core of steel. What would be, would be.

The flirting with Jack continued throughout the next two weeks of rehearsals. She found herself warming to him more and more. And his acting was a revelation. She had thought that he was completely wrong to play Bottom because he was so good-looking and assured, but on stage he transformed into the buffoon the role demanded. He was pompous, self-important and he even managed to make himself look less attractive by adopting a slightly buck-toothed smile. It was a fantastic performance. Valentine, meanwhile, was the femme fatale of the fairy world, doing her best to seduce him, while he was oblivious to her charms. VPL, who so far had doled out precious few compliments, praised her performance, telling her she was conveying just the right mix of comedy and sensuality. Her growing attraction to Jack was further heightened by Finn's distance. He finally called back but gave her no chance to tell him her big news; he was too full of his own as he was about to fly to the States to audition for a *CSI* something. 'This could be my big break, V,' he told her excitedly. Valentine was pleased for him, but couldn't help feeling that conversation with Finn was a one-way street.

However the downward spiral that would usually have been triggered by his lack of interest didn't materialise. And she tried not to dwell too much on the fact that Piers had yet to reply to her letter, though she was fanatical about checking her email. She told herself that he was bound to be away filming. Thank God she was acting as she knew if she wasn't she would have been obsessing over Piers's silence. But acting always gave her such a high. Not only did she feel good, she was convinced she looked better too. Her skin appeared brighter (probably because she'd massively cut down on alcohol and junk food), her eyes had a sparkle to them and even her hair seemed more manageable than usual. She loved working in a company again, getting to know everyone and feeling part of something. With a few exceptions (the wanker Xander and the ravishing and annoying Emily, who fancied the arse off Jack) she adored her fellow actors. It was like falling in love with everyone. She hung out mostly with Toby, Zara (a lovely Twirly), Kitty and Rufus (who were now a couple) and Jack after rehearsals and they invariably ended up going to the pub they'd nicknamed the Orange Peril because of its vile orange-patterned carpet that was so tacky with dirt that you felt you were going to be stuck like a fly on flypaper every time you stepped on it. There they would gossip and giggle and practically no subject was off-limits. That was the other thing she loved about other actors: when you bonded, you *really* bonded and confidences were quickly shared.

At the end of the second week her group were all deeply involved in discussing when they lost their virginity. Jack was in the middle of telling them how he lost his, aged sixteen, to a married woman he met when he was in an Am Dram production of *Noises Off*. Very Mrs Robinson in *The Graduate* they all agreed.

'Dirty cow!' Valentine exclaimed. 'You were practically jailbait!'

'I looked older than I was, plus I'd been working on a building site so I looked very muscular and tanned, though I say so myself.' He rolled up his sleeve to emphasise the point. Valentine found herself staring at his very lovely muscular arm. She did love a muscular arm and he had a striking tattoo on his shoulder of a dragon. She also loved a tattoo on a man.

'So you were her bit of rough trade,' Kitty put in. 'How did she seduce you, then?' There was a pause then Jack gave a wicked grin. 'She gave me a blow job backstage in the men's loos. I got the impression that she'd done it before to other members of the cast.'

'Or to other casts' members!' Valentine put in as she, Kitty and Zara laughed raucously, seeing the expressions of total envy on the other men's faces.

'And then she invited me round to her house the following morning, on the pretext that she needed some gardening doing. I didn't do any gardening, needless to say.'

'Just Mrs Robinson,' Valentine said dryly. 'Well, good for her; I expect she got the best of you. They always say a man's reached his sexual peak at eighteen, whereas a woman is a constant voyage of discovery.'

Jack moved closer to her and said quietly, 'Horrible mixing of metaphors there, Fleming, and you're so wrong; I'm in my prime. So there, sexy lips.' He gave her a challenging, come-and-test-out-my-theory-if-you-want look.

Valentine found herself holding his stare and thinking that, yes, that was a very tempting prospect.

'Oh, Jack darling, are you telling that story? Isn't it an absolute peach!' They had all been so engrossed in Jack's deflowering that they hadn't noticed the arrival of a very attractive forty-something woman. Valentine recognised her as the actress Julia Turner. She looked as if she'd just come from some event and was glammed up in a midnight-blue sleeveless dress, with killer black patent heels. She was beautiful, with pale skin, deep blue eyes, full lips and long silky black hair. 'I hope you don't mind me dropping in on you all like this, but I was in the area. Can I get anyone a drink?' she said in her trademark husky voice. She had cornered the market in lucrative sultry voiceovers for years. No one did husky quite like Julia Turner: *This is not just ordinary husky, this is Julia Turner husky*, kind of thing. She stroked Jack's arm possessively as she spoke, then Valentine heard her whisper, 'Why haven't you returned my texts?'

Jack muttered something about being busy. Valentine had been so intent on staring at Julia that she hadn't registered Jack, but now she glanced at him and saw that he looked furious. They were probably in the middle of some lovers' tiff. If she was honest she felt a little put out by Julia's arrival; she had been enjoying Jack's company and his flirty comments. And hadn't he said that he didn't have a girlfriend? She was sure that she wasn't jealous of Julia. It was just that Julia was an outsider and had broken up the lovely feeling of intimacy that the others had been building up. That was it, wasn't it? Jack pulled himself together sufficiently to make the introductions, ending up with Valentine. 'Valentine, this is Julia, Julia, Valentine.'

'Valentine? Isn't that a boy's name?' Julia said, looking Valentine up and down.

'It is,' Valentine admitted, wondering why Julia was giving her the once over. Surely she didn't see her as any kind of competition? There was Julia looking like a glamorous screen siren and there was Valentine practically looking like a crusty in clothes which were covered in dust from one of Vince's role plays where he'd had the cast charge around as wild animals, as he said the energy in the theatre was sluggish. She had no make-up on apart from mascara, so her face was no doubt as shiny as the moon, and her hair had gone completely unruly.

'Didn't you go to LAMDA?' Julia asked. 'You must have been there at the same time as a really good friend of mine, Eva Francis.'

Valentine nodded noncommittally. 'I didn't know her because she was two years above me.'

'I expect you knew her boyfriend, Finn Steele.'

Shit, if Julia was a friend of Eva's she was bound to know all about Valentine's affair with Finn.

'Yes, I knew him,' Valentine tried to say as evenly as possible, but she was aware of her heart racing. Julia was not exactly looking at her with the milk of human kindness.

'I know you did,' Julia said, her voice dangerously quiet.

Valentine suddenly wanted to be anywhere but the Orange Peril. She did not want Julia Turner picking over her life, judging her. She looked appealingly at Toby, hoping he would change the subject. Mercifully he was quick to react, and asked Julia what she was working on at the moment.

'Oh I'm in *Street Car*, at the Donmar; we start rehearsals next month.'

'Blanche Dubois, I presume?' Toby continued, as Julia nodded while Kitty and Valentine shared looks of complete jealousy at Julia landing such a fantastic role.

'I'd fucking love a part like that!' Kitty exclaimed while Julia went to the bar with Jack to buy a round. Julia's presence seemed to have unsettled all of them; even the charming Toby seemed rattled. It was as if her glamour and success were throwing a spotlight on them, showing up the fact that they were only in a small off-West End production while she was appearing in a cutting-edge West End theatre.

'I didn't know Jack was seeing Julia Turner,' Valentine said, wondering why he had lied and said he didn't have a girlfriend when Julia seemed to think that she occupied that role.

'Well,' Toby looked behind him to check the couple weren't in earshot, 'they were together but I think Jack broke up with her about three months ago.' Just as he finished speaking Julia and Jack returned with drinks.

'Cheers, everyone!' Julia declared, holding up her drink. 'Good luck with your play.'

'And good luck with yours,' Toby replied graciously. Now Julia was with them, much of the pleasure in the evening had gone for Valentine. She was unsettled by Julia's comments about Finn, and dreaded her bringing up the subject again. However, Julia seemed more intent on monopolising Jack. As Valentine chatted to Toby she kept hearing snatches of Jack's conversation with Julia – they seemed to be talking about Julia's daughter, Ruby.

'So where's Ruby tonight?' Jack asked.

'Oh she's at a sleepover,' Julia replied airily, then lowered her voice still further, but Valentine heard her say huskily, 'Why don't you come back?'

'No, Julia,' Jack replied, sounding exasperated. 'Please don't ask.'

'Please don't make me then,' Julia said emotionally, then lowered her voice still further so Valentine couldn't hear. She suddenly wanted to go home; she needed to clear her head. She quickly drained her drink, then stood up.

'Well, I'm off. See you all tomorrow.' She went round the table kissing everyone good night but simply blew Jack a kiss. Did he look disappointed that she was leaving? She couldn't tell. She was in a bad mood all the way home. Damn Julia Turner and her long silky hair; damn her for getting such a great role. And from out of nowhere she thought *damn her for being with Jack*. Now where did that come from?

'You obviously fancy him,' Lauren told her when she arrived back home, still seething. 'That's why you've got the hump.'

'He's got a hairy chest!' Valentine exclaimed.

Lauren frowned. 'What's your problem? I like them – they're very retro. Sexy. All that back, crack and sack waxing makes me nauseous. It looks too much like plucked chicken skin for my liking.'

'That's rich coming from you, Miss Brazil. Is there a hair left on your fanny by gaslight? And anyway, it's not about his chest. There's obviously unfinished business between him and Julia I'm-so-gorgeous-husky-voice Turner.'

Valentine was surprised how angry she felt. She and Jack had got into the habit of phoning each other late at night. When midnight came and went without a call from him she felt angrier still. He was probably shagging Julia Bloody Turner right now. Valentine imagined Julia sitting astride him, her lithe, slender body moving rhythmically, while Jack had his hands clasped round her waist (her bloody tiny I-can-fit-into-children's-jeans waist), his dark-brown eyes darker still with lust, she caressing his hairy muscular chest, as he groaned with pleasure at every movement of Julia's supple body and . . . WHAT was she doing thinking about the pair of them in bed? She was still angry the next day when she got up and went for her run. The anger and nipple-tassels fear combined to make her run faster and further than ever. But it did nothing to improve her mood. She stomped into the theatre determined to ignore Jack, but he sought her out and handed her a skinny latte.

'Thanks,' she muttered; she didn't feel like being gracious.

'I'm sorry about Julia bringing up the subject of your ex last night. She can be blindingly insensitive.'

'I'm sure she's told you that I had an affair with him,' Valentine said defiantly, though she felt anything but. 'I expect you're going to judge me for it.'

He sighed and ran his fingers through his thick dark-brown hair. He had black circles under his eyes and looked knackered. 'I wouldn't do that.'

But that wasn't enough for Valentine and she continued nastily, 'Kept you up last night did she, your girlfriend?'

'I told you, I don't have a girlfriend.'

'Yeah right.' Valentine felt as spiky as a sea urchin.

'I don't.'

'Oh, I get it. You don't *call* her your girlfriend, you just see her every now and then for sex. Ha! So fucking predictable.' Valentine was aware that her anger at Jack was out of proportion. Maybe he was just like Finn – why had she allowed herself to get even slightly close to him? At least with Finn she knew where she stood, knew what to expect.

'You're wrong; I don't treat women like that.'

'Oh really? Well, whatever you say doesn't matter; I've learnt not to trust any man.' Now she was sounding like the blurb on the back of a chick-lit novel – *Valentine Fleming can't trust any man, but will Jack Hart break down her defences?* She was being ridiculous, but she couldn't help it. Any minute now she'd flick back her hair and stamp her foot.

'He really messed you up, didn't he?' He didn't wait for her answer but moved closer to her, so close she got a hit of his musky, delicious aftershave. 'Well Valentine,

I'm not like that.' A beat. 'And I would never have let you go.'

Valentine was saved from having to reply by Vince calling a start to the rehearsal.

But much as she lost herself in her role, every time there was a break she'd think of Jack and his words. She treasured them as if she was holding up a diamond necklace and watching the jewels sparkle. He must like her to have said something like that. *It's just lust,* she told herself sternly, *nothing more.* Maybe she should have a no-strings shag with him? Just one, to get him out of her system. They could have sex all night, in a variety of positions; do everything to each other – well not quite everything; there were some things Valentine drew the line at. Then she snapped out of it. She was not a one-night-stand sort of girl. She knew herself too well and if she slept with him, she'd end up obsessing over him for the next six months, convinced she was in love with him – no way was she going down that route. It was a one-way street to Loserville, a place she'd visited too many times in the past. But not this time.

6

Family Values

Valentine had hardly spoken to her mum since the Piers revelation and she could only partly blame the hectic rehearsal schedule for that. The truth was that she did feel confused and shaken up by the news. Her mum had left several messages and Valentine felt slightly guilty for not returning them. Since Chris had died she had got in the habit of phoning her mum every other day and going to see her once a fortnight. When rehearsals finished unexpectedly early that day she took the opportunity to go and see her mum in East Sheen.

Sarah still lived in the terraced Edwardian house that she and Chris had bought when three-bedroomed houses in nice areas were affordable to people who worked in nursing. Every time Valentine went round she still half-expected to see Chris working on his mountain bike in the back garden, smoking the inevitable roll-up and drinking endless cups of tea, bantering with Sarah. They'd had such a good relationship, still in love after twenty years, still the best of friends. His death had left such a hole in all their lives. Matt, her brother, or rather her half-brother as she supposed she now had to think of him, had gone completely off the rails for a time, taking shedloads of drugs and dropping out of college, driving Sarah nearly out of her mind with worry. He was OK now, thank goodness and was back in college and off the drugs. Valentine rang the bell and Matt opened the door to her. He gave a mock bow and said, 'Welcome, my lady! To what do we owe the pleasure?' They were always teasing each other. Matt took the piss out of her for being an actress, and in his view pretentious; she took the piss out of him for being her annoying younger brother.

'I suppose Mum's told you the big news,' she replied, walking into the house.

'I always suspected there was something different about you, V,' he replied. 'It explains all your delusions of grandeur.'

She punched him affectionately on the arm and followed him into the kitchen. Matt's jeans were so low-slung it was frankly a mystery to Valentine why he was bothering to wear any at all – practically the whole of his boxers were on display. She instantly reverted to older sister mode. 'Pull your trousers up, Matt! No one wants to see your arse.'

'Actually, several people do,' he replied, giving her the finger.

Lottie and Sarah were sitting at the kitchen table, an open bottle of red wine between them. Clearly they had made up. Valentine kissed both of them and sat down. Lottie immediately poured her a large glass.

'Sorry about your birthday, V, I didn't mean to drop that bombshell on you and your mum like that,' Lottie said. 'I got a bit carried away; you know me.'

'It's OK Lottie,' Valentine replied. 'I think it had to happen sometime.' She looked at her mum, trying to gauge her feelings. She hated to think of Sarah worrying about her.

Sarah sighed. 'It was a bit of a clusterfuck though, wasn't it?'

Valentine and Matt rolled their eyes. Sarah grinned sheepishly.

'Sorry, when I was round at yours the other week I heard Lauren say it and I've been dying to use it ever since.' Lauren had a lot to answer for. Sarah rarely used to swear until she met her.

'It was, it is, Mum,' Valentine replied. 'I thought I should let you know that I wrote to Piers.'

The smile went from Sarah's face and she was back to looking anxious. 'And have you heard anything?'

Valentine shook her head.

'Try not to think about it,' Sarah urged her. 'Maybe he's away filming.' She used the exact same excuse that Valentine had to herself.

'Maybe he just doesn't want to know, Mum,' Valentine replied, and to hide how hurt she felt, took a large sip of wine.

'Oh Christ! Why didn't I keep my big fat mouth shut!' Lottie said with feeling. 'I'm sorry you two, I thought I was doing the right thing and now I've exposed you both to a world of pain. Can you ever forgive me?'

'She's off on one,' Matt said dryly, reaching into the fridge for the orange juice and drinking it straight from the carton.

'Matt!' the three women chorused.

He shrugged. 'I'm going to leave you three ladies to it; I'm seeing Daisy.' He paused and looked momentarily serious. 'V, don't stress about Piers. Chris was your dad and he loved us just the same; nothing's changed. You're still my sister and I love you.' Wow, emotional engagement from her brother; that was unexpected. She actually felt tears prickle her eyes. Matt snapped out of it. 'And don't drink all the wine, V, no one wants to see a bloated lush of an actress.'

'No one wants to see the crack of your hairy bum,' she shouted after him.

'It's not hairy anymore, Daisy waxed it,' he shot back.

'That was an over-share!' Valentine exclaimed as Matt slammed the door.

'He could wax his entire body so long as he isn't taking drugs anymore,' Sarah replied. She reached out and put her hand over Valentine's. 'We're OK V, aren't we?'

Valentine nodded. She couldn't bear to think of her mum agonising over whether she had made the right decision all those years ago.

Back home there was still neither letter nor email from Piers. He clearly wasn't interested in having a long-lost daughter. Valentine tried not to let it get to her. Lauren was in the living room cursing for England as she attempted unsuccessfully to light the fire, fag hanging out of her mouth, a super-sized glass of red wine next to her.

'Fuck, shit, piss, wank! Have you read this bollocky, sycophantic interview with Tamara Fucking Moore? All the crap about luminous skin this, wildly talented that, stylish, beautiful and wait for it – intelligent! Instead of what she's really like – a talentless, mean-natured, fat-arsed, botoxed stupid cow!' She picked up the magazine and hurled it across the room in disgust. 'Just once I want to read an honest interview with an actress, just once! Why do these magazines all conspire to make out that all successful actresses are perfect?'

Valentine shrugged. 'Because otherwise the actress would never do an interview with them again,' she suggested. 'Any wine left?' She definitely needed a drink after seeing her mum.

Lauren poured her a large glass, then retrieved the magazine and began colouring black spots on to Tamara's perfectly airbrushed skin, like a woman possessed. It was a little scary to watch, but then Tamara aroused strong feelings in both of them. 'Would it make you feel better to do the role play?' Valentine asked, realising that she was never going to be able to have a sensible conversation until Lauren had calmed down.

Lauren made Tamara's eyebrows meet in the middle and blackened out one of her teeth. 'Yes,' she said emphatically. 'You be the actress, I'll be the journalist.' The role play was something they did every now and then when they wanted to get certain issues about the acting world out of their system. Lauren always said it was cathartic, while Valentine wondered if it actually wound them up further. None the less she got into character as an internationally renowned movie star promoting her latest film. She sat up straighter and tucked her legs under her, and adopted a coy, dreamy expression, while Lauren spoke. 'When you – Valentine Fleming – agreed to do this interview, I was so thrilled. I mean, you are one of the leading, or rather *the* leading young actress of the day. Not only are you beautiful and talented, you also have the most amazing social conscience. Valentine, how many children have you adopted so far?'

'Three,' Valentine replied. 'Two girls and a boy.' She paused. 'I think.'

'And how on earth do you manage to juggle motherhood with your amazing acting career?' Lauren asked eagerly.

'I believe that being a mother is the most awesome role any woman can play.' Valentine put on an earnest voice. 'I just want to be there for my kids. I love seeing them at bedtime, when they've had their bath and I can tuck them up and read them a story. Well, of course I'd like to read them a story, but often my commitments mean that the nanny has to. But my picture is on all their walls, so they can look up at night and know that Mummy is watching over them.'

'But I suppose you're out somewhere incredibly glamorous, with other A-listers,' Lauren said sycophantically.

'I will not talk about my private life,' Valentine snapped, losing the coy expression and instead looking sulky.

'That was supposed to be one of the conditions of the interview. That, and copy approval.'

'Of course, of course, I'm *so* sorry,' Lauren said soothingly, and dutifully changed the subject. 'I have to say that you look incredible. I'll be saying in my piece that your skin is luminous and that you're not wearing a scrap of make-up.'

'Not a scrap,' Valentine agreed.

'And I'll be saying that you're so much smaller than I had realised, so fragile and ethereal-looking. I'll be writing that you've got a tiny, almost birdlike frame. How do you achieve that?'

'Well obviously I eat very healthily,' Valentine said defensively. 'I do some exercise, but I suppose I can keep the weight off because I'm always running after the children.'

'But I thought you said you only saw them at night?' Lauren put in.

Valentine wrinkled her forehead, trying to frown, then put a hand to her head in consternation. 'I see them as much as my busy filming schedule allows! And please don't make me pull a facial expression. The surgeon said not to make any sudden moves for a while—' She stopped as if regretting her words. 'Don't quote me on that.'

'So you'd say you had a normal attitude to food?' Lauren persisted. 'Can I offer you one of these pastries?'

Valentine gave a tinkly little laugh. 'Of course, I'd love one!' Her hand hovered over the imaginary plate of pastries as if a battle was being waged inside her. Should she or shouldn't she? Should won and she mimed picking up a pastry and stuffing it into her mouth, an expression of near-ecstasy on her face, and said, 'As you can see, my attitude to food is completely normal. Completely normal.' Ecstasy was then replaced by sheer horror. Valentine put a hand over her mouth, mumbled 'Excuse me,' shot out of the room and into the bathroom, where she made loud retching noises. Looking pained and studiously avoiding eye contact with Lauren she returned to her position on the sofa.

'Is everything OK, Ms Fleming?' Lauren asked, wincing as if she could smell something bad.

'Absolutely.' Valentine furtively mimed squirting breath freshener into her mouth.

'And what do your parents think of you acting? Were they pleased that you chose to follow in their famous footsteps?'

'They were both really cool about it, but I've made my own way in this profession; it had nothing to do with them.'

'Of course, so if I can get this clear . . . the fact that your mum is a famous Oscar-nominated actor and your dad is also a famous actor really had nothing to do with your success?'

'Nothing at all. I've worked so hard for my success. I haven't had a leg up at all.'

'Valentine Fleming, it really has been such a pleasure to meet you, truly one of the highlights of my journalistic career. Can I kiss your arse now?'

'No, but you can send your article to my publicist – I've

got copy approval, remember?' Valentine flicked back her hair dismissively.

Lauren sighed and was out of character, 'And now I've got that out of my system, let us pray to our patron saint.' Both girls turned to the mantelpiece and made the sign of the cross, where a picture of Kate Winslet occupied pride of place, surrounded by flickering tealights. 'Dear Kate, help us to be more like you in your transcendent acting ability, but grant that we never make embarrassing award speeches. Amen. So do you want to hear the really bad news?' Without waiting for a reply, Lauren ploughed on, 'NTM has invited us to one of her parties tomorrow night,' she said, holding up a fancy cream card with silver writing on it. 'How short notice is that? She's probably had nos from her A-list "friends" and so she's had to resort to asking us. I swear she only does it so she can feel superior when she asks what we've been in lately,' Lauren grumbled.

Suddenly both girls looked up as a stunningly hand-some twenty-something man appeared in the doorway, flaunting an incredibly toned and tanned torso, dressed only in a small white towel around his waist.

The gorgeous one spoke in an American accent. 'Hi there.' He strolled over to Lauren, draped his arms round her possessively and kissed her neck. 'Had you forgotten about me, Lauren?'

Lauren rolled her eyes; she hated displays of affection outside the bedroom. 'This is Mitchell, he's a model. And she's Valentine.'

The model looked annoyed. 'No, it's Nathan,' he

replied abruptly and shivered. Lauren turned the charm up, 'Sorry darling, I'm crap with names. Isn't Nathan lovely, Valentine? And he's got the most gorgeous—' Lauren hesitated, and Valentine winced in anticipation. Not the cock conversation again, or at least not in front of the guy! Lauren carried on, '. . . teeth. Go on, show them to Valentine.'

Nathan shook his head. 'What am I, a fucking horse?' *Ah*, Valentine thought, *This one's got spirit*. Usually Lauren's men did exactly what she wanted.

'Just for me, baby,' Lauren turned on the charm, kissing his neck and running her hands over his chest. Reluctantly Nathan opened his mouth, showing off his dazzling, perfectly straight white teeth. 'And they are all his own! God bless American orthodontists! Why wasn't I born there? Then I'd have teeth like that!' Lauren had a thing about teeth. There was nothing wrong with hers – they were very white because she was always bleaching them – but she had several ever-so-slightly crooked teeth on the bottom row, which she moaned about constantly.

'Very nice, very white,' Valentine answered, struggling not to giggle.

Nathan shut his mouth. 'I don't know what the big deal is. I prefer your teeth,' he told Lauren. 'They've got character.'

Lauren had a face like thunder and she narrowed her eyes. 'You mean like someone out of a Dickens story! All crooked and yellow, like a fucking hag's!' she hissed. Then added 'Motherfucker!' for good measure in her American accent.

Nathan laughed. 'I can't decide what's worse — you saying motherfucker, or that accent which is *so* bad.'

'See, I told you,' Valentine put in. 'Only Americans can say motherfucker; Nathan said it much better than you and he's not even a drug dealer.' She glanced at him again; surely he was too wholesome-looking. 'You're not, are you?'

Now it was Nathan's turn to roll his eyes.

'Anyway, please don't mention the *teeth*,' Valentine appealed to Nathan. She didn't think she could stand another night of Lauren's teeth fixation.

He shrugged and muttered, 'Whatever.'

'So what time are we due at Fi-fi's?' Lauren asked. For a split second Valentine hadn't got a clue what she was on about, then she twigged. This was the routine Lauren always used when she wanted out of a situation. Fi-fi didn't exist except in Lauren's imagination, which was just as well given her wanky name, and she was very useful when Lauren needed to rid get of some man sharpish. Valentine made a show of looking at her watch. 'We should leave in ten minutes.'

Nathan folded his arms across his chest. 'So am I invited?'

'Darling, I'm sorry but Fi-fi is very fragile. She's just split up with her husband. Well, he left her and now he's demanding that she move out of the house. She's in an appalling state, crying hysterically.'

'Well maybe I could help,' Nathan said calmly. What was going on? Valentine wondered. This never happened. It was surely time for Lauren's masterstroke.

'Oh, that's so sweet of you, but she's really off men at the moment and there are her three children – all under five – to look after. It could get very . . .' – she paused for dramatic emphasis – *'emotional.'*

'I used to work at a summer camp for inner-city kids; I'm pretty much not phased by shit like that.'

Lauren looked at Valentine in dismay and Valentine shrugged helplessly. Lauren's routine had always worked in the past; men hated the thought of raw emotion on show. Throw in the children and it was a dead cert that they would scarper.

'But if you don't want me to come, that's cool. Can I have your digits?' Nathan asked.

'My what?' Lauren exclaimed. 'I thought we'd just done all that.'

'He means your number,' Valentine interpreted.

'Nathan, you've so got to stop talking like a Lily Allen song. You're American, right?'

Now it was Nathan's turn to roll his eyes. 'And you're British, so quit saying *so* like some high-school bimbo. And the motherfucker has gotta go.'

Lauren pursed her lips, she *so* hated to be criticised. 'I've just lost my mobile. Give me your digits and I'll call you.' Another regularly deployed tactic of hers when she didn't want to be in contact with someone again. She hadn't lost her mobile.

'OK.' And wandering over to the table he picked up a felt pen, walked back over to Lauren, took her arm and wrote down his name and number on her bare skin. 'Don't forget to call me.'

'Couldn't you have found some paper?' Lauren said in outrage. 'I think that was my CD marker pen; it's never going to come off!'

'Well, you'll have no excuse not to call me then,' Nathan replied.

'Sure, I'll call you,' Lauren answered, crossing her fingers behind her back so that only Valentine could see them. And with that Nathan turned and took his beautiful body out of the room. Valentine gave a *what the fuck* look to Lauren, who sniffed dismissively. Nathan had seemed like a genuinely nice guy – a first for Lauren. Lauren shrugged, had another sip of wine and poked ineffectually at the fire. Nathan returned to the living room dressed in jeans and a blue sweater, the exact colour of his eyes. He looked adorable and any other woman would have been clinging on to him like a limpet. 'I thought you guys had to be somewhere.'

Lauren looked faintly guilty. 'We do,' she insisted. 'We're just having a drink to give us strength; it's going to be a tough night.' Then she blew him a kiss. 'I'll call you.'

Nathan looked sceptical and said, 'Well if you don't, I know where you live, and when I next come round let me make the fire. Motherfucker! This flat is cold!' Then he left.

Valentine waited a few minutes until she heard the downstairs door click shut, then spoke. 'Lauren, he seemed really nice – why didn't you want him to stay?'

'How long have you got? He's a model, so he'll be vain, self-centred and boring. I can't be arsed.'

'He didn't come across like that.'

'No, he just came all over me!' Lauren laughed loudly at her own joke.

'You're evil! You're going to end up a bitter and twisted old woman, living on her own, with just her memories and cats for company,' Valentine teased her.

'And the wine, don't forget the wine; I could bear anything so long as I had the wine! And you have to scrap the cats, because I'm allergic. Can't I have a horse instead? A lovely palamino?'

'In your tiny bedsit, lit by the single-barred electric fire, which you can't afford to have on, with the flocked wallpaper and garishly patterned carpet? I don't think so, sunshine. You can have a poodle.'

'*No!*' Lauren exclaimed dramatically, then snapped out it. 'Forget it, I'm only twenty-fucking-seven; I've got years of this ahead of me.' She stretched her slim arms over her head and yawned adding, 'Actually, Nathan was very good. I might have to see him again. In fact I might even ask him to Tamara's – he's so good-looking she's bound to be jealous. And his teeth were sublime. Gods among teeth.'

'I can't believe you can base a relationship on the state of someone's teeth!'

'Obviously he's got a massive cock as well,' Lauren retorted, then cackled with laughter. 'So you'd better take someone – you don't want Tamara thinking you're a saddo single on top of being a struggling actress – what about that Jack? I really want to meet him.'

Now it was Valentine's turn to try and look nonchalant.

'I expect he'll be out with Julia husky Turner, or another of his lovely ladies. He is catnip to the female population, I swear, especially the older ones.'

'Well, text him now and ask him,' Lauren demanded.

Valentine stubbornly shook her head, not wanting to admit that Lauren's idea was a good one. The truth was she would be mortified if he said no. 'Anyway, I'm going to Tesco. Do you want anything?' Valentine asked, keen to deflect Lauren.

'Just tobacco and I fancy some chocolate eclairs.'

Valentine tutted, thinking of her own virtuous planned purchases of spinach, carrots, cucumber and houmous. 'You *so* deserve to be fat,' were her parting words.

On her way out she checked if Lily and Frank needed anything but Lily informed her, a little smugly, Valentine thought, that she'd just done an online shop. 'Honestly Valentine, you should do it; it's so much easier! Gives you time to concentrate on other things.'

Valentine couldn't help noticing that as she said it Lily gave Frank a flirtatious little smile, and Frank winked back. Surely she didn't mean that they'd been up to anything this afternoon? Valentine wondered as she walked round Tesco Metro on Portabello Road. She adored Frank and Lily, but really didn't want to think of them *at it* at their ages. *Then again*, she thought as she sifted through the cucumbers in the fruit and veg section, *good on them*.

'What the fuck did you do that for?' she said aghast, when Lauren revealed that in her absence she had texted Jack from Valentine's phone to invite him to the party and he had replied that he would love to come.

Lauren rolled her eyes. 'Keep your knickers on; you're only inviting him to a party, that's all.'

And the thought popped into Valentine's head that maybe she didn't want that to be all.

'Anyway, just think of the expression on NTM's face when she sees him – if he really is as gorgeous as you say, she'll be so jealous. You know how much she hates it if anyone has anything or anyone prettier than she does.'

'You're right,' Valentine admitted. 'It would be worth it for that alone.'

7

Primrose Hill Poison

God, I loathe North London,' Lauren grumbled as she, Valentine, Nathan and Jack got off the Tube at Chalk Farm station. 'It's so right that the Northern line is black on the map, because that's what North London is like: gloomy, depressing, with too many houses too close together.'

'You should really learn to have an opinion,' Nathan teased in his Californian drawl.

Lauren insisted on walking up the stairs as she had a phobia of lifts, and Nathan went with her, so Valentine and Jack waited for the lift together. Jack had his hands shoved into the pockets of his battered black leather jacket with the collar turned up. He looked so sexy and Valentine got a thrill every time she sneaked a glance at him.

'I'm glad you asked me tonight,' he said. 'I was going to ask you out, but you beat me to it.'

'You make it sound like a date,' Valentine replied, 'And this is not a "date" date.'

'I thought that was exactly what this was,' Jack replied.

Valentine was on a mission to play it cool, and side-stepped the comment. 'Oh look, the lift's here.'

As the steel lift door closed, Jack moved closer and said, 'You look beautiful in that dress.' Valentine was sure it wasn't just the speed of the lift that made her stomach flip so deliciously.

Lauren and Nathan had already climbed the stairs and were waiting outside the station. Lauren was lighting up one of her roll-ups while Nathan looked on with an expression of disgust. 'You know you really should think about giving up,' he said. 'Hypnotherapy might help.' Lauren blew out one of her perfect smoke rings and said, 'I like smoking. When I don't, I'll give up. If you don't like it, well . . .' She shrugged, leaving Nathan in no doubt what he could do.

'Whoah, you're harsh!' Jack exclaimed.

'She's a pussy cat really,' Valentine hastily put in, fearing the evening was about to go spectacularly tits up. Lauren did not take kindly to criticism.

'She's no pussy cat,' Nathan said dryly. 'But I like her anyway,' and he put his arm round Lauren. Valentine was waiting for Lauren to push him away, but she didn't. She must like him.

'So what's Tamara like? I hope you don't think I'm being rude, as she's a friend of yours, but she's not a great actress, is she?'

Valentine liked Jack all the more for recognising Tamara's talent bypass. 'I can't stand her actually, but Lauren thinks we might meet someone useful there. I know that sounds shallow, but frankly she deserves it. She's probably only

asked us so she can feel better about herself. We needn't
stay long; we can just see if there are any people worth
talking to, down the champagne and then split.'

They walked slowly through the elegant, wealthy streets
of Primrose Hill. Valentine wished they weren't going to
the party; she was enjoying being alone with Jack far too
much. But within ten minutes they had arrived at Tamara's
three-storey house. Lauren and Nathan had got there first
and the four of them stood outside for a minute, taking
in the view of the stunning white Georgian building. The
party had already started and they could see the guests
milling around the vast, elegant living room, while waiters
circulated with trays of champagne and canapés. It was
a scene of such wealth and opulence. Valentine suddenly
felt conscious of how shabby her second-hand black fake
fur coat from Portabello market must seem and how her
red suede heels had really seen better days. She shivered.

'You cold?' Jack asked. 'I can warm you up.' And he
raised her hand to his lips and softly kissed it.

'Smoothie!' Valentine shot back, but she didn't pull her
hand away and after Jack had kissed it he continued to
hold it as they walked up the stone stairs to the imposing
front door.

Moments later one of the waiting staff had taken their
coats and had ushered them into the palatial living room.
It was lit by two dazzling chandeliers, flickering Jo Malone
candles on the white marble fireplace filling the room
with their heady scent. Tamara was holding court with
some well-known actors. She spotted them and waved,
but carried on talking.

'We're not important enough for her,' Lauren whispered to Valentine. 'But what the fuck, let's get some champagne.' She quickly got the attention of one of the waiters and they each took a glass of champagne from the tray he offered. As a stroke of luck, Lauren recognised him from one of her castings and managed to persuade him to leave them the bottle. 'And keep them coming,' she winked at him.

'Will do, Lauren,' the waiter said adoringly.

'Tell me you didn't,' Nathan demanded when the waiter had trotted obediently off to get Lauren more champagne and a tray of sushi.

'Could have,' Lauren replied, narrowing her beautiful blue eyes, 'but I chose not to.'

Conversation flowed easily between the four of them. Lauren clearly liked Jack, as she was particularly cheeky to him, taking the piss out of him for falling for the fluffers lie, which was always a sign that she approved of someone. The time to worry about Lauren was when she was coolly polite.

It was a good fifteen minutes before Tamara got round to saying hello to them, making them fully aware of their position in the status stakes, not that any of them cared. 'Hi guys! I'm so glad you could make it!' Tamara exclaimed, sweeping over to their group, a vision of loveliness in a Grecian-style white silk dress. There then followed the obligatory introductions and air-kissing rituals, where Valentine couldn't help noticing how Tamara's gaze lingered longest on Jack. Even though nothing had happened between her and Jack, she felt a sudden flash of jealousy.

'So how are you Tamara?' Lauren asked her, summoning their waiter over for yet more refills.

'Absolutely exhausted,' Tamara declared. 'I've been filming back to back for the last six months!'

She didn't look tired, Valentine thought bitterly; she looked as good as ever. She might possess very little acting talent, but Tamara's stunning good looks meant that the camera loved her face with her huge blue-grey eyes, regular features, shoulder-length honey-blonde hair and a naturally petite body, which she kept small through rigorous exercise and dieting. Though she did have one Achilles heel – her arse was really quite large for someone with such a small frame. Valentine and Lauren had been known to call her Five Mile Bottom behind her back. Tamara was extremely conscious of it, hence the floaty number that disguised it. Arse aside, Valentine even at her thinnest – a size ten as she was now – always felt like a cart horse next to the miniature Tamara. Instinctively she crossed her arms over her chest, feeling self-conscious that she was revealing too much cleavage in her low-cut figure-hugging black dress. Lauren rolled her eyes at Valentine. They both knew what was coming next: time for Tamara to revel in their lack of work.

'So what have you two been up to? More theatre work? It must be so lovely doing stage; I've really missed it.' And without waiting for their reply she pressed on, 'I've said to my agent that when I've got a decent break between films, I would so love to do some stage. Film just isn't the same; I really want a role I can get my teeth into.'

'Perhaps you could be in *Chicago*,' Jack put in. 'They're

always looking for guest stars.' And Valentine wanted to kiss him for puncturing Tamara's bubble.

'Oh no!' she exclaimed, looking horrified, 'I meant serious theatre, darling! You know, like Nicole Kidman appeared in *The Blue Room*!' She looked most put out and curled her lip petulantly. Then Valentine saw her give Jack another appraising look as she clearly decided to give him a second chance. She tilted her chin up and looked coy. 'So what would I have seen you in? You look very familiar.' Lauren had been spot on in her comment that Tamara would fancy Jack – she probably fancied Nathan too, but he had his arms draped round Lauren and had eyes only for her.

Valentine grabbed another glass of champagne from their waiter, who was hovering nearby, neglecting his duties to gaze at Lauren. She'd been wrong to listen to Lauren and come to the party. She could feel her self-esteem plummeting; any minute now she'd be attacking the canapés. Jack might have said that Tamara had no talent, but he couldn't fail to be impressed by her looks, her wealth and her connections. Out of the corner of her eye she noticed Tamara's famous movie-star mother holding court. Still a beauty in her late fifties, she had however seriously OD'd on the Botox. Her face was almost completely immobile; probably she had to hold up flash cards to indicate what emotion she wanted to express.

Valentine turned back to Tamara and Jack. Was it her imagination or had Tamara moved closer to Jack? So close in fact that one of her small, perky breasts, small enough to be bra-free, was nearly brushing against his arm.

'I'm sure you must be a fantastic Bottom!' Tamara giggled, and Valentine had to fight the temptation to grab the tray of exquisite sushi and throw it all over her shiny, poker-straight (it bloody would be, wouldn't it?) hair. 'You must tell me when the play's on and if I'm not in LA I'll come and see it.'

'I think we're sold out,' Valentine lied.

'Really?' Tamara replied, wrinkling her perfect little nose in disbelief. 'Well, if you say that *I* want to come then surely they'll be able to russle me up a ticket.'

'Actually, I don't know if they can,' Jack put in. 'Fire regulations, you know.' And Valentine gave him a warm smile, thrilled that he clearly hadn't been taken in by Tamara. At that moment Tamara's attention was claimed by one of her starry guests, Lauren took Nathan off to meet someone she recognised and Valentine and Jack were left alone.

Jack smiled and whispered, 'She's a bit up herself, isn't she?'

'She's very pretty, though. With her luminous skin. And tiny birdlike frame,' Valentine replied. She was tempted to add that she had a massive arse, but thought it made her sound too bitchy, so she kept it zipped.

'I'll give her that,' Jack agreed. 'But nothing like as pretty or as sexy as you in that dress.' He was gazing right at her. He was so delicious. Valentine felt light-headed from desire. Or maybe, she tried to tell herself – not very successfully, given the feelings of lust that were fizzing round her body — it was the fact that she hadn't eaten all day, and the no-carb rule she had imposed on herself because of the nipple tassels was really getting to her. She could imagine it being responsible for many an affair as carb-deprived women lost the ability to think rationally. And there was the fact that she still hadn't heard from Finn.

'Aren't I a bit too young for you?' she bantered back. 'What with your liking for the older ladies.' Before Julia, Jack had revealed that he'd been out with another forty-something actress.

Jack shrugged. 'Older ladies can be more appreciative and you can always learn something from them.'

'Yeah, but I bet there are some drawbacks. They're not exactly honeymoon fresh anymore, are they?' Valentine said cheekily and instantly regretted her words.

'Now, now,' Jack replied, laughing. 'Isn't that being unsisterly? Or are you trying to draw my attention to your much tighter, fresher—'

Valentine frantically interrupted him. 'Just forget I said it, please!'

'I can't!' Jack said, laughing. 'Now all I can think about is your—'

Valentine put her hand over his mouth, but Jack continued trying to talk. His lips felt gorgeous. He held her wrist and moved her hand away. 'I won't say another word about your superior anatomy if you kiss me.'

Valentine hesitated, then stood on tiptoes and lightly kissed him on the lips. A kiss that he returned. And the kiss, which she had hoped would stop something, was turning into a hot, hard kiss of desire. It was irresistible, but somehow Valentine found the strength to pull away and she realised that she had wrapped her arms round Jack's neck, and that she'd been pressing her body against his. Bad, very bad. And far too good. She moved away as if she'd been scalded, then tried to pull some gestures as if nothing had happened, flicking back her hair and taking a sip of her champagne. But Jack wasn't going to let her get away with it; he leaned right over to her and whispered, so she could feel his warm breath against her skin. 'And now I just want you even more. Come back to my flat.'

Valentine nodded, not giving herself time to think of all the reasons why she shouldn't.

'I'll just grab us a bottle of champagne,' Jack added, looking for their waiter. Valentine felt as gloriously fizzy as the champagne, bubbling up with happiness and desire and anticipation. But then Tamara sidled over to her.

'Guess who I saw last week, Valentine?'

Valentine shrugged. She was certain it was not going to be good news for her. It wasn't.

'Finn!' We were both at Adrian's thirtieth.' (Adrian was another actor who owed his career to his famous parents.)

'Oh.' Valentine tried to keep her expression neutral, but she could feel the happiness she'd just experienced beginning to slip away. Tamara always had that effect on her. She was like one of the Dementors in the Harry Potter books, sucking all the joy out of her.

'Yeah, he's doing really well, isn't he? And Eva is looking

so gorgeous. Do you know, I think she's lost even more weight.'

Valentine's happiness levels fell fifty per cent.

'And they've just got engaged.' And kept falling. 'Apparently Finn proposed the day after Valentine's Day. Funny that he didn't do it on Valentine's Day, isn't it? Oh course, I remember now! Valentine's Day has bad memories for all of you, doesn't it?' Happiness levels down to zero. Job done, Tamara.

'What are you two talking about?' Lauren demanded, walking over to them. She was a little the worse for wear; her cheeks were flushed and her eyes glinted dangerously. She'd taken off her gold sandals – her long vintage green silk dress trailed on the floor and was already a little grubby, but she still looked stunning.

'Tamara was just updating me about Finn,' Valentine said, trying to keep her voice steady. 'Apparently he's engaged.' She felt utterly miserable now and just wanted to go home.

'That was nice of her,' Lauren said insincerely. She turned to Tamara. 'Thanks for a lovely party, Tamara. Good luck with getting that part in *Chicago*. Spanx can do wonders with big arses nowadays.' And not giving Tamara the chance to answer back, Lauren took Valentine's arm and practically frogmarched her out of the room. In the hall she muttered, 'I'll go and round up the boys. Meet me outside. You need to get away from Toxic Tamara.'

Valentine grabbed her coat. Outside the cold March air was like a slap in the face. *I must not think about Finn,* she told herself, digging her fingernails into her palms and shivering in her fake fur. A few minutes later the others emerged from the house. As Lauren ran down the steps she gleefully opened her coat and revealed two bottles of champagne, which she'd lifted from the party. 'Come on, let's get a taxi back home and we can crack this open.'

'You're very quiet,' Jack said to Valentine halfway through the taxi ride home. He had quickly realised that Valentine was in no mood to come back to his. While Lauren had been chatting away about the people she'd met, laughing about the actress who wouldn't even eat the olive in her Martini for fear of putting on weight, and about Tamara's mother, who'd tried to chat up Nathan, Valentine hadn't said a word. In her head she'd gone back a year ago to the night Finn had chosen his girlfriend over her, despite telling her that he loved her. She suddenly felt as vulnerable and raw as if it had been yesterday. The confident, teasing, flirtatious persona she had adopted with Jack lay in ruins.

'I'm just tired,' she lied.

'Not too tired to drink Tamara fucking Moore's champagne!' Lauren interrupted, brandishing the bottles of Dom Perignon in the air.

'Actually too tired even for that,' Valentine replied and she saw Jack look at her, clearly wondering what had happened to change her mood so dramatically. He was perceptive, she had to give him that, and when they drove past Paddington station Jack asked the taxi to stop, saying that he was going to call in on some friends.

He hesitated at the door and Valentine wondered if he expected her to go with him. Then he simply said, 'See you on Monday, Valentine. Cheers for inviting me tonight,' and waved to Lauren and Nathan.

Back home Lauren, sensing her friend's mood, tried to get Valentine to have a drink with them, but Valentine refused and shut herself up in her bedroom. Champagne was not going to make her feel better. The memory of kissing Jack and of the feel of his body against hers did not make her feel better. As soon as she was alone she reached for her phone and texted Finn, her resolve not to contact him overtaken by events. She had to know if he really was engaged. *Please call me, I really need to speak to you. Vx.* She suddenly thought of Piers – he hadn't wanted her and now Finn didn't want her either. She felt completely worthless. She switched on her laptop, convinced that the SGF would have posted up a message about such dramatic news. She was trembling as she logged on and took several attempts to type in her Facebook password. *Please don't let it be true*, she thought, biting her nails as she went first to Finn's page, where there was no mention, and then on to Eva's. There was nothing. But that wasn't enough for Valentine.

She paced round her room, wishing she had some cigarettes. She had to speak to him. She jumped when her phone beeped with a text message; it had to be Finn. But she was bitterly disappointed when it was from Jack, asking her if she was OK. Fuck, this was no good; she couldn't stand it. She had to speak to him and if he wasn't going to call, she was going to have to go to his house. She didn't stop to consider that Eva was bound to be with him, as she grabbed her coat and tiptoed out of the flat.

Outside, the temperature had fallen even lower and it had started snowing. Valentine shivered as she walked briskly to Westbourne Park Tube station. She sat on the train in a perfect cocoon of misery, oblivious to the other passengers. She had been feeling slightly drunk from all the champagne, but Tamara's words had sobered her up. At Richmond she got a taxi to Finn's place. He owned the top-floor flat in a Victorian house. She hesitated for a few seconds as the taxi pulled up. Did she really want to do this? But the thought of not knowing drove her forward. She paid the fare and positioned herself on the opposite side of the road to Finn's flat, in the shadow of a large horse chestnut tree. The lights were still on and she could see people sitting round the dining table in the bay window. Finn was entertaining. It was probably his fucking engagement party. Once more she reached for her phone and texted him: *I am outside, I have to see you now. Vx.*

God knew if he would even get the text that night. She shoved her hands into her pocket wishing she was wearing gloves; she was freezing and the snow was falling more heavily. But after a few minutes her phone rang.

'V, where the hell are you?' he was whispering and sounded like he was walking down a flight of stairs.

Valentine told him where she was and watched as he emerged from the flat and quickly crossed the road. He looked angry as he approached her.

'Christ, we can't talk here! Eva mustn't see you. Come on, my car's round the corner; we'll go and sit in that.'

He swiftly strode down the street, not bothering to wait for Valentine, and unlocked his pride and joy – a silver Audi TT convertible that had been a twenty-first birthday present from his doting mother. Valentine had zero interest in cars and only knew what model Finn's was because he'd gone on about it enough times when they were together.

'You pick your moments, V,' he said as she slid into the seat next to him.

'I'm sorry, I didn't mean to drop you in it. It's just that I saw Tamara Moore tonight and she told me.' Valentine paused; she really didn't think she could bear it if what Tamara had said was true. She had been living in the hope that one day soon she and Finn would be together.

'What?' Finn said impatiently.

'That you're engaged,' Valentine said quietly.

Finn burst out laughing. 'No fucking way! That woman is a complete fantasist!'

'So you're definitely not?' Valentine asked, feeling a small glimmer of hope force its way through the misery. 'Tamara said Eva told her you had proposed the day after Valentine's Day.'

'V, I swear I didn't. Come here.' He put his arm round her and pulled her towards him, even though it meant the handbrake was digging painfully into her thigh. Then he kissed her. She had always thought Finn was a great kisser, but somewhere in the back of her mind came the thought that he wasn't actually as good as Jack and unlike

Jack, whose eyes had stayed open, Finn's were closed. Valentine suddenly felt as if she could have been anyone. He slipped his hand inside her dress and began caressing her breasts, not particularly gently. Then he murmured, 'Do you remember the last time we were in this car together? How about it? They think I've gone to the off-licence, so I've got a few minutes.' Valentine did remember; she had nearly put her back out.

'It was so good, V. I always think of you when I'm in the car. I've really missed you, baby. Take your knickers off.' What followed was apparently very good for Finn, judging by the groans he made, and not quite so good for Valentine, who was in a very uncomfortable position, and kept banging her head against the car roof. She was paranoid that someone would see them and think they were dogging and that really was not Valentine's scene. And then because they didn't have a condom Finn had to withdraw, and came all over her silk dress, which was dry-clean only. It was too cold in the car to stay and chat. Valentine had at least hoped for one 'I love you', but Finn was clearly anxious about getting back to the party.

'V, I'll see you soon,' he said, slamming the car door. 'It would be better if you went ahead.'

She should have been glad that Tamara's little bomb-shell had turned out to be a lie, and happy that Finn still wanted her. Instead, as she curled up in bed later that night, she felt used. Jack had texted her again: *Are you okay? Jx.* She didn't want to lie so she ignored it. She so wished she hadn't gone to Tamara's party and been poisoned by her. Jack must think that she was a complete mentalist – kissing him passionately one minute then pushing him away. Thank God she didn't have to face him tomorrow as it was Sunday. Maybe by rehearsals on Monday she would have worked out how to explain her behaviour – and worked out her feelings for him.

She was all set to brood the following day, but at half eight (after just four hours' sleep) Frank knocked smartly on the flat door. 'Sorry to wake you,' he said cheerfully, 'But I wondered if you wanted to come and help out on the stall. It's going to be a nice day and there should be plenty of tourists. There'll be thirty quid in it for you.'

Valentine was about to refuse, but then the thought of spending a day obsessing over Finn and Jack prompted her to agree. At first as they set up the stall she still felt under a dark cloud, lethargic and miserable, but Frank's good humour and good nature was infectious. He sold a mixture of jewellery, some total tat and some quality on his stall, which occupied a prime location on the Portabello Road outside a row of antique shops. He knew everyone as he'd had his stall for years, so she was forced out of herself, to chat and joke with Frank's friends. Frank was a fantastic salesman, bantering with the customers, telling the girls they were beautiful, while trying to strike a deal with them.

As if sensing Valentine's mood he gave her plenty to do so she couldn't brood, sending her off to get bacon rolls, getting her to display the jewellery and then to hold it up for the customers and take the money as his arthritis was particularly painful that morning. Valentine felt chastened next to him. She could tell that he was in pain, but he kept going; his good spirits never faltered. By lunchtime some of the dark cloud was lifting from her and she realised that she was enjoying herself. It was a cold, crisp day but the sun was shining – she loved these sorts of days.

'Hello!' trilled a familiar voice. Valentine looked up from the tray of silver rings she was busy arranging to see Lily, arm in arm with Jack. Her heart skipped and the sun seemed to shine brighter. 'This young man called round for you and I thought I'd bring him to you,' Lily continued. She looked very glam in her full-length black sheepskin coat and white fur hat. It was mink, though she always pretended it was fake. She refused to get rid of it, saying it had sentimental value as it had been her mother's, and it was better to keep her head warm than clog up a landfill site and add to global warming. Valentine doubted that anti-fur protestors would see it like that, but she had given up trying to argue with Lily.

'Hi Valentine,' Jack said. 'I was in your area and I thought I'd drop by. You don't mind, do you?'

Valentine smiled and shook her head, aware that Lily and Frank were watching her like a pair of hawks – subtlety was not the old timers' forte.

'In your area?' Lily sniffed. 'How unromantic! Why don't you just admit that you wanted to see her?'

'And why wouldn't you want to see her, a lovely girl like Valentine?' Frank put in loyally.

Valentine shrugged. 'My number-one fans,' she said ruefully.

Jack smiled, 'OK, I wanted to see you.'

'That's more like it!' Frank said gleefully. 'Life's too short to go beating round the bush! You like a girl, you tell her! Now who wants some coffee? It's brass monkey weather and I for one could do with some warming up.'

As Lily and Frank fussed over the cups, Valentine finally felt able to talk to Jack. 'I'm sorry about last night,' she said quietly. 'It was something Tamara said, something to do with my past, and it sent me on a bit of a downer.'

'Something you want to tell me about?' Jack asked sympathetically.

Valentine shook her head and fiddled with the tray of silver rings, 'Not just yet if that's OK.'

'That's OK.' Jack replied.

Valentine expected Jack would simply have coffee and leave; instead he spent the afternoon with them and proved himself to be a master salesman, especially with the ladies. *No surprise there*, Valentine thought, watching a couple of young girls buying far more than they had intended as Jack told them how good the necklaces looked on them. He was such a charmer. Frank was delighted as he cleared far more stock than usual, and insisted that Jack and Valentine come round for supper that evening.

'You don't have to if you don't want to,' Valentine told him as they walked the short distance back to the house, each lugging a large wooden jewellery case. Lily and Frank were walking ahead and safely out of earshot.

'No, I'd like to,' Jack replied. 'Frank and Lily are great and anyway, I want to see you.'

'So you don't think I'm a mentalist?' Valentine asked.

'Not too much,' Jack teased her. 'Borderline, I'd say.'

'Cheeky bastard!' Valentine shot back, trying to swipe a punch at him. And as they bantered away, the events of the night before – the mad dash to Finn's house, the furtive sex in his car – receded into the back of her mind like a bad dream. She was back to feeling confident and flirtatious.

Spending any length of time in Frank's flat always made Valentine feel stoned, even if she didn't have a joint, as the unmistakable sickly sweet tang of dope was everywhere. She stuck to vodka while Jack accepted one of the super-sized joints Frank had rolled earlier. 'You'll regret that,' Valentine told him. 'It will knock you out.' As she knew only too well from past experience.

Jack rolled his eyes. 'I'm a big boy; I can cope and I'll still be ready for whatever you've got planned for later.'

He winked at her while Valentine laughed and said, 'You won't be fit for anything once you've finished that. You'll be away with the fairies and not in a good way.'

Half an hour later Valentine's prophesy was fulfilled. Jack was laughing hysterically – at what? Valentine had no idea, while Frank and Lily looked on indulgently.

'Did you give him the strong stuff?' Valentine suddenly asked.

Frank nodded. 'I wanted to see what he was made of.'

'I can't believe you did that!' Valentine exclaimed. 'He's going to be wasted!'

Frank shrugged. 'He'll be all right.' They all looked on as Jack stopped laughing and stretched out on the ancient leather Chesterfield.

'I think the roast is done,' Lily declared.

Valentine tried to get Jack to come to the table to eat but he shook his head and grabbed her hand. 'Come here baby, lie down; we can look at the ceiling rose. It's amazing.'

Valentine laughed. 'It's a lovely offer, but I'm going to have dinner. I did warn you about the dope!'

'I'm fine!' Jack protested sleepily. But she slipped easily out of his grasp and joined Lily and Frank at the table.

'I might have had designs on that young man,' she said cheekily as Lily handed her a plate laden with roast chicken and vegetables. 'He's going to be good for nothing now!'

'We had to see if he was good enough for you!' Frank replied, tucking into his roast potatoes.

'And what's the verdict?' Valentine demanded.

'I like him,' Lily declared. 'Of course, I quite liked Sam in his suit and his briefcase.' Lily's face assumed the dreamy expression it always had whenever Sam's accessory was mentioned. 'But Jack will pass. No, more than that: I think he's lovely. And he thinks you are too – I saw him looking at you, Valentine. He's totally smitten.'

'No way!' Valentine replied, feeling secretly delighted. 'So what did you think, Frank?'

'Well, he knew nothing about free jazz,' at which Valentine and Lily shared a mutual eye-roll – nor did they. In fact whenever Frank insisted on playing it, it always made Valentine feel as if she was going mad, because of the lack of a discernible pattern in the music. 'But he seems sound.'

From the sofa, Jack was snoring loudly.

'Just as well then, isn't it?' Valentine replied, spearing a carrot. 'Seeing as how you're going to be spending the night with him.'

'No worries, I've got a spare duvet and if he wakes up I'll find out what his intentions are towards you. I'm not having another gutless bastard ruin your life.'

'I would hang on to this young man,' Lily told her as they cleared the table after supper.

'What, even though he's a total lightweight?' Valentine joked back.

'Valentine, I'm serious,' Lily replied and she looked it. She also looked very pale, Valentine noticed. 'I know you think you still have feelings for Finn.'

Did she? How did she know that? Valentine tried not to give anything away. Lily had an unerring ability to know things about her. She had often speculated to Lauren about the possibility of Lily being a white witch. 'But he's not the one for you. He never was, or he would never have treated you so appallingly. Jack's different – he's got integrity; he would never do something like that.'

'And you can tell that from one meeting?' Valentine asked sceptically.

'Yes I can,' Lily replied. Then she winced, a spasm of pain contorting her face. She put out a hand to steady herself on the kitchen table.

'Are you all right, Lily?' Valentine asked, instantly concerned.

'Yes, yes, it's nothing, just a bit of indigestion. You get off now. We'll send Jack up if he becomes conscious.'

8

The Ex Factor

'Can I cook you dinner to make up for last night?' Jack asked as they travelled on the bus to rehearsals the next morning. Even hungover and unshaven he still looked sexy – if anything more than ever, because he had that just-rolled-out-of-bed look. 'I can't believe I passed out like that,' he added sheepishly. 'I hope Frank and Lily don't think I'm a complete tosser. They're cool, by the way.'

Valentine laughed. 'I did warn you that it is very strong stuff. And yes, OK to dinner,' she said more cautiously.

'Good,' Jack replied, sounding pleased. 'I feel like I need to eat something healthy and you look like you need to eat something.'

Valentine gave him a sceptical look. 'Yeah, I'm just wasting away, aren't I? I'm surprised there aren't news articles devoted to the disappearance of Valentine Fleming.'

'Just don't go all extreme on me; you're gorgeous the way you are,' Jack replied, giving her one of his appraising

120

looks. There was a pause in conversation where Valentine was aware of his gaze and felt as skittish and shy as a teenager.

'So can you cook?' she asked.

Jack nodded. 'I've been told my puttanesca sauce is unsurpassed.'

'Was this by one of your older ladies?' Valentine said cheekily.

'I haven't forgotten what happened last time we had this conversation,' Jack replied, raising his eyebrows meaningfully.

Nor had Valentine. She felt hot all over just thinking about it.

'I thought I'd ask Rufus, Kitty and Toby as well,' Jack continued. And Valentine couldn't help feeling slightly disappointed that it wasn't going to be just the two of them.

'Mmmm that was absolutely delicious!' Toby exclaimed, leaning back contentedly in his chair. 'I just hope I'm still going to be able to fit into my costume!'

'Me too,' Rufus replied.

'It's OK for you, Valentine; you don't have that problem, do you?' Kitty put in wickedly. The five of them were sitting round Jack's dining table. Crammed would be a more fitting description, as the table was tiny and it was almost impossible to sit round it without brushing against someone else. Valentine had given up trying to move her leg away from Jack's and was secretly enjoying the feeling of his thigh against hers.

'Ah, but Valentine didn't finish hers; what was wrong with it?' Jack demanded in a deliberately bad French accent, folding his arms and adopting the pose of a top chef.

'It was lovely,' Valentine answered, hoping she didn't have any basil caught in her teeth – not a good look. 'I'm just trying not to eat too much at the moment.' And it had been delicious, but the combined forces of the prospect of the nipple tassels and Jack so close to her had effectively suppressed her appetite. He had cooked Italian and even though it looked delicious Valentine had not been able to manage more than a few mouthfuls. Damn Finn for putting her off her favourite food.

'Well, you must have some of my tiramisu,' Jack declared, getting up to clear the plates away. 'It's home made.'

'Is there no end to your talents, Jack?' Kitty asked, winking suggestively at Valentine. Valentine stuck her tongue out. It had not taken the other actors long to detect the undercurrent of attraction, or more accurately raging torrent running between Valentine and Jack – even though she had told Kitty several times now that nothing had happened.

'Nothing's happened *yet*,' Kitty had said meaningfully.

'Are you taking Jerry Hall's mantra to heart then?' Kitty continued now, 'A maid in the living room, a cook in the kitchen and a whore in the bedroom? Your flat is very tidy, you're a very good cook and dot dot dot.'

Jack laughed. 'I've got a merciless landlady, which is why the flat is so tidy. And I never kiss and tell about the bedroom.' He was looking at Valentine and she stared right back at him, wondering just what he would be like in the bedroom. In his lovely bedroom, with the honey-coloured stripped wooden floors, the silver art deco fireplace, the king-size bed with the wrought iron bedstead, painted in the white distressed fashion that Valentine had always loved and dreamed one day of owning. In the meantime the only distressed thing in her flat was herself.

'Anyway, great view.' Valentine was the first to drag her eyes away and look out of the bay window at the stunning view of the London skyline, Canary Wharf winking conspiratorially in the distance. 'It almost makes me like North London.'

'God, you're as bad as Lauren! West Londoners are so judgemental!' Jack shot back. 'You're going to have to spend a weekend up here and then you'll change your mind. We can go out for breakfast, go for a walk on Hampstead Heath and end up at the Everyman watching a film. And you'll be converted.'

'Sounds like a tempting offer, Valentine. You can get to sample all Jack's talents,' Kitty said mischievously.

Valentine ignored her and held up the bottle of red, 'More wine anyone?'

After dessert – also delicious, apparently, as Kitty, Rufus and Toby practically licked their plates clean while Valentine passed again, given it was another Italian job – the others were very unsubtle about leaving Valentine and Jack alone together. Kitty booked a taxi for the three of them and when Valentine asked if she could share it, Kitty said that they weren't going anywhere near her, which was a blatant lie. Then the three of them practically sprinted out of the flat.

'Stay for one more drink,' Jack asked her, as she was about to call a taxi.

'Just one,' she agreed. 'I'm in at nine tomorrow with the Twirlies and I don't want to be hungover.'

Jack poured her a glass and they both sat on the sofa (on the lovely, comfortable cream sofa – no springs going into buttocks here, unlike her sofa, which doubled as an instrument of torture). It had been over a week since Tamara's party, where they'd both made their feelings for each other obvious – a week that had been so hectic with rehearsals that they hadn't been alone together. But Valentine remembered vividly what it had felt like in Jack's arms, how wonderful it had felt to be that wanted and desired.

'Cheers,' Jack said, clinking his glass against hers. 'Here's to getting to know each other better.'

It was such a corny line and Valentine wanted to come back with a witty reply, but found that she couldn't. She did want to get to know him better.

'Sorry that was such a cheesy line,' Jack groaned, putting his glass down on the table in front of him and frowning. 'But it's true. Of all the plays in all the world, I'm very glad you're in mine, Valentine Fleming.' Another corny line, but Valentine let it go. 'So am I,' she replied quietly, taking a sip of her drink, as desire pulsed through her.

'Put the glass down,' Jack said softly.

'Why? Do you think I've got a drink problem?' Valentine shot back, but her heart was racing as Jack shook his head, took the glass away from her, and pulled her towards him. It was a very practised move, her head told her, while her body said yes and so what? Then it was kiss number three.

Desire had freed Valentine from her inhibitions. She put her hands up to his hair and ran her fingers through it, which was what she'd been dying to do ever since they'd met. Then she slipped them under his T-shirt, along his thankfully hair-free back (though frankly right now she was feeling so turned on she wouldn't have cared if she'd discovered hair neck to toe), feeling his smooth, warm skin as he expertly undid the buttons on her black silk shirt and caressed her breasts. She moved her hands round his neck and gently pulled him down so he was lying on top of her and she could feel the whole of his body against hers. He kissed her breasts, sending fireworks of pleasure shooting round her body. She longed to feel him and she boldly reached down and caressed him through his jeans, feeling his hardness. She felt very sexy as she popped open the buttons on his jeans. He inched up her skirt and Valentine thanked God that for once she was wearing hold-up stockings and not her usual eighty-denier black tights, which were about as alluring as – well, she couldn't think right now because of what Jack was doing to her.

'You look so sexy,' Jack murmured, kissing her thighs just above the stocking and then kissing her inner thigh, then higher and higher. Valentine lost herself in the feel of his lips against her skin. Then he broke away to kiss her mouth while his fingers caressed her through her underwear in tantalising circles. Jack knew what he was doing. Then he was gently sliding her silk briefs down and Valentine was pushing his jeans down and saw he really did have a fantastic big cock. The old saying that size didn't matter had never held true to Valentine. It bloody did. But by the look of it Jack had no worries in that department.

Suddenly the door buzzer went off, shattering the moment of intimacy. Jack groaned, 'Just ignore it; it's bound to be someone ringing the wrong bell,' and sensing that Valentine was going to move he once more kissed her, silencing her protests. 'God, I want you so much,' he said, looking into her eyes. And she wanted him so much, really she did, with an intensity that almost took her breath away, and she was about to tell him when someone, a someone who sounded a lot like Julia Turner, knocked loudly on the front door and called out Jack's name.

'I'm not going to answer it,' Jack murmured, kissing her again. But now the someone who was unmistakably Julia was hammering on the door and shouting. 'Fuck!' Jack exclaimed with feeling. 'I'll have to speak to her or she'll wake up the whole house. But don't move,' he ordered Valentine as he reluctantly peeled himself off her body and buttoned up his jeans. 'I'll get rid of her.'

Bloody Julia Turner! Did she have an inbuilt radar for detecting when women were getting close to Jack? Valentine heard him open the door and tell her to calm down. Julia was still shouting and she sounded drunk as she slurred, 'Jack, please, I just need to talk to you and then I'll go.'

'This is not a good time right now; you can't come in,' Jack said firmly.

'Why? Have you got someone here?' Outrage in her voice. 'Am I spoiling your lovers' tryst?'

Valentine sat bolt upright, pulling down her skirt and clutching her shirt to her, which was just as well, as Julia burst into the living room, closely pursued by Jack. She was clearly the worse for wear and had to hold on to a chair to stop herself swaying.

'Julia, I really would like you to go,' Jack said, angry now.

'Oh would you?' Julia said sharply, without a trace of her trademark husky tone. 'That's not what you said a few weeks ago, is it? You see, Valentine, Jack might protest now, but back then he was only too happy when I called round. We might have split up but he still wanted me. And I know he still does, don't you?' She managed to go husky again for the last comment.

Oh God, this was horrible! Valentine sat on the sofa, frozen in embarrassment.

'Julia, really you need to go,' Jack insisted, his jaw clenched angrily.

'What? So that you two can screw!' The husk was gone again. 'Just tell me Jack, what's she got that I haven't?' She pointed an accusing finger at Valentine, who was tempted to reply, 'Fifteen fewer years,' but she wasn't that bitchy.

'I know all about her from Eva – how she tried to wreck her relationship with Finn.'

'That's enough, Julia,' Jack replied.

'Who encouraged you to go into acting in the first place? It was me, darling. I've championed you all the way and now you want to throw away everything we had together for a quick fuck with her!' She turned to Jack, her beautiful blue eyes glinting with tears.

Valentine took the opportunity to get up from the sofa with as much dignity as she could muster, and still clutching her shirt to her, hobbled to the bathroom. There she attempted to calm her wild hair and did up her bra and her shirt. Her face was flushed and her lips were slightly swollen from the kisses. Bugger it, her knickers were on the sofa. Matching her appearance, her mind was all over the place, the doubts were creeping back in. What had she been thinking of? She didn't need this complication in her life. The play opened in three days; she should be focusing on that. She had to escape the scene of emotional carnage. She grabbed her bag, intending to creep out of the flat without saying goodbye; the knickers would have to be sacrificed.

But Jack was waiting by the door. 'Don't go. I'll get rid of her, I promise.'

'I really think I should, don't you? You've obviously got lots to talk about,' Valentine said brusquely, trying to banish the image of him kissing her body. He was a player; he'd slept with Julia when it suited him and he probably had a string of other women. He was probably just like Finn. She was a fool to ever get involved. 'I'll get the bus; thanks for dinner. I'll see you tomorrow.' And without giving Jack a chance to reply she opened the front door and marched down the stairs, ignoring Jack calling out after her and feeling very proud of her composure. It was only when she got to the bus stop that she realised she hadn't pulled her skirt down at the back and had been mooning most of Ferme Park Road, N8.

There was no denying that she liked Jack a lot. Wanted him, desired him, fancied the absolute arse off him and something else besides. But Julia's untimely arrival last night had unsettled Valentine. She knew she had to put the brakes on, whatever she had going with Jack, for the sake of her work – the show must go on and all that; she could not afford to be in emotional turmoil right now. The very next day, while they both had some time to kill between scenes, she asked him to go for a walk with her. Outside the sky was an oppressive grey and it was raining heavily – a perfect accompaniment to her mood. To cap it all her hair was bound to go crazily curly in the damp. She would no doubt end up looking like she'd had a tight perm, circa 1977. She was willing to bet that Julia Turner never had a bad hair day. As they walked along the road, trying to avoid getting drenched by the cars driving through the puddles, he tried to apologise about Julia again, but Valentine cut across him.

'Are you still seeing her?'

Jack sighed. 'I did sleep with her a couple of times after we split up, but we're not together anymore.'

'She still carries a torch for you though, doesn't she?' Valentine persisted. 'That was obvious.'

'Yes, but it's completely one-sided.'

'She's very beautiful,' Valentine said.

'Very,' Jack agreed. 'And very high-maintenance, neurotic, jealous and possessive, which is why I split up with her.'

'So why still see her?'

'I try hard not to, but as you've noticed she's very persistent. I've figured out it's better to see her every now and then, as friends, because I want to keep in touch with her daughter, Ruby. Anyway, please let's stop talking about her; it depresses the hell out of me. I'm not interested in Julia; only in you and me.'

A pause. 'Jack, I can't see you, at least not until the play's finished; it's too much.'

'Are you going to shut your eyes when we're on stage together then?' he said, trying to make light of her declaration.

'You know what I mean,' she replied, looking ahead so she didn't have to see his face.

'So you'll see me when the play's over?' he asked hopefully. 'I'll hold your knickers captive until you do.'

'Let's just see how it goes,' she replied, proud of herself for appearing so cool, but inside feeling the loss of his company already. 'You seem to have so much going on in your life.'

'And what about you?' Jack asked. 'There are plenty of things you haven't told me, aren't there? What about Finn?'

Valentine ignored him and quickened her pace.

'Wait.' Jack put his hand on her arm to get her to stop, then reached inside his jacket for his diary. He took out a pen and flipped through the pages, then he circled a date and held it up for her to see. He had marked the nineteenth of April, the day after the last show. 'So we have a date then?' he asked hopefully.

'OK,' Valentine replied, suddenly wondering how she was going to last five weeks.

There then followed the final week of rehearsals, where Valentine felt she was going cold turkey. The fact was that she really missed Jack. She restricted herself to only looking at him when she thought he couldn't see, to only talking to him when there were others present. And he kept to his side of the bargain: not seeking her out, no more intimate late-night phone calls. She felt bereft. She hadn't realised how much she loved his company. But she tried not to be distracted – she had the play to focus on and it was really coming together. During rehearsals there was a sense of energy as the drama unfolded and connections were made – except with Xander who had a wonderfully rich voice, but who delivered his lines as if he had no idea what he was actually saying, however many times VPL went through it with him. But Valentine, whom VPL had praised repeatedly for her comic and sensuous performance, felt completely ready for the play to open. That was, until she was presented with her costume.

'OK, tell me honestly, what do you think?' Valentine was standing in front of Lauren dressed only in the gold briefs (mercifully VPL had agreed that she didn't have to wear the thong) and matching gold nipple tassels that made up her Titania costume. All that was missing was the gold body paint.

Lauren wolf-whistled. 'Have you ever considered a career in lap dancing?'

'I meant, do I look fat?' Valentine exclaimed in exasperation. Lauren never got it, because she had never felt or looked fat in her entire life.

'No, you look curvy and delicious,' Lauren replied.

'So I do look fat then,' Valentine shot back, unable to take Lauren's words as a compliment. She'd been working so hard to lose weight, running and swimming every day and cutting down on the evil carbs. But evidently it had all been in vain. She was still a porker.

'You don't look fat at all!' Lauren told her. 'I promise.'

'I can't believe that I've actually got to wear this outfit!' Valentine groaned, peeling off the cursed nipple tassels and dropping them on to her dressing table with an expression of complete disgust.

'Tomorrow's the dress rehearsal and I've got to wear them in front of Jack for the first time. It's going to be mortifying. It will definitely be the end of him fancying me – if he does still fancy me, after I gave him the brush-off.'

'He fancies you,' Lauren told her. 'He's burning for you, baby.'

'No, no, he'll see Emily flitting about in her white see-through dress all slender and size zero and realise his mistake. Who wants a golden porker when they can have a beautiful nymph?'

A massive eye-roll from Lauren. 'I'm here for you, girlfriend, but if you keep going on about how you're fat when you're not, I will start talking about my teeth.'

'Deal.' Valentine reached for her dressing gown. Lauren could talk about her teeth all night.

By the time the dress rehearsal arrived she was in a state of near-meltdown over the tassels. Usually she loved getting changed into her costume – it was part of the transformation into the character – but not today. It was an hour and a half before the play started and in the dressing room the Twirlies had already stripped off and were wandering around half-naked, totally un-self-conscious about displaying so much flesh, but Valentine reflected that if she'd had a body like theirs she'd be the same. She sat hunched up in front of the mirror, delaying as long as she could the awful moment when she would have to strip off in the less-than-glamorous dressing room. It smelled of damp, stale perfume and hairspray. The facilities were limited to a sink, a shower (both of dubious cleanliness), a kettle and a rail for their costumes, but at least it was single-sex. Valentine had been dreading that they might have to share one with the boys, as she had on other productions. There was a long horizontal mirror on one wall, against which was a dressing table with space enough for six chairs. Valentine had made sure that she was sitting next to Kitty and Zara and at the opposite end of the table to Emily, who was openly continuing her pursuit of Jack, even though he'd given her no encouragement. Probably someone as ravishing as her wasn't used to rejection.

Valentine fiddled with her make-up, which she'd carefully arranged. Like a lot of actors she was a bit OCD about dressing-room rituals and she always had to have a purple towel and Chanel foundation and eyeliner.

'Shouldn't you be getting changed?' Kitty asked, sitting on the chair next to Valentine. She was already in her costume, a pretty lilac chiffon dress with a fitted bodice and flowing skirt. *No nipple tassels for her*, Valentine thought enviously. She sighed. It was now or never.

Under the cover of a black towelling robe she reluctantly took off her clothes put on the gold bikini briefs and immediately wrapped herself back in the robe, which had a hood and which she was sure made her look a little like Obi-Wan Kenobi. The four other fairies – Pease-Blossom, Cobweb, Moth and Mustard-Seed had by now put on their briefs and nipple tassels and she tried to tell herself there was safety in numbers, even though they all had bodies to die for.

But at least she didn't have to wear a thong like Robbie, who was playing Puck. He had arrived at the dress rehearsal in a complete state after opting for a back, sack and crack wax, in order to pull off the skimpy garment. He had tears in his eyes when he came into the girls' dressing room and recounted how excruciatingly painful the procedure had been. But he had come to the wrong place for sympathy. Kitty gave him short shrift. 'Robbie, women have been waxing for centuries, or maybe even millennia, so get over yourself ! Also we have to undergo a little thing called childbirth, remember? And what's that compared to a few ripped-out follicles?' Exit Robbie, much chastened.

'Oh, don't be so hard on the poor boy,' answered Dixie

the make-up artist, who was doing their make-up free for her CV. She was a complete sweetie. She had obviously read the make-up artist bible which stated: *Thou shalt only ever be lovely to thy clients and make them feel good about themselves, however bloody annoying and demanding they are.* 'Now come on Valentine, I need to do your body paint.'

Dixie was Welsh, slightly overweight – the fate of many a make-up artist, doomed to spend so much of their time sitting around – but gorgeous, channelling a Marilyn Monroe look with platinum-blonde hair and scarlet lips. She had a lovely temperament: calm, unflappable and tactful; she was bound to go far in her profession. 'You'll need to take off the robe, my love,' Dixie told her gently, and sighing heavily Valentine obeyed. Quickly Dixie got to work, expertly smoothing the paint over Valentine's bare skin, giving her instructions about how to stand and what part of her body to move. 'Just open your legs a little wider could you? I need to get to your inside thighs; that's lovely,' she said, kneeling in front of her.

'I just hope you've got enough paint to cover the massive surface area,' Valentine said bitterly, as an unpleasant image flashed into her head of a turkey being basted.

'Valentine, you're going to look absolutely lush when I've finished with you, I promise – like a fairy Bond girl!' Dixie continued.

'She died you know,' Valentine said gloomily. 'If you mean the one in *Goldfinger*.'

'Ooh, I'd forgotten all about that! I wonder what would be the quickest way to go? Poisoned by gold being sprayed over your entire body or drowning in that lift like that poor Eva Green in *Casino Royale.*'

'Probably drowning,' Valentine replied, feeling grateful to Dixie for taking her mind off her thighs, even if it was by discussing death.

'Still, at least she copped off with Daniel Craig first,' Dixie continued. 'That scene when she's in the shower and he sucks her fingers gives me goosebumps, and don't even get me started on the blue trunks! I tell you he can solace my quantum any day of the week!'

Lovely as the thought of Daniel Craig solacing anything was, Valentine was not to be distracted from her current situation. 'Are you sure you can't do that body-contouring thing that all the stars have done to make me look slimmer?' she whispered.

'Sorry love, I don't have a spray gun and anyway you don't need it, I promise! There now, all done.'

Finally Valentine got to see the result in the mirror. To her huge relief it wasn't nearly as bad as she'd feared. She had been dreading looking like a monster from Dr Who circa nineteen seventy-five, but the gold paint had a sheer texture and gave her skin a glittery, luminous glow which was actually quite flattering, though probably not one she was planning to repeat off-stage. Her hair had been curled to make it even wilder than usual, and the tips sprayed with gold – she looked exotic, and actually, sexy. She was about to reach for her Obi-Wan Kenobi robe but Dixie stopped her. 'You can't wear anything I'm afraid; the paint will come off. I'll go and get an electric heater so you can keep warm.'

Valentine could have done without being practically naked in front of the ravishing Emily, who had absolutely no worries about stripping off. She had been wandering around in a sheer bra and thong for what seemed like ages before finally putting on her costume.

'I bet she was hoping Jack saw her in her undercrackers, silly cow,' Kitty whispered to Valentine. 'Not because he wants to, but because she wants him to,' she added hastily, seeing the look on Valentine's face.

'I bet he would like to,' Valentine said gloomily. But Jack didn't come into their dressing room. All the other male members of the cast popped in at various intervals for a chat or to make themselves a coffee, or in Xander's case to have a good gawp at the Twirlies. Rufus came in to give Kitty a good-luck kiss; Toby sweetly gave all the girls a flower each for luck. Valentine steeled herself for cheeky comments about the costumes but none came – in fact no one even commented on the nipple tassels. It was both reassuring and slightly bonkers, as if they were all ignoring the elephant in the room.

The half was called and the boys left the dressing room. The half was actually thirty-five minutes before the performance started and even though it wasn't the real thing, Valentine got an adrenalin-charged rush as if it was. It became quieter then, with less gossiping and giggling. Every actor was different in how they prepared to go on stage – Kitty went into some yoga stretches, while Valentine just liked to be silent and get into character in her head. From next door they could hear Xander doing some frankly annoying vocal warm-ups. Then Zara, the lovely Twirly, started whistling 'Always Look on the Bright Side of Life'.

'What the fuck are you doing?' Emily shrieked at her like a banshee, her pretty face contorted with outrage – not so pretty now, Valentine thought. 'Go outside this minute, turn round three times, knock on the door and then come back in. And no fucking whistling!'

'Oh take a chill pill!' Kitty replied. 'You're not seriously hung up on that old superstition, are you? I bet you don't even know where it comes from, do you?'

Emily curled her lip petulantly and gestured to Zara to get out. Zara decided to humour her and elegantly tiptoed out of the room on her demi points like a prima ballerina, closed the door behind her, then knocked on it a few seconds later and arabesqued back in.

'It doesn't matter that I don't know where it comes from; I just know it's bad luck, as bad as naming the Scottish play!' Emily shot back.

'Well, I shall tell you,' Kitty replied, clearly delighting in getting one up on Emily. 'In the olden days scenery changes were cued by whistles. So someone whistling for pleasure could be mistaken for a cue, causing the scenery to be dropped on an actor's head by mistake. So it's obviously completely obsolete – oh by the way, that means out of date.'

'I went to bloody Oxford!' Emily hissed. 'Of course I know what it means!' And turning away from Kitty she picked up a make-up brush and applied more eyeshadow.

Kitty mouthed 'One nil to me,' to Valentine, who shrugged and closed her eyes and practised her relaxation techniques.

By the time she was waiting in the wings to go on stage she was in the zone. She was Titania, queen of the fairies, and her anxieties about her costume had melted away. She confidently stepped out on stage, totally in control. The enchanted forest was her kingdom. There was a tiny budget for lighting and scenery, but Vince had worked wonders. A huge screen was the backdrop on to which were projected different abstract images, giving the stage a dreamlike quality. The lighting had been designed to give off the effect of moonlight filtering through leaves, dappling the stage with mysterious shapes and shadows.

Her first scene with Oberon went perfectly and she exited stage right on a complete high. Then she walked straight into Jack. *Here goes.* She took a deep breath and shook her hair back defiantly, preparing for the inevitable cheeky comment about her costume. Instead he looked her straight in the eye, definitely not in the nipple area, and said, 'That was great Valentine; I'll see you on stage,' and walked away. Valentine didn't know whether to be pleased or offended by his response.

In fact Jack's silence about her appearance continued after their scene together, through VPL's notes back to them and into drinks at the Orange Peril. Surely he had some opinion on how she had looked? Everyone else had said something – Toby had told her that she looked sublime, which was undoubtedly an exaggeration but welcome as a compliment all the same; Rufus had said she looked gorgeous; even Xander had said she looked 'cracking'. But so far Jack had said nothing. All in all very disappointing and frustrating because the thrill she had got from being on stage was making her feel reckless, making her forget her determination to keep him at a distance. Now as he sat opposite her in what had become their corner, she longed to be sitting next to him, longed to touch him, but right now it was Emily sitting next to him, making sure that she was close enough for their bodies to touch. Bloody sylph-like skinny minnie Emily!

Valentine stayed for a few drinks, chatting away to Toby and Kitty as if she didn't have a care in the world, but every now and then she found herself looking at Jack. *Talk to me!* she willed him. Finally, when she could bear the situation no longer, she got up to go. She said her goodbyes and blew kisses to everyone and had just walked out of the door when Jack called out her name. She swung round expectantly and saw that he had followed her out.

Finally he spoke. 'I wanted to tell you that you looked beautiful on stage,' he said softly, his dark eyes almost black in the fading light.

'You mean in a pervy, lap-dancer type of way,' Valentine laughed, but the laugh was to disguise how thrilled she was by the compliment.

'No, I mean in a beautiful way,' he replied, completely serious.

Wow, cartwheels of pure happiness were turning round in Valentine's head, but even then she couldn't let it lie. 'And what did you think of the nipple tassels?' she demanded, and got the rare experience of seeing Jack look less confident than usual.

'There are many things that I want to say, but I respect

you too much as a performer. When the play's over I'll tell you.' And with that he turned back into the pub, leaving Valentine wondering why on earth she was trying to play it cool with him. Could she really wait the weeks until the show ended? Right now all she wanted to do was get close to him. Oh all right then, shag his brains out.

Valentine returned home that night high on the success of the play and high on desire for Jack. She decided that she would break her own rule and call him. Lauren was still up so Valentine popped her head round the living room door to say hi. Her flatmate was curled up on the sofa with a magazine, staring transfixed at something. She visibly jumped when Valentine walked in and stuffed the magazine behind her back guiltily.

'Hiya,' Valentine said, 'What were you looking at?'

'Nothing,' Lauren replied, 'just this season's must-have accessories.'

'Really?' Valentine said dubiously. Lauren followed her own fashion path – she didn't give a stuff about must-haves. 'Can I see them?'

'No!' Lauren shot back. 'You'll hate them.'

'OK, Lauren,' Valentine said, 'I know you're lying, because you're the world's worst liar, so what were you really looking at?'

Lauren sighed. 'Just tell me how you're feeling at the moment.'

Valentine considered. 'Really good, really happy; the play's going well. I feel a bit odd about the whole Piers Hunter dad thing, but apart from that, good.'

'And how do you feel about Jack?' Lauren asked.

'Well . . .' Valentine hesitated. She could play it cool or she could confide in Lauren. She felt she would burst if she didn't tell someone. 'Actually I really like him.'

'Good, so absolutely no need to see this then,' Lauren said brusquely.

'Oh come on! Now I've got to, otherwise it's going to torment me.'

'No, I really don't think it's a good idea. I know what you're like.'

'It's not another article about NTM, is it?' Valentine asked.

Lauren shook her head. And suddenly, with a sickening feeling, Valentine knew exactly who it was about.

'It's about Finn, isn't it?'

Lauren nodded. 'Please don't read it, V.' But Valentine held out her hand and Lauren reluctantly handed over the magazine and muttered 'Page one hundred and five, but don't say I didn't warn you.'

Valentine quickly turned to the page. Then she froze and all the joy went out of her day. It was a picture of Finn, featured in a glossy two-page spread as one of Britain's rising young acting stars. There he was, looking impossibly handsome – those blue eyes, dark-blonde hair, sexily dishevelled in black tie with the shirt and tie undone. And there he was coming out of a restaurant, his arm round Eva. 'Oh no,' she whispered as she read that Finn and Eva had recently become engaged. She sat down on the sofa next to Lauren, not even noticing that the springs viciously dug into her.

'V, he's been with Eva for four years; you can't be that surprised. It was bound to happen.'

'He lied to me,' Valentine said without thinking.

'Oh my God! Have you been seeing him?' Lauren demanded. 'V, you're mad!'

Valentine ignored her. She sat gazing at the pictures of Finn, feeling as if he had betrayed her all over again. She was such a fool, a stupid, stupid fool to have believed him.

Suddenly Lauren pulled the magazine out of her hands. 'Enough!' she declared and raced downstairs.

'No!' Valentine shouted, following her. 'I haven't finished reading it! Give it back to me!' They ended up fighting over the magazine on the landing outside Lily's door. 'Stop torturing yourself! You don't need to look at it anymore!' Lauren panted.

'Give it to me!' Valentine shouted, almost beside herself. She was considering whether to pull Lauren's hair in a desperate last-ditch attempt to get the magazine when Lily opened her front door, looking elegant in cream silk pyjamas and a fur coat – her flat was freezing too. 'Ladies, what on earth is going on?'

'I'm trying to save Valentine from herself!' Lauren shouted back, still holding firmly on to the magazine.

'I don't need saving!' Valentine shot back. 'I'm fine about Finn; I just wanted to read the article.'

'Fine about Finn? Do me a fucking favour!' Lauren shouted back. 'Every time his name is mentioned or we come close to discussing what happened with him, you go into a major depression. I know what it does to you,

Valentine. And now I know you've been seeing him! He's completely fucked you up!'

'Fuck you, Lauren! I don't need you patronising me. It's not like you've got the most well-adjusted attitude to relationships. Miss dysfunctional of the fucking century! You're so fucked up you don't even know a good man when you meet him! I expect it won't be long before you get rid of Nathan.' Valentine had lost it. She wanted to hurt Lauren, anyone, as much as she was hurting inside right now.

'Valentine, I'm sure you don't mean that; why don't you come in, have a drink and we can talk about this,' Lily put in reasonably.

'Leave me alone, Lily!' Valentine shouted back. 'And you're a fine one to give advice on relationships! All those years you wasted when you could have been with Frank!'

It was such a cruel thing to say, and as soon as the words were out of her mouth she bitterly regretted them. 'Maybe Finn is my Frank! I still love him, don't you get it? Just leave me alone.' And with that she grabbed the magazine, ran down the stairs and out of the house.

She had no idea of where she was going. All she could think about was Finn. Her feelings for Jack were pushed out by the toxic mixture of pain, betrayal, and longing evoked by Finn. She walked for several hours, through Notting Hill, along the Bayswater Road, round Marble Arch, along Oxford Street, then into Soho. She was oblivious to the chilly March air. She felt rejected all over again. Finn had promised, *sworn* that he was going to leave Eva – Valentine would never have got involved with him again if he hadn't. But when it came to it, it was Eva he chose yet again, leaving Valentine to wonder why it hadn't been her.

It was close to midnight and press night was tomorrow; she should have been at home in bed. Eventually exhaustion got the better of her and she caught the night bus. By now her feelings of anger towards Lauren had ebbed away and been replaced by a deep sense of shame that she had been so vile to her best friend and that she had said such a terrible thing to Lily.

The flat was in darkness when she let herself in. It was after one a.m. but even so she softly knocked at Lauren's bedroom door. There was no answer. Valentine quietly opened the door, determined to say sorry. But Lauren's bed was empty; she was probably with Nathan. Valentine felt awful. Lauren had done nothing wrong. She had only been trying to protect her. She reached for her phone and simply texted *sorry x*. She didn't expect a reply that night, but just as she was getting into bed her phone beeped. Lauren's text read *I understand, now go to sleep mother fucker! X*. There was just the matter of Lily.

Even though Valentine had gone to bed so late, she made sure she got up early in order to buy flowers for Lily. She headed straight for a flower stall on Portabello Market, buying a huge bunch of pale pink peonies, which she knew were Lily's favourite flowers. Then she raced back, wanting to catch Lily before she went out. Frank opened the door when she knocked.

He looked tired, but at least he wasn't looking at her

like she was the Antichrist. 'Oh hi Frank, I just wanted to give these to Lily and apologise for last night.'

'Come in, she'd like to see you. She's been worried about you.'

Stepping into Lily's flat was like going into a vintage treasure trove. Lily did not do minimalism and every possible surface was covered in wonderful ornaments and pieces of art deco china, glorious art deco lamps and photographs from Lily's heyday as an actress – she'd been such a beauty. In the corner of the living room she had a glass cabinet displaying the jewellery she'd collected over the years. She hated beautiful things to be locked away. Usually Lily would have been darting round the flat making tea, but this morning she was lying on the sofa, a beautiful green embroidered scarf around her shoulders and a pink satin eiderdown covering her legs, while Frank fussed round the fire.

'V, how lovely to see you!' Lily said, no trace of resentment in her voice for Valentine's cruel words of the night before.

'I'm so sorry for what I said,' Valentine said, handing her the flowers and perching on the end of the sofa.

Lily smiled. 'My favourites. How sweet of you, but there was no need. I understand. Have you got time for a cup of tea? Frank, can you be a darling and make it? I fancy lapsang souchong.'

Valentine waited for Frank to make a cheeky remark, as he would usually if Lily mentioned one of her posh teas, but he just nodded and padded out to the kitchen. And usually Lily would never trust Frank to make her tea, teasing him that he was only good for making the strong builders' cups that he preferred. But Lily didn't look as if she had the strength to do anything.

'Are you OK, Lily?'

'Oh I'm fine, darling, just struggling to get over this virus.'

'Well, have you been back to the doctor?' Valentine persisted.

Lily smiled gently. 'Yes, I've been back to the doctor. I'm fine. It's you I'm worried about. Try not to think about Finn. He belongs to the past. It's time to start again with Jack. He's perfect for you, I just know it.'

Valentine wished she shared Lily's certainty.

'Anyway, I have a little good-luck present for you.' Lily ignored the doubtful look on Valentine's face and handed her a small box. Inside she found one of Lily's favourite cocktail rings, a fabulous turquoise gem in a gold setting.

Valentine looked up at Lily all set to tell her that she couldn't take it, but Lily smiled and said, 'Please V, I can't wear it anymore. I'd like to think of you wearing it. And good luck tonight.'

Even though she had made her peace with Lauren and apologised to Lily, Valentine felt blue all day. She should have been looking forward to the first night, but instead she felt vulnerable and on edge. She kept trying not to think about Finn, but then she'd remember. An all-too-familiar feeling of worthlessness invaded her. Why was he engaged to Eva and not her? Had he been lying to her all along when he said he still loved her? She put off going to the theatre as long as possible, not wanting to see anyone and especially not wanting to see Jack. She just wanted to escape into her role, not have to deal with the world right now. But Jack was the first person she saw when she walked into the theatre.

'Hi,' he said, looking at her warmly. 'I texted you today; didn't you get it? I wondered if you wanted to have coffee. And I meant *just* coffee, not anything else, cross my heart.'

Valentine had got the text. 'Sorry, I was busy.' She knew she sounded cold, but couldn't help it. She felt the need for defences against him, against anyone.

'Are you OK?' Jack asked, looking at her closely. 'Your eyes look sad. Has something happened?'

'No, nothing. Just tired, I think, and nervous. Anyway, I'd better get ready, see you later.' And without waiting for his reply she headed for the dressing room. *Well done Valentine, you really know how to keep a man.*

Everyone else was already in costume and in the middle of putting on their make-up. 'You're late!' Kitty exclaimed when Valentine walked in, 'VPL was starting to get jittery. It doesn't take much to push him over the edge.'

'I know I cut it a bit fine, but I just needed some head space before coming in and I knew I wouldn't get any here.'

Both paused to watch the Twirlies warming up – stretching their long legs ridiculously high above their heads and then effortlessly sliding into the splits – truly they were like creatures from another galaxy. Emily moaned loudly to Dixie that she had a spot on her cheek.

'I can't see anything, sweetheart,' Dixie patiently

reassured her. 'You've got perfect skin. You all have,' she added, looking around the room, anxious not to offend anyone. Rule number two from the make-up artist's bible – never tell your clients the painful truth; just reach for the concealer. Lots of it.

'We haven't, Dixie,' Kitty shot back. 'But no doubt we will when we've trowelled on enough make-up.' At that Emily gave her an evil look, no doubt objecting to the implication that her skin was less than perfect.

Valentine looked at Kitty and shrugged, 'See what I mean?' She had been dreading coming in, but gradually as she started putting on her costume and make-up, some of the darkness began to lift. For now at least she was no longer Valentine with the disastrous love life who had made all the wrong decisions. She was Titania again. Beautiful, powerful, in control – well at least until she got drugged and ended up falling in love with a donkey! Valentine had often wondered if the reason she loved acting so much was that it offered escape from the real world and above all escape from herself. She sat down at her place in front of the mirror and tried to shut out the activity around her, the men coming in to make coffees and flirt with the Twirlies, Emily fidgeting and constantly going in and out of their dressing room – either it was nerves or she was on the lookout for Jack. Kitty was quick to point it out to Valentine. 'I see Princess Precious is still on the prowl for Jack,' she said quietly when Emily was out of the room.

Valentine shrugged. 'He doesn't belong to me.'

'Not yet,' Kitty replied cheekily, 'but we all know it won't be long.'

This was the very last thing Valentine needed to hear right now. 'Look, I don't give a shit to be honest, Kitty. Yes, I admit that I fancy Jack – who doesn't? But I don't know if I could ever trust someone like him.'

Unluckily for Valentine that was the moment Jack knocked at the door and walked into the dressing room. She wasn't sure how much if anything he might have heard. If he had heard he didn't give anything away. Immediately Emily came back into the room and made a beeline for him, telling him he could have some of her tea if he wanted.

'It's not herbal, is it?' Jack asked. 'I can't be doing with that. I only like builders' tea.'

'Is that because you're so manly?' Kitty teased him. 'Do you go weak if you don't eat red meat once a day?'

'Nope, don't eat red meat at all,' Jack replied. He looked at Valentine as if expecting her to join in the banter, but she just turned away and put on more lipstick. She didn't even care that she was half-naked in front of him.

'Well good luck everyone,' Jack called out, leaving the dressing room.

Valentine replied, 'And you,' but avoided looking at him.

'What's the matter?' Kitty whispered, sitting down next to Valentine, ostensibly to check her make-up.

'Nothing, I'm just centring myself.'

'Good work everyone!' Vince declared afterwards, as everyone gathered in the girls' dressing room to get their notes. 'In a nutshell, I think he just means faster, better!' Kitty whispered to Valentine as VPL droned on.

Valentine was last to leave the dressing room. She had scrupulously avoided eye contact with Jack throughout Vince's feedback. The performance had gone well but she still didn't feel up to being around people, or more precisely being around Jack. She felt too shaken up. She'd just go for one drink, she decided, so the rest of the cast didn't think she'd completely lost the plot, then go straight home. All the other women had glammed up in honour of press night, but Valentine felt too drained. She simply wiped off the gold paint, tied her hair back and put on a baggy black jumper, leggings and biker boots. Upstairs, the tiny theatre bar was rammed. Vince had managed to get in a number of critics – maybe he really was going places, as Sylvia her agent had promised. Kitty waved to her from one of the tables and Valentine wove her way through the crowds, steeling herself. Lauren and Nathan were also at the table, along with Rufus, Toby and Jack. And Julia Turner. Valentine's spirits took a further nosedive.

'You were fantastic, V!' Lauren declared. 'We got you a drink – double vodka OK?'

'OK, yes, unaccustomed as I am to alcohol I will do my best to force it down,' Valentine said dryly.

'You weren't unaccustomed the other night when you drank all those tequila shots,' Jack put in. Valentine turned briefly in his direction, then quickly turned back. She couldn't stop the pang of jealousy at seeing Julia next to him and the I-told-you-so feeling. Julia looked stunning in a black figure-hugging Roland Mouret Pigalle dress.

'Come and sit down,' Toby said, shuffling up to make room for her on the wooden bench.

'I'm loving the look, V. Are you channelling *Prisoner Cell Block H* as your style guru?' Lauren said sarcastically.

Valentine shrugged, 'I just wanted to wear something comfortable.'

'Next time why not go the whole hog and wear a sack?' Lauren replied. 'It's press night, V! You should have worn your red silk dress.'

'You look adorable as you are, Valentine,' Toby said chivalrously.

Valentine smiled and took a sip of her drink, and as she did so she caught Jack's eye. 'Are you OK?' he mouthed to her. She nodded and looked away. If anyone was too kind to her she was likely to lose it completely.

'Well, we should have a toast,' Julia declared, holding up her glass. 'To a great first night!' Everyone held up their glasses and Valentine heard Julia murmur, 'And to a fabulous Bottom,' as she leaned over and kissed Jack on the cheek. Even though Jack didn't look as if he was relishing her attention, Valentine couldn't help feeling crushed. He probably still had feelings for Julia and why wouldn't he? Julia might be possessive and neurotic, but she was still beautiful and successful. Valentine sipped her drink morosely.

Then Jack took up the toast and declared, 'To a wonderful Titania!' Julia looked sulky. Valentine then toasted Toby and so it went on round the table. Julia snapped open her chic black velvet clutch bag for a cigarette and was about to light up when Jack said, 'Julia, it's no smoking.'

'Bugger! I always forget. Will you come outside with me, darling?' she asked, stroking his arm. Jack shook his head. Julia did a double-take – clearly not used to being turned down. She narrowed her beautiful blue eyes, looking at Jack and then at Valentine. Then she spoke. 'So Valentine, that was quite something you had to do on stage, baring so much flesh and being surrounded by such ravishing creatures as the Twirlies.' Valentine waited for the sting in the tail and here it came: 'I was so impressed that you hadn't gone on an extreme diet and that you had all your curves. It was so very *brave* of you.'

Bitch. 'I'm a size ten to twelve, Julia. Last time I checked that wasn't on the morbidly obese spectrum. And yes I do look different from the dancers, but that's the point,' Valentine replied, aware that her cheeks were flushing with anger and embarrassment. Maybe everyone else had been lying when they said how good she had looked; maybe she had looked like a golden porker all along. She was probably a laughing stock.

'Oh I didn't mean it as a criticism! As I said, it was very brave of you!' Julia continued, tapping her zippo lighter on the table in what seemed like a deliberately irritating way.

'So, Julia, where do you stand on the face/body dilemma?' Lauren was quick to leap to her friend's defence.

'What do you mean?' Julia asked warily.

153

'You know, when a woman gets over a certain age, let's say forty? She needs to decide whether she keeps a skinny body but ends up with a wizened face or goes for a more relaxed approach, and has a fuller figure but with plumper younger-looking skin on her face. Though it's a cruel twist of fate that whatever she does, even if she has work done, the hands and neck always give it away, don't they?' Lauren looked meaningfully at Julia's hands, which actually still looked pretty good.

Julia gave a forced laugh. 'I'm wondering if I should be offended that you think I'm over forty.'

Lauren rolled her eyes. 'Julia, I know you're over forty, so you can cut the denial crap with me.'

'Well, so much for female solidarity,' Julia hissed, all pretence at being charming abandoned. 'Do you know how hard it is keeping this body?' she gestured at her lithe figure, then held up her arms and savagely tugged at the taut skin on the underside. 'Working out every single bloody day to make sure you don't get bingo wings; the hundreds of sit-ups just to keep a flat stomach; the constant dieting. Trying to keep age at bay at all costs because while society seems to think men improve with age – look at Anthony Head, a sex symbol in his fifties, or Harrison Ford, still supposed to be hot at sixty-four.' She took a swig of her wine and then continued her tirade. 'Forty-year-old women are rarely considered sex symbols or even sexual beings! We're character actors or we're someone's mother! And why should I be someone's mother just because I'm forty? Why can't I be someone's lover!' Julia was raising her voice now; she'd lost the husky tone and sounded positively screechy.

If it had been any other forty-year-old actress railing against the unfairness of it all, Valentine would have been totally on their side. She really did think it was outrageous how actresses became sidelined when they reached a certain age and how fifty-something actors on screen ended up with women often half their age. However, she felt decidedly unsympathetic towards Julia and her barbed comment about her figure.

Julia pointed an accusing finger at Lauren, Kitty and Valentine in turn. 'One day you'll be forty and then you'll discover the painful truth. You won't keep that peachy-looking skin for ever, you know. Your tits will sag, you'll get lines and you'll have to fight to keep the weight off.' She paused to survey their faces, her eyes flashing with anger. Hell hath no fury like a forty-something actress under threat. 'I really had expected more from my fellow actors.' She abruptly got up. 'Come on Jack, we're leaving.'

Jack remained sitting, 'I'm staying. This is press night, remember?'

Clearly struggling to keep her composure, Julia tossed back her long black hair and stormed out of the bar, killer heels clicking reproachfully on the wooden floor. There was a pause.

'Aren't you going to go after your girlfriend?' Valentine asked snidely.

'She's not my girlfriend. That situation's vacant, remember? I split up with her over three months ago. We're just friends.'

'Yeah right, friends that fuck, according to Julia,' Valentine shot back. Suddenly she was directing at Jack all the anger and hurt that had been building up inside her because of Finn. Jack looked furious.

'Whooah!' Toby put his hand up. 'I think that's enough! Who wants another drink? We don't need a public dissection of Jack's private life, do we?'

'No, we haven't got nearly enough time,' Valentine replied. 'God knows how many other older women he's got in his closet, lining up to pleasure him with their lithe bodies, wizened faces and monkey paws. Oh so grateful for a bit of young cock inside them! There's probably a queue of them waiting outside right now to suck your dick! And you probably wouldn't mind, would you, because a blow job's a blow job isn't it!' She knew she had crossed a line – the combination of depression mixed with jealousy was causing her to say terrible things.

'Is that what you really think?' Jack demanded. 'That I'm some kind of gigolo rent boy? God, you have a low opinion of me. I'll tell you what, I'll leave you to your character assassination.' And with that he got up, grabbed his leather jacket and marched out of the room.

There was stunned silence round the table. Valentine couldn't bring herself to look at anyone. Toby cleared his throat and was the first to speak. 'First nights can be very emotional events. I'm sure a well-timed apology to Jack tomorrow will iron everything out.'

'Or paying a pensioner to give him a well-timed blowie!' Lauren said cheekily. Whenever there was a line, Lauren always liked to cross it.

Valentine ignored her and turned to Toby. 'I just don't know what came over me. It was that woman being so rude and everything and oh my God!' She covered her face with her hands, mortified by her behaviour. 'I can't believe I said those things to Jack.'

Toby put his arm round her. 'Come on, you're just tired and emotional; I'll get you a taxi home, my treat.'

'Thanks Toby,' Valentine replied gratefully. She did need to get out of there fast.

'When you said older women, just how old did you mean?' Nathan asked. 'I'm feeling vaguely turned on by all this talk of pleasuring.'

'Shut up, Nathan!' Lauren replied, punching him on the arm. 'Or I'll give you pleasuring.'

'Time to go,' Toby said, steering Valentine out of the bar.

The following day Valentine arrived at the theatre early in the hope of seeing Jack. She had already texted him to say sorry, but he hadn't replied. Well, she couldn't exactly blame him, could she? It was time to eat a large (hopefully carb-free) slice of humble pie. She hung around in the corridor outside the boys' dressing room, chatting to Toby, hoping to see Jack before she had to get changed. She didn't want to make the apology in nipple tassels. She needed to get some dignity back. But there was no sign of Jack and by six forty-five she couldn't delay getting ready any longer and reluctantly went into the dressing room.

'No sign of him?' Kitty whispered sympathetically. Valentine shook her head. A few minutes later Toby popped in and said that Jack had arrived. Apparently he wasn't saying very much to anyone. Emily went on one of her flirting missions and came back looking very petulant, saying that Jack had snapped at her for no reason.

It wasn't until Valentine was backstage that she finally saw him. Usually they would have a whispered chat before their scene. Not this time. He stood as far away from her as he could in the wings, with his arms folded, staring straight ahead. Everything about his body language said *leave me alone*. But Valentine couldn't bear to go on stage without at least saying sorry to his face. She tiptoed over and lightly touched his arm. He remained looking ahead.

'Sorry Jack,' she whispered. No reaction. 'I'm really, really sorry, I didn't mean those things.' Still no reaction.

Then just as she thought she was going to have to go on stage without getting any response, Jack finally turned to her. 'I had no idea you disliked me that much. I promise to leave you alone from now on,' he said, face expressionless.

Valentine was about to protest that on the contrary she liked him very much, when it was their cue to go on.

For the next three days Jack kept his distance from Valentine. The play was going well, better than Valentine could have predicted, but she felt wretched about Jack. Kitty told her she had to tell him how she felt, but Valentine was convinced she had completely blown it with him. And suddenly she realised just how much she wanted him. Really wanted him, yearned for him, ached for him. She realised that in spite of her emotional reaction to Finn's engagement, deep down she'd always suspected it would happen. She thought about how different Jack was from Finn – how warm and open he was, how he had made her feel so good about herself. Oh God, why had she pushed him away?

Finally on the fourth day of presenting a cold front Jack joined the other actors for a drink in the Orange Peril. Usually he would have sat next to Valentine on what had become their sofa, but tonight he sat next to Toby. He studiously ignored Valentine. He had never looked so desirable or so unobtainable. Kitty exchanged a sympathetic glance with Valentine, who sighed and despondently swirled the vodka and ice around in her glass and wondered whether to blow her no-carb rule and eat a bumper bag of Walkers.

'That's fantastic news, Jack!' Toby suddenly exclaimed and everyone looked over expectantly. 'Jack's just been offered a part at the Manchester Exchange in *King Lear*, without even having to audition.'

'You jammy bastard!' Kitty exclaimed then added, 'Congratulations, that's brilliant.' She got up and gave him a big hug.

'Well done, Jack,' Valentine said, wishing she could do the same.

'Thanks,' he muttered but he still didn't look at her. 'So when do you start rehearsing?' she continued, desperate to hold his attention somehow.

Her question earned her a further mutter, 'Two weeks after we finish.' Then he added, 'Perhaps there'll be a wizened-faced, lithe-bodied crone I can get off with.'

No one knew whether to laugh. Kitty turned purple trying to stifle a giggle.

Valentine took a deep breath, sensing it was now or never to make Jack aware of her feelings. 'I didn't mean what I said; it was completely out of order. And you're wrong, I do like you; I like you very much. It was just something from my past that shook me up and I took it out on you and I shouldn't have. Please say you forgive me.'

It was a full-on speech to have to deliver in front of everyone else. If he ignored her she would be mortified. But at last he looked at her and the coldness had gone from his eyes. 'Julia was out of order as well. You're right, she does still have a thing for me and in the past I did encourage it, but not anymore. And in answer to your other comment – there's only been one other older woman. Hardly a harem, is it? You're the only woman I'm interested in.'

Valentine suddenly felt very warm and her stomach did that delicious-scary free-fall thing. 'So why don't you cheer the fuck up and come and sit on our sofa?' she demanded.

Needing no further encouragement Jack came and sat down next to her. The others, who had been listening to the exchange open-mouthed, suddenly pretended to be engrossed in conversation. It wasn't subtle but Valentine appreciated the effort.

'So do you accept my apology?' Valentine asked tentatively.

'Only if you can guarantee what you just said was true,' Jack replied.

'I can say it again or I can do this,' Valentine answered

160

and she leaned forward and kissed him – a sensuous, this-kiss-is-going-places sort of kiss, a get-a-room sort of kiss. She pulled away and whispered, 'Do you want to come back to mine?' Suddenly she wanted him so badly, she didn't care about anything else.

Jack nodded and his whispered 'Yes,' sent a shiver of lust through her.

As they got out of the taxi Valentine said, 'We should have champagne to celebrate your new play.'

Jack took her in his arms. 'How about celebrating us, here together.'

'Good idea, and also if you're crap in bed the champagne will help me get through,' Valentine said, winding her arms round his neck.

'I'm not crap in bed,' Jack whispered.

Valentine's stomach did another lurch; she didn't doubt it. As soon as she pushed open the off-licence door Robbie and Tom went into their prisoner routine. 'Miss Fleming, ma'am, it's so good to see you!' Robbie called out, 'We've missed you something awful. Is there any news of our pardon?' Valentine glanced at Jack, who was looking bemused.

'Boys, I have no news for you,' she replied in her Southern Belle accent. 'As you can see I have a gentleman caller and would appreciate you got me my liquor. It's champagne tonight.'

'Oh,' Robbie stared back at her with a crestfallen expression, while Tom reached for a bottle of whatever champagne they had on offer.

'It's just a thing we do,' she explained to Jack in her normal voice.

'So you're the prison governor and they're your prisoners?'

'They're on death row,' she replied.

'But Miss Fleming is trying to get us pardoned,' Robbie put in. He looked seriously put out by Jack's presence.

Jack's mouth twitched as he said, 'And I'm the pervy one with an older-woman fetish? Whereas you've got two young men in prison. Who's the pervert now?'

'It's not like that,' Valentine reverted to Southern Belle, 'I've been encouraging these young men in their Bible studies.'

'Come on, Scarlett O'Hara,' Jack answered, handing over the money for the champagne and ignoring Valentine's protests that she should pay.

Outside they both burst out laughing and Valentine said, 'Now you must think I'm a complete mentalist.'

'No, just a pervert. And you do know that poor Robbie fancies the arse off you, don't you? I thought he was going to hit me. I was relieved the glass was there to protect me.'

'Well, unlike your ladies, I'm not into younger men,' Valentine replied as they crossed the road and walked up the steps to the house. Inside the flat the banter deserted her and nerves took over. Lauren was round at Nathan's, so Valentine had the place to herself and while she grabbed the wine glasses Jack wandered into the living room. There was a loud expression of pain as he sat down on the sofa.

'Sorry!' Valentine called out, 'I meant to warn you about the springs.' She walked into the living room to discover Jack ruefully rubbing his thigh.

'Interesting sofa you've got, sort of like an instrument of torture. And it's fucking freezing in here!' His voice became softer. 'I need warming up. Come here.' He held out his hand.

For a moment she hesitated, then she took it and he pulled her towards him. And then in spite of the wickedly uncomfortable sofa they kissed, and kissed, and kissed. And Valentine gave in to her desire for him, exploring his beautiful body. Then she knew what she wanted to do; she was going to show him that there were blow jobs and blow jobs. She got down to business and enjoying the whole activity far more than she did ordinarily. In fact, she felt very turned on. He really did have the most magnificent . . .

Jack groaned, 'It's no good.' Immediately she sat up, offended; she'd always been complimented on her technique. Jack caught sight of the look on her face and said, 'No, no, it's not you! It's the spring! It's like I'm having a lumbar puncture. It's like being tortured and going to heaven at the same time.'

Ha, so he did like her technique. 'OK, let's move to the bedroom,' Valentine said, trying to put on a husky voice like Julia and getting up from the sofa. 'And don't lose that.' She pointed to his impressive erection.

'Is there something wrong with your throat?' Jack asked, pulling up his jeans and following her out of the room.

'No,' Valentine replied. 'Be quiet and get on the bed. And don't look like that,' she continued, seeing the dubious glance Jack gave her double futon. 'Futons are very good for the back.'

'I never realised you were a sadist, Valentine Fleming,' Jack said, obeying her. They lay down together and as Jack leaned over her to kiss her he took his T-shirt off with one hand, in one fluid move – revealing his toned chest. And yes it was hairy, but actually it was sexy hairy, not repulsive hairy, and his back had none. But oh God, who cared about all that now, because Jack's chest and back, in fact his whole body was a thing of beauty . . .

'So much for waiting until April,' Jack said when they were finally lying in each other's arms, enveloped in a blissful post-sex haze. 'I knew you wouldn't.'

'Yeah well, I only did it with you tonight to keep warm,' Valentine said teasingly, while thinking what a truly delicious experience it had been. Making love with Jack had none of the awkwardness she usually associated with having sex with someone for the first time. Instead everything had felt so right and for once Valentine hadn't felt self-conscious about her body. Usually she was paranoid about being completely naked with a man. Whenever she was with Finn she always kept her skirt or a camisole on, certain that he would be comparing her to Eva. But Jack had freed something in her and in his arms she had felt beautiful and sexy. When he had unbuttoned her red silk dress he had done it gently, reverently, as if he was unwrapping a beautiful present and wanted to appreciate every second.

'So you didn't find that a mindblowing, bone-melting

sexual experience, up there as one of the best ever?' Jack demanded and when Valentine didn't answer he whipped off the duvet and exposed her to the freezing air.

'Put it back on,' she squealed. 'All right I admit it, it was very good.'

'Just good?' Jack replied, still withholding the cover.

'Fantastic!' Valentine confessed and Jack wrapped her up in the duvet.

'Fantastic is the right answer,' he replied, pulling her on top of him.

'But,' she murmured, kissing his neck, 'there's always room for improvement. And what did you mean "one of the best"?'

'Fleming, that was just the start.'

9

Last Night

Valentine's prediction that Jack was a player was proved
way off the mark. He made no secret of their romance,
to the obvious dismay of Emily who became even more
petulant in the dressing room, and to the delight of the
rest of the cast, who were pleased for them and also
relished the chance for a good gossip. Being with Jack
was a revelation. She felt as if she'd gone from winter
to summer emotionally. He made her feel as if anything
was possible. She loved the fact that everything with him
was straightforward and clear-cut. When he said he
could meet her, he met her, and when she texted him,
he replied. There was no skulking around in the middle
of the night, no furtive secret encounters, no lies to be
told or to be lived with. She felt cherished, desired, good
about herself. She was discovering that love didn't have
to hurt. And although she had vowed not to tell anyone
apart from Lauren about Piers, she found herself
confiding in Jack.

'I can't believe you've had so much going on,' Jack

exclaimed when she told him the whole story late one night as they lay in bed together. 'You've handled it so well.'

'I haven't really; I just haven't been allowing myself to think about it and the play has been a great distraction.' And it was true Valentine had been so caught up with acting and with Jack it was as if she had put her feelings about Piers on ice. 'But I know I'll obsess about it when the play ends.'

Jack held her tighter. 'Don't obsess; you can always tell me how you feel. I don't want us to have any secrets.'

Valentine didn't want them to have any secrets either. But while she had opened up about her father, there was one area of her life where she couldn't bear to let Jack in. Jack knew she'd had an affair with Finn, but she couldn't bring herself to reveal the hold he'd had over her for so long, or tell him about their clandestine meetings. Finn was her guilty secret.

'I can't believe I'm about to say this, but I think I'm really going to miss the Orange Peril.' Jack was speaking as he and Valentine and the rest of their gang were out drinking on the play's penultimate night. Valentine nodded and looked round the table, which was crammed with glasses and empty crisp packets, at the people she'd grown so close to over the last two months; she was going to miss them. She would probably even miss Emily, who had finally loosened up and got off with Xander, which had put a smile on her face, though probably not for long according to Kitty, who revealed that a friend of hers had had a fling with Xander on another play and ended up with an STD.

'Hey, why the sad face?' Jack asked, putting his arm round her. She leaned back against him.

'I hate things coming to an end,' she replied. 'I hate not knowing what, if anything, I am going to be doing next.'

'Something will turn up. And there's a couple of weeks before I go to Manchester. We can hang out together loads – but only if you promise to keep wearing the nipple tassels, just for me – my private show,' Jack replied.

'I am going to be burning those things!' Valentine shot back. 'Never again and I mean *never*. They have chafed my breasts and humiliated me!'

'You've always got me to kiss them better and as for humiliation – no way – you were magnificent.'

Valentine appreciated the compliment but that didn't stop her coming out with her next comment. 'I bet you'll forget all about me when you go to Manchester.' There, she'd come out with it – the thought that kept sneaking into her mind ever since their first night together.

Jack looked at her, surprised. 'Valentine, I want you and I'll want you even more when I'm away. Why don't you come up and stay for a couple of months?'

'Because you'll be wanting to bond with the other actors and I don't want to be the saddo out-of-work actor girl-friend,' Valentine said slightly bitterly.

'There's only one actor I want to bond with right now, and that's you. Take me back to your place and I'll show you how much.'

* * *

After Jack had proved not once, but twice how much he wanted to bond with her, they lay curled up together. 'I've got something to tell you, Valentine Fleming. I've wanted to say it practically from the moment I met you,' Jack whispered.

Valentine almost held her breath, and traced her finger round his dragon tattoo. Was he talking about what she thought he was? Lauren had told her never ever to say *I love you* before the man. It was one of her many commandments, along with, 'Sleep with a man once and he doesn't make you come, shame on him; sleep with him twice and still no result shame on you.'

'I love you.' There, he said it.

Valentine's heart gave a cartwheel and backflip of sheer joy, while the judges held up cards with perfect tens. Jack looked at her expectantly and Valentine left it as long as she dared before replying, 'I love you too.'

'You bastard!' he exclaimed. 'I thought you weren't going to say it!'

Valentine softly kissed his lips. 'I was always going to say it.' Later, when she thought he was asleep, she whispered, 'So would you come back for me?' She was referring to their film, *The English Patient*, to the scene where Katharine is lying, injured in the Cave of Swimmers and Almásy her lover has to leave her and cross the desert for help.

'Yes, I would come back for you. I would never leave you.' He curled his body around her so she was encircled by his warmth. In contrast to Finn, Jack held her all night, and never let her go.

* * *

The final show went fantastically well – one of those nights where everything came together and the action felt fluid and seamless. Valentine was left on a high. She would keep the demons away, tonight at least. There was still silence on the Piers front. Maybe he hadn't got her letter; she would write again. Tonight was for celebrating and living in the moment, forgetting that there was uncertainty about tomorrow.

But that all changed when she walked into the bar at the end of the show, and there sitting in the corner were Finn and Tamara. What the fuck were they doing here? She was strongly tempted to leave, but just at that moment Finn noticed her. Immediately he walked over and kissed her. 'V, that was a brilliant performance.' Then he whispered, 'Tell me you're keeping the costume; I have got to get you alone with those nipple tassels.'

'What the hell are you doing here?' Valentine demanded, pulling out of his embrace.

'Seeing the show, of course! I've been wanting to see it for ages. This is the first chance I got. I'm so proud of you V, you really were great. Come and join Tamara and me for a drink.'

'Dragged yourself away from your fiancée, did you?' Valentine was determined not to be taken in by him again.

Finn pulled his hurt expression, 'I feel just awful about that, V. It was wrong of me not to tell you. I'm so confused about everything. Please come and have a drink. I can't bear for us not to be talking.'

Part of Valentine wanted to turn round and walk out of the bar, but she was so programmed to doing what

Finn asked that she muttered about just having one drink and trailed after him. How ironic that he should come now. The number of times she had wanted him to see her in a show! This was not one of them.

'Hello Tamara,' she said, giving the obligatory air kisses, 'I didn't think this was your kind of thing.'

Tamara smiled. She looked every inch the star in a Missoni maxi-dress and stood out a mile in the shabby-round-the-edges theatre bar. 'But I absolutely adore Shakespeare, Valentine! In fact I'm going to be in a Shakespeare myself.' She paused, just long enough for Valentine to think *smug cow*, before she continued, 'I'm in *Lear* in Manchester; I'm playing Cordelia. Didn't Jack tell you?' Inside Valentine felt as if she'd been punched, she shrugged, trying to keep her face as expressionless as possible, aware of Tamara staring at her and weighing up her reaction. Fortunately at that moment one of the audience came over and asked Tamara for her autograph. Tamara gave a coy smile and signed with an extravagant flourish on the programme the man handed her.

'You really should ask Valentine; she was actually in the show!' Tamara trilled, but the man said, 'Oh thank you but no, I just want *your* autograph.' Trust Tamara to make her feel bad. But then she was a master in the art of self-esteem crushing. Really she should run classes on it.

At that moment Jack walked into the bar. He looked more than a little surprised by Valentine's company. She smiled ruefully at him and he walked over.

'Jack – what a great Bottom you were,' Finn said, reaching out and shaking his hand.

'And you are?' Jack asked, but Valentine had a feeling he already knew exactly who he was.

'Finn Steele. And you know Tamara Moore, don't you?'

'Hi again Jack. I can only second what Finn said; you were marvellous. I can't wait for us to be on stage together.'

Valentine seethed inside. God, how she loathed Tamara.

'I don't think Edmund is ever actually on stage with Cordelia,' Jack replied abruptly.

'Anyway, let me get you both a drink; your usual I presume, V?' Finn sounded so possessive, so knowing and at any other time in the last year Valentine would have loved it. Now she wanted him to shut up. She nodded. 'And for you, Jack?'

'Just a bottle of Becks, thanks.' Jack's answer was barely audible.

'And Tamara, please don't ask for Veuve as I'm completely broke,' Finn continued.

'Don't be silly, Finn! I'll have a vodka and tonic – slimline.'

Tamara talked at Jack while Finn was getting the drinks in. 'I am nervous of course; it's been so long since I've done stage, but Alan, the director, has been absolutely lovely.' She was clearly expecting Jack to gush that she would be wonderful blah blah blah; instead he replied, 'I can see why you would be nervous – shooting a film and being on stage night after night, when you've only got yourself, no special effects, no editing, just you, doesn't really compare does it?'

Tamara gave one of her annoying tinkly laughs, but

looked slightly peeved that Jack hadn't come out with the sycophantic comments she was used to.

Another fan approached the table at that moment and Tamara signed another autograph, leaving Valentine free to tackle Jack.

'Why the fuck didn't you tell me?' she whispered.

Jack sighed. 'I didn't want to put you on a downer for your last show – I only found out today.'

'She's got her eye on you,' Valentine said gloomily, imagining how eager Tamara would be to get her talons into Jack. And as she was so beautiful and so skinny, who was to say that Jack wouldn't be tempted?

'And I've only got eyes for you,' Jack replied, leaning over and kissing her.

Finn returned at that moment with the drinks, lightly touching Valentine on the shoulder as he handed out the glasses.

So there they were – the boyfriend, the girlfriend, her ex and the woman who was giving out signals that she would so like to step into Valentine's shoes where Jack was concerned. It made for a supremely awkward ten minutes. Finn was looking at Valentine with his I-want-you eyes; Jack was glaring at Finn; Tamara was gazing at Jack and Valentine was trying to give Jack reassuring I-am-your-girlfriend vibes.

'So what else have you been in?' Finn asked Jack, the two of them sizing each other up in that Alpha male sort of way, which Valentine would have found funny if she hadn't known both of them.

'This is only my second play,' Jack replied. Was it her

imagination or was he suddenly sounding more Norf London? And less RP?

'I see,' Finn answered, raising an eyebrow as if to say *loser*.

'Jack has only just started acting,' Valentine put in. 'He's a trained barrister.'

'Oh right, couldn't hack it?' Finn replied.

'No, I could hack it,' Jack said in low voice, almost a growl, 'I just didn't want to.'

Any minute now they'd be squaring up to each other. In fact maybe it would be better if they had a fight and got it out of their systems. There was so much testosterone swirling around (mainly from Jack) that Valentine could almost smell it.

'Anyway,' Valentine cut across their macho fest, 'Jack and I have to go now. Thanks for the drink; see you later,' and she got up and practically dragged Jack from the bar. At the doorway he paused and pulled her to him and kissed her hard. Kissing Jack was always a gorgeous experience, but this felt too much like he had something to prove, that he was putting his mark on her.

'Jack,' she said, breathless, when he had finished, 'I'm with you.'

'Are you sure you don't still have feelings for him?' he demanded. 'I saw the way he was looking at you. And why the fuck did he turn up anyway?'

'I've no idea, I didn't ask him. And I'm with *you*,' she repeated. 'Now, come on, let's go to the Orange Peril. I want to get away from those people.'

* * *

But that night in bed after they'd drunk long into the night with the cast, saying their emotional goodbyes, after she'd made love with Jack and he lay sleeping next to her, Valentine couldn't sleep. Her mind felt as if it was on overdrive. There was the unresolved matter of her father and there was Finn. Now he couldn't have her, it seemed he wanted her. It was both bitterly ironic and entirely predictable. Well, he could carry on wanting her; he was never going to have her. And Valentine tried to hold on to that thought, even when he texted her at four in the morning: *Want you Fx*. For the first time ever she didn't reply.

10

First Contact

For the two weeks before Jack left for Manchester Valentine tried not to think too much about anything – not her father, not Finn, not Tamara, not the fact that she didn't have any work lined up – she just wanted to enjoy the time with Jack. And they made the most of it, spending every minute together, mostly in bed, as if they could store up the memories for the time they were apart.

'You know I would never be unfaithful to you,' he told her as she sat cross-legged on his lovely bed watching him pack his clothes. 'You can trust me. I'm not attracted to Tamara Moore one little bit; you've got nothing to worry about on that score, I swear.'

Valentine was relieved. She hadn't wanted to bring up the subject, as she didn't want to sound paranoid and jealous, but it had of course been preying on her mind.

'So can I trust you here in London? Finn still seems very interested.'

Valentine hadn't replied to his text, but she hadn't

deleted it, and there had been several times when she had sneaked a look at it – even imagining a scenario where she met Finn. In her fantasy her plan was to humiliate him in a restaurant as he had her. She would be looking particularly sexy in a green silk dress and black sky-high Christian Dior heels, as worn by Carrie Bradshaw in the *Sex and the City* movie – all right she didn't have any, she was never likely to have any, and even if she did she would never to able to walk in them, but this was her fantasy; she was allowed them. He would say something like, 'God, I want you so much V, I love you,' and she would pause for a beat, letting him have one last look at her before she replied, 'But I don't love you anymore.' It was so tempting – she could even hear her heels clicking emphatically on the pavement as she walked away from him, while he called her name in vain.

'You can trust me,' Valentine replied, silencing any further questions with a kiss and pulling him back down on the bed with her.

When Jack left for Manchester she was determined not to go on the downward spiral. She would give herself three weeks off before she resorted to temping. Her plan was simple – she would keep busy. She would exercise every morning, then she would read a play for the rest of the day and write to directors she wanted to work with – not that this tactic had ever yielded any results in the past, but you never knew. It was vital to be optimistic. She would also write to Piers again. There was going to be no lying in bed, obsessing about being a failure and stuffing her face with peanut butter, no incidents of self-loathing, no drinking too much. She had one day following this pattern, which nearly finished her off, and then she got an urgent call from one of her friends who had sprained her ankle and begged Valentine to take her place at the yummy-mummy toddler music group she worked for in Hampstead.

It was a week of pure, undiluted hell. The group was run by Maria, a scary ballet-teacher type who was in fear of the yummies defecting to another music group. 'It's dog eat dog in the world of children's music groups, take it from me.' She told Valentine, 'If we don't put on a show, they'll go elsewhere. Tiny Tigers round the corner is proving very popular, as they perform songs in Chinese to reflect the growing Asian economy. Do you speak Chinese, by the way? Maybe we could do a quick Chinese number to show that we're on the case? I expect you to give your *all*!

Maria's fervour came as a bit of a shock. Valentine had imagined singing a couple of verses of 'Old Macdonald', 'The Wheels on the Bus' and 'Row Row Row your Boat' and if things got really wild shaking some maracas. The reality was four forty-five-minute carefully choreographed shows a day, complete with costume changes, where Valentine was indeed expected to give her all. After each performance Maria actually gave her notes. She told Valentine that her Queen of Hearts lacked conviction and accused her of relishing her bottle of rum too much in the pirate song. When Valentine retorted that she was simply getting into the role of the pirate à la Stanislavsy method, Maria replied, 'We don't want to give out the message that alcohol dependency is a good thing.' Alcohol was just about the only thing that got Valentine through the week. She got her revenge by playing 'Old Macdonald' as an Old Queen, giving him a faraway wistful look in his eye, as if secretly he longed to be vegetarian and wear a dress; by giving the yummies full-fat milk in their coffees and by eating Maria's entire supply of chocolate digestives.

Meanwhile Jack's rehearsal schedule was absolutely frenetic. She hardly got to speak to him at all – just first thing in the morning and last thing at night and by then he sounded knackered and they barely got to speak. Valentine missed him, and missed his optimism. They talked about Piers and how Valentine might have to prepare herself for him never getting in touch – it had been over two months since she'd written to him. Valentine was starting to wish that her mum had never told her, as now she didn't have the distraction of work or of Jack, Piers's silence cast a shadow over her days. Her own father was not interested in knowing her. It wasn't the greatest boast to her self-esteem.

She also couldn't help feeling jealous of Tamara spending all that time with Jack and much as she tried to hold on to the thought that Jack had told her that she could trust him, it was hard. She had trusted Finn and look at what had happened there. She wanted Jack to bitch about Tamara and tell Valentine what an atrocious actress she was, anything to make Valentine feel better.

Instead he told her that he felt sorry for her as she was so clearly out of her depth and that she was actually quite sweet. Not words guaranteed to cheer Valentine up. She could feel herself sliding into the blues.

Then when she was feeling particularly down about her acting career she bumped into someone she had been at drama school with. She had been browsing the hair care products in Boots as part of her ongoing quest to find something that would tame wild curls. While curly hair looked great on Sarah Jessica Parker for example, Valentine always thought that her own hair would look much better straight. As a child she had been obsessed with the fairytale of Rapunzel. She spent ages poring over her Ladybird book with its pictures of the girl with the beautiful, long, poker-straight, golden hair and kept asking her mother when her hair was going to look like that. Valentine knew in her heart that if she'd been Rapunzel the prince would never have been able to scale the tower because her curly hair would have bounced him off and she would have been stuck there for ever – just one more example of how the odds were stacked against the curly-haired.

She was absorbed in reading the many promises offered by a new product – perhaps finally this was the one, her hair's nirvana! – when someone called her name. She turned round and there was Stella. She had been two years above Valentine at drama school. She was so talented, a naturally gifted comic actress and everyone was convinced she would be a star. Though Stella hadn't had a big break, Valentine had always assumed that she was doing all right. 'Hi, Stella!' she exclaimed warmly, 'I haven't seen you for ages!'

'Valentine, how lovely to see you!' The two women hugged each other.

'You look so well,' Valentine said, standing back and looking at her, trying to work out what was different about her.

'Yes, I've put on a stone and a half since you last saw me.' Stella had always been incredibly skinny, too skinny in fact, and was rumoured to have an eating disorder, but that was no big deal in a profession that was ruthless about looks and size.

'Really? You look great; so what are you up to?'

Stella sighed. 'I thought you knew. I've given up acting. I work in PR now. Our main clients are some of the country's leading cosmetic dentists. Oh, don't look like that.'

Valentine snapped her mouth shut. 'I'm just a bit surprised, that's all. You're such a good actress, Stella. Why?'

At this Stella's pretty face hardened. 'Because I was sick of it! Sick of always feeling out of control, sick of never getting auditions, then being treated like dirt by directors when I did get them. And I was sick of never being able to eat anything apart from fucking rice cakes! The constant dieting, the constant feeling bad about myself.' There was a display of muffins next to the shampoos. With the speed of a frog flicking out its tongue to entrap a fly, Stella suddenly reached out, grabbed a double-chocolate-chip one and swiftly pulled off the wrapper. 'Now I can eat what I like!' she exclaimed, shovelling the cake into her mouth and showering crumbs all over her suit. Stella clearly still had issues.

'I do understand. It is really tough,' Valentine said sympathetically, anxious to pacify Stella, who really did seem on the edge.

Stella took another bite of the muffin and then continued her tirade. 'If I got a part, it was never a main one, but it was just big enough to give me a glimmer of hope that something better was round the corner, so I never quite gave up. But all the time I was being ground down. One day I woke up and thought, I'm twenty-fucking-nine and I've got no security whatsoever. And one day I would like to have children and I don't want to be living in a poky little flat above a kebab shop, working in a bar but saying that I'm an actress just because once in a blue bollocking moon I get to be in a play that no one comes to see and for which I get paid a pittance!' Stella was shouting now and Valentine was aware of the other customers walking warily around them, trying to avoid the crazy woman and the shower of crumbs.

'How about a cup of coffee?' Valentine suggested.

Stella shook her head. 'I have to get back to the office; I've got a really important press release to send out about the latest teeth-whitening technique. It really works, you know. It's up to twenty per cent more effective than other teeth-whitening products currently on the market.' At this she burst into tears, proper noisy sobs, snot and all.

Valentine took her arm and said gently, 'Let's just pay for the muffin and have that coffee.'

She spent the next hour trying to calm Stella down and get her in a fit state to return to work, which involved three lattes (two for Stella, one for Valentine) a large chocolate-chip cookie (Stella), a pain au chocolate (Stella), a slice of cherry cheesecake (Stella) and an almond croissant (Valentine, who simply couldn't hold out on the carbs any longer in the face of Stella's misery eating). Then she slowly walked back home, her spirits now as flat as her pumps. Stella might have been describing *her* acting career. How much longer could she hold on to the hope that her big break was just round the corner? Was she being completely deluded that her moment would come? She had been holding on to her dream that something would happen. But what if it didn't? She didn't want to end up bitter and frustrated like Stella. And God knew she had no interest in cosmetic dentistry. What should she do? Valentine was using up her store of hope. What if nothing happened? She was almost tempted to turn back and have another almond croissant. Instead she went back to the flat and got roaring drunk with Lauren.

She woke up the following morning with a hangover of evil proportions. The noble, self-disciplined side of her intoned, *Must get up, go for a run and go swimming.* She didn't move. *Must lie in bed, eat peanut butter on toast, buy Red Bull,* countered the undisciplined side of her.

'Are you still in bed?' Jack asked her accusingly when he called her at half nine, about to go into rehearsal.

'No!' she lied. 'I'm just doing some stretches before I go for a run.'

'You're such a liar, Fleming,' he replied.

'All right, I'm lying in bed completely naked, waiting for you and your big—'

'Don't tell me that,' Jack cut across her, groaning, 'I've been fantasising about you all night as it is. Please tell me you're coming up this weekend; I want you *bad*.'

She finished the call promising that she was going to go running and woke up to the sound of the doorbell, two hours later. Grabbing her lilac and gold vintage kimono (a present from Lily, who believed that a woman should always look glamorous in the bedroom and didn't hold with towelling) she staggered downstairs and opened the door. A smartly dressed thirty-something woman – pinstripe trouser suit, killer heels and crisp white shirt, sleek ponytail, expensive perfume – stood on the doorstep. She must have the wrong house; Valentine couldn't imagine Lauren, Lily or Frank would know anyone who would dress like an executive.

'Are you Valentine Fleming?' the smart woman asked. She was American, possibly a New Yorker.

'Yes,' Valentine mumbled behind her hand, not wanting to asphyxiate the woman with her hangover breath.

'I'm Greta Cox, Piers Hunter's personal assistant.'

'Oh my God, is he here?' Valentine asked, anxiously looking past Greta. This was definitely not how she imagined meeting her father, dressed in her PJs, accessorised with breath that could kill a man at ten paces.

Greta shook her head and her ponytail swished. 'No, no, I need to talk to you before any such meeting. May I come in?'

Shit, what exactly was the state of the flat? The fragrant Greta was going to report back to her father that she was a complete and utter slob. Valentine nodded and led the way upstairs. She showed Greta into the living room, which thankfully looked reasonably OK apart from several mugs, two wine glasses and two empty bottles of wine.

'My flatmate,' Valentine lied. 'Would I be able to have a quick shower before we talk?'

'Of course,' Greta said graciously, sitting down on the sofa and letting out a yelp of pain before Valentine had a chance to warn her about the dodgy springs.

'Sorry! It's best to sit the other end.'

'I realise that now,' Greta replied sarcastically.

Valentine hit the shower in record time, got dressed and slapped on some make-up to stop her looking quite so much like one of the undead. 'Hi again,' she said to Greta, who was busy tapping away at her BlackBerry, probably telling Piers right now what a loser he had as a daughter. 'I'm usually up earlier than this, running.'

Greta looked sceptical.

'Can I get you a tea or coffee?'

'Do you have any herbal tea?' Greta asked. She pronounced it 'erbal,' which always gave Valentine and Lauren the giggles. Valentine didn't feel like giggling right now.

'We might have some ancient camomile tea, but to be honest I wouldn't risk it.'

Greta sniffed. 'OK I'll just have a cup of hot water and lemon.'

'Sorry, can you do without the lemon?' Honestly, where did she think she was, bloody Champneys?

Five minutes, two paracetamol and a black coffee later, Valentine was all ears as Greta explained the reason for her visit.

'Piers was most surprised to get your letter, Valentine. He had absolutely no idea that he had a daughter. In fact his first reaction was to imagine that it couldn't possibly be true.'

Valentine was determined to play it cool, but she found herself bursting out, 'Why would I want to lie about something like that!'

'You'd be surprised how many people would when there is the potential of making money.'

'Hold on a minute, are you accusing me of being some gold digger?' Jesus, where did she dredge up an expression like 'gold digger'? The alcohol must be destroying her brain cells faster than she'd realised.

'Valentine, no one is accusing you of anything, but you must consider Piers's position.'

Valentine made a big effort to calm down.

Greta paused to take a sip of her hot water. She pulled a face. 'Is this filtered?'

Valentine shook her head. 'London's finest.' Greta put down the cup with an expression of disgust.

'But Piers must know about me – my mum's written to him several times.'

Greta's perfectly made-up face and botoxed forehead gave nothing away. She ignored Valentine's comment and resumed her speech. 'Rather than make this a long drawn-out affair, Piers wants the matter resolved as soon as possible one way or the other. With that end in mind he would like you to take a DNA test. Then if you are his daughter, we can plan the next stage.' She handed Valentine a card. 'Here are the contact details of the clinic; if you give them a ring, they will arrange an appointment for you.' It seemed reasonable, if a little cold to Valentine's sensibilities. But maybe Piers had lots of long-lost children claiming to be his.

As soon as Greta left Valentine called Jack, desperate to tell him her news. They had both come to the conclusion that Piers didn't want to know, and now this! She got his voicemail. She tried Lauren but her phone was off – she was probably doing something tantric with Nathan; her mum was also on voicemail. She went downstairs and knocked first on Lily's door, to no reply, and then on Frank's – no reply either. It was so frustrating. She really needed to talk to someone.

While she was in the middle of buying a Red Bull and a packet of salt and vinegar crisps from the off-licence – surely she could not be expected to run at a time like this – her phone beeped with a text message. *Really need to see you. Fx.* She had ignored Finn's *want you* text of a few days earlier, so she could ignore this one as well. She marched back to the flat, phoned the clinic to arrange her DNA appointment for the following day, tidied up (i.e. picked up mugs and wine glasses and dumped them in the sink), put on a little more make-up, fiddled with her hair, lay on her futon reading Pinter's *The Homecoming*, then had to switch to *Grazia* as her head was hurting too much and all the while the siren call of Finn's message was in her head. What did he need to talk to her about? Was the engagement off? Was he phoning to declare his undying love for her? He could declare away; she wasn't interested.

It was pathetic, weak and showed no backbone whatso-ever — she knew all of that — but an hour later when she had read the same page on this summer's must-have beauty products about five times without taking in a single word (her make-up was going to be *so* last season), when she had called Jack yet again and left another message, she called Finn.

'V! Thanks for calling me back.' He sounded so pleased to hear from her, and in spite of her best intentions Valentine was pleasantly surprised. 'Any chance we can meet today? I really need to see you. Can I take you out for lunch?'

'What about Eva?'

'Oh, she's filming in Edinburgh. Please V, we don't need to talk about her or Jack. It'll be just about us.'

Finn had fed her the perfect line. 'There is no us, Finn,' Valentine retorted, then added, 'I can see you briefly, but I can't stay long. I've got so much to do.' She was impressed by how assertive and kick-ass she sounded.

'Have you got an audition?' Finn said, impressed. 'That was quick work.'

And then because Valentine really was so desperate to tell someone her news she blurted out the whole Piers Hunter long-lost-father story. Finn was suitably impressed.

'V, that is amazing news! This could seriously change everything for you. It could be your big break – no more fringe plays, but movies, V!'

'What do you mean?' Valentine asked.

'If he's your dad, just think of the film roles he can give you!'

'I hadn't thought of it like that,' Valentine replied. 'I don't know if I'd want to be in one of his films on those terms.'

Finn laughed. 'Oh don't give me that "I want to make it off my own back" shit! Our world isn't like that. If you've got connections you need to use them! Everyone else does.'

Valentine didn't like how calculating Finn was sounding. She was saved from having to answer by her phone alerting her to another call. 'Finn, I'm going to have to go. And actually I can't make lunch.' Finn protested but Valentine cut him off and took the other call. It was Jack. It was a relief telling him. In contrast to Finn his only concern was how she felt – no mention of film roles. But it was only a quick call and ended with Valentine hearing Tamara in the background saying that they had to go.

'Are you out somewhere with NTM?' Valentine asked, suddenly wary.

'Just a quick coffee.' He lowered his voice. 'She's having a hard time fitting in. I feel sorry for her. And the stuff she's told me about how her mother treated her – Jesus, that woman sounds like a witch. Did you know she put Tamara on a diet when she was seven?' Valentine was all set to give him the many reasons why he should absolutely not feel sorry for NTM when Jack said, 'I'm sorry, I've really got to go. I'll call you later.'

Valentine was left feeling decidedly unsettled and slightly jealous. She rather wished she had gone out for lunch with Finn after all.

11

A Kiss is Just a Kiss

A week later Valentine was standing outside a huge wrought-iron gate topped with vicious-looking spikes to deter any would-be burglars, while a CCTV camera clicked and whirred above her. She pressed the intercom and a woman with an East European accent asked her who she was, then buzzed her in. The iron gates smoothly opened and Valentine walked along the drive towards the imposing black front door. Piers Hunter's front door. Her father's front door; the front door to his enormous four-storey Victorian mansion, complete with several wings and turrets. The results of the DNA test had come back last week. It was official. She was Piers's daughter. She had expected Piers would want to see her straight away but Greta had informed her that he was away filming for a week and not even a long-lost daughter could distract him. The film was already way over budget.

As she drew closer to the house she noticed that every single window had bars across it, marring the beauty of the house. The front door was opened by a middle-aged woman, looking very upstairs downstairs in a black dress and brilliant white apron and rather eccentric white cotton slippers. 'Good afternoon, Miss Fleming. Do come in. I am the housekeeper,' and the owner of the East European accent. 'Mr Hunter has been detained in a meeting but says he will be with you within the hour.'

'Oh, hi.' Valentine stretched out her hand in welcome, which appeared to startle the housekeeper, who cautiously put her hand out to shake Valentine's. She was in her forties and had a serious, unsmiling face.

'I am Ivana. Now before you go any further can I ask you to please put these on?' Ivana held up a pair of white cotton slippers identical to her own. 'Mrs Hunter is most particular that all visitors should wear these.'

'Can't I just go barefoot?' Valentine asked, thinking that the slippers would ruin the elegant and sophisticated look she was aiming for in her purple silk dress and gold sandals.

Ivana shook her head disapprovingly. 'No, barefoot is not hygienic. There will be germs.'

Valentine tried not to be insulted by the comment and reluctantly unfastened her sandals and put on the slippers. She followed Ivana across the black and white marble hall floor – easily bigger than her entire flat – into the vast living room. The first thought Valentine had when she walked in was that it was like the Snow Queen's palace – everything was either white or silver. The effect was stark. Valentine was no fan of such a look, preferring cosy clutter. The sofas were white leather, the fireplace white marble, the floor white marble – which felt decidedly chilly through her cotton slippers; the curtains and cushions were all silver silk; even the flatscreen TV that occupied an entire wall was silver. Valentine suddenly felt incredibly self-conscious in her vivid purple silk dress. And cold. The air-con seemed excessively powerful.

'Is it me or is it cold in here?' she asked, shivering.

'I will turn air-conditioning down,' Ivana replied. 'Drink while you wait? There are also magazines.' She walked over to a sleek white table and slid out a drawer revealing a selection worthy of a newsagent. 'And films you can watch.' She pressed a button and a section of white wood panelling slid back, revealing floor-to-ceiling shelves of DVDs.

'I'd love a coffee,' Valentine replied, trying to stop her teeth from chattering.

Ivana nodded and left her alone.

To keep warm Valentine paced round the room. She paused at the DVD collection. There were two rows devoted to Piers's films – of which she had seen only two, and even then not all the way through. Maybe she could start watching one of them; that should make a good impression, shouldn't it? Piers was renowned for his block-buster action movies – usually the very films she steered away from. She reached up for one in which the hero (an ex-soldier with issues, naturally) had forty-eight hours to stop central London being blown up by a terrorist cell. Well, at least it wasn't twenty-four hours.

Ivana returned with a cafetiere of coffee. 'Mrs Hunter allows no dairy in the house so we just have soya milk; I hope that is acceptable.'

Valentine loathed soya milk. 'I'll have it black,' she replied.

'And the coffee is decaf,' Ivana added.

'Perfect,' Valentine lied.

She had spent the last week in a state of high anticipation about the meeting; a mix of nervousness, apprehension, but also excitement. Maybe as soon as she and Piers set eyes on each other they would experience a deep connection; it would be some kind of life-changing moment for both of them. But she also felt sadness – if she got on well with Piers would she be betraying Chris? She had the chance for a whole new relationship with her father, but Chris was the one who had been there for her and she wondered if she had ever really told him how much she loved him and appreciated him.

An hour later and Valentine felt as if hypothermia was about to set in. She imagined slowly freezing to death in this white room; Piers would return to discover a block of ice for a daughter. She paused the film, which she wasn't enjoying at all, and resumed pacing round the room. There was a large photograph of Piers and Olivia on the marble fireplace. Olivia had been a very successful Hollywood actress, a great beauty, the Angelina Jolie of her day. But since she had hit her late fifties the roles seemed to have dried up for her. Now she devoted herself to Piers and raising money for her horse-sanctuary charity. Valentine wondered why they had never had children or adopted as so many other celebrity couples had.

She paced some more. Then watched some more of the film. Another half-hour passed. Any nerves she had

had about meeting Piers had gone; all she could think about was that she was very very cold and very very bored. *Maybe if I was a fifteen-year-old boy I would enjoy it*, she reflected as yet another person was shot, not once but about fifty times. Now on top of feeling cold she needed a wee. Knowing her luck the moment she chose to go to the loo would be the time Piers showed up. But when you've got to go, you've got to go.

Cautiously she opened the door and stepped out into the hall. She tried one door and that turned out to be the dining room, also in white; another door led to a library. She headed upstairs and thankfully the first door on the right led to a bathroom – also entirely in white. As she sat on the loo and looked around she was startled by the number of antibacterial soaps on the shelf by the sink. There were at least ten all neatly lined up and facing the same way. She looked over to the towel rail where the pristine white towels were arranged in size order. It instantly reminded her of that Julia Roberts film *Sleeping with the Enemy* where the evil husband lines up all the tins and towels in a scarily regimented way. But maybe it was Ivana, the housekeeper; she looked like she had it in her to be a neat freak.

Valentine was just making her way back downstairs when, speak of the devil, Ivana appeared in the hall. 'Miss Fleming, you haven't just used the upstairs bathroom, have you?' she asked accusingly.

'I did actually,' Valentine replied, wondering what the big deal was.

Ivana uttered a series of what could have been Serbian

swear words, then reverted to English, 'That is Mr Hunter's personal bathroom. Mrs Hunter permits no one else to use it.' Valentine was about to apologise when Ivana turned away and called out loudly, 'Sergei! Deep clean Mr Hunter's bathroom now!'

By the time Valentine had reached the bottom of the stairs, the summoned Sergei was running into the hall wearing a white boiler suit and clutching a bucket filled with an array of cleaning products. Now Valentine was remembering another film clip – *Silkwood*, when the heroine has been contaminated with radioactive waste and has to be scrubbed down. Except in this instance Sergei and Ivana seemed to believe that Valentine was the one doing the contaminating. She was now somewhat offended – just how dirty did they think she was?

Ivana held the door open to the living room. 'Please, Miss Fleming, wait in here. Mr Hunter will not be long.'

Was it Valentine's imagination or did the room seem even colder as she walked in. She was about to ask Ivana to adjust the air-con again, but she had already clicked the door shut behind her. This was ridiculous! Valentine began jogging on the spot – no small achievement in the slippers, which slid against the marble floor making this a potentially perilous undertaking. If the hypothermia didn't get her first, a crack to her head from the marble floor would finish her off.

She was just doing star jumps when the door swung open and Piers walked in. He looked just as handsome and distinguished as in his photographs.

'Wow! An exercise freak! You'll get on well with my wife!'

Why oh why did she have to be doing star jumps when her father saw her for the first time? This was supposed to be an emotionally charged meeting; now it felt more like a comedy.

Piers strode over to her. 'I'm so sorry to have kept you waiting.' He stuck out his hand, which Valentine took. It all felt very formal, as if she was in a business meeting. But then Piers smiled and said, 'This is weird, right?' his voice had a slight LA twang – Valentine remembered reading that he spent half the year in the States.

'Yes,' she replied, smiling back.

'Come on, let's get to my study. I never sit in here; it's way too minimalist and cold for me. My wife, Olivia, has got a bit of a thing about air-con and filtered air.'

Valentine followed him as he strode out of the living room, up the stairs and into a snug little room filled with books and magazines. Piers sat down behind the desk and Valentine sat opposite him in a comfortable, battered brown leather armchair.

'Ever since the results came in, I've been dying to meet you.' Piers didn't exactly look like a man who was dying to meet anyone, and seemed cool and detached. But then Valentine knew she wasn't giving much away either. It was clearly a tense time for both of them. What followed resembled a job interview as Piers fired a succession of questions at her.

Where did she live? What plays had she been in? Did she know such and such a director? 'I just want to know everything about you, Valentine,' he said at one point during the interrogation. 'By the way, you do know that's a boy's name, don't you? Maybe that's why the roles have been a little slow coming in for you.'

Valentine shrugged; it was all very well her thinking that her career wasn't going well, and quite another for someone else to say it, even if that person was her father. And where was the emotional connection she had hoped for? She remembered with a sudden pang one of the last times she'd seen Chris. It had been Halloween. As usual Chris had gone to town, throwing a huge fancy-dress party. He'd spent ages festooning the house in fake cobwebs and skeletons, and put carved pumpkins on the doorstep to welcome trick or treaters. Chris had dressed up as a witch and took great delight in opening the door to trick or treating children and making them choose between two bowls – one full of sweets and one full of jelly – though of course he ended up giving sweets to everyone. He was so exuberant and so full of life. She couldn't imagine Piers behaving like that.

She was pulled back to the present by his next comment. 'I've just realised that I know someone you were at drama school with. Tamara Moore – such a delightful girl and doing brilliantly now.'

Valentine checked his face for signs of irony. There were none. This probably wouldn't be a good time to say that she loathed Tamara.

'Oh yes,' she replied. 'In fact she's in *King Lear* at the moment with my boyfriend, Jack Hart.'

'Would I have seen him in anything?'

She shook her head. 'He's just starting out, but he's hugely talented.'

'Well, Tamara's mother is an old friend, so maybe we should go see Tamara and Jack in *Lear*.' He paused. 'That's the kind of high-profile play it would be good for you to be in.'

This was not exactly turning into her dream meeting with her new-found father. After a further twenty minutes of questions, another vile decaf coffee and no offers of lunch, even though it was after one p.m., Piers's Blackberry beeped.

'There's the alert for my next meeting. I'm going to have to go. It was lovely to meet you, Valentine. I'm sorry if it sounded like I was firing so many questions at you – I just really want to know as much as I can about you. Greta will be in touch to arrange another meeting. I'm sure you'll agree that we need to take things slowly. Olivia, my wife, has been very unsettled by your arrival in my life and I need to be sensitive to her feelings. Also I must ask that you tell no one yet that we are related. I feel we need time to get to know each other and we can't do that if there is some God-awful media feeding frenzy. You know what the press are like. You haven't told anyone, have you?'

'Well, my mum obviously, and my boyfriend,' Valentine admitted, thinking she'd better be economical with the truth.

'If we could just keep it to those two just now, that would be good.' He stood up to show Valentine out and at the front door he shook her hand again.

Valentine felt incredibly deflated and disappointed by the lack of emotional connection. She wasn't sure what she had expected, but something more than the sense of anti-climax she was experiencing now. Piers's comment about Tamara hadn't helped. Valentine couldn't help thinking that he would have preferred to have discovered a successful daughter. Maybe he even regretted getting in touch with Valentine. She hardly matched up to Piers's A-list life. As soon as she was safely out of sight of the CCTV cameras she called Jack. He was reassuring, telling her that it was bound to be strange and that she and Piers needed time to get to know each other. In fact he said all the right things until yet again in the background she heard the unmistakably annoying tinkly laugh that could only belong to Tamara.

'Are you out with NTM?' she said accusingly.

'Don't you think that name is a little childish?' Jack said quietly. 'I'm just having lunch with her and two other members of the cast.' He sounded slightly put out that Valentine was questioning him.

Valentine knew that Jack hated any kind of jealousy or possessive behaviour in his girlfriends. Julia had made him wary, but Valentine couldn't stop herself from coming out with her next sarcastic comment. 'Oh well, have a lovely time bonding, won't you?'

Jack sighed. 'Valentine, don't be like this; there's no need. Look, I'll call you tonight.'

Valentine had to bite her tongue to stop herself making any more snide remarks about NTM, but the thought of Jack and Tamara getting close was almost unbearable. And so when Finn called later she was a little more receptive than she had previously been. When he picked up on how low she felt, he immediately suggested meeting that afternoon.

'V, it's just for a coffee. You sound really down, come on.'

'All right, but just coffee: no alcohol, no funny comments, no outrageous flirting; I've got a boyfriend, remember?'

'V, I can't help my feelings for you,' Finn said reproachfully.

'That kind of comment is exactly what I mean,' Valentine replied.

A bottle and a half of wine later – coffee really hadn't seemed like a suitable drink after all – Valentine was feeling slightly more mellow. Finn had been incredibly sweet and attentive, wanting to know every single detail of the meeting. When Valentine mentioned how Piers hadn't even kissed her, Finn suddenly remembered reading that Olivia was fanatical about cleanliness and had a terror of germs, bordering on OCD. Apparently she hated her husband kissing anyone except her.

'So V, there was nothing personal in him not kissing you,' Finn told her, filling up her glass again.

'You think?'

'Definitely – you've just got to give the relationship time to develop.' He paused and looked pensive. 'Did he mention anything about film roles?'

Valentine shook her head, annoyed with Finn for bringing up the subject again. 'That's really not why I got in touch with him.'

'I know,' Finn said smoothly, 'but it could be really good for your career, V. Look at someone like Tamara; you're way more talented than her.'

'D'you really think so?' The comment was exactly what she wanted to hear after Jack's support for NTM.

'Absolutely – there is no comparison between you. Do you seriously think Tamara would have got on without her connections? Come on V; don't you think you deserve a break?' He reached out and took her hand. 'I think you're on the cusp of a life-changing moment.'

If Valentine hadn't been feeling quite so drunk and annoyed with Jack, she might have moved her hand away, and told him not to be so ridiculous. As it was, she liked his concern for her. And when he said he was going her way and would walk with her, she thought that perfectly reasonable. She also thought it perfectly reasonable that he put his arm round her as they strolled along Notting Hill Gate, down the first part of Portabello Road with its row of pastel-coloured Victorian terraces – after all, she often walked arm in arm with her friends. She even thought it reasonable that when it was time to say goodbye on the corner of Portabello Road and Westbourne Park Road outside Coffee Republic, he kissed her. Friends kiss goodbye, right? Though maybe not like this – as the light kiss on her lips turned into a proper serious let's-get-down-to-business kiss. But it didn't mean anything, she tried to tell herself as she finally managed to extricate herself from his embrace and walk home. It was just a kiss. Admittedly tongues had been involved, but that was because she'd had such an emotionally charged day, and she was slightly drunk. It would never happen again.

Just then her attention was caught by an elderly well-dressed couple walking slowly arm and arm on the opposite side of the road. It was unmistakably Frank and Lily. Shit! Surely they hadn't seen her with Finn? She was just about to pretend that she hadn't seen them when Frank noticed her and raised his arm in greeting. No escape. She crossed the road, feeling horribly guilty.

'Hiya,' she said, falsely cheerful. She noticed that Lily looked paler than ever and even though it was a warm day was wrapped up in a white mohair cardigan with a red velvet shawl round her shoulders. The old timers just looked at her. Was that sadness she could see in their eyes? Disappointment? Disapproval? They must have seen her.

'It was just a kiss, Lily,' she said defensively.

'A kiss is never just a kiss,' Lily replied sternly.

'Oh please, don't be like this!' Valentine exclaimed. She tried for their sympathy. 'I'd just met up with Piers, which was a bit stressful, so I had a few drinks with Finn. But the kiss meant nothing.'

'It's not like you to behave like that.' Now Frank was putting his oar in. Any minute they'd be pinning a scarlet A to her breast to mark her out as an adulteress.

'And it's not us you should be justifying yourself to; what about Jack?' Lily again.

'OK, OK, it was a mistake.' Valentine hung her head.

'We won't say anything.' Lily again. 'But don't throw away what you have with Jack for *him*.'

'He can't hold a candle to Jack,' put in Frank. 'Not a fucking candle. He's a gutless bastard who nearly destroyed you.' Bloody Lauren and her bloody mantra.

* * *

Valentine spent much of the train journey to Manchester the following morning obsessing about whether to fess up to Jack about the kiss, rehearsing how best to break it to him: *Jack, I've got something to tell you, but I swear it didn't mean anything; I kissed Finn.* Somehow saying it made it sound as if it *had* meant something. Also it was Jack's birthday on Sunday and revealing that you've snogged your ex didn't exactly make for the best birthday surprise. By the time she arrived at Manchester Piccadilly station she was resolved. She would say nothing. Whatever Lily had said about a kiss never being just a kiss simply wasn't true. It had just been a kiss.

Her heart flipped when she saw Jack waiting beyond the barrier. He looked more gorgeous than ever – really he should carry a health warning. As soon as he saw her he ran over, wrapped her in his arms and kissed her. 'Very *Brief Encounter*,' she murmured once she'd come up for air.

'Nope,' Jack said. 'No sex in that film if you recall, Fleming. Just lots of yearning, longing and sacrifice. Three emotions that I do not expect to be feeling over the next forty-eight hours. To which end I have booked us into a hotel. My digs are not built for passion. I think my carpet has fleas, the landlady is an alcoholic insomniac and there's a pink crocheted lady over the loo roll.'

'A nice one?' Valentine asked hopefully. 'The hotel, I mean.' She didn't often get to stay in good hotels. Finn had once taken her on a mini-break to some posh country hotel when Eva was away filming, but his credit card had been declined and she'd had to pay with hers. In fact, she was probably still paying for it.

It was indeed a very nice one, Valentine reflected once she and Jack had got all the yearning and longing out of their systems, which took most of the afternoon. Taupe walls (she knew that only very expensive hotels ever used taupe); five-hundred-thread-count Egyptian cotton sheets; a carpet so luxuriously thick you practically sank up to your knees when you walked on it; lovely Molton Brown products in the bathroom. It must have cost Jack a fortune.

'So what else have you been up to, apart from meeting Piers?' Jack asked as she lay with her head on his chest, he with his arm round her.

'Not much,' Valentine mumbled and as soon as the words were out of her mouth an image of kissing Finn popped up in her head. She was convinced that Jack would be able to tell that she was lying; instead he asked if she was hungry. Reprieve for the guilty.

Over a Thai meal Jack filled her in on how rehearsals had been going. Apparently the director was so precious that he made VPL look laid back. The two actresses playing Lear's evil daughters Goneril and Regan hated each other. Regan thought Goneril was too old to be playing the part and kept making barbed comments behind her back. The actress playing Goneril thought Regan was fat and made equally snide comments. The actor playing Lear had a formidable reputation as a stage actor who, despite many offers of film work in his youth, had never done a movie, believing the stage to be infinitely superior. And now he believed that he was superior to any film actors. Subsequently he loathed Tamara, who represented everything he despised about film actors.

'I really do feel sorry for her,' Jack said again. Valentine nearly choked on her green curry. 'I mean, she is spoilt and no great actress – we're all agreed on that – but Clive, who's playing Lear, is so vile to her.'

'I wouldn't worry about her,' Valentine said, when she could finally speak. 'She's got thicker skin than a rhinoceros. It serves her right if he's giving her a hard time. She thinks she can waltz into a serious role like that and everyone will love her, when the truth is it exposes that she actually has no talent whatsoever!' She was getting impassioned now. 'I can't wait for that moment she's carried on stage dead!'

'Nor can Clive, as he frequently tells her. Seriously, Valentine, she's been in tears more than once after one of his tongue-lashings. He told her she delivered her lines with all the emotion of the speaking clock.'

'As much as that? I always used to think she sounded like a Dalek.' Valentine replied, not at all liking Jack's show of sympathy for NTM. 'So how's your other girlfriend, Julia Mentalist Turner?'

Jack curled his lip. 'Don't say *girlfriend* and Julia Turner in the same sentence – that woman took ten years off my life. She's getting rave reviews in *Street Car*, which has thankfully got her off my case. She was born to play Blanche Dubois.'

'That's because she *is* Blanche Dubois!'

'OK enough! I don't want to talk about Julia or Tamara

or anyone but you. And have you nearly finished your green vegetable curry? Because I've got another bad case of yearning. Our Egyptian cotton temple awaits us.'

They spent most of Saturday in the Egyptian cotton temple. Their desire for each other had only grown more intense in the three-week absence. Valentine was feeling blissfully happy. The illicit kiss, the unsatisfactory meeting with Piers, the no-work scenario – all were forgotten as she basked in being with Jack. On the morning of his birthday she surprised him with smoked salmon, bagels, strawberries and champagne, which she'd smuggled into the hotel the night before, and hidden in the mini-bar.

'Sorry it's not room service,' she said.

'I like it all the more because you got it,' he told her. If he was lying it was a sweet lie.

'So, happy birthday old man!' she joked, handing him a small package. Jack ripped off the paper and opened the black velvet box.

'That is so cool!' he exclaimed, lifting out the thick silver chain bracelet she'd bought him from Frank's stall.

'Well, I thought you were metrosexual enough to carry it off,' she said, fastening it on his wrist.

'You're so cheeky, Fleming. Do you know what your present is?'

'A dirty old man with a big package, I hope,' she replied, giggling as Jack pinned her down on the bed.

'You're only three years younger than me! I am going to take such delight in your thirtieth birthday,' he exclaimed.

'Oh shut up,' she murmured. 'I've never shagged a thirty-year-old before; aren't you going to get on with it? Or do you need me to get you a fluffer to get you going?'

Apparently not, as after round one, Jack was up for an encore. Maybe it was just a myth that men reached their peak at the age of eighteen. Valentine was just wondering if they could go for a hat trick when Jack's phone rang. Go away world, Valentine thought as Jack sat up and took the call.

'Shit! I'd completely forgotten! Sorry, we'll be with you in a half an hour.' He snapped his phone shut and looked over at Valentine, 'We're supposed to be meeting some of the cast right now for drinks.'

'Who's going to be there?' Valentine asked cautiously.

'Regan, Gloucester, the Fool and Tamara.'

Valentine did a major eye-roll.

'Don't give me that look. We won't stay long, I promise. When they offered to take me out I couldn't really say no.'

Couldn't you? Valentine felt like saying, slightly put out that she was wasting her last day with Jack in the company of strangers and they wouldn't be seeing each other for at least another two weeks.

'Happy Birthday, Jack!' Tamara squealed as soon as they walked into the bar. Valentine tried not to grit her teeth too much at the sight of Tamara's slender arms wrapped round Jack. She could get through this. She would be calm, sophisticated, aloof. Barely acknowledging Valentine, Tamara led Jack to a table where other members of the cast were sitting.

Valentine trailed behind. Tamara installed Jack next to her at one end, leaving Valentine sitting at the opposite end, next to the fool (Timothy) – was Tamara trying to tell her something? – and Gloucester (Seb), who fortunately were both charming. Especially Seb, who paid her outrageous compliments about how lovely she looked. And so she bloody should! The moment she'd found out about the drinks she'd spent an hour getting ready. Tamara, of course, looked ravishing in a white sun dress that showed off her beautiful golden-brown skin, her blonde hair with a just-got-out-of-bed-but-actually-it-cost-a-fortune-to-achieve-this look.

'To the birthday boy!' she called out, holding up a glass of champagne – vintage, naturally. Valentine had a sudden pang for that morning when she and Jack had shared the cheapest she could find in Sainsbury's. Then Tamara handed Jack an exquisitely wrapped present. Jack looked slightly awkward as he unwrapped it to reveal a copy of *To Kill a Mockingbird* – one of his favourite books.

'Tamara, this is too much,' he said, sounding embarrassed, especially when he opened the cover and saw it was a first edition. 'Really too much.'

Tamara looked like the cat who had got the cream – fat-free in her case. 'It's just a little thank you for being so sweet to me and helping me through this difficult time.'

Valentine felt a flash of jealousy at the thought of Jack giving NTM any attention.

Jack shrugged. 'I really haven't done anything.'

But Tamara lowered her voice, making the exchange between them intimate, 'You have, Jack, you've been my rock.' Her voice caught with a sob as she carried on,

'You've been like Atticus Finch standing up to the bullies who would bring me down.'

The woman was an egomaniac! Fancy comparing her situation to that of the persecuted African American falsely accused of rape! She was just a bad actress and she only had herself to blame for that.

Still, Jack was simply being nice to Tamara because that was the kind of person he was, Valentine tried to tell herself. She should be happy that she had such a lovely, generous, warm-hearted boyfriend. The pep talk didn't work. Her mood grew darker.

Seb pulled her back from the brink by asking her about *A Midsummer Night's Dream*. 'Jack said you were absolutely sensational!'

'Not sensational enough, apparently,' she said. 'I've heard nothing from my agent.' She took another sip of champagne, but the drink, which had made her feel so high this morning, was now having the opposite effect. She just wanted to go. She looked appealingly at Jack, but he was still being monopolised by Tamara. Valentine hated to admit it but she felt jealous and insecure. She was just hours away from getting the train back home, leaving Jack with Tamara. And Jack's plan to have a quick drink then leave did not materialise as the director of the play turned up and ordered more champagne.

At five o'clock – just half an hour before Valentine's train – they finally left.

'I thought we weren't going to stay long,' Valentine said, aware that she sounded petulant, but unable to stop.

'I know, I'm sorry.' He put his arm round her. 'I'll make it up to you next time, I promise.'

'You know NTM really fancies you,' Valentine continued.

'She doesn't,' Jack protested, but he didn't look Valentine in the eye. 'I told you she's having a hard time and she sees me as an ally.'

'Do you have to be her ally?' Valentine persisted. 'Couldn't you just keep a cool and polite distance?'

Jack removed his arm. She'd exasperated him. 'Clive is bullying her. I hate bullying, that's all.'

'So if the situation was reversed and say it was me and Finn and he was having a hard time and I was just being kind and he was buying me expensive presents, you wouldn't mind?'

'It's completely different! You've got previous with Finn. Tamara is just a colleague. I really don't know what your problem is with her. Yes, she can be annoying and she isn't as talented as you and it is a shame that she's got to where she has because of her connections, but that's just the way of the world. She's completely harmless and actually quite sweet when you get to know her.'

Valentine saw red. 'You've got no idea! She was vile to me at drama school, never missed an opportunity to put me down, and she's been like that ever since.'

'She's probably just insecure because she knows that you're the better actress.'

'Oh yes, that must be it! She's jealous of my glittering career! Who knows what exciting roles the coming week has in store for me! Maybe I'll get another booking to be a party fairy and be groped by some lecherous dad, or I can help out at the yummy mummy music group again and be criticised for not putting my all into "The Wheels on the Fucking Bus"! No wonder NTM is jealous of me; I mean, how can the role of Cordelia compare with all of that?' The anger and jealousy was pouring out of her.

There was a pause when they both stood glaring at each other in the station – a direct contrast to their romantic meeting two days earlier. Oh God, she couldn't part like this!

Jack was the first to speak. 'Don't let's argue. It's not important.' He put his arm round her again. 'Are you sure you can't stay tonight? I could smuggle you into my digs. I promise I won't let the bed bugs bite and I'll hide the pink crocheted lady loo roll cover.'

'Really? That cover would have been one of the highlights of my stay,' she attempted to joke. 'But no, I can't, Jack.' It was tempting, but she knew she would feel ten times worse in the morning when Jack left for his rehearsal and she had an empty day ahead of her.

'I love you, Valentine,' Jack said as they hugged by the ticket barrier. She buried her face in his neck, getting one final hit of Jack and Eau Sauvage. So much more romantic in the past when lovers could wave each other off at the platform. 'Love you too,' Valentine said. There was nothing at all romantic about going through a ticket barrier on your own.

It was a miserable journey back to London. The train was packed. The air-conditioning had broken and it was sweltering. 'We should be able to get our money back,' the large man opposite her kept repeating at regular intervals. The heat didn't seem to have suppressed his appetite and Valentine watched him put away a Big Mac, fries and an apple pie. In the heat of the carriage the smell of the fast food seemed to linger. Valentine had brought one of Jack's T-shirts back to snuggle up with in bed because it carried his scent, but at this rate all it was going to smell of was bloody McDonald's – hardly the Proustian memory she had hoped for. Her iPod battery had gone flat, but she put the headphones in anyway, hoping to protect herself from any more comments from fast-food man, and shut her eyes for good measure. She was already missing Jack and hating the fact that they had nearly quarrelled as she left. Had she been in the wrong to be so negative about Tamara? She didn't want to seem like a bitch, but she really couldn't stand her. Just thinking about her again and about the way she had hijacked Jack's birthday made Valentine feel angry, irrational and very insecure.

12

Lord, What Fools
These Mortals Be . . .

'Does this say "daughter of famous film director" to you?'
Valentine demanded, walking into the living room where
Nathan was doing sit-ups (proper Army-style hardcore
ones, she noticed in some awe) while Lauren lay on the sofa
languidly eating Ben and Jerry's Cherry Garcia from the
tub.

Valentine was off to meet Piers and his wife Olivia for
lunch at Nobu in Mayfair. It was to be her second meeting
with Piers and her first with Olivia. Since she'd met Piers
in Hampstead they had been sending each other emails
regularly. And Valentine had found herself warming more
to Piers. She discovered he had a very dry sense of humour
– but it still felt strange every time she remembered who
he was. She was nervous about Olivia, certain that she
would be a force to be reckoned with, and she wanted to
make a good impression. All her dresses, a mixture of
Vintage and Top Shop, appeared a little shabby by
daylight. In the end she'd chosen a green halterneck with
a fitted waist and full skirt, with a little black cardigan

over the top. She'd spent ages taming her hair so it hung in soft forties-style waves and not in a mad frizz. The question was, would she do?

'V, you look great, but I don't know what a daughter of a famous film director is supposed to look like, except Sophia Coppola. And you don't look like her, sweetie.'

'Because she's so slim,' Valentine said gloomily.

'No! Because you have a completely different look, birdbrain!'

'You look gorgeous V,' Nathan panted, now doing press-ups.

'I don't mean to witter on,' Valentine sighed, perching on the end of the sofa. 'It's just that I really want Piers to like me.'

'Do you like him?' Lauren demanded.

'I don't know him yet. But he is my father. I'm still hoping for some kind of connection.' Valentine couldn't bring herself to say "dad". She'd already had a dad – Chris. Piers could never replace him.

Lauren put down the empty tub of Cherry Garcia. 'V, if he doesn't like you then he is some fucked up motherfucker.'

'*Lauren*!' Nathan and Valentine chorused. Nathan fully supported Valentine's campaign to get Lauren to stop saying "motherfucker".

'Oh shut up American Boy and get on with your press-ups. I thought your abs seemed a little slack this morning,' Lauren shot back.

'Nothing to what yours will be if you keep mainlining ice-cream,' Nathan replied, but they were smiling at each other. It was definitely love, Valentine thought as she headed out of the house.

'So Valentine, isn't that a boy's name?' That original question came from Olivia. She was several years older than Piers, in her late fifties, but still intimidatingly beautiful in an ice-blonde sort of way, with cheekbones to die for. She had not been giving off especially friendly vibes. Valentine had tried to see things from Olivia's point of view. It was understandable that she would be wary of her husband's daughter suddenly appearing on the scene. All the same, her cool manner had been disconcerting.

Valentine nodded and launched into her usual explanation, all the while aware of Olivia observing her, and not just Olivia. Piers had also brought along Saul Morrison, one of the screenwriters he worked with, explaining that he wanted Valentine to get to know the people he was closest to. Valentine would have preferred one-to-one time with Piers. She hadn't warmed to Saul one little bit. Alongside Olivia, he had interrogated Valentine about her acting CV and the looks he gave her made it clear that he thought she was a loser. He seemed to be dissecting her every move and every expression, as if storing them for future use. No doubt people were just source material to him. If that wasn't enough he was wearing the loathsome chinos. She felt supremely awkward. Piers was making an effort with her, but Saul and Olivia were so aloof. No one was drinking alcohol and in Olivia's case, not eating anything either. Valentine had long wanted to taste black cod in miso, but she was too aware of Olivia monitoring her mouthfuls to enjoy it.

'Valentine was at drama school with Tamara Moore,' Piers told Olivia when there was a lull in the conversation.

'Such a lovely girl!' Finally the ice queen looked animated. 'And isn't she in *Lear* at the moment? We'll have to go, Piers. Though,' and here she seemed to shudder slightly, 'isn't it in Manchester?'

'Not a fan of the North?' Valentine asked teasingly. 'I love it myself.'

'Of course I like the North; what are you suggesting?' Olivia demanded, her grey eyes bulging slightly, a vein pulsing in her lovely long neck. 'One of my horse sanctuaries is in Cheshire; I'm always going up there.'

'Nothing at all,' Valentine mumbled. Maybe Olivia just had no sense of humour and preferred horses to people. Valentine had long been wary of horse people since her days as a horse-mad ten-year-old and having to deal with Mrs Trimmer, the fearsome owner of the stables. Mrs Trimmer strode around in mud-caked boots, a filthy Barbour, fag hanging out of her mouth and woe betide you if you hadn't groomed or mucked out her horses to her satisfaction. In fairness she adored her horses – it was just the people she didn't care for. Maybe Olivia was like Mrs Trimmer – except a beautiful, non-smoking version.

'And Valentine's boyfriend is in the play too,' Piers carried on, oblivious to any discord. 'So we can all go together. It's Jack Hart, isn't it? Great name for a movie actor.'

'Jack Hart?' Olivia said, 'That name sounds familiar. Yes, I remember. I saw a picture of him in some magazine with Tamara.'

'Did you?' Valentine asked, slightly rattled. 'Was it about the play?' Jack hadn't mentioned that he'd been interviewed.

'Actually I've got it on me.' She reached into her pink Hermès Birkin bag, which Valentine knew cost thousands, and pulled out a copy of *Grazia*.

Valentine froze as she took in one of the headlines on the cover: 'Does Tamara have a new leading man?' She suddenly felt sick. There was a whole article devoted to Tamara's stage appearance. That didn't concern Valentine, though ordinarily it would have got right up her nose. It was the picture that was holding her attention right now. The picture of Tamara and Jack sitting outside a cafe, laughing together and looking intimate. The strapline underneath it named Jack and there was a quote from Tamara's agent saying there was a new man in her life but it was early days and she was not prepared to name him. However the juxtaposition of the photograph and the comment made it clear what conclusion people were supposed to draw. How stupid she'd been to trust him. She was a complete and utter idiot. She should have realised there was something going on when he started defending Tamara. With some effort she dragged her eyes away from the magazine. Olivia and Saul were watching her intently to gauge her reaction. Self-preservation kicked in; she wasn't going to let these two know how this really made her feel.

'Oh, Jack's been helping her out with the play. Apparently the actor playing Lear has been giving her a hard time because she hasn't done much stage work and has been saying that she can't act.'

'Oh,' Olivia replied. And it was interesting just how much meaning could be conveyed in that tiny word. Olivia's 'oh' read like *You silly, stupid girl, he's shagging her. You're history.*

'If you'll excuse me, I'm going to find the bathroom,' Valentine said as calmly as she could.

As soon as she was out of sight she practically sprinted to the ladies', where she locked herself in the cubicle and promptly threw up her lunch. Probably this was the only thing she had done so far that Olivia would approve of. She scrambled in her bag for her phone and called Jack. No answer. He was either rehearsing or shagging Tamara Moore in her penthouse apartment. Silly, stupid Valentine. Of course he was going to be interested in Tamara, with her glittering career and beauty. Men didn't care about massive arses if the rest of the package was so slim. Hadn't he said that he loved Valentine's backside? And that was more of a J-Lo than a Li-Lo. She left a garbled message about seeing the magazine and needing to speak to him urgently. She closed her eyes and tried to chant Lauren's core-of-steel mantra. No good. She felt crushed. But somehow – the lack of steel notwithstanding, she managed to pull herself together. She went through the motions of repairing her make-up, then slowly walked back to the table.

'Are you OK Valentine?' Piers asked, sounding concerned.

'I expect she had a phone call to make,' Saul put in. God, he was horrible. A chinos-wearing poisonous toad.

'Actually my agent rang; I've got an audition tomorrow. Would you mind if I left now, so I can prepare?'

'What's it for?' Olivia asked.

'Just a small role in a new Jane Austen TV drama.' Oh God, they'd all been done, hadn't they? Why did she say that?

'And who's directing it?' Olivia carried on.

Valentine shook her head. 'I didn't ask, actually.'

'Well you should find out. It's important, isn't it, Piers? Now Valentine is associated with you.'

Piers shrugged. He seemed embarrassed by Olivia's comment.

'I probably won't even get it,' Valentine replied, desperate to get out of there.

'Well, with that attitude you won't!' Saul put in. A chinos-wearing poisonous motherfucker of a toad. Valentine ignored him.

'Thanks for lunch, Piers,' she said, putting out her hand to shake his. 'Lovely to meet you, Olivia, and you, Saul.'

She scuttled out of Nobu at high speed, but just outside walked straight into Julia Turner arm in arm with a very good-looking young male companion. Jack Mark Two. Were there no other restaurants in London that a successful stage actress could have gone to with her latest arm candy? Bloody Julia husky Turner! She was all set to ignore her but Julia had seen her. She waved a copy of *Grazia* at Valentine. 'Interesting reading, Valentine.'

'I'm in a rush actually, Julia.'

'A word of advice – I've known Jack far longer than you and one thing you might not be aware of is just how ambitious he is. He probably kept that side of himself under wraps as he was in an off-West End play. But he wants to make it. And I think he'll do whatever it takes to get there. I was useful to him for a while, you were a diversion and now he's got Tamara. You have to agree it's a perfect match.'

Valentine so wanted to make a cutting remark, but she was too hurt. All she could do was repeat that she had to go and walk away from Julia as quickly as she could. She was in complete turmoil. She couldn't face going home to an empty flat and she knew Lauren was at a casting. As soon as she was far enough away from Nobu, she phoned Jack again. No reply. Now on top of the hurt she was starting to feel angry. She stormed through Mayfair, cried all the way down Oxford Street and ended up in Soho Square. The bright sunshine, the people lying on the grass, chatting and having lunch, seemed to mock her. She phoned Kitty, Rufus and Toby and got their voicemails. She phoned three more friends, also on voicemail. And finally she called Finn. 'Can I see you?'

On the journey to Richmond she kept hoping that Jack would ring. He didn't. It was five in the afternoon – Jack must have had a break from rehearsals by now; he must have got her messages. There could only be one possible reason for him not replying to her. He was Tamara Moore's new leading man. He just didn't have the guts to tell her. Valentine's self-esteem plummeted to an all-time low. Jack didn't want her anymore. It was such a beautiful June evening, the horse chestnuts in full bloom, the gardens backing on to the river a riot of colourful flowers, the river glinting in the last rays of the sun. But Valentine was blind to the scenery.

Finn was already sitting at a table outside the pub by the river. As soon as he saw her he took her in his arms and held her tight. 'Poor V, sit down and tell me all about it. I've got you a double vodka. I thought you might need it.'

Valentine slumped next to him. 'I just can't believe Jack would do this to me. He made such a big deal about how I could trust him and it was all fucking lies!' She rapidly drank the vodka and Finn went to get more drinks. Right now, self-medication with alcohol seemed like the only option. She kept checking her mobile. No message from Jack. She tried texting – *Saw the magazine. Have to speak to you.* She was well on the way to becoming drunk, a dangerous thing to be around Finn, but she couldn't stop. She felt as if there was a demon of rage and hurt inside her waiting to explode.

'And with Tamara fucking Moore of all people!' she exclaimed as soon as Finn returned from the bar.

'Don't let it get to you V, he's not worth it,' Finn said soothingly.

Valentine was in no mood to be pacified. 'I mean, I expect that behaviour from someone like you!'

'Oh, you mean a gutless bastard who nearly destroyed you,' Finn said dryly. Lauren had told Finn that to his face. 'I am sorry about what I did, V. Truly.' He put his arm round her. 'And if you let me get a word in edgeways I can tell you my big news. I've split up with Eva.' He paused for extra effect. 'The engagement's off. Forget about Jack. We're meant to be together. I won't let you down again, I swear. I want you, V, always have done, always will.'

'Really?' Valentine struggled to take on board what Finn was saying.

'I love you, V.' And he kissed her.

Valentine let him make all the moves and then she kissed him back. Jack was probably kissing Tamara and the rest. He didn't want Valentine any more; she had just been a distraction easily discarded when someone better came along. Valentine was beyond being rational and reflecting that of course Julia would say anything to make her feel bad. More drinks followed, then more drunken snogging. And when Finn suggested that they went back to his flat, she hesitated only long enough to check her phone, still hanging on to the fragile hope that Jack would have left a message saying it was all a horrible mistake. There was nothing. By now it was last orders. Well, fuck him. She wasn't going to sit around being a victim. She switched her phone off.

It was hot, desperate, feverish sex. She pulling off his T-shirt, unbuttoning his jeans, he ripping off her underwear, lifting up her dress and driving into her, grabbing her wrists and holding them over her head, kissing and biting her breasts, she raking her fingers down his back.

She ordering him to change positions, with her on top, then him changing again.

'I fucking love you,' he panted, thrusting into her.

'Then fuck me harder,' she gasped. And with every thrust it felt as if she was being wrenched away from Jack, away from the tender, sensuous, passionate sex they'd had. This was hard, selfish sex, both wanting to get their satisfaction first and despite the waves of pleasure pulsing through Valentine, when she came it felt like the end of something. It felt like a destruction.

'Where the fuck have you been?' Lauren demanded as Valentine let herself into the flat the following morning. 'We've all been out of our minds with worry about you! Couldn't you have phoned?'

Valentine shrugged, too hungover and too disconsolate to speak. She trudged into the kitchen and put the kettle on. She had regretted her night with Finn as soon as she had woken up.

Lauren followed her, arms folded, looking like she meant business. 'Jack rang, desperate to speak to you. He left his mobile behind when he went to rehearsal and came back to all these messages from you. He's on the train now.'

'Oh, so he's managed to drag himself away from Tamara, has he?' Valentine said bitterly.

'What are you on about? There's nothing going on between him and Tamara! He told me about that magazine article; it was a complete fabrication. A fantasy on Tamara's part.'

Valentine suddenly felt very wobbly. She sat down at the table.

'Where have you been, V?' Lauren persisted.

She looked down at her hands as if she could somehow avoid the question. But there was no getting away from it. She couldn't lie. 'I've been with Finn,' she said flatly.

Lauren's mouth fell open in astonishment; she couldn't even say her mantra.

'I slept with him. I thought Jack was having an affair with Tamara Moore, so I thought I may as well.' Her voice was cold and robotic. She was in shock.

Now Lauren had put her hands up to her mouth. 'You are joking, aren't you?'

Valentine shook her head.

'Jack will be here in an hour. What are you going to tell him?'

'The truth,' Valentine replied, giving a bitter little smile. 'I've always hated liars. I wouldn't do that to Jack.'

'Oh V,' Lauren said with feeling. 'What a bloody mess.'

Valentine felt numb in the hour before Jack arrived. She spent ages in the shower, as if the hot water could erase what she had done, but all the perfumes in Arabia weren't going to get this situation clean. She could hardly bring herself to look at him when he walked into the flat. Lauren had tactfully gone out.

'I'm here, see? I would never be unfaithful to you,' Jack said as he went to hug her. Instead of returning it Valentine stood stiffly with her arms by her side. She didn't deserve the hug.

'Let's go into the living room,' she mumbled, as if they were acquaintances.

'I was thinking more on the lines of your futon,' Jack said playfully and then froze as he caught sight of Valentine's stricken face. She turned and walked away from him. He sat down on the sofa while she stood by the window. 'I'm really sorry about that magazine story. It's all lies. Yes I was out with Tamara, but we were having coffee and what the picture doesn't show is that Seb was with us as well and he'd just gone to the bathroom or something. I admit that Tamara does seem to have a thing for me, but I don't have any feelings for her. I swear you can trust me.'

Valentine felt as if her mouth were full of dust. She had broken what she had with Jack, smashed it into a million pieces. He didn't know yet, but she would have to tell him.

'But you looked so loved up in the picture,' Valentine said sadly. 'And you were being so nice about her when I was last up in Manchester. And she so obviously wants you.'

'I felt sorry for her, that's all.' He paused then said with passion, 'Valentine, you sound so strange. Has something happened? Because you can trust me; I would never be unfaithful to you. *Never*. Where were you when I rang last night? I was really worried.'

'I was just out,' she replied, hanging her head in shame. She had been so sure of Jack's guilt. Now she believed him. She had jumped to the wrong conclusion; she had ruined everything.

'Who with?' Jack asked quietly. Then when Valentine didn't answer, he said with more urgency, 'Tell me, who were you with?'

'Finn,' Valentine said, her voice barely audible. 'You see, I thought you were with Tamara, and when you didn't phone I believed that the story must be true.'

Jack had got up from the sofa and was standing in front of her. 'Tell me you just had a drink with him.'

Valentine shook her head; she couldn't speak. But she didn't have to. Her silence said it all.

He gripped her arms tightly, and repeated, 'But it was just a drink, wasn't it?'

Valentine could not bring herself to look at him; she was crying now, hot tears coursing down her cheeks, weeping with shame for what she had done and for what she had lost.

'No!' Jack exclaimed, letting go of her and taking a step backwards as if he couldn't bear to touch her, be close to her. 'You screwed that worthless, gutless shit! How could you? After everything we had together! You were the one, Valentine.'

Now she looked up at him and the full force of what she had done hit her.

'Well, I hope it was worth.it for you.' Hurt, anger and something worse in his voice – he despised her.

Valentine wanted to beg him to forgive her, that it was a one-off, that it would never happen again, but the words sounded so hollow and empty even inside her head.

'I love you, Jack,' she whispered.

'No, you don't fucking love me! That's not what love

is. You were so quick to believe that I had been unfaithful, all because of what that shit did to you. Maybe you two are meant to be together.' He walked away as if he couldn't bear to look at her anymore. At the doorway he paused and said coldly, 'You deserve each other. For all I know you've been shagging him all along.'

'I haven't, I swear. I made a mistake. I know it sounds mad but I really believed you were with Tamara. Can't you forgive me?'

He shook his head. 'It's over.' And he carried on walking out of the flat.

13

If Only . . .

The next month was a blur. So many times Valentine was on the verge of calling Jack and begging him to forgive her, but she kept remembering the expression on his face when he realised what she'd done. If only she hadn't been so quick to jump to conclusions. If only. If only. If only. The world did not run on 'if only's. Lauren was a true friend, never once saying, 'What the hell did you do that for?' She listened to her endlessly talking about Jack, made her cups of tea, poured her glasses of wine. Never judged her. Her mum and Lottie were brilliant as well and insisted on taking her out to the cinema or inviting her round for dinner, not that she felt like doing anything other than lying in bed. But she appreciated their efforts.

Acting would have been a distraction, but no auditions came through for her. She got a series of temping jobs and felt as if she was sleepwalking through the days, with just misery for company and the painful knowledge that she only had herself to blame. Her nights were given over to fantasising that Jack could forgive her and they'd get back together. She didn't give Finn a second thought. He was away in the States again for another audition and despite proclaiming that he and Valentine were meant to be together she hardly heard from him.

Then Lauren announced that Nathan had invited her to spend a month with him in San Francisco but that she had said no, because she didn't want to leave Valentine in such a state. Valentine wouldn't hear of it and urged her to go, though she felt the dark side beckoning. Lily and Frank were on her case. She had dreaded telling the old timers about breaking up with Jack, fearing that Lily especially would have a real go at her and tell her how monumentally stupid and selfish she had been. But Lily had just hugged her and said, 'My poor dear Valentine; how wretched you must feel.' And Valentine had cried, and cried and cried till her face was red and blotchy and her eyes were so sore she could hardly open them. Frank had taken to bringing up fresh fruit smoothies every morning which he'd made especially for her, because he and Lily were worried that she wasn't eating. And she wasn't. Not even the siren call of peanut butter could tempt her. How ironic; it seemed she could be fat and happy or thin and unhappy.

She hadn't seen Piers since the disastrous lunch at Nobu, as he'd been away filming, but the day after Lauren's departure she received a call from Greta. Olivia had arranged a birthday surprise for Piers; was Valentine free on Friday? Yes, Valentine was free – her diary was wide open. She was feeling so low she didn't even ask what the surprise was, just registered that she needed to dress for dinner and pack an overnight bag. On the day itself she barely had the energy to get dressed and put on make-up, but she forced herself to go through the motions. Piers seemed pleased to see her and gave her a warm welcome when the chauffeur-driven people-carrier picked her up. Well, warm by his standards – he shook her hand slightly longer than usual. Olivia seemed as cool as ever and the supercilious Saul gave her one of his 'you're not worth my while engaging with' greetings, his gaze fixed just past her shoulder as if looking at someone far more interesting.

'Happy Birthday Piers,' Valentine said, sinking back into the leather seat and handing him his present. She'd had no idea what to buy Piers. What did you buy someone who had absolutely everything? In the end her mum had come up with a suggestion that she give him a photo-graph album full of pictures of her through the years. Valentine had no idea how this would go down; she only hoped that Piers didn't feel that she was trying to make a point of how he hadn't been there for her.

In the event Piers's reaction was startling. As soon as he saw the photographs his eyes filled with tears and he reached out for her hand. 'Thank you, Valentine. This is a wonderful present. I'm only sorry I wasn't there for you, but I want you to know that I'm here for you now.' He seemed to be struggling to compose his feelings as he said, 'Olivia, take a look at this. Isn't it absolutely charming?'

Olivia was sitting in the front seat; she briefly turned around and said, 'I will later, darling. You know how car-sick I get.'

Olivia's travel sickness meant that she required everyone to be silent on the journey. Piers and Saul both put on headphones and watched films on their laptops while Valentine gazed blankly out of the window. She had imagined they were probably headed for some luxury hotel for dinner. Three hours later they were driving into the centre of Manchester and pulling up outside the The Lowry Hotel. Valentine knew it was supposed to be a luxury hotel, but even so it seemed a long way to come. It was also a coincidence as Frank and Lily were up in Manchester as well, seeing Jack's play. Valentine started to have a bad feeling about this whole Manchester trip, the bad feeling just got a whole lot worse with Olivia's next comment. 'We just have an hour to freshen up before the play begins.'

'What play is that?' Valentine asked, with a sinking feeling.

'*Lear*, didn't Greta tell you?'

Valentine shook her head. Of all the plays in all the world, why, oh why did it have to be that one? How could she see Jack again and know that she had lost him? It would be unbearable. But now she was here, how could she not?

'I'm really looking forward to meeting your boyfriend,' Piers put in. 'We're hoping he'll join us for dinner.'

Valentine's heart sank further still; this just got worse. She felt as if Olivia must have arranged this surprise just to torment her. 'Actually, I'm not sure if that will be possible.' She hesitated. 'We broke up a month ago.'

Olivia's 'Oh,' said *I told you so*.

Piers looked at Valentine. 'I'm sorry to hear that. We had no idea, otherwise we never would have put you in this situation, would we, Olivia?'

Olivia shook her head. But Valentine couldn't help wondering if she was telling the truth. Wasn't she supposed to be good friends with Tamara's mother?

'Are you going to be OK coming to the theatre?' Piers continued. 'I understand if it's too painful for you.'

'I'll be OK,' Valentine managed, thinking of Lily and Frank. Perhaps if Jack saw her with the couple he'd think less badly of her, remember that he'd once loved her. Perhaps there was a tiny flicker of hope.

The Royal Exchange was packed. Valentine scanned the rows for Lily and Frank, but couldn't see them anywhere. She hoped the train journey hadn't been too much for Lily; she'd been looking so frail lately. Valentine's party was in the third row from the front. Now she was not only feeling apprehensive about seeing Jack after the play, she was feeling nervous *for* him. This was a really big deal. She desperately wanted it to go well for him.

She need not have worried. From the moment Jack appeared as Edmund, bastard son of the Duke of Gloucester, in Act I he was mesmerising. He was sexy, brutal, and persuasive. A man of no conscience, who didn't care what he had to do to get what he wanted. Valentine had thought that she wouldn't be able to see beyond the fact it was Jack, but he played his part so well that she almost forgot she knew him. It was a tour de force and she sensed that this would be the making of him.

The same could not be said of Tamara as Cordelia. She was toe-curlingly bad, playing her as a simpering girl rather than a strong-minded, principled young woman, and she murdered her wonderful speeches. As Valentine had predicted it was a relief in Act V when Lear carried her lifeless body on stage after she'd been hung; no doubt most of the audience had been itching to strangle her themselves from Act I.

'An utter triumph!' Piers declared, clapping loudly at the end.

'Valentine, I know it's awkward but do you think you might be able to introduce Jack to Piers? He would be perfect for his next film,' Olivia whispered, so Piers could not hear. Clearly a woman with an empathy bypass.

'I'm not at all sure that Jack is even speaking to me,' Valentine said quietly. 'And anyway, won't Tamara wonder why I am with Piers?'

'Tamara knows about the situation.' She said 'situation' as if the thought of Valentine being related to Piers was distasteful to her. 'Tamara's an old family friend and I trust her completely.'

Valentine felt a sudden flash of resentment because Piers had been so insistent that she tell no one. Olivia and Piers led the way to the bar, with Valentine trailing behind, accompanied by the still-chinos-wearing Saul. Did he not possess any other trousers?

'Piers has something in mind for Jack. Tamara has

been telling him how talented he is.' He paused. 'And he is. It's a pity you're not still with him; looks like he'll really be going places. It would have been good for your career. Any parts yet or are you still "resting"?' A most vile chinos-wearing traitor!

She ignored the comment about her work and said sarcastically, 'With your degree of sensitivity you should think about having a relationship column.'

Saul gazed over her shoulder. 'Actually, I'm too busy writing successful movie scripts.' As they walked up to the bar, Valentine wrung a tiny piece of satisfaction out of the situation by doing the whatever-minger signal behind his back.

A table had been reserved for Piers and his party, with champagne on ice. 'Jack is exactly what I've been looking for, with that combination of menace and raw sexuality,' Piers said enthusiastically to Valentine. 'He couldn't be more perfect.'

'No he couldn't,' Valentine replied sadly.

'Sorry,' Piers said. 'That was tactless of me.'

At that moment she spotted Lily and Frank and waved. The pair walked slowly over to the table, Lily clinging to Frank as if she could hardly manage to walk. 'Piers, these are my friends Lily and Frank,' she said as the couple finally made it to the table.

Piers smiled. 'Good to meet you. You'll join us for a glass of champagne?'

Valentine noticed that Olivia looked slightly peeved by Piers' offer of hospitality and while Piers made polite conversation with the couple she sat in glacial silence, only nodding when Frank told her how much he had loved her performance in one of her films.

'Oh look!' Lily exclaimed. 'There's Jack! He's coming over!'

Valentine's heart was racing so fast she felt like the time Lauren had made her take poppers as a dare. His hair was still damp from a shower; he was dressed in jeans and a black T-shirt. He'd had to pump up for the part of Edmund and his body looked fitter, in both senses of the word, than ever. His lovely muscular arms were now even more lovely and muscular. He looked briefly at Valentine, then quickly looked away without acknowledging her. That hurt, but then what did she expect? She watched Lily and Frank congratulating him, Lily doing her usual over-the-top 'You're such a star, darling,' routine, while Jack smiled and shook his head.

Then Piers introduced himself, sticking out his hand. 'Piers Hunter. I just wanted to congratulate you on an awesome performance. Won't you join us for a drink?' Piers briefly looked at Valentine as if checking it was OK; well, it was too late now. Jack sat down next to Lily and continued to avoid eye contact with Valentine. She hung her head and picked at her thumbnail. It was very hard holding it together in front of him. Saul poured everyone a glass of champagne, while Piers continued to enthuse about Jack's performance.

'And of course Tamara was divine too,' Olivia put in. 'I can imagine you would both look fantastic on film together, such chemistry between the pair of you.'

236

Valentine had a sudden urge to throw her champagne into Olivia's smug face. Why was she being so insensitive?

Just as Valentine thought things couldn't possibly get any worse, they took a turn for the so much worse as Tamara turned up, put her arms round Jack's neck and kissed him. And this was not a 'well done for your perform-ance' kiss, this was a 'you belong to me' kiss. Just in case anyone was in any doubt that this was what it signalled, after she'd said her hellos to everyone else (a particularly gushing one to Piers), seeing that there was no seat, she slid onto Jack's lap. Her tiny frame was no doubt light as a feather. Valentine looked at Jack disbelievingly, as Tamara whispered something in his ear and giggled. How long had this been going on? Had he been lying about his relationship with her? She looked at Lily, then at Frank, who both looked equally shocked. To pull herself back from the abyss she was hurtling towards she tried her trick of listing everything she had to be thankful for in the world. She had wonderful friends, she had a great relation-ship with her mum, she had her health, she'd lost weight . . . but it was no good. She felt utterly crushed. Tamara chose this moment to speak to her.

'So what's new with you, V?'

Valentine was about to shrug and mutter, 'Nothing,' feeling too dejected even to pretend. But Lily spoke up for her. 'V has got several auditions lined up, one with a very prestigious director.' Valentine appreciated the lie.

'Oh, what parts?' Tamara replied.

Lily tapped a finger against her nose. 'All hush hush I'm afraid.'

'Well now,' Olivia spoke, clearly expecting everyone's attention, 'I suggest dinner – Tamara, Jack? We'd love it if you could join us.' Her invitation was not extended to Lily and Frank.

'Thanks, but I am taking Lily and Frank out for dinner, as they came all the way up here to see me,' Jack replied.

Olivia was forced to back-track. 'Well, of course they must come too.'

'Thank you,' Lily replied graciously, 'but I am going to retire with Frank. The journey has tired me more than I anticipated.' She stood up and swayed slightly. Immediately Frank got up and put his arm round her to steady her.

'I'll walk out with you,' Valentine said, getting up.

'Me too,' Jack said.

Lily seemed very frail as she walked through the bar, leaning heavily on Frank for support.

'Here, let me take the other side,' Jack said, putting his arm round Lily. 'Thank you, sweetheart,' she said gratefully, adding, 'You were a revelation on stage.'

'I wasn't Lily, but thank you anyway,' Jack replied.

'You were and you need to get used to being gracious about your talent.' She paused. 'And I know you might not want to hear this and you'll think that I'm meddling, but I'm old and I'm allowed to, so here goes: Jack, perhaps you need to be a little more forgiving in other areas of your life.' She looked meaningfully at Valentine. Where Angels feared to tread Lily stormed right in.

Jack caught the look. 'Lily, I know you mean well, but I've always believed that infidelity is a deal-breaker.

238

You can't have a relationship without trust.' Valentine's tiny flicker of hope was extinguished.

'Oh Jack, I wish you knew what I did about life, then you'd realise that in the grand scheme of things it is something that can be forgiven,' Lily said sadly. She put her hand up to Jack's face. 'Lovely Jack, try to forgive.'

Jack took her hand and kissed it. 'Lovely Lily, let's get you that taxi.'

After they had seen Frank and Lily into a taxi, Jack and Valentine stood outside the theatre. The ex and the ex. Jack staring after the departing taxi as if it were a thing of great fascination.

'Lily was right, you were fantastic,' Valentine said quietly, willing him to look at her. If only he would do that he would surely see how sorry she was.

But Jack wouldn't look at her. 'Thanks and congratulations on your auditions.'

'There are no auditions. Lily was just putting a positive spin on my lack of career.'

'Oh.' A beat, then a muttered, 'So how's it going with him?'

'If you mean Finn, there is no me and him. I told you, I made a mistake; I wish you would believe me, Jack,' Valentine replied, twisting her diamante bracelet round and round her wrist in anguish. 'I wish you could forgive me.' He still wouldn't look at her.

'It's a big ask, don't you think?' he said finally. 'How would you feel if you were me?'

Valentine hung her head. 'Devastated, just like I do.'

'You threw us away. I don't think I can ever forgive you.'

Valentine did her best to blink back the hot tears. 'And now you're seeing Tamara?'

'*Now* I am,' he said meaningfully. And he was about to go on when Tamara appeared.

'There you are!' she said a little huffily, linking her arm through Jack's. 'Olivia was wondering where you'd got to. It's time to go.'

If there had been any excuse Valentine could have thought of to get out of dinner, any at all, she would have used it. As it was there was nothing she could say. She ended up sitting opposite Jack and Tamara, the latter continuing to mark her possession of Jack – feeding him some of her risotto with her fork (Valentine had a particular loathing for couples who did that), running her hand down his back, smoothing back his hair. She literally could not keep her hands off him. *I don't know why she doesn't just fuck him in front of me and get it over and done with,* she thought bitterly. Piers meanwhile was talking to Jack about his current project, another of his action blockbusters. Valentine endured the starters and the main course making small talk with Olivia.

'I see you've lost weight, Valentine,' Olivia commented at one point. 'What diet have you been following?' The I'm-broken-hearted-and-so-miserable-I can't-eat diet, was the correct answer.

Valentine shrugged. 'I just haven't been very hungry.'

'Well it suits you,' Olivia said and she nodded

approvingly when she noticed that Valentine had barely touched her food.

Jack continued to ignore her, not even looking at her. By dessert she could bear the situation no longer. She made a feeble excuse about having a migraine – Piers wasn't to know that she didn't get them – and said her goodbyes. Finally Jack looked at her as she got up to go, but his brown eyes were completely unreadable.

Now she'd seen Jack again she couldn't even hold on to that tiny flicker of hope that he might be able to forgive her. There could be no more fantasies about getting back with him. She looked back to the night she'd slept with Finn and saw it for what it was – a moment of complete madness. She felt at an all-time low, worse than she ever used to when she was having the affair with Finn. Now that seemed like a rehearsal for experiencing pain – this was the real thing.

Finn was back in London – the audition hadn't gone well; he hadn't got the part. He phoned her a few times trying to persuade her to go out with him; each time she said no. Finally he called round and insisted on taking her out for dinner. She'd run out of excuses for saying no. Finn's treat was oysters at an uber-trendy pub on Westbourne Park Road, which was no treat at all for Valentine, who hated oysters. Even the sight of people eating them made her feel queasy. Finn was in a bad mood after the rejection and spent most of the evening ranting about how unfair it was that he hadn't got the part. He barely asked her anything about herself. How had she never noticed before how incredibly self-obsessed he was?

'So did you miss me, V?'

She shrugged.

'Oh, you're not still hung up on Jack, are you?' He paused. 'You do know he was shagging Tamara before you broke up?'

'How do you know?' Finn's answer suddenly became very important.

'She told me. So I don't know why he acted all moral-high-ground with you.'

'When?' Valentine couldn't let this go.

'I don't know the exact time and date but I just know that it was before you broke up, after someone's party I think.'

Valentine felt sick. She remembered Jack going to a birthday party of one of the members of the cast. He had promised to call her afterwards but never had. She'd thought nothing of it at the time. Nor did she stop to think now that Finn might possibly be lying.

'So are we done talking about him? Those two deserve each other anyway – the high-maintenance princess and the hypocrite.'

'Funny, that's exactly what he said about us – deserving each other.'

'Well we do, don't we?' Finn said, oblivious to the bitterness in Valentine's voice.

He slurped down another oyster. Valentine took a large sip of wine and looked away. Finn had clearly decided the subject of Jack was now closed. 'So when am I going to meet Piers?'

Valentine shrugged. 'I'm not sure. It's very early days with us getting to know each other. Probably in a couple of months.'

'A couple of months!' Finn said in outrage. 'I was thinking more like next week! He's your father, V, and I'm your boyfriend!' Was he? That was news to Valentine. 'I should be introduced to him.'

Valentine didn't point out that he had never been bothered about meeting Chris. 'He's got a really full schedule,' Valentine replied. 'I'm not even sure when I'm seeing him.'

'Well, perhaps I could come along next time you see him,' Finn persisted.

'Finn, those meetings are about us trying to establish a bond – you know, father/daughter – trying to get to know each other.' God, he really was insensitive.

'Well, I can help with that' Finn blustered. 'It would probably make it less intense to have me there.'

'And this keenness to meet Piers has nothing to do with you hoping he might offer you some movie role?' She was feeling seriously pissed off with Finn now.

He laughed, but it was hopelessly unconvincing. 'Of course not V, my only concern is you.' He had juice on his chin from the oysters, which Valentine found infuriating.

She pointed at his mouth. 'You've got something there.'

Finn absently wiped his mouth with his hand, then leaned towards her. 'Shall we go? You know what a turn on I find oysters.'

Valentine thought about saying no, she had no particular desire to go to bed with Finn, but then she thought of Jack lying to her about Tamara. She stood up. 'What are you waiting for?'

'Oh God V, I'm close, yes, yes,' Finn was thrusting energetically into her and in the past she would have been right there with him. It wasn't as if he'd done anything different, in fact he'd actually gone out of his way to please her before himself (a first for Finn). But as he lay with his head between her legs she kept having flashbacks to him sucking at the oysters, which really wasn't going to hit the spot, so she put an end to that activity. And now she felt as if she was having an out-of-body experience, completely unmoved by his exertions. In fact, all she could think about was that she wished he'd bloody hurry up and get it over with. This had never happened before. She had always loved sex with Finn.

'Do that thing, babe,' he panted.

Fuck! Because she was feeling so angry with him she really didn't feel like doing that thing, not one little bit. Then again, if she did that thing it might speed it up. She slid her hands over his buttocks and, well, there was no other way of dressing this up – put her finger up his arse. Finn quivered at her touch and the thrusts got more intense, the groans deeper.

'Oh God, I'm coming . . .' One final pant and then he collapsed on top of her.

Halle-fucking-lujah, it was over.

'That was so good, V! You see, we do belong together.'

Valentine couldn't bring herself to answer. All she could think about was Jack shouting that she and Finn deserved each other.

It was a relief when he left the following morning. Ironically during the night he had been the one who had put his arm round her as they slept. All those times she had longed to be held by him and now she felt suffocated by his embrace. She managed to get out of seeing him that night, instead watching *Breakfast at Tiffany's* with Lily. Frank was out with his some of his musician friends, something that Valentine knew made Lily tense. Frank had been dry for five years, but it hadn't been easy and the people he was seeing tonight were all hard drinkers. The film was to distract Lily from worrying, but Valentine had forgotten how emotional the ending was – what with Holly Golightly abandoning her cat, which made Valentine cry and she didn't even like cats, then leaving Paul Varjak, the writer she was in love with, then the scene of them being reconciled in the pouring rain in Manhattan. But as Valentine cried, Lily remained resolutely dry-eyed. As the credits rolled to the haunting strains of 'Moon River' (the tune that had already made Valentine cry earlier on in the film) she turned to Lily and exclaimed, 'I can't believe you didn't cry.'

'Real life is so much more upsetting,' Lily replied. 'And anyway I prefer the book, which doesn't have a happy ending. So much more realistic.'

This wasn't like Lily; she was usually a hopeless

romantic. Valentine hadn't wanted to upset Lily by telling her about Finn's revelation about Jack. But as she appeared to be in a cynical frame of mind, Valentine thought she may as well.

'Jack was seeing Tamara before we broke up.'

Lily frowned. 'I don't believe it. Why do you say that?'

'Finn told me.'

'And he would have no vested interest in you thinking badly of Jack?' She sighed and said more gently, 'The last thing Finn would want is for you to be obsessing over Jack. V, sometimes you're very naïve.'

'Oh.' Suddenly Valentine wanted to end the conversation. It was too painful. She offered to make some tea.

Lily smiled and shook her head. 'Actually I think I'll have a small brandy while I wait for Frank. But you go to bed; you look exhausted.'

Valentine stifled a yawn. 'I'll stay up if you want me to.' The nights spent obsessing about Jack had taken their toll.

'No, no, I'll be fine. Frank said he would be back around midnight.'

Upstairs Valentine looked yet again at the production website of *King Lear*, which carried several photos of Jack. Googling Jack had become her new guilty and torturous pleasure – more pain than pleasure it had to be said. She read his reviews, which were just glowing. Jack was clearly destined to go far. But not even the less-than-glowing reviews of Tamara could cheer her up. She was on the rack.

She was just about to go to bed when she heard Frank banging on Lily's door and shouting. He sounded drunk. Oh God, poor Lily. Valentine padded downstairs, but as she opened the front door and looked down to the second-floor landing she froze, transfixed by the scene in front of her. A very drunk Frank was slumped against the wall with Lily beside him. Tears were coursing down his face. 'Don't leave me, Lily,' he kept saying over and over again. 'Please don't. I can't go on without you. We waited all this time to be together; don't leave me now.' Valentine didn't know whether to go to the couple or stay out of it. Was Frank saying these things because he felt guilty for getting drunk, or for some other reason? Lily didn't seem angry, more resigned. She caught sight of Valentine and mouthed, 'It's OK.' It didn't seem OK, but Valentine quietly shut the door and tiptoed upstairs, wondering what had triggered Frank's drinking. Then she reached for her phone and read through all the messages Jack had ever sent her. Was Lily right? Were happy endings unrealistic?

The following day she knocked on Lily's door before going swimming, but there was no reply – she was probably exhausted after her late night. As she walked back from the Porchester Centre after a mile of front crawl, Greta called. Piers had an unexpected window; could she meet him for a coffee? After establishing it was just going to be with Piers – she really didn't think she could face seeing Olivia and Saul – Valentine agreed to meet him at The Connaught in Mayfair. Its timeless elegance and air of wealth suited Piers – anywhere luxurious suited Piers, whereas Valentine felt like an imposter. This time, to her surprise, Piers hugged her in place of the usual handshake. He seemed less in control and less sure of himself than usual.

'Valentine, I do hope that Manchester wasn't too upsetting for you. I thought it about it afterwards and it must have been difficult seeing Jack with Tamara. I wanted to say that I'm really sorry that we put you in that position.'

'It wasn't a barrel of laughs,' Valentine replied, reluctant to divulge any more details.

Piers sighed. 'I think Olivia is finding the whole father/daughter thing very challenging. I know she hasn't been quite as welcoming as she might have been.'

Valentine was in no mood to contradict him.

'You've probably gathered that we couldn't have children. We tried every possible treatment.' He shook his head sadly. 'It took its toll, especially on Olivia. That's where her obsession with hygiene started.' Valentine had never seen this side of Piers; he was really opening up to her. His expression brightened. 'Which is why, for me, finding out about you has been so wonderful. Though I am mindful of all the wasted years. I keep looking at that photograph album you gave me. I so wish I'd known about you earlier.'

'Mum did write to you,' Valentine said gently.

'So you said; I just don't understand why I never received the letters. Anyway, I suppose it's pointless to dwell on the past; I want to think about our future.' He paused. 'I wondered if you might consider moving into

248

the flat at my Hampstead house for a while. At the moment my schedule is so manic and I feel I've hardly seen you.'

Valentine hadn't been expecting this. 'Won't Olivia mind?'

'I don't think so. I've taken things slowly and respected her feelings, but right now I'm more concerned about you and me.' He paused again. 'I would like to help you further your career and I know Olivia agrees with me on this. You'll have everything you need at your disposal – a personal shopper, a chef, a personal trainer.' He looked slightly awkward. Was this about establishing a relationship or getting Valentine to lose weight?

'Do you think I'm too fat to get on then?' she asked, feeling hurt. God! Wasn't it enough that her heart was broken? Now her own father thought she was fat.

'Not at all! I just want to help you. You know how ruthless the film industry is about size.'

'So you're offering me a place at Fat Camp?' Valentine retorted, still smarting from her interpretation of Piers's offer.

'Please, Valentine, I'm sorry if it sounded like that. I asked because I would like to see more of you.'

'Don't you mean you want to see less of me?'

Piers shook his head. 'It was Olivia who suggested the personal trainer. I think she was just trying to be helpful.'

Valentine doubted it, but even with the fat-camp angle, it was still quite a tempting offer. The flat was horribly empty without Lauren and maybe (though she didn't hold out much hope on this score) a change of scene would help her get over Jack, or at least distract her from thinking about him quite so obsessively. 'Can I think about it?'

'Of course,' Piers replied. 'Take as long as you want.'

Back home she knocked on Lily's door and this time she answered. She was still dressed in her pyjamas and not wearing a scrap of make-up, which was most unlike Lily, who usually was in full make-up from the moment she woke up. 'How's Frank?' Valentine asked.

'He's sleeping it off. He's just been to AA.' She sighed. 'It's going to take him a while to get back on track.'

'Why did he do it?' Valentine asked.

Lily shrugged. 'It just happens, but he'll be all right.'

'And what about you?' Valentine persisted. 'Are you all right?'

'Of course I am.' And before Valentine could press her further she changed the subject. 'Now tell me what you've been up to today. I haven't been out because of Frank and feel as if I've got cabin fever.'

Valentine quickly filled her in on Piers's offer, thinking that Lily was bound to tell her not to do it.

'What a fabulous idea! And Hampstead, how lovely to be by the heath in the summer. And it will give you more time to get to know Piers. I definitely think you should go.'

Valentine was taken aback; she hadn't expected this reaction, but if Lily thought she should, maybe she should. After all, she had nothing to lose. Right now the flat felt so full of memories, it would be good to go somewhere new. Her mum had the same reaction when she told her, as did Finn. In fact, Valentine could practically see him rubbing his hands in glee at the prospect of a luxury pad and a chance to network. Valentine still wasn't convinced. But then on her late-night Google she found a picture of Tamara and Jack leaving a restaurant in Manchester arm in arm. Maybe it was time to move on.

14

Hampstead Hell

As Valentine waited at the ferociously spiky gates of Piers's mansion for Ivana to buzz her in she wondered if she was doing the right thing. True, it would be good to spend more time with Piers and to get to know him better. He still seemed so different from her. If she hadn't had the results of the DNA test herself she doubted she could have believed that they were related. But there was also Olivia to contend with, and whatever Piers may have said, somehow Valentine doubted that she wanted her there. The gates slid open and Valentine picked up her case and walked towards the front door. Ivana opened it, as unsmiling as ever – maybe she hadn't forgiven Valentine for the deep clean.

'Good afternoon, Miss Fleming. Mr Hunter has asked me to show you to your new apartment.' She handed Valentine the regulation white cotton slippers. 'Now if you'll please follow me.' Valentine reached for her suitcase, but Ivana stopped her. 'Please leave. Sergei will do that.'

'Isn't Piers here?' Valentine asked, surprised that he wasn't there to meet her on her first day as she trailed after Ivana, who was marching briskly across the marble floor, quite a feat in the cotton slippers. No wonder Ivana had such over-developed calf muscles.

'Mr Hunter was called away unexpectedly with Mrs Hunter. They will be back in five days.'

'Oh.' Surprise turned to disappointment.

At the far end of the hallway a door led to the basement flat. 'You will also be able to access the flat from outside. I will show you later,' Ivana said as they went down the stairs and into a huge living room. It was furnished in a similar minimalist style to the upstairs living room, with far too much white for Valentine's liking, and it was just as chilly. She walked over to the heavily barred French doors that led out to the garden, intending to open them and let in some warmth. There was a sharp intake of breath from Ivana. 'Miss Fleming, none of these windows or doors must be opened; Mrs Hunter insists on it. There is air-conditioning and the temperature is strictly regulated. Also the air is filtered. And we had a break-in last year, so security is of the upmost importance.'

Suddenly Valentine felt extremely claustrophobic; she was an open-window kind of girl.

'Now please see this,' Ivana went on, sliding a panel on a white fitted cupboard to reveal row upon row of DVDs. 'These are all films that Mr Hunter recommends you should see.'

'Not all tonight,' Valentine joked, while Ivana stared at her blankly; she clearly didn't do humour.

'Of course not. It would take at least a month to see all of them.'

Ivana then led her to the bedroom, another vision in white, which reminded Valentine of a hotel room. Everything looked incredibly expensive and brand new, as if no one had ever lived here. It made Valentine feel profoundly ill at ease, as if she was in a show flat. Ivana showed her the kitchen next.

'These must be a bugger to keep clean,' Valentine joked, pointing at the shiny white units.

Ivana frowned. 'No, it is easy.' Though possibly no one had ever even boiled a kettle, never mind cooked in the cutting-edge but decidedly uncosy kitchen. Valentine had a sudden pang for her ramshackle Westbourne Park kitchen, yellow walls and all. The bathroom turned out to be a wet room with no bath – just a massive shower head in the middle of the room and floor-to-ceiling black marble tiles. There was no window. Valentine had a horror of bathrooms with no window. She also preferred baths. A long bath with a glass of red wine at the end of the day was one of her most favourite things. Showers just said 'morning' to her; they were too wash-and-go for her liking.

'Is there a bath?' Valentine asked hopefully.

'No bath. Mrs Hunter thinks they are unhygienic. And it is true.' Ivana suddenly sounded impassioned. 'All that wallowing in your own dirt and dead skin, like swine. Disgusting! Vile! Filthy!'

Valentine looked at her. Oh. My. God. The woman was deranged. Possibly she'd been breathing in too many chemicals from all the cleaning products she had to use to keep the house up to Olivia's exacting standards.

Ivana seemed to collect herself. 'I apologise, that was extreme. I just don't like baths.'

'Why not?' Valentine couldn't resist asking.

'I have my reasons,' Ivana replied mysteriously. 'Anyway, you like the apartment?'

'Yes, it's lovely,' Valentine lied, thinking that she must be the most ungrateful person in the world.

'There are just a few things you need to know. The apartment will be cleaned every day, with a complete change of linen and towels.'

Valentine interrupted her. 'Oh no, there's no need to do that! It's so environmentally unfriendly.'

Another frown from Ivana, who probably thought she was a filthy beast. 'Every other day if you prefer. You will be able to order food and drink from this list.' She handed a small booklet to Valentine. 'For tonight the chef has prepared you a salad. It is in the fridge. I understand that you are on a special diet, no?'

'Well, yes, I am trying to lose a little weight,' Valentine replied, slightly put out as she flicked through the menus.

Ivana nodded. 'Just so you know, we have been asked not to supply you with any items of unhealthy food.'

'Oh my God!' Valentine couldn't help exclaiming. 'So I *have* been sent to fat camp!' At size ten she was now the slimmest she had ever been. Did Olivia and Piers really believe that she had further to go?

Ivana frowned. 'Is not fat farm, is Mr Hunter's house. Mrs Hunter simply feels it is best to take temptation away.

255

It is the regime she herself follows. Also Kelly, your personal trainer, is arriving at eight tomorrow morning. If that is all I will leave you to get settled in.'

Valentine nodded, too stunned to speak. As Ivana padded silently to the door she turned and said, 'There is just one more thing. Mrs Hunter asks that you do not have red wine in the apartment. And of course no smoking.' Valentine had a sudden and powerful craving for a large glass of red wine and a cigarette.

It took less than ten minutes to unpack all her belongings. There didn't seem to be any bookshelves, so she had to stack her books on the white dressing table and almost immediately she felt comforted by seeing the familiar titles. Then she wandered into the kitchen and checked out the fridge. All it contained were rows of bottled water, wheatgrass, a bottle of champagne (now that looked promising) and the salad. *The tiny salad*, Valentine thought as she took it out of the fridge. She had often fantasised about having a personal chef to make her meals, but frankly if this was the best they could come up with, they could stick it. It was some kind of tuna salad, consisting mainly of a variety of leaves and fresh seared tuna. There didn't appear to be any dressing. Valentine only really liked tuna when it was smothered in mayonnaise and even though she was hungry she just picked at it. How very A-list of her.

She checked out the other cupboards, which contained a variety of healthy food and drink; miso, tofu, brown rice, green tea and aduki beans, absolutely nothing that she felt like eating. God, she needed a drink, but it was only four o'clock and it didn't seem appropriate to open the bottle of champagne, though if she and Lauren ever had any booze in the house they always drank it. Lauren declared that deferred gratification was for wimps. Valentine had imagined having a leisurely lunch with Piers and then going for a walk on Hampstead Heath for some more daughter/father bonding time. She sighed; she didn't feel comfortable enough in the apartment yet to curl up and read the Sunday papers and if she was honest the lack of fresh air was already bugging her. She was developing the itchy nose and scratchy-eyed feeling that air-con always gave her. She'd go out, have a coffee, get to know Hampstead – maybe go to the Everyman and see a film on her own. How very grown up.

But Hampstead on a Sunday afternoon did not improve her mood. Everyone was out with friends or family and as she strolled down the High Street she suddenly felt overwhelmed with loneliness. She reached for her phone and was about to call Lauren but realised it was eight in the morning in San Francisco and Lauren did not do mornings. She then tried Kitty, but her phone was switched off. Her mum was at work and Lottie was rehearsing a student production. So even though she was trying to break her dependency on Finn she called him, but got his voicemail too. She wandered into Caffè Nero and without thinking ordered a frappe latte. She was halfway through her favourite drink when she remembered she wasn't supposed to be drinking such calorific things. Bollocks! She really should leave half of it, but no, it was her favourite drink, and the salad really hadn't hit the spot – she'd work out

extra hard with the personal trainer. She carried on
drinking and just hoped that Olivia hadn't sent Ivana to
spy on her. She could just imagine Ivana stalking her with
a long-lensed camera, her thin lips pursing in disapproval
as she saw Valentine sipping her drink. Or maybe it was
the lack of food making her hallucinate. She finished the
latte, then walked up to the Everyman cinema.

Thank God the classic *An Affair to Remember* was on –
she really didn't think she was up to a double bill of
Tarkosvky. She relaxed for the first time that day as she
sank into one of the seats and the lights dimmed. Here at
least she didn't feel as if she was being judged; she could
even nip out for a box of popcorn or a Green and Black's
ice-cream and no one would notice. In fact she restricted
herself to popcorn (salted, fewer calories) and a glass of
red wine – a large glass and admittedly calorific, but red
wine was good for you, wasn't it? And as she wasn't going
to be able to drink it at home, she'd have to make up for
it when she was out. Valentine had expected the film to
be a bit of froth – all lovely nineteen fifties outfits and quips
between Deborah Kerr and Cary Grant. There were indeed
lovely fifties outfits, but what she hadn't bargained for was
quite what a tearjerker it was. It was so tragic! She didn't
know which was worse – the part where Terry, Deborah
Kerr's character, gets hit by a car on her way to meet Nickie
(Cary Grant's character) at the top of the Empire State
building and he thinks she doesn't love him anymore and
that's why she hasn't turned up; or the scene at the ballet
when they meet by chance and he doesn't realise that she
is paralysed from the accident as she is sitting down.

Valentine left the cinema feeling an emotional wreck, her state of mind accessorised by streaks of mascara. More wine was needed. She went into an off-licence on Hampstead High Street. There she had another pang of homesickness – there were no boys to fool around with, only a rather haughty-looking man. Nor were there any three-for-two offers. Valentine didn't recognise any of the wines and ended up buying a couple of bottles at around the six-pound mark. The haughty-looking man looked even haughtier; evidently Valentine had just purchased the wine equivalent of Diamond White.

Back at the apartment, Valentine opened one of the bottles of wine. In spite of the popcorn and the latte she was starving again. It was fortunate then that she had also bought a packet of pistachio nuts from the off-licence. She wandered aimlessly round the living room, not knowing what to do with herself. It was so quiet here. She was used to hearing the sound of traffic and people walking by. She felt sealed off from the world. *Now come on, where's your backbone?* She tried telling herself. *This is the perfect opportunity to get to know Piers and get in shape at the same time.* She walked over to the cabinet with the DVDs and looked through the titles. There were many that she had seen and many others that she knew she should – *Citizen Kane* for example. But she was so emotionally drained from *An Affair to Remember*, she really didn't feel up to watching anything else. She set up her laptop on the elegant glass table in the living room and let out a shriek of horror as she shifted it into position and managed to make a large scratch on the glass. Oh my God, could you French polish glass? Why did rich people always have such wildly impractical furniture? Was it just another way of flaunting their wealth? She took a large slug of wine to steady her nerves, hoping Ivana wouldn't notice the scratch, and switched on the computer. It was Google Jack time. She found an article detailing his relationship with Tamara, full of quotes from her about how Jack was her rock, her soulmate, how he completed her, blah blah blah. The celeb mag was in raptures over Jack's physique – *phwoar* just about covered it – and they'd printed a picture of him as Edmund, looking particularly manly, stripped to the waist. Even the celeb mag, which usually drooled over waxed chests, was quite taken with the hair.

She put her head in her hands; she couldn't bear to look anymore. She picked up her phone. Maybe she could text him, say well done again, open up some kind of communication with him, tell him about her worries over Lily and Frank. She got as far as selecting his name and then put the phone down again. In the end there was nothing for it but to go to bed. She couldn't face the power shower, even though the air-con was making her feel cold. She curled up in bed in her PJs and socks, holding on to Jack's T-shirt as if it were a talisman that could bring him back, but it was losing its scent; soon there would be nothing left.

She woke suddenly at one a.m. and for a few disorientated seconds couldn't work out where she was. It was so dark in the apartment and she was used to the comforting orange glow of the street light filtering through her curtains back home. The only sound was the monotonous click and hum of the air-con. She needed fresh air. Forgetting all about Ivana's warning, she padded into the lounge and opened the French doors and stepped outside. It was a beautiful night, a full moon holding court in the sky. She breathed in the air, relishing its sweetness and freshness after the recycled air of the apartment. This was what she needed − maybe she could ask Piers to let her have the air-con off.

She walked further into the garden, down some stone steps and on to the perfectly kept lawn − silvery green in the moonlight. Suddenly a spotlight was shone directly into her eyes, while a male voice shouted from behind her: 'Armed Response guard. Put your hands in the air and do not move!'

Fuck! 'But I live here,' Valentine protested, praying there weren't any Dobermanns lurking nearby. She'd never trusted them after seeing *The Omen*. She heard an ominous growl. She wondered if she could outrun the dog. She had been working really hard at her running. Any plans for escape went out of her head as the guard came into view, struggling to control a large and ferocious-looking Dobermann, which was straining at the leash and salivating at the prospect of sinking its teeth into Valentine.

'I don't know anything about that,' the guard replied. 'Stay standing right where you are.' The dog gave a backup growl and glared at Valentine with its devil eyes. The guard spoke into a walkie talkie: 'Black Knight to Queen of Diamonds, I have apprehended the intruder.'

'I'm not an intruder!' Valentine interjected, but Black Knight gave her such a look that she shut up. As he had a gun and a dog, it was probably better not to say anything to annoy him.

'The subject claims that she lives in the house; can you verify that?'

Scratchy, crackling sounds from walkie talkie, then a female voice, sounding suspiciously like Ivana: 'Does subject have wild curly auburn hair, green eyes, around five foot seven, a hundred and thirty-three pounds?'

'Excuse me!' Valentine forgot about the dog and the gun in her outrage. 'I did weigh a hundred and thirty-three pounds but now I weigh a hundred and twenty-six.' Though in all honesty after the latte, wine and nut combo of the day she was most likely back up to a hundred and thirty-three.

Black Knight took his time looking Valentine up and down, in a way she did not like one little bit.

'Roger that, Queen of Diamonds.' Nor did she like the way he emphasised the word 'Roger'.

More crackling, then, 'It is Miss Fleming; please escort her back to her apartment immediately. I will meet her there.'

Valentine had thought there could be no more fearsome sight than Ivana in her black and white uniform, topped off with her sucking-on-lemons expression, but it seemed there was – Ivana in a baby doll hot pink satin robe, matching slip and marabou-trim slippers. She obviously liked to feel off-duty when out of uniform. Valentine averted her eyes from the expanse of thigh. 'I do apologise,

Ivana. I didn't know that would happen. I just needed some fresh air; the air-con was bothering me.'

Ivana ignored her – she had eyes only for Black Knight, her usual expression replaced by a coy, girlish look. 'Thank you Black Knight, excellent work,' she simpered.

Black Knight simply bowed his head. He was no looker, with a straggly moustache and slightly bucked teeth, but he clearly rang Ivana's bell. 'I live to serve Queen of Diamonds.' And then he left. Valentine had an unpleasant thought – the pair of them were probably swingers. Uggh, it didn't bear thinking about.

Ivana turned her attention to Valentine and the sucking-on-lemons expression returned. 'Please do not open the door again.'

She paused as she walked out of the lounge and Valentine had a horrible feeling what was coming next. 'I will send the table away to be repaired. It is Lalique. I will get you another more suitable for your requirements. I won't say anything about the table if you do not say anything about these.' She pointed at the marabou-trim slippers.

Valentine nodded. She didn't know much about Lalique's work, she just knew it was expensive, very expensive. What a great start she had made living at Piers's house.

The following day didn't go any better. She overslept for the appointment with Kelly, the personal trainer. She had hoped for someone she could talk to honestly about her body and what she wanted to achieve – i.e. I am never going to be a supermodel – I just want to tone and tighten; starving myself does not make me happy. But she was presented with Kelly, a vision of athletic loveliness in hot pink Lycra shorts and a white vest. Her long shiny blonde hair was pulled back in ponytail and she had slim fake-tanned limbs, the pertest bum Valentine had ever seen, and abs of iron. Terminator Body, Valentine privately named her.

'So Olivia tells me you want to get down to an eight,' Kelly said, making notes on a clipboard as she looked at Valentine. They were standing on the lawn and Valentine was feeling highly self-conscious. She could have sworn that she saw Ivana watching her out of the window, clearly channelling Mrs Danvers from *Rebecca*.

Valentine shook her head. 'No, I don't think I can get to an eight; I'd like to be a very toned ten.'

'Now come on Valentine, of course you can get there!' Kelly was speaking like some kind of cheerleader; any minute she'd say *Go Valentine* and start kicking her legs up in the air and waving pom poms. 'It's all about setting goals.'

'OK,' Valentine said, deciding the best option was to humour Kelly.

'Great!' Kelly beamed at her. 'See, didn't it feel good saying that?'

No I lied, you pert-bummed moron.

'So this is the programme I suggest. We'll run eight kilometres today and build up to twelve by the end of the week. Next week we'll go from twelve to fifteen. After running we'll do weights and core training for a couple of hours.'

'Is that including or excluding the running?' Valentine asked with some trepidation.

'That's on top of the run.' Another beam from Kelly. 'So let's go inside to the gym and do a quick warm-up on the bike, then we can get going!'

Frankly Valentine felt knackered after the three-minute warm-up. She hadn't had breakfast and was feeling almost dizzy with hunger as they set off for the heath with Kelly talking all the way. After the first two kilometres Valentine stopped replying, and tried to tune Kelly out. It was just white noise in the background, Kelly droning on and on about how Valentine should visualise herself running on the beach in her ideal body shape, her ponytail swishing from side to side like a well-groomed horse's tail. *Yeah right*, thought Valentine, *like I'm going to be running on a beach! If I'm on a beach I want to be lying there drinking a beer!*.

'Piers runs ten k every other day,' Kelly informed her, just as Valentine thought she might have to stop; Kelly had made her run at a much faster pace than she did usually. 'So does Olivia, and then we do pilates for two hours. She has incredible stamina. She could be a good role model for you, Valentine.'

'She must be able to shoot cannon balls out of her vag after so much pilates work,' she couldn't resist saying and was rewarded with a completely baffled look from Kelly and then merciful silence.

Finally, hallelujah praise Jesus, the spiky gates came into view. Nearly there, Valentine urged herself on, nearly there. As soon as they got inside the gates she jogged to the lawn and collapsed in a heap. 'No no no! Don't let your heart rate slacken,' shouted Kelly, sprinting over to her. 'We'll just have some water and then on to the gym. Keep visualising that body, Valentine. It can be yours, but you've got to work for it!'

Someone else can have it, if this is what it takes, Valentine thought bitterly as Kelly had her doing squats, followed by an hour of weights and core exercises.

The morning of unmitigated pain at least had one benefit – it stopped her thinking about Jack. It had stopped her thinking about pretty much anything. Her mind was a blank, except for one thing – she was starving. The moment her session with Kelly finished she headed to her apartment to see what delicious lunch the chef had prepared. Sushi would be good; didn't lots of the stars eat that? She opened the fridge and pulled out a dish containing two jumbo prawns on a bed of wilted spinach. That didn't seem like nearly enough, especially since she had skipped breakfast. Then she noticed a note on the pristine marble work surface. 'Miss Fleming, as you will see lunch is less than it should be, owing to the pistachio nuts consumed last night. I'm sure you will be back on track by tonight. Regards, Ivana.' How did she know about the nuts? Valentine was aghast. She looked around the apartment. Was there CCTV in it? Or had Ivana gone through the bin? Valentine felt outraged by the invasion of her privacy and it wasn't just down to her low blood sugar levels. This was not reasonable behaviour. *Don't push me Ivana,* she thought. *Remember I know about the marabou-trim slippers.* Then again Ivana was staff – she was probably simply following orders from Olivia, who clearly thought she had a porker for a step-daughter. And was this the reason Piers hadn't told anyone about her? He was ashamed of owning up to being her father because he thought she was fat? She stomped into the wet room and took a shower. Yes, the water was hot and powerful, she gave it that, but it wasn't a pleasant experience. The black tiles made her feel as if she was in a coffin.

Piers no doubt expected her to be watching one of his recommended movies that afternoon; instead she met her aunt in Regents Park. As usual Lottie wasn't hard to spot – today wearing a turquoise satin prom dress, which was fighting a heroic battle to contain Lottie's full figure, purple footless tights and gold pumps. Lottie had come prepared with a picnic: a French stick, squishy brie and a bottle of red wine. She and her new boyfriend were about to go camping in the South of France and Lottie was getting into the spirit.

'So Jack hasn't called?' Lottie asked. She knew the whole story of the break-up and if she thought Valentine was a fool for what she did, she hadn't said so, for which Valentine was grateful.

She shook her head. 'He won't. I think he must hate me, Lottie. You should have seen how he was with me in Manchester.'

'Well in fairness you broke his heart. He was totally in love with you; we all thought that, even your mum, and you know she rarely comments on matters of the heart.'

Valentine groaned. 'Don't say that! I can't believe I

did what I did, but I was so convinced that he must be seeing Tamara.'

'Not all men are like that gutless bastard Finn,' Lottie replied, who knew that whole story now.

'I know that *now*,' Valentine replied. 'I'm supposed to be seeing Finn tonight; he's coming round to the flat. And in the past that's all I would have been thinking about all day. And now I'm not bothered and I don't even want to have sex with him. And that's all we ever used to do. In fact last time, and I'm sorry if this is an over-share, I had to fake it.'

'Well there's a saying – the fanny never lies,' Lottie replied, completely deadpan.

'What!' Valentine choked on her red wine.

'It's obvious. You don't fancy him anymore, and probably don't love him; that's why you don't want to have sex with him. The fanny never lies.'

'OK OK, you didn't need to say it again. Though maybe if I drink enough wine I won't care and it will be able to lie its way through.'

Lottie shrugged. 'Why would you want to?'

Valentine sighed and picked at the bread. 'I keep thinking of Jack saying that Finn and I deserved each other.'

'He only said it because he was so hurt. You don't deserve Finn – yes you made a mistake, but is Finn really the best you can do? He's all over you now, but I bet in a few months or maybe even a few weeks he'll revert to his gutless bastard behaviour.'

'Oh God, it's so depressing. Let's change the subject. Tell me about your holiday.'

As Lottie chatted Valentine tried to push thoughts of Jack and Finn away and just enjoy being with her aunt. But it was hard. Every time Lottie mentioned her new boyfriend her face lit up. Finn did not make Valentine feel like that anymore. By the time she met up with him that evening, she was feeling as unlit up as it was possible to be.

Finn was in a state of high excitement when she let him into the flat, though some of that diminished when he discovered Piers wasn't there. 'Can I have a tour of the house then?' he demanded.

'I think it would be weird without Piers here,' Valentine replied.

'Really?' Finn's lip curled petulantly. 'I'm sure he wouldn't mind; you are his daughter.'

'It's not him I'm worried about,' and Valentine quickly filled him in on Ivana and how she was sure she was snooping on her.

Finn had very little imagination, so his immediate reaction was that Valentine was being absurd. 'And anyway, V, isn't it a good thing that you're losing weight? You can have too much of a good thing.' He reached out and pinched her bottom.

'Thanks Finn,' Valentine said sarcastically. 'You always know exactly how to make me feel good about myself.'

'Oh come on, V! Don't be such a baby. So if you're not going to give me a tour of the house, what are we going to do?' He stretched back on the sofa, his T-shirt riding up and revealing an expanse of brown perfect skin, a line of hairs running from his naval into his Armanis

– a sight that usually she found such a turn on. Now she just thought, *Put it away!* He looked at her meaningfully. He obviously knew what he wanted to do. It was the last thing Valentine wanted to do. A chasm seemed to have opened up between her and Finn. Was Lottie right? Did the fanny never lie?

'I need a drink,' she mumbled, getting up from the sofa. She wandered into the kitchen and grabbed the bottle of champagne. She didn't particularly want it but neither did she think she was up to sex with Finn sober. But as she walked back into the living room, she suddenly thought, *Why am I doing this? Why am I going to have sex with him if I don't want to?* It was like a lightbulb turning on in her head: *I don't want to have sex with him, and so I am not going to have sex with him. And Lottie is right, the reason I don't want to have sex with him is* – now the lightbulb had turned into an enormous flashing neon sign, worthy of Las Vegas – *because I DON'T LOVE HIM ANYMORE!*

'Champagne! The good stuff, way to go V,' Finn exclaimed from the sofa. 'I could get used to this lifestyle, and isn't this apartment great? I love the minimalist look.'

'I don't like it actually,' Valentine replied, putting the champagne down on the replacement glass table.

'Shall I open the champagne?' Finn asked, not appearing to hear Valentine's comment – but that was Finn all over, he only ever really heard what he wanted to hear.

'No,' Valentine replied. 'Actually it would be best if you left.' She had his attention now.

'Why?' he demanded. 'I thought we were going to spend the night together.'

'Finn, it's over,' she said.

'What is?'

'Us.'

'What, because I said it wouldn't be a bad thing if you lost more weight?' He laughed. 'You've got a great body, but there's always room for improvement.'

'Not because of that comment, although that is symptomatic of what you think of me, but because . . . She paused for a beat, wondering how best to put it and then decided that being direct was the only possible way. 'I don't love you anymore.' There, she'd said it. She felt suddenly light as a feather, her spirits lifting as if she'd just drunk a glass of bubbly.

Finn was frowning now. 'Don't piss around V, of course you love me and I love you. We are meant to be together, you know that.'

She shook her head, 'No we're not, Finn; it's over. I don't love you anymore.'

Finn's face had gone through shock, disbelief and now anger was taking over. 'Are you seeing him again?' he demanded.

'I suppose you mean Jack, and no, I'm not. I just don't love you anymore.' Now she couldn't stop saying it; she wanted to shout it from the rooftops.

'Well who are you fucking seeing then?' Finn clearly couldn't imagine ending a relationship without the replacement already lined up.

'No one. I don't love you anymore.'

He stood up. 'I fucking heard you the first time! Well don't fucking come crawling back to me, V. If I go now, that's it.' He stood waiting for her to change her mind and when she didn't say anything, he grabbed his jacket and stormed towards the door. A comical sight it had to be said, as he was wearing the compulsory white cotton slippers and it was hard to have any kind of dignity in them. When he reached the door he suddenly realised he was wearing them and pulled them off and threw them on the ground in disgust. He slammed the door shut behind him.

Valentine waited to be seized by a storm of emotion, waited for the feelings of regret to envelop her, but there was nothing. She felt completely calm. She opened the bottle of champagne and poured herself a glass.

15

Brief Encounter

The following day she fully expected to regret her actions, but found she felt nothing of the sort. The only sense of loss she had, which had become her familiar companion these last weeks, was entirely to do with losing Jack. Nothing whatsoever to do with Finn. By the end of the week she remained certain that she had made the right decision. Instead of wallowing in an emotional quagmire she was focusing on herself, on catching up with friends, going to the theatre and getting fit. She was actually quite enjoying the personal training sessions, though the temptation to strangle cheerleader Kelly was very strong at times. Food was another matter – the portions had continued to be minuscule and several times Valentine had to supplement them with secret trips to Pret, but on the whole she had stuck to the diet. On the Friday she was feeling particularly proud with herself for having run fifteen kilometres with Kelly. She was sunbathing by the pool and feeling quite OK, until a shadow fell across her face. She opened her eyes to discover toady Saul standing by the lounger, dressed in his regulation chinos.

'Hello, Valentine. I wondered if I could have a word?'

'Sure,' Valentine replied, reaching for her robe. She wasn't going to have a conversation with loathsome chinos toad in her bikini. 'Outside or in?'

'Here is fine,' Saul replied, sitting down on the adjacent lounger. He was wearing sunglasses and Valentine couldn't see his eyes – always disconcerting when you were dealing with someone like Saul. She reached for her own dark glasses – two could play at that game. 'I've been asked to run some paperwork by you. It's all very straightforward. You may remember that Piers asked that you keep the matter of his paternity confidential?'

She nodded, wondering where this was leading.

'And you said that you had only told your mother, your aunt and your then boyfriend, Jack Hart.'

'I do remember my ex-boyfriend's name,' Valentine bit back. She was not feeling quite so OK anymore.

'I'll get to the point. The lawyers have advised that you and anyone else you have told about your relationship with Piers should sign a confidentiality agreement.'

He handed her a document and with a feeling of disbelief Valentine flicked through the pages. It was written in highly legal language and was hard to follow, but she got the gist. She was to sign, shut up and if she did speak to the press there was the threat of legal action against her. A growing feeling of outrage was building up inside her. Did Piers really expect her to sign this? What about trust and integrity?

'See, it's all very straightforward isn't it?' Saul pulled out a pen from his jacket and offered it to her.

Valentine shook her head. 'I'm not signing this; I'll give my reasons to Piers in person.'

'Oh come on, Piers is very busy; that's why he delegated the task to me. You really don't want to piss him off.' Saul's arrogant drawl thoroughly set her teeth on edge.

Resisting the temptation to tell him to fuck off, she got up from the lounger with as much dignity as she could muster, wrapping her robe tightly around her. 'If you'll excuse me, I've another appointment.' Dignified, moral high-ground intact, Valentine turned to go.

'I meant to say Valentine, you're looking really good. The new fitness plan must be really paying off.'

Valentine wasn't prepared for the compliment; was this Saul's way of wrongfooting her? She turned back round and glared back at him. 'I wondered if you wanted to go out for dinner sometime.'

Ha! Did the chinos toad really think he was in with a chance? 'Thanks for the offer, Saul, but I'm really busy at the moment and as you know I'm on a diet.'

Saul's lip curled. Clearly he didn't like being turned down. 'Olivia wants to see you. She's expecting you in the living room.' Olivia had returned two days earlier without Piers and this was the first time she'd asked to see Valentine. *Just keep walking,* Valentine told herself. It was only when she was inside her apartment that she gave vent to her feelings.

'It's fucking outrageous!' she shouted, not caring if Ivana had got a hidden CCTV camera trained on her.

Valentine hated feeling as if she'd been summoned, but nonetheless she quickly changed into a black sun dress and put on a dash of red lipstick to give her confidence. Then she went upstairs, choosing not to wear the white slippers as a small gesture of defiance. Olivia was sitting on the white leather sofa looking effortlessly chic, in a white trouser suit. She gave a smile that did not reach her eyes.

'Valentine, do come and sit down.' Then she noticed Valentine was barefoot. 'Oh you've forgotten the slippers I see; let me ring Ivana for some more. It's one of the very few house rules.' Her own feet were clad in a pair of pale-gold ballet pumps. Clearly only guests and staff had unhygienic feet. She languidly got up from the sofa and pressed the intercom by the door, asking Ivana to bring replacement slippers. 'So, how's the fitness regime going?'

Valentine shrugged. 'OK I suppose.'

'I know it's only early days, but I am a little surprised you haven't lost more weight.'

At this point Valentine could only think it was just as well Olivia hadn't had a daughter, as she probably would have been one of those ghastly women who put their daughters on diets from the age of five.

'I have been working hard with Kelly,' she replied, wondering why she was justifying herself to Olivia. Though she supposed it would be unforgivable to tell her father's wife to fuck off.

'But not doing quite as well with the diet,' Olivia persisted. 'You've been drinking.'

'Well there was a bottle of champagne left in the fridge, I didn't think alcohol was banned, so I drank that and the odd glass of wine.' Valentine said defiantly.

'Bottle, I think,' Olivia corrected her. She sighed as if Valentine had let her down. 'Piers would never say this to your face, but he does think you need to get into better shape if you're to have any chance in movies. And he really does want to help you, but he has his own reputation to think of.' Another sigh. 'I'm sorry, but I do believe that in our profession brutal honesty is the best course. The bottom line is you have to lose more weight. Look at someone like Tamara. Her figure is really what you should be aiming for.'

Valentine was struggling to remember if she had ever been so insulted in her life. 'Tamara is a completely different build from me! I'm never going to look like her unless I get dysentery and don't treat it, and I'm sure we'd both agree that isn't a good look!' But it was hard to stay strong in the face of Olivia's assault on her self-esteem.

'I'm just being honest,' Olivia repeated, as if that excused everything. 'So let's talk about the premiere of Piers's film next week. It will be your first red-carpet event I presume?'

Valentine nodded, not trusting herself to speak.

'Greta will take you shopping for a dress. Piers wants to treat you to something special. So just work a little harder on the dieting; I am sure you want to make Piers proud when he sees you at the premiere.'

'Well I'm not going to show him up, if that's what you mean! Even though no one actually knows that I am his daughter. I hadn't realised that Piers was ashamed to acknowledge me! But with the confidentiality agreements and our little chat I'm beginning to wonder!' Valentine said with feeling.

For the first time in their conversation Olivia looked a little rattled. 'I'm sorry if I upset you – please don't mention any of this to Piers. He really can't have any conflict in the run up to his premiere. He's under a huge amount of pressure.'

'Of course I don't want to upset him!' Valentine exclaimed, getting up from her seat – as far as she was concerned the meeting was over and she wasn't going to wait for Olivia to dismiss her. She paused at the door, 'I will persevere with the training programme and cut down on the alcohol, but I will do that for myself and not to fit in with someone else's perception of what I should look like.' And without waiting for Olivia's reply she left the room.

Even though she was furious with Olivia she made a conscious effort in the week before the premiere to stick to a strict exercise regime and diet. The premiere would be the first time she would actually see Piers since she had moved in, as he'd been tied up with some budget meeting in LA. So much for father/daughter bonding. On top of the dieting and the exercise, she had a facial, manicure, pedicure, waxing, highlights and a subtle spray tan. The extensive preparations had been like having a full-time job – it was just as well she wasn't acting at the moment. The afternoon of the premiere itself was completely given over to hair and make-up – she and Olivia both had their personal team. They had avoided each other since the meeting. It was probably better that way.

Valentine actually enjoyed getting ready; it was like dressing up for a part in a play. She'd managed to book Dixie as her make-up artist and the two girls had a great gossip as Dixie worked on her face. Nicky, the hairdresser, was a sweetie who achieved an amazing up do with her hair, but as it took him at least two hours it was not something Valentine planned on repeating. Then it was time to get into the Spanx and put on the dress. And oh my God, what a dress! It was a red evening gown by Valentino, simply stunning. Valentine had never worn anything so expensive before. She half-expected the heavens to open and for a booming voice to declare, 'Valentine Fleming, remove that dress at once! You are not worthy!' Dixie helped zip her in and was generous in her compliments. 'Are you sure it looks OK?' Valentine asked, anxiously surveying herself in the mirror, experiencing a sudden pang for Lauren.

'Fab. You look totally A-list. You've got star quality, Valentine.'

Valentine laughed. It was an outrageous compliment and only to be expected from a make-up artist. Just then there was a knock at the door and after she'd called out 'Come in,' Piers and Olivia walked in the room. Piers looked very handsome in his black tie. It was the first time they had seen each other for several weeks and Valentine was feeling quite nervous. Olivia was playing her ice-queen role to perfection in white silk. Valentine's heart sank at the thought of their verdict. She breathed in an extra notch and thanked God for Spanx. 'So will I do?' she asked, sounding more confident than she felt.

'Valentine, you look beautiful!' Piers had finally given her a compliment.

'So I won't let you down on the red carpet?'

Piers looked puzzled. 'Of course not! You look incredible, doesn't she Olivia?' It was with some effort that Olivia nodded.

Valentine was so astonished and pleased at the warmth of Piers's comments that she impulsively kissed his cheek in gratitude.

'Valentine!' Olivia hissed. 'What did you do that for! She turned to Piers, 'Darling, quickly go to the bathroom.'

'It's no problem, Olivia,' Piers told her, looking rather embarrassed at Olivia's reaction. He then lowered his voice and said, 'I thought your OCD wasn't so bad lately.' But Olivia was rubbing at the spot Valentine's lips had touched and then practically frogmarched Piers out of the room.

Valentine's faux pas with the kiss made for a frosty limo ride to the premiere at Leicester Square. Olivia practically ignored Valentine, apart from whispering, 'You know Piers could really have done without that incident.'

It was just a display of affection, Valentine felt like saying. *Remember what that felt like?* But her relationship with Olivia was rocky enough at the best of times without her defending herself. She looked away from Olivia and straight into the cold grey shark eyes of Saul, which she was appalled to notice had a lecherous gleam in them as he looked her up and down. Please let the chinos toad not fancy her! They were approaching Leicester Square now and Valentine couldn't believe the crowds pressing against the crash barriers, clamouring to get a glimpse of the stars. She was tempted to shout out, 'Get a life! These people are nothing special, they're just like you. But no doubt Olivia would have had her shot on the spot – Olivia really did not think she was like anyone else.

Piers was first out of the limo and while he was caught up with talking to one of the stars on the red carpet Olivia whispered, 'Valentine, you'll remember not to make any comment to the media about being Piers's daughter, won't you? And did your mother, aunt and ex-boyfriend sign those confidentiality agreements? We really don't want any stories leaking out to the press.'

Valentine tried to keep her cool. 'There's no need to get anyone to sign anything, I've asked them to keep it quiet and I trust them.'

'Hah!' Olivia exclaimed in shocked disbelief. 'You are so naive! Do you know what a big story this would be to the press and how much money they would be prepared to pay for it?'

'Neither my mum, my aunt or Jack would sell a story to the press,' Valentine insisted quietly. 'They're not those kinds of people.'

'Oh right, because they're all wildly successful and don't need the money,' Olivia shot back sarcastically.

'Money isn't everything,' Valentine replied, but now Olivia was getting out of the limo and into a volley of camera clicks and flashes.

'You really must get them to sign the papers,' Saul added. 'It will be easier all round.'

Easier for who? Valentine felt like saying, knowing that her mum and Lottie would be incredibly hurt if she presented them with such a document, which would be tantamount to saying that she didn't trust them. And she couldn't imagine what Jack's reaction would be. Olivia and Piers were already way ahead of them on the red carpet, pausing every now and then to be photographed. The press weren't interested in screenwriters, even very successful screenwriters like Saul, so Valentine and Saul walked up the red carpet without being photographed. Valentine concentrated on walking as elegantly as possible in the evening dress, wanting to make a good impression, but she couldn't help wondering again why Piers was still so reluctant to name her as his daughter. It wasn't as if she had asked for any of his massive fortune. Maybe it was down to Olivia; perhaps she felt threatened by Valentine? Whatever the reason Valentine wished the situation could be resolved. She felt as if she was in limbo, waiting for something to happen.

In the star-studded foyer – here a Sienna Miller, there an Orlando Bloom, but alas no George Clooney – Valentine realised that she'd forgotten to get a picture of herself in the dress, and she'd promised her mum. She scrabbled for her phone in her Chanel clutch bag (another gift from Piers, after Olivia had seen the vintage gold bead bag she had planned to take and vetoed it – she probably thought vintage was unhygienic). 'Saul, please could you take a picture of me?'

Saul looked taken aback at the request. 'This isn't really the place, Valentine,' he replied huffily. 'It makes you look like a tourist, and you're supposed to belong here, remember?'

'Take a chill pill Saul, it's just a picture,' Valentine replied. Saul was the last person she wanted to ask a favour of, but needs must. 'I could always ask someone else if you think it's such a big deal.'

'Don't draw attention to yourself,' Saul shot back. 'Just give me the fucking phone.' She handed him her mobile and he furtively took the shot, barely giving Valentine time to pose, then tossed it back at her. She checked the image and saw to her dismay that he'd only got her head and shoulders. He was such a git.

'Saul, you haven't got the whole dress,' she started saying, but Saul's attention had been claimed by another guest and she was left standing there holding her phone and feeling self-conscious, even though she knew for a fact that Piers had asked him to look after her. She scanned the crowd looking for Piers, then realised that she had no reason to seek him out. What was she supposed to do now? She'd never been to a film premiere before and had no idea of the etiquette. She didn't know anyone. Should she go and introduce herself to some people or should she just stand here like a lemon? Albeit a lemon in a very expensive dress.

'Well, well, Valentine Fleming.'

Oh my God, it couldn't be, could it? She spun round at the sound of the familiar voice – adrenalin pumping through her along with that tiny flicker of hope because there standing in front of her was Jack. He looked devastatingly sexy in black tie, his dark-brown hair cut shorter than the last time she'd seen him. Valentine felt suitably devastated. Even in the tightly fitted Spanx Jack had an impact and Valentine was reminded of Lottie's saying.

'Here with Daddy, I see,' he continued, dryly.

'He doesn't want anyone to know yet, so promise you won't say anything.' She couldn't bring herself to mention the confidentiality contract.

Jack shrugged. 'What's the big deal, aren't you good enough for him? Though I see he's got you dressing the part.' He whistled as he took in the Valentino dress. 'Not sure about the hair, though. It's a bit First Lady, isn't it?'

'Oh.' Instinctively Valentine put a hand up to her hair. Jack had always liked her to wear it down, as wild as possible, but Ivana had told her that Olivia had a phobia about finding stray hairs anywhere near her and had asked that Valentine always wear her hair tied back in her company.

'And have you got fake tan on?'

'I might have.'

'Be careful Valentine, it's a thin line to becoming one of the orange people.'

Valentine looked at her arms in alarm. No way was she orange; she had a sunkissed glow, damn him. To hide her discomfort she changed the subject. 'So why are you here?'

'I'm here with Tamara.'

Wham, that was a blow. The flicker of hope went out again. Valentine had hoped by now the novelty of Tamara would have worn off.

'And Piers invited me.' Jack curled his lip dismissively. 'He seems to want to offer me a role in his next movie. *Big wow.*'

Valentine was stung by Jack's disdain, even though she knew he had always preferred art house over block-busters. 'You don't have to audition,' she answered. 'There are plenty of other actors out there who would jump at the chance of working for my—' she lowered her voice to a whisper – 'dad. His films are very successful. Don't be such a snob because they're main-stream. Not everyone can be Alejandro González Iñárritu!' She stumbled over the pronunciation of one of Jack's favourite directors.

'That's not the reason. Piers's films are so crushingly predictable, where the actors get to show the emotional range of fish.' He paused. 'So, are you here with Finn?'

She shook her head. 'I did see him for a while, but then we broke up. For good.'

Jack gave a bitter laugh. 'So he went off with his other girlfriend, did he? I could have predicted that one.'

'Actually I broke up with *him*,' Valentine replied, not at all liking Jack's tone of voice.

'Well that's probably the best thing you've ever done. Pity it all came too late in the day.'

She was shocked and hurt by the venom in his voice. He sounded as if he hated her. She was about to reply when he said, 'There's Tamara. I'd better go. Enjoy the film, Valentine.'

Stung as she was by Jack's words and by his tone, she knew she couldn't be that surprised. She had hoped that by now he might have been feeling more forgiving, but clearly this was not the case. Nonetheless she spent the time before the film started scanning the vast auditorium for him, still longing to see him.

'Stop looking around,' Saul hissed. 'It's so uncool to be star-spotting here.'

She ignored him. She couldn't see Jack anywhere, but Piers was sitting several rows in front. 'Why aren't we on the same row as Piers?' she asked.

Saul rolled his eyes at her naivety, and said bitterly, 'I'm only the writer, remember. I'm surprised they asked me along at all.' Valentine didn't add *you're one of the writers*, because it had taken ten of them to put together the screenplay.

A sudden hush fell in the auditorium as the lights dimmed and the midnight-blue velvet curtains rippled back revealing the huge screen. Usually Valentine loved going to the cinema and losing herself in the drama, but right now she knew she had to concentrate one hundred per cent on the film, so she could come up with something penetrating and intelligent to tell Piers afterwards. It was an action movie – Piers's speciality – set way in the future, when the earth had been decimated by global warming, and invaded by aliens, who had enslaved the surviving humans. Naturally only one man could save mankind and defeat the alien hordes. She so wanted to see the good in it, but it was devoid of humour and nuance, *Die Hard* minus the comedy and great one-liners. Halfway through, Valentine felt her concentration waning. She was in the uncomfortable position of agreeing with Jack – the actors only got to show a fraction of what they could do. But they were showing more range than fish, she decided; it was more like the range cats would show. To entertain herself she recast the film with cats. The hero would be half pedigree, making him sleek and arrogant, and half moggy, making him streetwise and fearless. The heroine would be Siamese, pretty and pampered with bewitching blue eyes and the villains would be white Persians, all with one green eye, one blue, a shocking cat stereotype she knew, but what the heck. She was in formulaic hell.

'Why are you smiling?' Saul hissed in her ear. 'This is supposed to be the really emotional part.'

Oops, Valentine had been trying to imagine if a cat would be able to work the controls of an Uzi automatic while before her the hero lay dying, shot so many times that surely he had no chance of surviving. The heroine was cradling his head in her hands, tears raining (she was watching clichés, she sure as hell could use them) down on his face as she told him she was pregnant. This was unusual in Piers's films – the hero never died, but credit to him for breaking the pattern; she'd have to remember to mention that. Then again not, as the hero's unfeasibly blue eyes opened and he croaked, 'I'm going to be there for my son.' Not dead at all. In fact the door was wide open for a sequel.

Cheers and wild applause rose up from the auditorium as the credits rolled. Valentine turned to Saul. 'That was brilliant,' she tried to say with as much sincerity as she could muster, conscious of how fake she sounded.

'Do you think so?' Saul asked anxiously, temporarily not his usual confident, poisonous-toad self.

Valentine knew only too well from her own acting career that after any performance you *always* said the person was marvellous, even if they weren't, and left the savaging to the critics. She figured the same rule applied to the film world. 'Absolutely,' she continued. 'That's going to be such a huge hit.'

'What?' he looked horrified. 'Did you say pile of shit?'

Valentine resisted the urge to giggle. 'Of course not, I said huge hit!'

The after-film party was being held in the ballroom of one of the swish hotels lining Hyde Park. It had been dressed to look like a desert in homage to the film. Sand, about a metre deep, had been scattered all over the floor, which was frankly annoying as it made walking in heels difficult and waiters had to keep rescuing guests whose heels had got stuck. There were huge artificial palm trees with girls in skimpy silver bikinis performing trapeze acts from them while silver-suited waiters – no doubt intended to mimic the aliens' silver skin – handed out champagne. Valentine quickly noticed that she was the only guest who ever seemed to thank them. She'd done her share of wait-ressing and had vowed never to treat waiters badly. She wanted to have a wander around and see if there just might be someone she recognised, but Saul gave her strict instructions to stay with him. 'I don't need babysitting,' she told him petulantly.

'Piers wants us to stay together,' was Saul's answer. So she was forced to stand at Saul's side, smiling supportively while people congratulated him on the film. Inevitably, after the guest had heaped enough praise on Saul, they would ask her the question dreaded by struggling actresses the world over: 'So what are you in at the moment?'

'I'm between projects,' she replied, smiling fixedly, and would see the instant waning of interest in the other person's eyes.

Sometimes they would go on to ask an additional question. 'So what movies have you been in?'

'Oh I've only been in one film; I'm not sure if you would have seen it. It was only shown at film festivals,' Valentine would reply. And that would be the final nail in the coffin of the conversation, and they would make their excuses and go off and talk to someone way more interesting and higher up the food chain.

'These people make me feel so worthless,' Valentine said bitterly to Saul after she'd endured another such conversation.

'Well you don't exactly sell yourself, do you?' Saul replied nastily and for a second Valentine almost felt like telling him what she had really thought of the film. But then Piers and Olivia joined them.

'So what did you think?' Piers asked.

Valentine took a deep breath and launched into her

carefully prepared speech. 'I thought it was amazing! Such a powerful film with such strong themes about life and death and survival and identity. It was an epic really, wasn't it?' She knew she was gushing, but she really wanted to impress Piers.

'Good, good,' he replied, nodding in agreement. 'I'm glad you got all that. Did you pick up where I was influenced by Bergman? Anyway, we can talk about this tomorrow in more detail; I've got a window after my training session with Kelly. Shall we discuss it over breakfast? And I really want to talk about your career Valentine. I definitely want you to have a part in my next film.'

Valentine was simultaneously thrilled at the prospect and horrified at the thought of having to come up with something else to say about the film. It really had been the most dreadful load of predictable bollocks. And what the hell had been the Bergman influence? She took a super-sized sip of her champagne. Hopefully there would be some reviews already up on the net and she would be able to glean something from them. She looked round the room, half-hoping, half-dreading that Jack would be there. Saul and Piers were chatting to a journalist, Olivia was deep in conversation with the very good-looking hero of the film, and she was left feeling like a lemon again.

Suddenly she caught sight of Jack and Tamara walking towards them. She noticed that Tamara didn't look quite so polished as usual – she had bags under her eyes, her usually glowing skin looked sallow and she seemed to have lost even more weight. What was that about? Valentine wondered. As Tamara went into raptures over the film to Piers (she hadn't lost her ability to be really annoying), Jack stood at her side looking moody. He caught Valentine's eye and moved next to her. 'Shall I tell you what the reviews will say tomorrow?' he whispered in her ear. 'They'll all say that it was a turkey. No, that's too generous; it was a Turkey Twizzler.'

She turned to him. 'Shut up! It was not! It had all these really strong themes in it, and had so much to say about the planet. I think it will be a classic. Didn't you pick up on the Bergman influence?'

'You know that's bollocks,' Jack replied, smiling at her feeble attempts. It was the first time he'd smiled at her since the break-up.

'Come on, let's go outside and talk. I can't hear myself think with so much sycophantic crap flying around.'

Maybe this was the moment Jack was going to tell her that he'd made a huge mistake and that he wanted her back. Her heart did the crazy racing thing as she followed him out of the room, the small flicker of hope reignited. Seeming to know exactly where he was going, Jack led her down the long corridor and into an empty conference room.

'So Fleming, have you missed me then?' Jack asked once they were inside. His question definitely sounded promising, even flirtatious and he'd called her Fleming, as he always used to when they were flirting.

'You can't ask me that when you've just been so horrible to me!' she protested. She leaned against the wall and tried to act cool, doing her best Greta Garbo 'I want to be alone' impression, while inside her thoughts were tumbling round, with the answer: God yes, I've missed you, I miss you so much that sometimes I can't bear it. Do you know I still sleep with your T-shirt and I still can't drink coffee because it reminds me of you and how you always had to drink coffee in the morning. And I'll never be able to watch *The English Patient* again.

'I'm sorry I was rude earlier. I guess it was just the shock of seeing you again. But you haven't answered my question. Have you missed me, Fleming?'

'Have you missed me?' she countered.

He moved in closer. 'What do you think?' He was so close his lips were almost brushing against hers. She got a hit of Eau Savage, always her favourite, and he gently ran his hands along her bare arms, sending fireworks of anticipation shooting down her spine all the way into her Spanx. She instinctively moved closer to him so their bodies were touching, willing him to kiss her. As if he had read her mind his lips were on hers and they were kissing, opening the floodgates of memory and desire in her. She wanted him so badly. He broke away from kissing her lips to kiss her neck and shoulders, slipping down the thin straps of her dress. Desire made her reckless; she didn't care that anyone could walk in on them. She returned his caresses, undid his shirt buttons, ran her hands over his chest, his flat, hard abs and lower still. *God*, this was going to be like that really intense scene in *The English Patient* when Katharine and Almásy have slipped away from a party to make love. So long as she didn't end up trapped in a dark cave on her own to die, with only a notebook and tinned meat for company – Valentine knew she wouldn't have come up with such poetic musings as Katharine had in her final hours – more like *Help! I don't want to die!* And she hated corned beef. Though true enough, she wasn't quite sure how they would negotiate the passion-killing control pants. Nothing mattered except how good kissing Jack felt and feeling his body against hers. But suddenly, just as Valentine was wondering if she could race to the bathroom and take off the Spanx before resuming activities – whatever Hugh Grant's character in *Bridget Jones' Diary* had said about them, they really were not a turn on – Jack abruptly pulled away.

'What's the matter?' Valentine asked, disconcerted by the change.

'I just remembered I had to be somewhere else.' His voice was clipped and cold.

'What d'you mean?' Valentine, suddenly aware of how much of her body was on display, quickly pulled up her straps.

He gave a small smile that didn't reach his eyes and said, 'That was just a taste of what you've been missing all this time.'

She looked at him in dismay. He hadn't wanted her at all; this had just been about humiliating her and getting some kind of revenge. It was so needlessly cruel, so unlike Jack.

He started walking out the door; then he turned back and said, 'I miss the old Valentine. Do you want to know why I stopped just then? I realised I didn't even know you anymore. You obviously love this kind of world, and seem to fit right in, but it's not for me. And you can tell Daddy dearest that I'm not interested in working for him, not now, not ever.'

Valentine watched him go, willing herself not to cry. *He's not worth it*, she tried to tell herself, but her words sounded so hollow, because yes he was worth it – Jack Hart was definitely worth it. She had been the one to blow it; she blinked back the hot tears. All she wanted to do now was go home, but how would she explain that to Piers? *Oh sorry, I just ran into my ex, nearly had sex with him but then he rejected me.* She spent a few minutes redoing her make-up, wincing at the sight of her flushed cheeks and swollen lips. Then she walked slowly back into the ballroom, trying to locate Piers. She had to accept once and for all that Jack belonged to the past. So why then as she looked around her, did she long for him? And not just him – suddenly, as she looked around at the famous faces, the lavish decor, the extravagant food and drink, she was overcome with longing for all of her old life. She wished she was back in her old flat giggling over a bottle of red wine with Lauren, Lily and Frank rather than standing here and sipping vintage champagne in her designer evening dress. She didn't belong here and she didn't want to either, even if there was a film role for her.

16

A Break

'Darling! I think you may be finally up for the part that could be the making of you!' It was Sylvia, her agent, in full flow.

'What is it?' Valentine realised that she was required to speak, even though all she wanted to do was crawl back to bed. It was the morning after the premiere. In the aftermath of her encounter with Jack Valentine had drunk a lot of vintage champagne. In fact she'd probably consumed an entire two days' worth of calories, Olivia had informed her when Piers was out of earshot. Valentine had simply drunk another glass as her answer; it seemed like the only way to deal with what Jack had said to her.

'It's the female lead in a major new TV drama about a private detective agency in London. A kind of British *Moonlighting* if you like. Yes, yes I know it was way before your time, but google it and you'll see what I mean. Lots of simmering sexual tension between you and your partner. Gorgeous. You're the Cybill Shepherd type character who runs the agency. I know you will be absolutely

perfect. It's a bit like *Spooks*; you know, all sexy slick
production values, plenty of gadgets and a scrumptious
male actor – think Rupert Penry-Jones meets James
McAvoy – but obviously not them as they're looking for
someone new.

'Did Piers line this up for me?' Valentine asked
suspiciously.

'Who, darling? No, the director saw you in *A Midsummer
Night's Dream* and in that film you did yonks ago and
thought you were wonderful – very powerful, very sexy,
just the qualities he's looking for. The audition's tomorrow.'

They finished the call with Sylvia telling her the script
would be with her in the next half-hour as she was biking
it over. Valentine had told Sylvia she was staying with
friends in Hampstead. How ironic that she'd got this audition at an all-time low. She was bound to fuck it up. Just
then Kelly knocked at her door. 'Hiya!' she said perkily.
Kelly had two tones – perky or bossy. Valentine didn't
know which one she loathed more.

'Kelly, there is no way I can go running just now. I'm
horribly hungover. I'm going out to a cafe for a fry up.
It's the only cure.'

Kelly's perfectly glossed lips formed an O of shock. 'A
fry up?' She could barely get the words out. 'What are
you going to have?'

'Scrambled eggs, bacon, grilled tomatoes, mushrooms,
baked beans and toast,' Valentine replied.

'White or brown bread?'

Valentine considered. 'Brown, I think.'

'Butter, or marg?'

What was this? The Spanish Inquisition? She'd never known Kelly ask so many questions.

'Butter, definitely.'

A battle seemed to be being waged inside Kelly. Then she spoke. 'I'd fucking love a fry up. I haven't had one for years. I always have a grapefruit and hot water for breakfast.'

'Come with me then,' Valentine replied.

Kelly looked behind her furtively and whispered, 'Promise you won't tell anyone, especially not Olivia.'

Valentine nodded.

'Can we at least run to the cafe?' Kelly asked.

Valentine shook her head and looked stern. 'Absolutely no running of any kind.'

'Power walking?' Kelly persisted. 'It can burn just as many calories as a run, if you do it fast enough.'

'If you do that I'll tell Olivia.'

'We'll walk,' Kelly replied.

Kelly ate her traditional English breakfast with enormous relish, finishing by mopping up the egg yolk with at least five pieces of white bread toast, slathered in butter. Her face took on a dreamy expression. 'That was fucking lovely.'

'Kelly! That's twice I heard you swear,' Valentine replied in mock outrage.

'I swear all the fucking time when I'm not at the Hunters'. Mustn't ever do it near Mrs Hunter. She sacked the last trainer for saying "bloody".'

'God, she's harsh.'

'Miserable cow. It's Piers I feel sorry for. She's always telling him to lose weight and train more, when the truth is he looks bloody amazing for a man his age. You look good as well Valentine, by the way. I know I've been hard on you, but Mrs Hunter's had me on performance-related pay for my work with you, and me and Dex, my fiancé, really want to get a deposit together for a flat.' Now Kelly had shed her cheerleader persona she was coming across as a really down-to-earth, nice girl.

'D'you really think that?' Valentine asked.

'Yeah really. Though I don't think you should lose any more weight. In fact I think you should put some on – you look better curvy, well-toned curvy. Get that balance right and you'll look fucking ace.'

'That's the nicest thing anyone's said to me in ages. But it has been lovely getting slimmer – well the result, not the process. Wearing jeans with no muffin top, being able to try on a size ten in a store and then calling out to the assistant for a size eight because the ten is just too big! I've loved it.'

'Yeah, but it's fucking hard work isn't it?' Kelly replied with feeling, adding wistfully, 'Sometimes I wonder what it would be like just to let it all go and eat whatever I like.'

'But what about your gorgeous pert bum? And your abs of steel?'

'Would I be any less of a person if I didn't have them? Do they define me? Am I a better person because I'm slim? Aren't we, as a society, outrageously discriminating against fat people? I mean, we're all for sexual and racial equality and outlawing discrimination against people with disabilities, but what about the way we treat people who happen to be overweight, often through no fault of their own!' God, Kelly was getting a bit deep. Valentine had never seen this side of her when Kelly was urging her to push herself harder. She would never judge a person by their pert bum again.

'Well, you probably wouldn't be able to work as a personal trainer anymore.' Valentine didn't want to be responsible for Kelly losing her job and any chance of owning a flat with her fiancé just because she'd had a fry up.

'You're right.' Kelly snapped out of it. 'Fuck it! I'm going to have to work out extra hard to make up for this.' She looked down at her now completely clean plate. 'Still, it was worth it.'

Valentine would have liked to stay chatting to Kelly, but the script was on its way and even though she felt she didn't have a chance in hell of landing such a fantastic part, she may as well go through the motions.

She left, swearing eternal secrecy on the fry-up front to Kelly. As she walked slowly back to the mansion she had flashbacks to the night before – memories of kissing Jack, jarring painfully against the look on his face when he said he didn't even know her anymore. But surely, the tiny flicker of hope tried to speak up – very persistent that flicker of hope – he couldn't have kissed her like that if he didn't still have feelings for her, whatever he may have said? Valentine hadn't thought she was even remotely close to getting over Jack, but she'd made small progress:

she hadn't woken up in tears for a while and she had stopped reading his old text messages, but now she was back to square one, of the wanting, aching, longing, hopeless feeling for him. It was like that man in mythology whom the Gods punished for giving fire to humans by chaining him to a rock and having his liver pecked out by vultures for all eternity, and just to make sure it really did go on for all eternity every night his liver would grow back ready for the bird to peck out in the morning. Well, obviously her situation was not *exactly* like that, but seeing Jack again had blasted any hopes she had that she was getting over him and the pain was repeated on a loop. Mind you, at least the guy in the myth got a new liver and frankly after the amount of champagne she'd drunk the night before that wouldn't be such a bad thing, if you could just get rid of the chains and birds of prey. Oh God, she must be still drunk to be wittering on like this.

She had just let herself into her apartment when there was a knock at the door. It was Olivia and Saul. The ice queen and the toad.

'Piers had to go out, so sends his apologies about breakfast,' Olivia said, wrinkling her nose as if she could smell the fry up, even though Valentine had just sprayed herself with practically a whole bottle of Coco Mademoiselle on the way home. A reprieve for Valentine for having to come up with a comment about the elusive Bergman influence. 'And this came for you,' Olivia said, walking down the stairs, followed by Saul even though Valentine hadn't invited them in. She handed Valentine the package and looked meaningfully at her feet. Valentine was still in her gladiator sandals. She chose to ignore the look and took the package, muttering, 'thank you.'

'You were seen, by the way.' Olivia said.

'What do you mean?' Valentine demanded. Surely Ivana hadn't tracked her and Kelly down to the greasy spoon?

'Last night – you and the ex, going at it some.' The chinos toad spoke.

Valentine and her hangover saw red. 'Shut up you motherfucking chinos-wearing toad!'

'It's rather unseemly, don't you think, Valentine?' Ice queen now. 'Piers is going to offer you a film role, even though frankly, I just don't think you're ready. He's getting ready to introduce you as his daughter and you're running around with someone else's boyfriend. A someone else who is a close family friend.'

'He was my boyfriend first, if you remember!' Valentine shot back. 'But whatever, this is absolutely none of your business.'

'Anything that affects Piers is my business! It's not enough that you burst unannounced into our lives and upset Piers!' She was losing her cool now, the ice queen in meltdown. 'We were perfectly happy until you came along and now you've ruined everything!'

Valentine was getting pretty wound up herself. 'What's your problem? All I want is a relationship with my father, and I think he wants one with me! Why can't you let us get on with it?' She realised she'd reached the point of no return in her dealings with Olivia; she simply couldn't stay at the house another minute. It was hopeless to imagine that she would get closer to Piers this way. 'I've had enough; I'm leaving right now. Don't worry, Olivia, I don't want any part of your world.' And with that she marched past the duo, into her bedroom and began throwing her possessions into a suitcase, running on anger and adrenalin. And if she could have she would have high-fived herself for finally telling the toad what she thought of him. Maybe Lauren had been on to something with that word. It had sure felt powerful saying it.

Back home – and never had the patches of damp, the bright yellow kitchen walls and the uncomfortable sofa seemed so welcoming – she settled down to read the script. For once Sylvia had not been exaggerating. It was an absolute peach of a role. A funny, sexy, feisty, strong female lead. Just the best part Valentine had ever been up for. A part that really could be the making of her. In contrast to other auditions where she was gripped by nerves and insecurities, she felt strangely calm. What would be would be. The worst thing had already happened. Jack had left her. If she didn't get the part it wouldn't matter, it wasn't the end of the world, because the end of her world had already happened.

'Valentine? Isn't that a boy's name?' Jamie, the director asked the following morning after Valentine had given her read-through. He was in his thirties, Scottish, very groomed, fantastic shaped eyebrows, she noted – he must get them waxed. The read-through had gone surprisingly well; she had a devil-may-care attitude about her this morning, not her usual air of being desperate to please.

She rolled her eyes at the comment. Usually she would

have given her bright little laugh and launched into her explanation, but today she just shrugged and said, 'Yeah. And isn't Jamie a bit of a girl's name?'

Jamie laughed, 'Yeah. Anyway, Valentine, it was good to meet you. We'll be in touch.'

Usually post-audition Valentine would have analysed her every word and expression, tormenting herself by speculating how she could have performed better, but today she was calm. She decided to go and see her mum. The last couple of days had been an emotional rollercoaster, what with seeing Jack again, then the row with Olivia. She'd left a message with Piers, wanting to set the record straight on why she had left the Hampstead house, but had heard nothing from him. She hoped Olivia hadn't poisoned him against her. She badly needed the reassurance that only her mum could give.

'Do you think I'm a bad person for not staying in Hampstead?' She was sitting in the kitchen drinking tea with Sarah.

'Of course not! But I'm sorry it didn't work out. It's obvious to me that Olivia found your presence very threatening,' Sarah sighed. 'But I do sympathise; I've been feeling quite threatened myself since Piers came into your life.'

Valentine frowned. 'Why?' She didn't like to think of her mum experiencing any kind of emotional turmoil.

'Because I've been wondering if Chris and me did the right thing by not telling you sooner about Piers.'

'Mum, you just did what you thought was right. If anything, I've been feeling guilty about Piers because every time we shared a moment where it looked as if we might have a connection I felt guilty about Chris. I'll always see Chris as my dad. Piers might be my father, but Chris is my dad. And I'm really glad he was, because if I'd been brought up with Piers I can't imagine how many hangups I would have.'

'There's something I want you to see,' Sarah said, getting up from the table and walking over to the dresser, where she opened a drawer and picked up a letter. 'I found this the other day when I was going through some of Chris's papers. I never realised he wrote it.' She walked back to the table and handed Valentine the letter.

Dear V,

It's odd writing this and knowing that you'll be reading it when I'm not around – I hope I had a bloody good send off ! I just wanted to let you know that I always thought of you as my own. Always. I couldn't have loved you more even if you'd been my own daughter. And I'm so proud of you: you're such a beautiful, wonderful person and so talented. I don't know much about your world, but I always loved to see you act. It seemed like it was what you were born to do. So I hope you don't judge me and your mum too harshly for not telling you the truth right from the beginning. We did it because we didn't want you to get hurt and if we were wrong then I hope you can forgive us.

Love always, Dad xxxx

Valentine was completely overcome when she read the letter. She felt as if she'd been blind to so many things lately – Piers, Finn, Jack . . . She didn't go back to the flat that night, preferring to stay in her old home – her old, un-conditioned, cosy, slightly shabby home. She watched *Spooks* with her mum and Matt, had an Indian takeaway and then had the best night's sleep she'd had for a long time.

'Are you sitting down, Valentine?' It was Sylvia, on the phone three days after the audition. As Valentine had heard nothing straight away she had convinced herself that she hadn't got the part. 'It's OK, Sylvia, I know I haven't got it,' she replied glumly. It really would have been a lovely role for her, a career-changing moment.

'You got it!' Sylvia shrieked, almost deafening Valentine.

'I did!' she shrieked back. 'Oh my God! Oh my God, Oh my God!'

Sylvia let her shriek some more before interjecting, 'Jamie, the director, is thrilled to have you. He just has one little request.'

'Don't tell me,' Valentine said, her mind racing to conclusions, 'nipple tassels and nudity. Can't I ask for a body double? I just don't know how I feel going nude on primetime TV.'

'No, no, it's nothing like that!' Sylvia replied. 'Jamie has just asked if you wouldn't mind putting on a little weight, taking you back to a size twelve.'

'But the TV puts on ten pounds as it is!' Valentine wailed back. 'I thought I was supposed to be playing the femme fatale, not the token fat girl! Do you know how hard I've worked lately to get this slim? And losing weight has been the only good thing to come from having a broken heart!'

'Darling, I know.' Sylvia went into agent-pacifying-difficult-client mode. 'It is a lot to ask. But think of the bigger picture. This series has the potential to be a massive success.'

'Just so long as I don't have to get massive!' Valentine retorted.

'Darling, do calm down. We're not talking morbidly obese, just more of your curves back. I always thought you looked better like that anyway. And one day you'll have to make the choice between your face and your body, anyway. And let me tell you that the people who choose their faces over their bodies always look better than the ones who don't. Although it's a tough call, I admit,' Sylvia said with real feeling. Valentine knew it was a dilemma the fifty-year-old Sylvia battled with daily.

'So shall I tell Jamie that you are up for gaining a few pounds? He's worried that all the female actresses look the same.'

'Great, so I will stand out as the fat one,' Valentine said bitterly.

'No, no! You'll be the curvy, sexy one! So is it a yes?'

'Yes,' Valentine mumbled. 'And by the way, who's my co-star?'

Sylvia hesitated. 'I'm not sure, to be honest. I think they've had tremendous difficulty casting it – so hard to get manly actors these days. Too many pretty boys. I'll let you know as soon as they do.' She went on to fill her in on some of the details. They would start filming in a month's time and her fee was fantastic compared to anything she had ever had before. Valentine was almost in a state of shock. This was what she had wanted for so long. But even as she was thrilled a small worm-in-the-bud voice said, *and how much better would this be if you had Jack to share the news with?*

'So darling,' Sylvia drew to a close, 'think of Renée Zellweger and all that weight she put on for Bridget Jones. Go and have a doughnut or three. Better still, a fried peanut butter sandwich.' She put the phone down before Valentine could think of a suitably caustic reply.

After she'd told her mum and Lottie and texted all her other friends with her big news she called Piers. His phone went straight to voicemail again. Valentine left another message, telling him about the part. At last something for him to be proud of her for. Her relationship with Piers seemed to hang by such a fragile thread. A few times she had glimpses that they might possibly be able to form some kind of bond, but these were few. He was consumed by his world and by Olivia. An hour later she received a call from Greta. 'Piers has asked me to call to offer his congratulations on your TV role.'

'Couldn't he have called me himself?' Valentine asked, thinking that this was the phone equivalent of a businessman getting his secretary to buy his wife's Christmas present.

'Piers was a little taken aback by your leaving the house. I think he feels a period of reflection and distance is needed. And,' Greta paused, 'For now the film role is on ice.'

'Can't I at least speak to him and tell him what happened?' Valentine asked with feeling.

'He knows everything from Olivia. Do not put him in the invidious position of having to take sides between his wife and his daughter. He's under a lot of pressure, Valentine. I'm sure he will get in touch when he feels able.'

Valentine was almost tempted to tell him not to bother, but something stopped her from closing the door entirely. She was hurt, though. It felt worse than when he took so long to contact her. Now he was rejecting her after he knew her. Even with the lead role to buoy her up she might have gone to the dark side, but thankfully Lauren returned from the States. It was so wonderful to have her best friend back, to have someone to confide in and laugh with, someone who knew her so well. Inevitably Jack was one of their main topics of conversation. Lauren could not believe that he was happy with Tamara.

'It's a total rebound shag. He was hurt and upset and there she was; it could have been anyone. I bet he'll dump her really soon.'

'Even if he does, it doesn't mean that he'll want me. You should have heard him, Lauren, he sounded as if he hated me.'

'He tried to get in your pants first though, didn't he?'

'Not quite. And anyway I was wearing Spanx. They would have repelled him, in both senses of the word.'

'I reckon he still wants you and that's why he was so vile to you. What's that quote – we always hurt the one we love?'

Nathan (who had practically moved into the flat – so much for Lauren's commitment phobia) looked disconcerted.

'Oh, not you darling!' Lauren exclaimed.

'And now Tamara's ill, he'll never leave her.' Valentine had recently read that Tamara was suffering from nervous exhaustion. 'He's too decent.'

'She's just tired; nothing that a holiday on some exclusive Caribbean island won't put right, no doubt.'

'Oh God, I expect they'll go together and do a photo shoot for some magazine and I'll have to look at the pictures of them being loved up on a yacht or strolling hand in hand on a beach. Him with his lovely muscular chest, her without an iota of cellulite.'

'She'll be wearing a sarong over her massive arse, you can depend on that. And you didn't mention Jack's hairy chest. Does that mean you're over your repulsion/attraction thing?'

'I love his hairy chest!'

'Did you tell him "hirsutes" you sir!'

Valentine rolled her eyes. 'Lauren! Here I am pouring out my heart, and you come up with a pun? Girlfriend, I am discovering new depths to your shallowness!'

'I thought of it when we were in San Francisco and I've been dying to use it. Anyway you look like you need cheering up.'

Ignoring Lauren, Valentine turned to Nathan. 'I've a question for you. Please answer it honestly; my life hangs in the balance.'

Nathan put down his beer and sat up straighter.

'Just humour her, cheri,' said Lauren, 'I think she might have PMT and there's no chocolate in the house. Be afraid.'

'Don't worry V, I'm ignoring her.' Nathan put his hand over Lauren's mouth and pulled her next to him so she couldn't say anything else. It was definitely love, Valentine thought as Lauren just kissed his hand and snuggled up to him. The old un-loved-up Lauren would have bitten any man who had done that for sure, and they would all have ended up in A&E, with the man in question having stitches and a tetanus shot in his bum.

Valentine went ahead with her question. 'So, if your girlfriend was unfaithful to you just once and had a good reason for it, would you ever be able to forgive her?' She had asked every other man she knew, so she may as well ask Nathan. So far her answers had come back as: a yes from Rufus (though possibly only because Kitty was giving him a Chinese burn at the time to make him come up with the right answer; Toby, yes (only because he was being nice to Valentine as he was such a gentleman, and couldn't bear to upset anyone): Frank, yes (life was too short – him she did believe). So she had three yeses against the five 'no's she'd had from her other male friends. It wasn't looking good.

Nathan sighed. 'I guess I wouldn't at first. I would find it really really hard to forgive her – so don't even go there, Lauren! But if there was a good reason maybe I would be able to, after some time had gone by. If I could see that she really was sorry.'

He looked hopefully at Valentine, who shook her head

and said, 'Jack said he couldn't forgive me. I don't think time will make any difference.'

'Don't go on a decline now!' Lauren urged her. 'You've got a fantastic part. You've finally got that gutless bastard out of your life. And you can even fit into my size ten skinny jeans.'

'Not for long,' Valentine replied, reaching for a doughnut and then putting it down. The one time in her life she was being encouraged to put on weight and she had completely lost her appetite.

17

Of All the TV Dramas
in All the World

Valentine was not used to being treated like a star. She had fully expected to make her own way to the BBC studios in Elstree so it was a pleasant surprise when Sylvia told her a car would pick her up. She spent the hour-long journey reading through the script for the first episode again, though she had already learned her part. She had barely done any filming before and the excitement she felt was mixed with apprehension. A vivacious looking redhead who introduced herself as Lynsey, the PA, met her at reception and whisked her through to the large conference room where the read-through was being held. Immediately Jamie shook her hand and introduced her to the team. It was quite overwhelming being surrounded by so many people – alongside the actors were the assistant director, producer, assistant producers, PAs – and that was excluding the technical team. The sheer scale of the production was suddenly brought home to Valentine. The six-part series was going to be filmed over three months and then would go out the following spring as one of the jewels in the TV schedule. It was a very big deal.

Jamie called everyone together. For the read-through the actors and production team were sitting round a vast circular table. Valentine even had her own name card and Lynsey kept offering her drinks. Valentine felt very pampered. She was happily getting her script out of her bag and checking her mobile was switched off when Jamie said something that stopped her in her tracks.

'Jack Hart's agent has rung to say that he's going to be a little late this morning, but as he's not in the first scene I suggest we crack on anyway.'

'You know Jack, don't you?' Helen, the actor playing Valentine's office manager whispered to her.

Valentine nodded, not trusting herself to speak. Her mind was working on overtime – had her agent known all along and not wanted to tell her? What the hell was it going to be like acting opposite Jack? Would he even speak to her off set? And what about the love scene in the penultimate episode? The thought of it had been worrying her even before she knew it was going to be with Jack. *Core of steel*, she tried telling herself as her core wibble-wobbled away and she thought she might have to ask to lie down in a darkened room. Thankfully Jamie put a stop to her wild thoughts by starting the read-through.

The first scene involved Valentine's character, Frankie, trying to recruit a partner for her private detective agency. She had recently given up her job as a high-flying detective, sick of all the bureaucracy and politics, and she

313

needed a change after the break-up of her marriage. Frankie was going to be a great character to play – strong, assertive, sometimes overly so, passionate and with plenty of emotional baggage. Frankie doesn't want a relationship and then Daniel, a sexy former SAS soldier with a carousel of emotional baggage himself walks into her office. The attraction between them is instant, though neither will admit it.

As if on cue there was a knock at the door and Jack, sexy former lover with plenty of baggage, walked in. He was wearing his battered leather jacket and Valentine had a sudden flashback to her wearing it-and nothing else as they lay in bed together. Did the fact he hadn't got rid of it mean something? Surely if he hated her so much he would have thrown it away? That persistent flicker of hope was sparking up again. Valentine blew it out by deciding that any memory Jack had of her wearing the jacket would have been supplanted by too many other ones of Tamara writhing around in it.

'This seems like a good moment to break,' Jamie said. 'But before we do, I'll quickly introduce you all to Jack.' He whizzed round the circle calling out everyone's names, Jack smiling at each person in turn. Quite how he would react when it was Valentine's turn she couldn't imagine. Would he freeze her out? Tell Jamie that he couldn't possibly act with her as he loathed her? The reality was a slightly smaller smile for her than anyone else, though only she would have noticed. Then everyone was getting up and heading for the coffee area. Valentine was about to join them when Jack walked over to her.

'I suppose we should get the hello out of the way.' He spoke with none of his trademark warmth.

Valentine smiled at him tentatively, but he did not respond. 'I had absolutely no idea you were going to be in this. Of all the TV dramas in all the world you end up in mine.' It was a feeble attempt at echoing something Jack had said to her at the start of their relationship. How very long ago that seemed.

'Or you end up in mine,' Jack replied. 'It was too good a part to turn down. So you're OK about all this?'

'Just peachy,' Valentine lied, and then because she felt hurt by Jack's abrasive tone she added, 'Don't give it another thought; this is the best part I've ever had, and I'm not going to let my personal feelings fuck it up.' With that she turned away.

'Great!' Jamie had overheard them. 'You two are getting into character already! Loving the chemistry!'

It was nearly ten at night when the car finally dropped her home. Valentine was exhausted. The read-through had been exhilarating but it was also incredibly emotionally demanding having to work with Jack. Every time she looked at him, every time she heard him speak, she was reminded of what she had lost. Apart from his coolness with her he was his usual lovely, charming self to everyone else. His stunning success in *Lear* and offers of film roles hadn't changed him.

She walked in the kitchen to discover Lauren, Nathan, Lily and Frank sitting round the kitchen table planning Lily and Frank's thirtieth anniversary, or rather it would have been their thirtieth anniversary if they'd stayed together all those years ago. They were going to hold it at Ronnie Scott's jazz club in the heart of Soho, where Frank had spent so many nights playing in the past. It promised to be an amazing night. 'A celebration of love,' Lily declared.

'It sounds wonderful,' Valentine said, joining them. Lauren poured her a glass of red wine.

'So we've been dying to know how today went,' Lily continued. 'It's so exciting, V. You're on your way now, I just know it! So when will the series be out?'

'Next March I think,' Valentine replied. There was a flicker of sadness in Lily's eyes as she replied, 'I can't wait to see it.'

'Who's your co-star? Some sexy motherfucker?' Lauren. Some things never changed. Valentine exchanged eye-rolls with Nathan; both of them had given up trying to stop her. She had worn them down with her relentless swearing.

'Actually yes.' She paused for maximum impact. 'Jack Hart.'

'Destiny!' Lily exclaimed. 'I knew it! It can only be a matter of time before you two get back together. Jack won't be able to hide his true feelings for you any longer.' Lily seemed so thrilled by the prospect that Valentine didn't have the heart to reveal just how cool Jack had been with her. 'And I'm asking him to our party – just him, not Tamara.'

'Lily, she's his girlfriend; you'll have to ask her,' Valentine replied.

'Rebound shag,' Lily corrected her. Lauren's swearing had even rubbed off on her.

'So do you get to snog him on set?' Lauren put in.

'Actually we have a love scene in the penultimate episode,' Valentine replied. 'I don't know if it will be worse filming it with Jack because I know him or if it would be worse with someone else.'

'It could be really hot because you do know him,' Lauren replied, ever the sexual thrill-seeker, 'like in that film *Don't Look Now*, where Julie Christie and Donald Sutherland allegedly got very carried away – you could really do *it*.' Everyone looked at Lauren, who shrugged and replied, 'Doesn't everyone have that fantasy?'

'What? Being filmed having sex and then having it broadcast to the world? Have you suddenly changed into Paris Hilton?' Nathan demanded. 'Just let me tell you, you won't be doing that on my watch.'

'Anyway, perhaps I could ask for a body double,' Valentine mused.

'Either that or a merkin,' Lily put in.

'What's that?' Frank asked.

'Pubic wig,' Lily and Valentine chorused.

'To think I have lived most of my life without knowing what it was.' Still, I'm the only one of you who has seen the ping-pong show in Bangkok. Did I ever tell you about it?'

'Yes!' everyone said in unison.

'Enough already with the ping-pong balls,' Lily told him. 'Take me downstairs and I can show you my collection of vintage merkins.' But even as she joked she looked exhausted and very frail. Valentine, Lauren and Nathan exchanged concerned looks as Frank helped her out of her seat and downstairs.

The following day both Jack and Valentine's cars dropped them off at reception at the same time. There was a fleeting moment when Valentine thought he might ignore her, then he seemed to change his mind and they walked into the building together. It was the first time they'd been alone together since the night of the premiere.

Valentine's heart did its usual scary racing. Jack just muttered 'hello' and seemed to be prepared to leave it at that. But Valentine spoke, longing to get some reaction from him. 'I saw Lily and Frank last night – they're planning their thirtieth anniversary party.' She was practically having to jog to keep up with him as he strode along the corridor.

He slowed down fractionally. 'How is Lily? I thought she looked terrible when she came up to Manchester to see *Lear*. Any idea what's wrong?'

Valentine sighed. 'She just says it's a virus, but I'm not sure if I believe her. I'm really worried about her and about Frank; he looks worn out as well.'

Jack slowed right down and looked at Valentine, his brown eyes full of concern. 'I'm sorry to hear that. They're such a great couple.'

'Yeah, they're not bad for old timers, are they?'

By now they'd reached the conference room.

'So keep me posted on Lily and let me know if there's anything I can do,' Jack said just before they went in.

Valentine was about to reply when Lynsey presented Jack with an enormous bouquet of autumn flowers, artfully mixed in with berries and twigs.

'Somebody loves you!' Lynsey said cheerily.

Valentine gave Jack her arched-eyebrow look. He seemed rather nonplussed as he opened the card.

'So who are they from?' Lynsey put in, asking the question Valentine was dying to ask.

'From my girlfriend,' Jack mumbled.

'It's not your birthday,' Valentine said.

Jack looked embarrassed. 'Two-month anniversary, apparently.'

'I hope you remembered to send her something.' Valentine couldn't stop the sarcasm. 'Though maybe you can make it up to her later.' She regretted that comment instantly as Jack gave her a WTF look.

'Actually Tamara's not feeling too well at the moment.'

'Nervous exhaustion?' Valentine did her best to lose the sarcastic edge from her voice.

Not that successfully, apparently, as Jack looked at her coldly, the warm concern gone from his eyes. It felt like standing in the shade after the sun had gone in. 'Actually yes. *Lear* really took it out of her, and having to withstand Clive's constant bullying. It's shattered her confidence. She's not like you, Valentine, she doesn't have many friends to confide in, who support her. She's going through a really hard time at the moment.'

She's got you, Valentine thought. 'Please tell me you don't expect me to feel sorry for her!'

'Now you've got this great part, perhaps you can take

off that chip on your shoulder. Isn't it getting a bit heavy, carrying it around all the time?'

'What do you mean? I haven't got a chip on my shoulder!' She was getting angry now.

Jack held his hands up. 'Listen to yourself! I rest my case.'

'I'll leave you to your bouquet then,' Valentine replied and tried to regain her composure by getting a coffee. How dare Jack say that she had a chip on her shoulder about Tamara? She just didn't like her and with good reasons. Now she had more reason than ever, seeing as Tamara had Jack. Just to add to the toxic mix swirling round in her head she now wondered what else Tamara had got planned for Jack that night for their bloody two-month anniversary – how cringey was that? Possibly she would have booked a penthouse suite somewhere. She would have ordered the staff to strew the bed with rose petals – she'd never do it herself. Then she would lie back on the petals and await Jack's arrival in some sheer Agent Provocateur number. He would enter the suite and make straight for the bed.

To puncture the very unwelcome image of the couple embracing, Valentine added a twist where the disgruntled hotel staff, sick of Tamara's incessant demands, had left some rose stems in the bed. As Tamara writhed in Jack's arms, she would be impaled by a thorn on the backside, calling an immediate halt to the amorous proceedings. Valentine imagined Tamara would have a very low pain threshold and so instead of shagging the night away Jack would have to apply antiseptic cream to Tamara's massive backside – all right, it was only massive in proportion to the rest of her slender body – while she screeched like a banshee about suing the hotel. Hmm, Valentine wasn't wild about the cream-rubbing bit; there still might be some pleasure to be derived for the pair of them as Jack was very good with his hands. Instead, Tamara could develop a sudden allergy to rose petals and come up with huge suppurating boils all over her body, and Valentine meant *all over*. Pus would definitely be a passion-killer; no one likes to get up close and personal with pus. Valentine sighed, and took a reality check. Even if Jack hadn't looked exactly overjoyed by the flowers, she probably couldn't read anything into it and now on top of whatever else he felt for Tamara, he clearly felt sorry for her. NTM was in a win-win situation.

Valentine felt in a bad mood for the rest of the day, though luckily that gave an extra edge to her reading with Jack, as they were supposed to be wary of and attracted to each other in equal measure, with plenty of spiky banter, in one of those ironic art-imitating-life moments. Jamie just loved their performance, said it was everything he had hoped it would be. *Well, that was something*, she thought as she made her way out of the building. Jack was already in reception waiting for his car; he seemed to have forgotten something.

'Where are the flowers?' Valentine asked.

Jack rolled his eyes. 'I gave them to Lynsey. As I'm hardly home at the moment it seemed a waste.'

'I hope Tamara won't be too disappointed when she sees you later.'

'I'm not seeing her tonight; I'm going for a run, then I'm going to bed,' Jack said curtly. 'What about you?'

'The same,' Valentine lied, thinking of the glass(es) of wine she planned on having and getting a lovely image of Jack's bed with Jack in it.

Jack's lips twitched and for a moment he was back to being the Jack she used to know. 'You're such a liar, Fleming. I bet you'll just go home and sink a bottle of wine with Lauren. Who's she seeing now, by the way?'

'Still Nathan. I swear I won't be surprised if they end up getting married, though I never thought I would see that day. If she makes me be a bridesmaid and wear something vile in violet, I'll hunt her down and kill her!'

Jack held her gaze for a beat before replying, 'Well, I'm glad it worked out for them.'

All the way home in the taxi Valentine tried to figure out if there was a subtext to Jack's words. Had he put an extra emphasis on the word *them* and did he mean therefore that it was a pity it hadn't worked out for him and Valentine? Or was he simply happy for Lauren and Nathan because he was a genuinely nice person? Then again, he had called her Fleming, as he used to when they were together. So could that mean he was thawing towards her? Just a little bit?

The following day however it was back to arctic conditions. Jack was distant with her, avoiding her when they weren't working on the script, but at the end of the day he sought her out. 'Valentine, can we talk?' No hint of flirtation in his voice.

'Shall we go for coffee?' she asked. He shook his head.

'No time; I have to go in a minute. I just thought we needed to clear the air and we didn't seem to get a chance yesterday. So here goes.' He avoided eye-contact as he spoke. 'I'm sorry for the way I behaved that night at the premiere. I was a dickhead.'

'Well, you had your reasons I suppose,' Valentine muttered.

'The fact that you slept with Finn—' they both winced at the mention of his name – 'didn't give me the right to behave like that. I just wanted to say that I hope we can be friends during the filming. We both need this to go well. So can we be friends?'

Valentine longed for the return of the flirtatious banter. Jack sounded so formal. She wanted to say, 'I can't be your friend because I still love you.' But Jack had left her no room for manoeuvre; there was nothing to indicate that he still had deeper feelings for her. Self-respect dictated that she agree they could be friends.

'Good, I'm glad that's sorted,' he replied. 'I'll see you tomorrow.'

This cool detachment became the pattern of their behaviour over the next month as they filmed. They were unfailingly polite to each other; Valentine didn't even make any more sarky remarks about Tamara. But the strain of keeping a lid on her feelings was almost unbearable. Practically every night she would dream about Jack, deeply erotic dreams of unfulfilled desires. Typical! Even her dreams conspired against her and every time she was about to do the deed with him she would wake up. Sometimes Valentine wished Jack would be horrible to her, as at least that showed that he cared enough about her to be angry. But the shutters had well and truly come down and every day that went by Valentine had the feeling that he was slipping further and further away from her.

18

Lily's Divers

Valentine had thought that they were at least a month away from filming the love scene; somehow she hoped that she would have more perspective by then. So it was a shock when at a production meeting Jamie announced that they'd be filming it at the end of the week. 'The whole feel of the series is going to be slick and sexy, and I would like the love scene between Frankie and Daniel to reflect that. Basically I'm asking you guys to push the boundaries.'

Valentine had a sudden wish that she had one of those ejector chairs and she could press the button right now and eject out of there and straight into a production meeting for a lovely classic drama, say *Pride and Prejudice*, where there would be no talk of pushing the boundaries on sex scenes and only a heaving of well-covered bosom or extra clenching of male jaw to indicate arousal. She looked down at her script as if the answers would magically appear there, but all it said was Frankie and Daniel 'kiss and then make love'. There wasn't even an adjective – not a passionately, wildly, frenziedly to be seen.

Valentine could only hope for a 'quickly' right now and 'in the dark' would also be good.

'So can we rehearse after we finish filming today? To map out the moves and get a feel for how the scene will roll?' Jamie again.

'It will be hard having sex with you at the end of the week as it's totally out of sequence,' Valentine tried to banter with Jack as they walked out of the meeting. 'Frankie still mistrusts you.'

'Won't that give the scene an extra frisson?' Jack replied, moving closer to her in the corridor to let someone get by. Just having him near was giving her an extra frisson; God knows how she would cope with simulating sex with him. She'd probably combust with suppressed longing.

'I suppose so,' she answered, aware that her voice sounded slightly higher-pitched than usual.

'It'll be OK, Valentine. It's just a scene like any other and they'll cut it up so it looks all moody and arty and nothing much will be on show. It's not going to be *Last Tango in Paris.*' Valentine had never cared for the infamous pack-of-butter sex scene but were Jack to be involved in such an act, she realised she just might change her mind . . .

'Or *Don't Look Now,*' she squeaked, appealing in vain to her vocal cords to be husky.

He frowned. 'Have you got a sore throat?'

She shook her head. 'I'm just nervous Jack, aren't you?' Really his I'm-not-bothered act was getting too much to bear.

Finally he nodded. 'What do you think?'

* * *

'Cut! Jamie called out. Frankie/Valentine was lying on the bed, Daniel/Jack had just been kissing her breast. Valentine remembered reading somewhere that they sometimes needed to fake erect nipples on set with a judicious application of cold water or blast of cold air. Her nipples didn't need any help in that department right now.

Daniel/Jack rolled off her and turned to face Jamie, while Valentine folded her arms across her chest. 'I'm sorry to do this to you, but can we go from the top? I promise I won't stop you again. I just need the first kiss to go on for longer.'

After one more take they were done. She had kissed and caressed her ex-lover, felt his body on hers, had been practically naked, had sat astride him, had felt him on top of her, had felt quite a bit of him actually – she was sure that didn't happen in other love scenes – had faked an orgasm (now that had never happened in real life with Jack). The one thing she didn't have to fake was the moment when they gazed into each other's eyes and Daniel/Jack said, 'I love you.'

'I love you too,' Frankie/Valentine replied, willing Jack to mean his lines. And Valentine longed to add, 'I've never stopped.' But Jamie called out, 'Cut.'

'Are you going to Lily and Frank's party?' Valentine asked as they sat up in bed and she did up her shirt – now this really did feel weird.

'Yes, I said I would, so I'll see you later,' Jack replied, pulling on his T-shirt. He stood up and looked back at her, a definite warmth in his brown eyes. 'So how was that for you, Fleming?'

Finally there was a flirtatious edge to his voice; she decided to play along. 'Good.'

'Just good?' Jack replied. 'So you didn't find that a mindblowing, bone-melting sexual experience, up there as one of the best ever?'

Oh God, he was using the same words he had when they'd first made love all those months ago.

'OK, fantastic then,' Valentine replied, in an echo of her own words. Now the memory was in full high-definition and surround-sound in her mind – she and Jack were lying wrapped up in each other's arms after the most mindblowing, bone-melting, sexual experience ever. Jack was teasing her, holding the duvet off her and she was freezing. They were both laughing, knowing they were at the start of something wonderful.

Jack held her gaze. 'Fantastic is the right answer.'

It was time to step out from the past and into her present. 'It always was, Jack,' she said softly.

His 'Yes,' was barely audible as he turned to go. 'See you at the party.'

'I don't bloody believe it, V! He's given you a hickey!' Lauren exclaimed as she examined the purplish-red bruise on Valentine's neck later that evening as they got ready for Lily and Frank's party. 'I bet that was because he was so full of suppressed longing and he had to let it out somehow, without getting jissum on your leg.'

'Nathan! Can't you do something with her? She gets worse.'

Nathan held up his hands. 'Apparently not.'

'Honestly! The face of an angel, the mind of a sewer rat!' Valentine exclaimed again, watching Lauren perform a twirl in her silver beaded flapper-style dress.

'So, do you want me to cover up your love bite?' Lauren asked, holding up a jar of concealer.

Valentine considered the mark in the mirror, 'No, I'll leave it as it is. It's the only thing Jack's given me in a while, so it can be my badge of honour.'

'So did he have a massive hard-on in the sex scene?' Lauren persisted.

'I would never kiss and tell,' Valentine replied coyly, but when Nathan's back was turned she made an appropriate hand gesture and mouthed 'massive' to Lauren. Ah well, she'd had to bare her soul and most of her body to a roomful of strangers and simulate sex with her ex; she was allowed to see the funny side of it.

While Nathan and Lauren went on ahead to the party to check everything was in place for Frank and Lily's big night, Valentine travelled in with Lily and Frank. Lily insisted on the taxi dropping them off at Piccadilly even though it was a fifteen-minute walk to Ronnie Scott's and she didn't seem up to walking any distance at all.

'I've got something to show you,' Lily said mysteriously as the taxi pulled over and they got out. 'Look up there,' she urged Valentine, pointing to the top of a building on the corner of Piccadilly and Haymarket. Valentine looked up and saw an entrancing art deco sculpture – three sleek, gold, female figures diving from the roof. 'That is one of my favourite sights,' Lily told her. 'Whenever I feel down I hop on the number seventy-three and gaze at my beautiful divers. They always pick me up. I think they're telling me that life is full of possibilities and you must dive in it. Don't you feel that too, V?'

The trio stood in silence for a few minutes looking up, while all around them people hurried on their way, oblivious to the beauty above them. Valentine took a deep breath. *I am going to be golden and lithe of spirit*, she told herself. Lily is right; life is to be dived into. And then it came to her. She had to tell Jack she still loved him. It came to her so clearly – a perfectly formed thought from nowhere – as if it had been hovering somewhere in space and only now had shape to it. It didn't matter if he didn't give her the chance – she had to make that chance. It was now or never.

Valentine was thrilled for Lily and Frank when she saw how many people had turned up to their party. It was touching to see so many old timers, all decked out in their best clothes. Lily and Frank of course looked the most stylish: Lily, channelling a fifties starlet in a long gold dress, matching silk gloves that went up to her elbow and a white fur stole; Frank in a pinstripe suit and trilby hat looking like he was auditioning for a part in *GoodFellas*. A jazz band was playing and it promised to be a brilliant party. But there was no sign of Jack.

'He'll be here, Valentine, don't you worry,' Lily reassured her, doing one of her mind-reading acts. 'Didn't I tell you that tonight was a celebration of love?' Lily seemed better than she had in a while, but there also seemed something feverish and desperate about her as if she couldn't wait for Valentine and Jack to get together. Valentine put it down to Lily's incorrigible romanticism.

She spent the early part of the party hanging out with Lauren and Nathan, endlessly scanning the room for Jack and drinking a lot of champagne. What with the love scene and then getting ready for the party she'd had no time to eat and the fizz was going straight to her head. Every time a tall dark man walked into the club her heart beat that little bit faster in case it was Jack. But by eleven she had decided that he definitely wasn't coming. Disappointment washed over her. They had finished the champagne and really she'd had enough, but she had the demon inside her and instead of switching to water as she knew she should, she headed off to the bar for vodka. As she wove her way slightly unsteadily through the partygoers, Robbie, the student from the off-licence, appeared at her side.

'Hiya,' he said a little shyly. 'Long time no see, ma'am.'

'Well good evening Robbie,' Valentine replied in her Southern Belle accent, and gave him a quick kiss on the cheek.

'Can I get you a drink?

'Why yes, even though I don't usually hold with hard liquor, I could manage a vodka and tonic.' Valentine swayed and Robbie grabbed her arm. 'Thank you, Robbie.' She stared at him, trying to focus on his boyishly cute face; he really wasn't bad-looking at all. True he was blonde and she didn't ordinarily go for blondes, but he was very sweet actually, with lovely skin. She would love skin like that! So what if he was too young for her? He wouldn't judge her so harshly after one mistake and then run off with a film star and break her heart. No, he would be loyal and good and true. Oh God, she really was drunk. She gave another lurch and Robbie put his arm round her waist and she leaned against him gratefully.

'Look, why don't you sit at this table and I'll go to the bar,' Robbie said, steering her towards a chair. Valentine sat down – she was starting to get that spinny-head feeling but it was better than obsessing about Jack. Robbie returned with a double vodka that Valentine found went down surprisingly quickly and he obligingly went off for more supplies. He sat down next to her and gazed at her with undisguised longing and asked all about her new role. Valentine babbled away. It was so good talking to someone who seemed interested in her, so nice to see the longing in Robbie's eyes – or maybe that was her vodka-head talking; who knew, who cared? Jack clearly didn't. Bastard! She was very drunk.

'I've really missed seeing you around, Valentine,' Robbie mumbled. 'I was wondering if we could go out some time – you know, just you and me. I could take you for dinner.'

'That would be so sweet!' Valentine exclaimed, reaching out and stroking Robbie's hair. Really she couldn't resist it; it looked so shiny and clean. He really was very cute. Robbie took that as an invitation to latch lips with hers and then he thrust his tongue eagerly into her mouth. It was not a good kiss. It was like being assaulted by one of those fish that are kept in aquariums to keep them clean by sucking up all the dirt. She managed to pull away and swore she could hear suction sounds as she disengaged her tongue. She sat back, wondering if he would notice if she wiped her mouth.

'That was nice, but d'you know what? I'd love a cigarette. Have you got any, Robbie?'

He looked flushed with excitement as he shook his head. 'I've given up. I thought you didn't like being around people who smoked.' He moved towards her lips, ready to re-engage.

Valentine moved sideways. 'Oh no! It doesn't bother me at all. Can you get me one?' She put her hands together and leaned forward, treating Robbie to a front-row view of her cleavage – a cheap trick, but she had to get rid of him. *'Please.'*

Robbie looked as if he'd much rather stay where he was, but he managed to tear his gaze away and promised to get her a cigarette. Whoops, what had she got herself into? Time to take stock and repair the damage Robbie had inflicted on her face. Out of the corner of her eye Valentine saw Lauren laughing at her. Valentine stuck her tongue out (her poor, violated tongue) as she made her way to the ladies'. The floor seemed to be undulating, which made walking in her heels tricky. Valentine felt rather proud of herself when she finally made it to the bathroom. She'd only fallen over twice – not bad. She was just squinting at her reflection in the mirror when Lily accosted her. 'What do you think you're doing with that young boy!' She sounded outraged.

'Havingadrink,' Valentine replied. 'What'stheproblem?'

'The problem is that you are throwing away your chance of happiness with Jack. What are you going to do when he turns up and sees you in the arms of another man?' Lily had drawn herself up to her full height and looked extremely formidable.

'Lilyhe'stheonewithagirlfriend,' Valentine replied.

'He's only with her because of what you did!' Lily shot back. Valentine was impressed by Lily's ability to understand her when she was having difficulty understanding herself. 'I could have been with Frank for the last thirty years instead of the last ten. We made such a mistake staying in our marriages. I know you look at me and think my life is nearly over and I should be knitting or collecting china figurines of Disney princesses or thinking that *EastEnders* is the highlight of my day just because I'm old, but I still feel the loss of those years in here.' At this Lily clasped a hand to her heart. 'Don't throw it away!' she said again, with tears in her eyes.

Lily's outburst had a dramatic sobering effect on Valentine, who put a hand up to her own face and found that it was wet with tears. 'Oh Lily, don't you see? I've already thrown it away – I did that when I slept with Finn. If Jack had any feelings for me he would have turned up tonight. The most I can hope for is to be friends with him.'

'No! I won't let you say that! Come on, sort yourself out. I know that Jack is up there now.'

'Have you seen him?' Valentine asked, getting the heart-racing feeling, worse than usual because she was drunk.

Lily shook her head. 'No, I just feel it.' She fussed around Valentine for the next few minutes, applying face powder, taking off the red lipstick that Valentine had so drunkenly applied. 'You looked more Coco the Clown than Coco Chanel,' she told her as she wiped it off, leaving just a subtle red stain on her lips. She stood back and surveyed her work. 'Much better now.' She took Valentine's arm.

Upstairs Lily paused by the bar and looked around. Even though Valentine just knew that Jack wouldn't be there, she was still disappointed when they drew a blank. Even Lily looked slightly crestfallen and usually (the last scene in the bathroom excepted) she was the queen of optimism. 'He'll be here,' she insisted, steering Valentine away from Robbie, who was frantically gesticulating with a cigarette, and installed her at a table as far away as possible from him.

'Right young lady, I'm getting you a glass of water and a black coffee, so stay here,' Lily told her and headed back to the bar.

Valentine watched as Lily was surrounded by friends, then she gestured to Robbie to come over. 'Let's go outside and have that cigarette,' she said as soon as he had bounded over eagerly, making Valentine think of the Andrex puppy, even though at over six foot Robbie was not in the least roly poly – it must be the hair, she thought, and the eyes. She got up and Robbie was quick to put his arm round her. 'Don't let Lily see us,' she whispered. 'And on the way out, grab my drink, will you?' She wanted to forget what Lily had told her, wanted oblivion. Jack was not coming.

* * *

Outside the air was cool on her bare skin. Valentine shivered and choked slightly on the cigarette Robbie had lit for her. She hadn't had one for ages and even as she inhaled, she regretted it. She was going to feel so rough in the morning. Robbie took off his denim jacket and put it round her shoulders.

'Thanks, you're such a sweetheart,' she said.

'So, do you want to come back to my place?' Robbie asked tentatively. 'Everyone's out and I've got a bottle of vodka.'

'Robbie that's very sweet of you, but—'

'Stop telling me I'm sweet!' Robbie cut across her angrily. 'I'm not sweet! I really like you, Valentine – I have done for the longest time.' He stood in front of her. 'I'm in love with you.'

Perhaps it was the prisoner/governor fixation? Robbie had really taken their role play very seriously – a little too seriously, perhaps. How was she going to get out of this one? She wished for the millionth time that she could have been more like Lauren; she'd have told Robbie to shut up – no hard feelings.

'But you just want Jack, don't you?' Robbie said bitterly.

There was no point in pretending she didn't know exactly what he meant, so Valentine just nodded and whispered, 'Yes.' And she handed Robbie back his jacket and went back inside. As if reflecting her mood the band were playing 'God only knows.' A drunken, heartbroken wreck apparently, Valentine answered to the line *God only knows what I'd be without you.*

Lily took her arm and frogmarched her to Nathan and

Lauren. 'Give this girl water and nothing else,' she ordered before joining Frank on the dance floor.

'Finished with toy boy already then?' Lauren demanded, ignoring the order and pouring Valentine a generous glass of white wine.

Valentine picked it up and took a large swig, then grimaced and said, 'You're not supposed to mix the grain and the grape, are you? Where does vodka come from?'

'Well it's not from a grape, is it?' Lauren shot back. 'You don't hear them say it's been a fine year for the Smirnoff grapes, do you? Anyway, answer my question: what have you done with Robbie? Is it the start of a beautiful friendship or a one-night stand?'

'I'm not like you, Lauren. I don't do one night stands, as you know.' She glanced at Nathan. 'Oh sorry Nathan, I didn't mean that to sound like it did.'

Nathan rolled his eyes. 'Let's hope Lauren doesn't do them anymore either.'

'Well make sure you keep me happy then,' Lauren replied, but she gave him a kiss to show she didn't really mean it. God, she really had mellowed. 'Come on, let's dance.' Lauren stood up and grabbed Nathan's hand. 'Will you be OK?' he asked, trailing after Lauren.

Valentine nodded and held up the bottle of wine. 'We'll be fine.'

She was back to feeling drunk. Lily's shock outburst had sobered her up temporarily, but now the units had caught up with her. Everything around her was ever so slightly out of focus, but that seemed like a lovely thing right now. The table lamps gave off a warm, fuzzy orange glow, like fireflies she imagined, not that she'd ever seen any in real life. Or did she mean glow worms? The music was making her feel very maudlin. She'd just sit here nice and quietly, drink her wine and go home. She took another sip and thought of how the scene would look in a film. There she'd be, the talented but tragically underrated actress, unlucky in love, drinking herself into oblivion, in a jazz club. It seemed very Billy Holiday. Very glamorous, though she probably should be smoking to complete the picture.

'There's nothing glamorous in drinking yourself into oblivion.' Lily was standing by the table with a cup of black coffee, which she placed in front of Valentine. 'Cirrhosis of the liver isn't pretty. You turn yellow eventually and you've always said that yellow isn't your colour. And you're right; you'd look bloody dreadful in it.'

'LilyIloveyoubutgivemeabreak.' She'd gone back to the slurry mad drunken speaking. But then everything faded into the background because there, standing next to Lily, was Jack.

'Happy anniversary Lily,' he said, putting his arm round her and kissing her. 'I'm sorry I'm so late.'

'You're here – that's all that matters,' Lily said, smiling. 'Anyway I'm sure you've got things to discuss with Valentine,' she said meaningfully. 'Do get the girl to drink some coffee.' Then she left them. As ever, Lily was about as subtle as a herd of marauding elephants. 'Subtlety – never Lily's strong point I remember,' Jack said as he sat down next to Valentine. 'Fleming, are you drunk?' So he was back to calling her Fleming again.

'Very.' And freed of any inhibitions, Valentine plunged straight in. 'Please sayyouforgivemeaboutwhatIdid. Iregretitsomuch.'

'Pardon?' Jack said, clearly lacking Lily's ability to understand drunken gibberish.

Valentine took a deep breath, and spoke as deliberately as she could. 'I am drunk but even if I wasn't I would still say this: please tell me you can forgive me for what I did.'

'So we're not going to do the polite "how are you?" "Oh I'm just fine," bollocks routine we've been doing for the last month,' Jack replied, gazing at her – or at least she thought he was, but there seemed to be two of him right now. 'I think I do forgive you.'

Now was the moment to tell him. She would dive into the unknown. 'I've got something else to tell you. I don't care if it messes up the filming; I have got to tell you.'

'No wait, I've got something to tell you.'

But neither of them got the chance to speak because just then there was a shriek of 'Jack! Darling,' and an all-too-familiar petite blonde raced towards the table. Tamara. Jack looked completely stunned to see her.

'Didn't you get my message?' he asked when Tamara finally stopped showering his face with kisses.

Talk about bad timing! Valentine thought bitterly. Now NTM was there she'd never know what Jack was about to tell her. But Jack didn't look at all pleased to see Tamara, and Valentine was sure she wasn't imagining this, even in her altered state.

'What message?' Tamara said brightly, 'I had to see

you!' She gazed at him, clinging on to his arm and totally blanking Valentine. She had thought it wasn't possible to loathe NTM any more than she already did, but found a new depth to her feelings.

Jack coughed and looked awkward. 'You remember Valentine.'

Tamara turned her face and looked at Valentine with her huge blue eyes. 'Of course! I'm so sorry I didn't recognise you! You look so different. I can't work out what it is.' She narrowed her eyes and looked Valentine up and down. 'Oh I can see now! You've lost weight. Piers must be so relieved; I know he was terribly worried that you might have an eating disorder.'

Bitch. 'Oh, because I actually eat something?' Valentine replied.

Tamara ignored the sarcasm in her voice. 'But I'm sorry to hear it didn't work out between you. I know he took the fall-out pretty badly.'

'What the fuck are you on about?' Valentine demanded.

Tamara's eyes widened. 'I'm sure I don't need to remind you! How you threw Piers's offer of a film role back in his face, told him you wouldn't ever want to appear in one of his movies. How you were vicious to Olivia.' Tamara had the look of a cat playing with a mouse.

'I don't know what you're talking about, Tamara, or why you're getting off on saying things like this. But that is definitely not what happened.' Valentine got up.

'Are you OK?' Jack asked, looking at her with concern.

Valentine felt like a woman on the edge, but no way did she want to let on how much Tamara's words had upset her. 'Fine. I think I have a phone call to make. Could you tell Frank and Lily that I've had to go?' She was utterly stunned by Tamara's comments.

'Sure, let me get you a taxi,' Jack replied.

Valentine shook her head. 'I could do with a walk.' The night no longer seemed full of possibilities, but dead ends and dead hopes. How foolish she'd been to think that she could tell Jack how she felt. It was all pointless. He was with Tamara, end of story. She found herself walking back to Piccadilly. She reached the corner of Haymarket and looked up. Lily's golden divers were tumbling through the sky. Now they did not seem such a symbol of hope. They were falling into the darkness and there was nothing to catch them. But suddenly Jack was by her side, out of breath from running to catch up with her.

'I wanted to see you were OK. Lily thought you might be here. I'm really sorry you had to hear that from Tamara.' He hadn't put on his jacket in his rush to catch up with her and was just wearing a white shirt and jeans. How Valentine longed to put her arms around him! If she could just hold him again then maybe she could be diving into hope and not despair. He reached out his hand and brushed a tear away from her cheek. 'Hey, don't cry. I'm sure you can sort things out with Piers. Tamara was most likely exaggerating; she has that tendency.'

'I'm not sure that I'm crying about that,' Valentine replied. 'Look up there: Lily's favourite sculptures.'

Jack followed her gaze upwards. 'They're perfect.'

'If only life could be like that,' Valentine replied. 'Simple, straightforward, no darkness, no shadows.'

'It's not like that though, is it?' Jack replied. 'It's dark, shadows, mess.' He looked back at her. This was the moment to tell him that she loved him.

'I'll get you that taxi.' And within what seemed a matter of seconds he had hailed her a taxi, was seeing her safely in and walking swiftly away.

Valentine watched him go. The taxi was stuck in traffic. *If this was a film*, Valentine thought, *he'd turn round and run back to me and tell me that he loved me.* He didn't turn round.

She expected that the late night would have taken its toll on Lily and Frank, but even so she was shocked by how drawn Frank looked when he opened the door to her the next day.

'Hi Frank, fantastic night wasn't it? I think.' Valentine winced. Even with painkillers her head was still throbbing, as if sadistic gnomes were drilling into her skull. But it wasn't just the hangover making her feel so bad. She kept replaying the events of the day before in her head. She was hoping that Lily might inject some optimism into her about her relationship with Jack, as well as have some wisdom to offer about what to do about Piers.

'Come in, V. I'm sure Lily would love to see you. She's in her bedroom.'

'Oh, drank a little too much champagne like me?' Valentine asked, following Frank through to Lily's bedroom, or rather boudoir because her room was a fabulous mix of burgundy velvet curtains, red and purple silk throws and an amazing gold headboard on her bed, shaped like a scallop. Lily looked tiny lying on the bed and not at all well.

'Valentine,' she croaked, 'why did you rush off like that? We were worried.'

Valentine quickly filled them in on Tamara's comments about Piers.

'You must contact him; don't leave it. I'm sure there's an explanation. Now tell me about Jack.'

'He said he could forgive me for what I did, but then Tamara turned up.' She shrugged. 'Bad timing.'

Valentine had hoped to pour her heart out to Lily, remembering how feisty she had been the night before, but Lily seemed exhausted. 'I expect he's going to end things with Tamara and then he'll be free to see you again. He's very honourable like that.'

Valentine shook her head sadly. 'I doubt it; he didn't give me any sign that he still has feelings for me.'

'Don't say that!' Lily said with feeling. 'I know he loves you and you love him.'

'I'm not sure,' Valentine replied, but didn't want to push it. Lily seemed so weak.

'Don't throw this chance of happiness away; life is just too short.' Lily repeated what she had said the night before. 'My ten years with Frank weren't enough.' Valentine frowned. Lily sounded so final.

'But you've got years ahead of you both,' she replied.

'No I haven't.' Her eyes flicked up to Frank as if seeking reassurance. He nodded. 'I've got cancer; I'm dying. There, I've told you – such a relief.'

Valentine's eyes swam with tears. 'What do you mean?

You can have treatment can't you?' She looked at Frank and Lily, appealing to them to tell her there was hope.

Lily shook her head. 'It's beyond all that. Ovarian cancer, so hard to detect and now it's too late. They offered me chemo, but even with that there was little chance. I'd rather leave this world as myself.' She reached out her hand and Frank took it. 'I'm going into a hospice today. Frank has been looking after me so beautifully but it's time. So you see why I've longed for you and Jack to get back together.'

'Oh Lily.' Valentine was crying so much that she couldn't speak anymore.

'Think of the divers!' Lily urged her. 'Dive into life.' And with that she closed her eyes and whispered, 'I'm sorry, I need to rest now.'

19

The Final Curtain

Valentine left Lily and Frank feeling completely shell-shocked. This couldn't be happening – not to Lily, vibrant, wonderful Lily with her zest for life. She spent the day with Lauren, who was equally devastated by the news. She rang Jack, who was on his way to Paris to film one of the episodes for the series, but only got his voicemail. She left a message explaining that Lily was seriously ill; it didn't seem the right moment to say 'and by the way I love you,' even though Lily's words about diving into life were a constant refrain in her head. She called Piers and left a garbled message saying that they needed to talk. Life suddenly seemed infinitely precious and even if Piers wanted nothing more to do with her, she wanted to give it one last go.

Frank returned from the hospice later that evening looking absolutely shattered. He had wanted to stay, but Lily had sent him home. Valentine and Lauren went down to his flat to keep him company. They tried to persuade him to eat something, but he resisted their efforts.

In typical tough trooper Frank fashion he managed to joke that it was only because they were such bloody awful cooks. He let them make him mugs of strong tea instead and because his arthritis was especially painful Lauren rolled him several joints to see him through the night.

'I wish Lily had told us how ill she was,' Valentine told him, bringing him his third mug.

'She wanted things to be as normal as possible. She wanted everyone to see her as Lily the person and not Lily the cancer victim.' He rubbed a hand across his face. Valentine wished she could say something, anything to make him feel better, but what was there to say when the love of his life was dying?

'It must have been a strain on you, Frank, having to keep it to yourself,' Lauren put in.

'I just did what she wanted,' Frank said sadly. 'It was the least I could do for my girl.'

Now Valentine realised why Frank had fallen off the wagon that time. Her heart ached to think of the couple soldiering on, never once letting on how tough things were.

Neither Lauren nor Valentine could face going back up to their flat after seeing Frank, so they headed off to a pub round the corner. Jack still hadn't returned her calls – clearly filming was over-running. Nathan joined them and Valentine noticed that Lauren sat closer to him than usual, held his hand and didn't tease him quite so mercilessly. They all felt shaken up about Lily. By the time they walked home it was nearly midnight. Valentine was surprised to see that Frank's light was still on. She was about to ring his bell and check that he was OK when his door opened and Frank stood there in his elegant black silk pyjamas and red velvet smoking jacket – both presents from Lily, who believed that men should be just as stylish as women in the bedroom.

'V, I'm glad you're back. You've got a visitor.' Valentine followed Frank into his living room and to her great surprise discovered Piers sitting on the brown leather Chesterfield, smoking a massive joint.

'Oh God Frank, you haven't given him the strong stuff, have you?' Valentine asked. She didn't think she could cope with Piers being high on top of everything else. Frank shook his head.

'Valentine!' Piers got up, strode over to her and enfolded her in a tight hug. He must be high; he had never been that demonstrative before. 'I need to talk to you.' He no longer seemed the aloof, in-control movie director.

Valentine managed to prize the joint away from Piers and took him up to her flat. She was expecting him to be dismissive of the flat's bohemian and shabby appearance, but instead he exclaimed how much he loved all the different colours and didn't even complain when he sat on the dodgy spring in the sofa. Powerful stuff, Frank's weed.

'First of all, Valentine, I have to apologise for how you were treated in my house. Olivia had no right to say those things to you. She put a very different spin on what had happened and for a while I believed her.'

Valentine shrugged; in view of what was going on in

the rest of her life Olivia seemed inconsequential. 'It doesn't matter.'

'It does matter! It matters very much. You're my daughter and Olivia had no right to sabotage our relationship because of her own insecurities.'

Valentine had never before heard Piers criticise Olivia. He stood up, reached inside his jacket and pulled out a bundle of letters. Valentine instantly recognised her mum's handwriting.

'When I got your message today I had a sudden thought and went through Olivia's private papers. I found the letters. She must have intercepted each one and hidden it from me. To think I could have known about you, that I could have seen you grow up! She kept me from you; it was such a wicked thing to do, I don't think I can be married to her anymore.' He seemed a broken man. 'And I found the confidentiality agreement she drew up for you to sign, believe me Valentine I would never have wanted you to sign anything like that. I'm proud that you are my daughter. I want the world to know. I was only cautious about you telling too many people at first because I didn't want the press to find out, but bugger that now! And of course I want you in my next film – that is if you still want to be.'

Valentine, grief-stricken about Lily, still longing for Jack, found it surprisingly easy to forgive Olivia; she didn't feel any anger towards her, just sadness for those lost years and pity for the woman who must have been desperate to do what she did. 'Piers – don't be too hard on her; she did it because she loved you, because she was devastated that she couldn't have a child. You have to forgive her.'

Piers shook his head, 'I just don't know if I can; it's too much.'

'You should try,' Valentine said gently. 'And it's not too late for us to try and get along as father and daughter, is it? And at least you missed out on all my bolshy teenage years.'

Piers smiled faintly. 'You really think that's possible?'

Valentine sighed. 'My lovely friend Lily is dying. I think life is too short not to forgive people.'

'She's drifting in and out of consciousness, but do talk to her. I'm sure she'd love to hear your voices,' Sally, one of the nurses at the hospice, told Valentine and Lauren as she directed them to Lily's room. Valentine had been dreading that Lily would be in some awful grey, depressing ward; instead she was in a pleasant room with pale yellow walls filled with sunshine flooding in from the large bay window, with just one other patient in it.

Frank was sitting by Lily's bed, holding her hand. He got up when he saw them. 'I'll leave you for a while, go and stretch my legs in the garden. I'm sure Lily would like to have a good gossip with you girls without me earwigging. She'll love the flowers; they were always her favourites.' He pointed at the bunch of pale pink peonies Valentine was holding. 'Did Piers get home OK?'

'He passed out on the sofa after he insisted on smoking that joint you gave him. But he left this morning to try and sort things out with Olivia,' Valentine replied.

Frank nodded his approval and walked slowly out of the room. He seemed to have lost the spring in his step overnight. Valentine and Lauren sat down either side of Lily, who seemed barely conscious. Her eyelids fluttered and her breathing sounded laboured and rasping. Valentine was no expert but it seemed as if she was reaching the end. Dear Lily, still making the effort even in her last hours, in a gorgeous peach silk nightdress trimmed with delicate cream lace.

Valentine picked up her hand. 'Hi Lily, lovely to see you. Your anniversary party was so magical. We all loved it.' There was no response. Valentine's eyes filled with tears and she suddenly couldn't go on. What did you say to someone who was dying? She knew that Lily was a fervent atheist so it wasn't even as if she could console her with thoughts of an afterlife.

'What we wanted to say, Lily,' Lauren took over, 'is that we both love you. You're our ultimate style icon. And I thought you'd want to know, given that you're a hopeless romantic, that I'm going to stay with Nathan as long as he'll have me. Yes, I am finally in a committed relationship, Lily. Bet you never thought you'd hear me say that!' Lauren looked across at Valentine. 'In fact he's moving in, V, if that's OK?'

Valentine smiled in spite of the situation. She had *never* thought the day would come when Lauren committed to a relationship. 'So you're not going to end up in a bedsit on your own, with just a poodle and a crate of wine for company?'

'No way – I hate poodles!' She paused. 'Prepare to be

amazed, Lily, but I'm actually thinking of having chil-dren with Nathan.' Now that really was too much to take on board – Valentine felt as if she'd suddenly fallen down a rabbit hole and entered a parallel universe, or maybe the real Lauren had been abducted by aliens, leaving this ideal, domesticated, sweet-talking Lauren as a replace-ment. Lauren continued with her mind-boggling statements. 'He's agreed that he'll stay at home and be a house dad, which I'm cool about so long as he doesn't go all sappy and let himself go. I don't want some pot-bellied motherfucker sloping around in tracksuit bottoms, watching daytime TV and going for coffees with yummy mummies. No, he's got to put the effort in.' Still the same Lauren, thank God.

'Lily,' Valentine finally got a word in, 'can you believe you're hearing this? Just promise me Lauren that you're not going to make me be a bridesmaid.'

'If we get married you can be my best woman and you can wear whatever you like. And Lily, you're not to worry about V – I just know she's going to get it together with Jack, even though she did snog the face off poor Robbie at your party. You know how stubborn she is – she won't believe it – but I saw the way Jack was looking at her at Ronnie Scott's. He still loves her. And she loves him.'

Valentine nodded.

'Speak up!' Lauren demanded. 'Lily can't hear you.'

'Yes, I love him,' Valentine said loudly. 'Love him, love him, love him!' She and Lauren paused to look at Lily. Was it her imagination or was there a glimmer of a smile on Lily's face?

Frank walked back into the room. 'Had a good chat then?'

'We've filled her in on all the gossip. D'you want to come back with us? You must be exhausted,' Valentine said. Frank shook his head and gently smoothed back a lock of silver hair from Lily's forehead. 'I'm staying right here with my girl. Sally – lovely woman, but no understanding of jazz – says she hasn't got long. I wouldn't like her to go anywhere without me next to her. I promised I wouldn't leave her.'

20

A Leap of Faith

'Only Lily's funeral could be this cool,' Lauren whispered as she, Valentine and Nathan walked into the church. Frank's old jazz band were accompanying a beautiful young woman singing 'Summertime' – Lily's all-time favourite song. The church was packed with Lily's friends who were dressed as if they were going to a party. Lily had left strict instructions that no one should wear black. Frank himself was dapper in his pinstriped suit. Instinctively Valentine scanned the rows of guests – another edict from Lily, who didn't want mourners – for Jack. He was due back from Paris that morning and in the briefest of phone calls had said he would come straight to the funeral. But there was no sign of him. 'He'll come, V,' Lauren told her.

The glorious strains of 'Summertime' came to a close and the minister began his address. Although Lily had not been in any way religious, the minister knew her from way back when he had been an actor and his speech was warm, full of personal recollections from friends and Frank, a fitting tribute to Lily. Valentine clenched her fists and picked at her thumbnail anxiously; she had promised Frank to read out the poem Lily had requested because he didn't feel able to. The minister came to the end of his address and introduced Valentine. She walked slowly towards the altar, hating the sight of Lily's coffin, even though it was beautifully decorated in peonies and white roses. She turned to face the rows of people, and took a deep breath.

'Lily was one of the most wonderful people I have ever known, but I'm sure I don't need to tell any of you that.' Her voice faltered and it was taking all her strength to carry on. 'So I hope I can do her favourite poem justice.'

At that moment the door opened and Jack walked in. For a moment he simply stood there, locking eyes with Valentine; then she began reading the Shakespeare sonnet.

'Let me not to the marriage of true minds admit impediments. Love is not love which alters when it alteration finds.'

Dear Lily. Even beyond the grave it seemed to Valentine that she was sending back the message that true love endured, that it could withstand anything, even infidelity . . .

Valentine finished the sonnet, made her way back to her place and saw Jack was sitting next to Lauren. Oh Lily, is it wrong of me that my heart is racing at the sight of him? She sat next to him and he put his arm round her. For a second Valentine thought he was simply being comforting, the gesture of a friend, but then he pulled her to him and held her close, so she could feel the warmth of his body against her and he whispered, 'We need to talk.' The feel of him next to her again made her feel giddy; she hoped Lily wouldn't mind that she was having carnal thoughts at her funeral. At that moment the pall-bearers slowly made their way down the aisle with the coffin on their shoulders, followed by Frank. He looked over at the couple and smiled.

There was no chance to talk intimately in the taxi over to the Chelsea Arts Club where Lily's party was being held, as they were with Lauren and Nathan, but Jack held Valentine's hand all the way. 'I was so sorry not to be able to say goodbye to Lily,' Jack said.

'She wouldn't have known; she was completely out of it by the time we saw her.' Valentine paused. 'I sent her your love.'

'She adored you, Jack,' Lauren put in.

'I adored her; I just wish I could have had longer to get to know her.'

'How do you think Frank feels?' Lauren replied with feeling. 'God knows what he's going to do without her. Imagine, you finally get to be with the love of your life and they die and leave you all on your own. And it's not as if you're young and can meet anyone else – you're old and have got nothing to look forward to – nothing!' Lauren, who never cried, was crying now, and so was Valentine. They had tried to keep it together in the church for Frank but now the full impact of Lily's death was bearing down on them. The wonderful music, the beautiful speeches, the guests dressed up in their finest clothes were all a distraction – Lily was dead and she was never coming

355

back. The four of them were subdued for the rest of the journey and still feeling low when they walked into the bar of the Chelsea Arts Club.

Frank was the first person they saw there. 'Come on you lot, stop looking like wet weekends! This is a party for my girl and I want to see you smile. Lily would be livid if she knew you were looking so dreary.'

Valentine hugged him. 'Frank, you're such a star. It's just we can't help being sad.'

'I won't hear of it. I expect you've been wondering what I'm going to do without her.' God, had Frank somehow inherited Lily's ability to know what people were thinking?

'In contrast to the life you think I might have – drinking myself to death in a flat full of memories, with only my vegetables and jazz collection for company – I'm moving to Sydney to live with my daughter and help run the jazz club she's just opened. You'll have to come out and see me.' He paused and looked meaningfully at Valentine and Jack. 'Yes, I've lost the love of my life and it will never stop hurting, but I had her; short as it was, I had her.' Jack reached out for Valentine's hand as Frank continued. 'So now you know I'm not going to be wallowing in a pit of despair, go and dive into life and get some bubbly down you!'

Lauren grabbed Nathan's arm and made a beeline for the champagne. Valentine prepared to follow them but Jack led her out of the bar and away from the other guests into the deserted living room. Once there he shut the door and pulled her into his arms. A lot of pulling had been going on that day, it seemed to Valentine, but she didn't mind one little bit. His fingers traced the contours of the faded love bite on her neck. 'Sorry about that, Fleming. I did get a bit carried away. Would it be inappropriate of me to say how sexy you look in that dress?'

Valentine smiled. 'Lily wouldn't mind one little bit.'

It was all the encouragement Jack needed; he ducked down and kissed her neck. Particles of pure lust rushed round Valentine's body. She could have given the Large Hadron Collider a run for its money right now. God knew she needed a big bang . . . Jack moved from kissing her neck to her lips. She closed her eyes, hardly daring to believe that this was actually happening.

'So Fleming, what were you going to tell me when we were interrupted at Ronnie Scott's?'

Valentine opened her eyes and looked straight into Jack's. So this was really happening. 'What were *you* going to tell me?' she countered; she didn't want to destroy the moment. What if she told him she loved him and pushed him away for ever?'

'I was going to tell you that I wasn't with Tamara anymore — in spite of how it might have looked,' Jack replied. 'We finished a month ago. I wanted time to know what I really wanted.' He paused. 'I know what I want now. Come back with me. Much as I want to ravish you here, that probably would be crossing a line.'

There were all kinds of things Valentine wanted to do with Jack in the taxi but they were both sober, it was still light outside, and everyone knows that you only get to behave outrageously in taxis under the influence and cover of darkness, when at least you can pretend the driver can't see you. Instead, sitting as close to him as she possibly could, they talked. It turned out that Tamara had been unable to accept that Jack had ended their relationship and had been stalking him for the last month, Julia Turner-style, hence her turning up unannounced at Ronnie Scott's. The journey seemed to be going on for ever, and wonderful as it was to be talking to Jack, Valentine thought she might combust if they didn't get to his place soon.

'Why are we stopping here?' Valentine exclaimed as the taxi pulled over at the top of Haymarket.

'Just a small detour,' Jack replied. 'Come on, it'll be worth it.' He took her hand and jumped out of the taxi and suddenly Valentine knew exactly where they were going. Lily's divers. She and Jack looked up at the sculptures. Then back at each other. It was six in the evening and people were rushing past them. Jack put his arms round Valentine's waist and pulled her close to him. 'I love you, Valentine. I wanted to tell you that night but you were so drunk and Tamara had turned up unexpectedly and it seemed such a mess and I wanted everything to be perfect. Now I know that there's never a right time. And I have Lily to thank – when she and Frank came round for dinner she talked at me all night about you, how wonderful you were and how Finn had messed you up so much that you found it hard to trust anyone, how I shouldn't throw our relationship away because of one mistake.'

Valentine sent up a silent prayer of thanks to her dear

friend. 'I love you, Jack. I always have, however it looked.'

'I know that now. It's not going to be easy and I know there will be times when I'm going to hate you for what you did, and it's going to take me a long time to trust you again, but I would rather have that conflict and pain than live without you.'

'How about we get some pleasure now?' Valentine said, standing up on tiptoes to kiss Jack – a deep, you-belong-to-me, get-a-room kind of kiss. High above them she could see the sleek golden figures catching the last rays of the sunset as they dived. It was time for her and Jack to dive as well and take their chances.

THE POWER OF READING

Visit the Random House website and get connected with
information on all our books and authors

EXTRACTS from our recently
published books and selected
backlist titles

**COMPETITIONS AND PRIZE
DRAWS** Win signed books,
audiobooks and more

AUTHOR EVENTS Find out which
of our authors are on tour and
where you can meet them

LATEST NEWS on bestsellers,
awards and new publications

MINISITES with exclusive
special features dedicated to our
authors and their titles

READING GROUPS Reading
guides, special features and all
the information you need for
your reading group

LISTEN to extracts from the
latest audiobook publications

WATCH video clips of
interviews and readings with
our authors

RANDOM HOUSE INFORMATION
including advice for writers,
job vacancies and all your
general queries answered

Come home to Random House
www.rbooks.co.uk